James Redpath

The Public Life of Capt. John Brown

With an Auto-biography of his Childhood and Youth

James Redpath

The Public Life of Capt. John Brown
With an Auto-biography of his Childhood and Youth

ISBN/EAN: 9783337074937

Printed in Europe, USA, Canada, Australia, Japan

Cover: Foto ©Raphael Reischuk / pixelio.de

More available books at **www.hansebooks.com**

THE

PUBLIC LIFE

OF

CAPT. JOHN BROWN,

BY

JAMES REDPATH,

WITH AN

AUTO-BIOGRAPHY

OF HIS

CHILDHOOD AND YOUTH.

BOSTON:

THAYER AND ELDRIDGE,

114 AND 116 WASHINGTON ST.

1860.

DEDICATION.

TO

WENDELL PHILLIPS, RALPH WALDO EMERSON, AND HENRY D. THOREAU,

DEFENDERS OF THE FAITHFUL,

WHO, WHEN THE MOB SHOUTED, "MADMAN!" SAID, "SAINT!"

I HUMBLY AND GRATEFULLY

Dedicate this Work.

JAMES REDPATH.

"THE Saint, whose fate yet hangs in suspense, but whose martyrdom, if it shall be perfected, will make the gallows glorious like the Cross." — *Ralph Waldo Emerson.*

"He was one who recognized no unjust human laws, but resisted them as he was bid. No man in America has ever stood up so persistently for the dignity of human nature, knowing himself for man, and the equal of any and all governments. He could not have been tried by his peers, for his peers did not exist." — *Henry D. Thoreau.*

"God makes him the text, and all he asks of our comparatively cowardly lips is to preach the sermon, and say to the American people that, whether that old·man succeeded in a worldly sense or not, he stood a representative of law, of government, of right, of justice, of religion, and they were pirates that gathered about him, and sought to wreak vengeance by taking his life. The banks of the Potomac, doubly dear now to History and to Man! The dust of Washington rests there; and History will see forever on that river side the brave old man on his pallet, whose dust, when God calls him hence, the Father of his Country would be proud to make room for beside his own." — *Wendell Phillips.*

PUBLISHERS' CARD.

In presenting this work, the publishers deem it proper to congratulate themselves and the public on having secured as the biographer of Captain John Brown, a gentleman so well qualified, both by personal knowledge and literary ability, for the task, and whose previous life has been so identified in feeling and character with the career of the sainted hero, as to enable him to do that justice to his motives and acts which a less friendly pen would fail to render.

They would also call the attention of the public to the fact that a large percentage on each copy sold is secured by contract to the family of Captain John Brown, and every purchaser thereby becomes a contributor to a charitable object, which appeals to all freemen with a force that is irresistible.

The publishers would remind the public, and especially the press, that the work is copyrighted, and any reprinting of the *Autobiography*, or the chapter entitled "The Father of the Man," will be prosecuted as an infringement, as it is the desire of the friends who contribute

1 *   (5)

it that it should appear exclusively in this volume, for
the benefit of the family.

The work is published with the sanction and approval
of the family of Captain Brown, as may be seen by the
following letters:

NORTH ELBA, Dec., 1859.

Messrs. Thayer & Eldridge.

Dear Friends: I am satisfied that Mr. Redpath is
THE man to write the life of my beloved husband, as he
was personally acquainted with him, and I think will do
him justice. . . . I think that the portrait is a very
good one.

Yours respectfully,
MARY A. BROWN.

NORTH ELBA, Dec., 1859.

Messrs. Thayer & Eldridge.

Dear Sirs: I was somewhat acquainted with James
Redpath in Kansas. I am also familiar with his writings,
and I consider him an able biographer, and THE MAN
ABOVE ALL OTHERS to write the life of my beloved father.
I believe him to be a man of undoubted veracity, and
fully believe he will do justice to the work he has undertaken.

Yours respectfully,
SALMON BROWN.

PREF.

WHEN the news of the arrest of John Brown reached
Boston, I could neither work nor sleep; for I loved and
reverenced the noble old man, and had perfect confidence
in his plan of emancipation. I knew him to be one of
earth's worthiest souls — the last of the Puritans; and yet
I heard, on every side, people calling him a madman, and
sneering at his "crazy scheme." Now, or never, was the
time to defend my friend, when no voice, however faint,
was heard to praise him. An opportunity offered; I
indorsed John Brown. A few years hence this will seem
absurd; as ridiculous, now, as an indorsement of Warren;
but necessary in October last — and pronounced insane!
I heard of no one man who fully approved my doctrines
or defence when my first article appeared; but, before the
series that I had contemplated was finished, I turned
again to other work — for already the highest talent of
the nation was marshalling to the rescue of the conquering
prisoner of Charlestown Jail. Like Samson, in a single
day, if not with the jawbone of an ass, yet with the help
of that of a Member of Congress, the mighty man of valor
had smitten his enemies, hip and thigh, "from Dan even
unto Beersheba, and all the region round about." Now

that the most skilful trained soldiers of Freedom were in the field to encounter the reserve forces of the enemy, I withdrew myself from the conflict for a time — for, a guerilla skirmisher only, unfitted both by habit and nature for a place in any regular army, I did not care to fight under any General, or to fire except where I wanted to kill.

A publisher of New York asked me to write a Life of John Brown. He wanted it as a Republican campaign document. I declined. I would not help to light cigars from the fire above the altar. The publishers of this book made a nobler request; they believed in John Brown; they wished to do him justice; and they desired to assist his destitute family. This volume is the result of their request.

I have written this book, because I could not resist it. Equally at war with the cant of conservatism, of politics, and of non-resistance, and a firm believer in the faith that made Bunker Hill classic, I think that John Brown did right in invading Virginia and attempting to liberate her slaves. I hold God in infinitely greater reverence than Congress, and His holy laws than its enactments. I would as soon think of vindicating Washington for resisting the British Government to the death, as to apologize for John Brown in assailing the Slave Power with the only weapons that it fears.

Therefore, reader, if you think that white makes right, or might makes right, or if the opposite doctrine is abhorrent to you, lay this volume aside at once, for I will not promise that I shall try to avoid giving you offence.

I have no apology to make for this book; not because I am unconscious of its defects, but because it is the best that I could write in the allotted time, and because nowhere else can so correct a biography of John Brown be found. It is compiled from hundreds of sources —newspapers, books, correspondence, and conversations. Much of it, also, is the record of my personal knowledge. Materials came to me from all quarters; and not always in the order of time. Thus, the third chapter of the first book was written two weeks after the account of his execution; the history of his Kansas exploits before I obtained the autobiographical sketch of his childhood and youth. Hence, if there be occasional repetitions, whether of fact or idea, the just or generous reader will overlook this defect. I do not think that there are such iterations; but it is a possibility that I desire to explain in advance.

Writing in this way, the volume grew faster than I foresaw. I had intended to write the Life of John Brown, private and public, and biographies of his men, also. But Kansas, and Harper's Ferry, and Charlestown, and an un- expected gift of materials from North Elba, compelled me to defer the biographies of John Brown's men, as well as a minuter record of his own private life and correspond- ence. For, on the return of my wife from the home of John Brown, I found myself in possession, in trust, of hundreds of private letters, — every one that has been preserved, — written during the long and active career of the illustrious Liberator, which exhibit his daily life in its every relation, and the exceeding beauty of the religion which inspired its actions. These records, with other memorials of him, will be published, in due time, in a supplementary volume.

The latest telegraphic news makes one correction necessary. I have spoken of Richard Realf as dead. I thought that he died a natural death on the ocean. It appears that he still lives in the body; but dead to honor, the voice of conscience, and the cries of the poor. He has chosen the part of Judas, and promises to play it well.

I am indebted to several friends for valuable aid in the preparation of this volume — first, to every one whom I have mentioned in the notes, or text, or whose letters I have quoted; and to Dr. Thomas H. Webb, of Boston, Richard J. Hinton, of Kansas, and, lastly, but not least among them, to "a nearer one still and a dearer one" for her visit to North Elba and its results.

I still desire information, (whether anecdotes, letters, or conversational remarks,) respecting John Brown and his heroic associates, and will be greatly obliged for all such contributions.

How unworthy soever this book may be, I shall not regard it as a useless work, if, in the minds of its destined readers, it shall arouse the inquiries:

How far, as men, have we strayed from the Mount where Jesus taught? and

How far, as citizens, have we wandered from the Hill where Warren fell?

MALDEN, MASS., *December 25,* 1859.

Book First.

HE KEEPETH THE SHEEP.

11. And Samuel said unto Jesse, Are here all thy children? And he said, There remaineth yet the youngest, and behold he keepeth the sheep. And Samuel said unto Jesse, Send and fetch him; for we will not sit down till he come hither.

12. And he sent and brought him in. Now he was ruddy, and withal of a beautiful countenance, and goodly to look to. And the Lord said, Arise, anoint him: for this is he. — *I Samuel*, Chapter xvi.

I.

The Child and his Ancestors.

December 2, 1859.

HOW, worthily, write the Life of worthy John Brown? The task is as difficult as the man was heroic. In every part and phase of it, numerous and serious obstacles present themselves. For to-day John Brown was hanged by a semi-barbarous Commonwealth, as a traitor, murderer, and robber, and fifteen despotic States are rejoicing at his death; while, in the free North, every noble heart is sighing at his fate, or admiring his devotion to the principles of justice, or cursing the executioners of their warrior-saint. Thus opposite are the views men have of him; and this is the first difficulty that confronts his biographer.

But putting it aside, by utterly disregarding the opinions and denunciations of the mob, looking steadily at the old man only, and drawing him as he strove to be and was, — a warrior of the Lord and of Gideon: to satisfy the public expectation, and, at the same time, to do justice to the hero of their hearts, is a far more important, and a still more embarrassing task. For an immediate publication is demanded; and it is impos-

2   (13)

·sible, at once, to collate all the facts that should be told of him.   But one alternative remains — to do the best that is possible for the present day, and, if a still more extended biography be demanded, to endeavor, at another time, to supply that want.

PATERNAL ANCESTRY OF JOHN BROWN.

Among the group of godly exiles who knelt at Plymouth Rock, on the 22d of December, 1620, and returned thanks to the Almighty for His goodness to them in preserving them from the dangers of the Deep, was an unmarried English Puritan, a carpenter by trade, of whose personal history all that now can be known is, that his name was Peter Brown.   That he came over in the Mayflower, is evidence enough that he feared his God, respected himself, and strove prayerfully to obey the divine commands; choosing rather to sacrifice the comforts of English civilization, and enjoy in the wilderness his inherent rights, than · calmly contemplate the perpetration of wrong by sinners in high places, or to rest satisfied* with the sophistical belief, that, by the philosophy of an enlightened selfishness, or the diffusion of correct principles of political economy, all the evils of the age would peacefully be rectified — in a century or two! He died in 1633.

Peter Brown, the second, was born in 1632.   A monument in the churchyard of Windsor, Connecticut, is his only biography.   It tells us that he married Mary Gillett in 1658, and died October 16, 1692.

He had four boys: the second-born named John Brown; who, in his turn, married Elizabeth Loomis in

1692, had eight daughters and three sons, the eldest of whom was his namesake.

. John, the second, had seven girls and two boys, of whom the first-born son became the third of the name in the family. He died in 1790, at the age of ninety, having been the husband of Mary Eggleston, (who preceded him twelve months to the spirit world,) for the long period of sixty-five years. Mary, the eldest child of this marriage, remained a spinster till her death at the age of one hundred.

John, the third, was born November 4, 1728; married Hannah Owen in 1758;* was the father of John, Frederick, Owen, and Abiel Brown; and the honored grandfather of Captain John Brown, the hero of Kansas and Harper's Ferry. John Brown, the third, at the outbreak of the revolutionary war, was chosen Captain of the West Simsbury (now Canton †) trainband; and, in the spring of 1776, joined the forces of the continental army at New York. His commission from Governor Trumbull is dated May 23, 1776. After a service of two months' duration, he fell a victim to the prevailing epidemic of the camp, at the age of forty-eight years. ‡ He died in a barn, attended only by a faithful subordinate, a few miles north of

---

* John Owen, the ancestor of Hannah, was a native of Wales. He was among the first settlers of Windsor, where he was married in 1650.

† In 1806, West Simsbury, with a narrow strip of New Hartford, was incorporated, by act of legislature, into a township named Canton.

‡ He served under Colonel Jonathan Pettibone.

New York City, where the continental army was at that time encamped. His body was buried on the Highlands, near the western banks of the East River. On a marble monument in the graveyard of Canton Centre, this inscription may be seen: —

"In memory of Captain John Brown, who died in the revolutionary army, at New York, September 3, 1776. He was of the fourth generation, in regular descent, from Peter Brown, one of the Pilgrim Fathers, who landed from the Mayflower, at Plymouth, Massachusetts, December 22, 1620."

Thus far we see that same spirit of resistance to wrong, which, recently, — nay, at this very hour, — men are branding as insane! Why did Captain John Brown, "of the fourth generation, in regular descent," risk his life — "throw it away," as our politicians phrase it — by opposing it to the hitherto resistless strength of a mighty empire? Why not wait until, by the aid of a "constitutional republican party," the evils then endured should have been peacefully abolished? What was he to Massachusetts, or Massachusetts to him, that he should leave his family and fight her battles? Personal liberty he had; his house was his castle; no power on earth dared molest his property, or wife, or children. It was only a petty question of taxation that called him to the field, but in it there lay embodied a political right; and, rather than submit to an infringement of it, he resolved to throw "his life away," if need be. We now honor him for it; for we see in it the spirit of the first Peter Brown, who would not wait for the convenient season of corrupt and heartless demagogues, but chose rather to abandon his native land, and enjoy his liberty at once. But it is far nobler than the first Peter's conduct; for it is not solely for himself, as in the Puritan's case, that he abandons home and friends. It is for a neighboring colony, and the rights of his race, rather than for his personal immunities. Only one step further was possible in the ladder of disinterested benevolence — to fight for a race, poor, despised, friendless, and inferior; and this crowning glory to the family of Peter Brown, the Puritan, was reserved for the grandson of the revolutionary captain.

Captain John Brown, the third, left a widow and eleven children, of whom the eldest daughter was eighteen years of age, and the first son nine years only. "They were reared by his widow, with singular tact and judgment, to habits of industry and principles of virtue, and all became distinguished citizens in the communities in which they resided. One of the sons became a judge in one of the courts of Ohio. One of the daughters had the honor of giving to one of our most flourishing New England colleges a president for twenty years, in the person of her son." *

" She was a woman of great energy and economy," writes a descendant, † " the economy being a needful

---

* My authority is William H. Hallock, of Canton Centre. The preceding facts were chiefly furnished by Lancet Foote, Selden H. Brown, of the same place, and by a pamphlet, now out of print, entitled, "Genealogical History, with Short Sketches and Family Records of the Early Settlers of West Simsbury, &c., by Abiel Brown," an uncle of the liberator.

† Professor C. F. Hudson, a distinguished theological author.

virtue. I have heard my grandfather tell of her cooking always just what the children needed, and no more,
and they always 'licked their trenchers,' when they
had done with knife and fork. They all grew up to
respectability. Their average age was considerable,
that of five of them being seventy years, and I forget
how much more."

Of the sons of these parents, John — afterwards
known as Deacon Brown — lived many years in New
Hartford, and died there. Abiel lived and died on the
old homestead in Canton, Connecticut, while Frederick
and Owen both lie buried in the State of Ohio.

MATERNAL ANCESTRY OF JOHN BROWN.

Owen Brown, the last named of these sons, and the
father of Captain John Brown, the greatest and most
heroic of the race, married the daughter of Gideon
Mills, " who was himself an officer in the revolutionary
army, and was intrusted with the command who had
in charge a large portion of the prisoners comprising
Burgoyne's army: thus proving that John Brown
inherits his military spirit through a patriotic ancestry."

A very brief record of John Brown's maternal ancestry, (all that it is now possible to write,) will prove
that his descent was as honorable and patriotic by his
mother's family, as from Peter Brown, the Puritan of
the Mayflower.

Peter Miles was an emigrant from Holland, who
settled at Bloomfield, Connecticut, near the confines of
Windsor Plain. He had seven sons, was a tailor by
trade, and died in 1754, at the age of eighty-eight.

Of these seven sons, Jedediah graduated at Yale College in 1722, and was a clergyman and theological author of considerable note. Pelatiah was a useful citizen, and an able attorney at law. John was the father of two clergymen. Peter had a numerous offspring, one of whom was the first minister of East Granby. Of two other and younger sons no record exists; of Return, a daughter, all that is told is the date of her death, 1689.

Gideon, the seventh son, and the great grandfather of John Brown, the liberator, married Elizabeth Higley, a cousin of the first Governor Trumbull, of Lebanon. He was the minister at Old Simsbury about ten years previous to 1755; and, after living and preaching one or two years at West Simsbury, was installed in 1759, and died there in 1772. His character may be judged by the following interesting incident of his life:

"At the time of his ministry in West Simsbury, he lived two and a half miles from the meeting house, over a very hilly, cold, and uneven road, which would now be called a hard Sabbath-day's journey for a clergyman or a layman. This road he travelled weekly, and sometimes much oftener. One incident respecting the Rev. Gideon Mills is thought worthy of notice. He was habitually fond of sacred music, and would request others that could sing to join with him, and he retained his relish for singing even to his dying moments. He died of a cancer in the face, which kept him in great suffering for many of the last weeks of his life. He dwelt much on the sentiments expressed in the thirth-eighth psalm, (Watts,) 'Amidst thy wrath remember love,' &c.; also, the thirty-ninth — 'God of my life, look gently down.' Just before he expired, he requested the friends in attendance to sing the thirty-eighth psalm — 'Amidst thy wrath remember love,' — and attempted to join with them, but when the fore part of the psalm was sung he expired; so that it was said by Mr. Hallock, on a certain occasion, that he died singing the thirty-eighth psalm."

This stout-hearted Puritan left three sons and three daughters. . Elizabeth and Faithe were married twice, and Anna was the third wife of the Reverend William Robinson. The biography of Jedediah is brief enough : " Born in 1755–6 — married Miss Wells."

. Rev. Samuel Mills, second son of the Rev. Gideon . Mills, graduated at Yale College in 1776, " with a view to the gospel ministry."

"Being full of the patriotism prevalent at that time, he entered the American army as lieutenant in the cavalry. In one of those actions which took place in 1777, this young officer received a wound from a horseman's sword in the forehead, was taken prisoner, and conveyed into Philadelphia with a deep and dangerous wound, the scar of which he carried through the remainder of his life. The sick and wounded prisoners in Philadelphia experienced far different treatment from that which those unfortunate American prisoners received from the British and tories in New York in 1776. A kind Providence furnished a goodly number of ministering angels, (if the expression may be allowable,) in the persons of some of the most accomplished ladies of Philadelphia. Those of superior rank and refinement took it upon them to visit and minister to the wants of the suffering prisoners. Among those worthy ladies was Miss Sarah Gilpin, a person of high refinement and accomplishments. Her labors of benevolence brought her and Lieutenant Samuel to an acquaintance which eventuated in his obtaining her hand and heart. He pursued and finished his theological studies, and was married to Miss Gilpin, and was settled pastor . over the church and society of Chester, then a part of Saybrook."

Gideon, the eldest son of the Rev. Gideon Mills, and the grandfather of John Brown, the liberator, was also a lieutenant in the American army, and died in 1813, at Barkhamsted, Connecticut, at the age of sixty-four. He left two sons and four daughters, of whom Ruth, the eldest child, married Owen Brown, the father of our hero.

JOHN BROWN BORN.

The town records of Torrington supply these dates :

"Owen Brown, now of Torrington, late of Simsbury, was married at Simsbury, on the 11th day of February, A. D. 1793.

"Anna Ruth Brown, daughter of Owen and Ruth Brown, was born in the town of Norfolk, the 5th day of July, 1798.

"*John Brown, son of Owen and Ruth Brown, was born in Torrington, the 9th day of May, 1800.*

"Salmon Brown, son of Owen and Ruth Brown, was born on the 30th day of April, 1802.

"Oliver Owen Brown, son of Owen and Ruth Brown, was born the 26th day of October, A. D. 1804."

John Brown, therefore, was born in the year 1800, at Torrington, Connecticut, where he lived, "about a mile north-west of the meeting house," until the age of five, when his father emigrated to Hudson, Ohio ; where, we are told, " he became one of the principal pioneer settlers of that then new town, ever respected for his probity and decision of character ;" was " commonly called 'Squire Brown, and was one of the Board of Trustees of Oberlin College ;" was " endowed with energy and enterprise, and went down to his grave honored and respected, about the year 1852 or 1853, at the age of eighty-seven."

II.

The Father of the Man.

TRULY says the poet, that the child is father of the man. This is why every incident of the childhood of great men is so eagerly sought and cherished by their friends and admirers. When the fruit is glorious, we desire to see the blossom, too. Happily, in the case of Captain John Brown, this desire can be amply gratified — and in a way, and by the pen, of all others the best fitted to do justice to it. Gladly I here step aside for the old hero; to permit him, in his own inimitable style, to narrate the history of his infancy, and early manhood.

All that it becomes me to write, by way of preface, is a brief statement of the story of this autobiography. When John Brown was in Boston, in the winter of 1857, among other noble friends of freedom here, he made the acquaintance of Mr. and Mrs. Stearns, of Medford; who, recognizing him at once as an historic character, — although clad in a plain suit of clothes only, and with a leathern strap for a neck-tie, — received him at their hospitable home with all the honor justly due to a hero and a saint. Their children soon learned

(22)

to love the old warrior; for, like all godlike men, he
loved little children; and, like all young souls, they
instinctively recognized the true hero. One of them
asked him many questions about his childhood, and he
recounted, with great interest, the incidents of his
infancy and boyish days. When the old man was preparing to return to Kansas, Master Henry (to whom
the letter is addressed) asked his father's permission
to give all his pocket money to Captain Brown. The
permission was readily given, and the old hero received
the money. He promised, at the same time, — if he
should ever find the leisure for it, — to write out for
his young friend an account of his own early life.

When crossing the State of Iowa, with military supplies, in the month of July following, — he himself
driving a team, — he was detained for some time by
the failure of certain parties to fulfil their promises to
send him money. He then fulfilled *his* promise, and
wrote this autobiographical sketch. I have copied it
with the fidelity of a Chinese artist: Italics, punctuation, orthography, and omissions. I add a few notes
only, and divide it into paragraphs. It fills six pages
of letter paper in the original manuscript, which is
very closely written, and contains two paragraphs only
— the letter and the postscript.

It is hardly necessary for me to say that the internal
evidences of its perfect fidelity are overwhelming: for
we see throughout it the same grand traits in the barefooted, bareheaded boy, clad in "buckskin breeches,
suspended often with one leather strap and sometimes
with two;" who idolized the "bobtail squirrel," and

had "a mourning season" at its death; and who, at
the age of twelve, swore eternal war against slavery;
which, when in the jail and the Court room and on the
gallows of Charlestown, Virginia, astonished and delighted the world.

This is the letter:

MR HENRY L. STEARNS

My Dear Young Friend

I have not forgotten my promise to write you; but
my constant care, & anxiety have obliged me put it
off a long time. I do not flatter myself that I *can*
write any thing that will very much interest you: but
have concluded to send you a short story of a certain
boy of my acquaintance: & for convenience and shortness of name, I will call him John. His story will be
mainly a naration of follies and errors; which it is
to be hoped *you may avoid;* but there is one thing
connected with it, which will be calculated to encourage any young person to persevering effort: & that
is the degree of success *in accomplishing his objects*
which to a great extent marked the course of this boy
throughout my entire acquaintance with him; notwithstanding his moderate capacity; & still more moderate acquirements.

John was born May 9th 1800, at Torrington, Litchfield Co, Connecticut; of poor but respectable parents:
a decendant on the side of his father of one of the company of the Mayflower who landed at Plymouth 1620.
His mother was decended from a man who came at an
early period to New England from Amsterdam, in Hol-

land. Both his Father's & his Mother's Fathers served
in the war of the revolution: His Father's Father;
died in a barn at New York while in the service, in
1776

I cannot tell you of any thing in the first Four years
of John's life worth mentioning save that at that *early
age* he was tempted by Three large Brass Pins belonging to a girl who lived in the family & *stole them.*
In this he was detected by his Mother; & after having
a full day to think of the wrong: received from her a
thorough whipping. When he was Five years old his
Father * moved to Ohio; then a wilderness filled with
wild beasts, & Indians. During the long journey which
was performed in part or mostly with an *ox team;* he
was called on by turns to assist a boy Five years older
(who had been adopted by his Father & Mother) &
learned to think he could accomplish *smart things* in
driving the Cows; and riding the horses. Sometimes he
met with Rattle Snakes which were very large; & which
some of the company generally managed to kill. After
getting to Ohio in 1805 he was for some time rather

---

* A correspondent thus writes of John Brown's father: "My recollections of John
Brown begin in the winter of 1806-7. I was then five years old. My father's family
lived that winter at Hudson, Ohio, which was then one of the remotest of the settlements made by Connecticut people on their Western Reserve. One of our nearest neighbors there was Mr. Owen Brown, who had removed to Hudson, not long before, from
Connecticut. I remember him very distinctly, and that he was very much respected
and esteemed by my father. He was an earnestly devout and religious man, of the
old Connecticut fashion; and one peculiarity of his impressed his name and person
indelibly upon my memory. He was an inveterate and most painful stammerer — the
first specimen of that infirmity that I had ever seen, and, according to my recollection,
the worst that I had ever known to this day; consequently, though we removed from
Hudson to another settlement early in the summer of 1807, and returned to Connecti
cut in 1812, so that I rarely saw any of that family afterwards, I have never to this
day seen a man struggling and half strangled with a word stuck in his throat, without
remembering good Mr. Owen Brown, who could not speak without stammering, *except
in prayer.*"

3

afraid of the Indians, & of their Rifles; but this soon
wore off: & he used to hang about them quite as much
as was consistent with good manners; & learned a
trifle of their talk. His Father learned to dress Deer
Skins, & at 6 years old John was installed a young
Buck Skin—He was perhaps rather observing as he
ever after remembered the entire process of Deer Skin
dressing; so that he could at any time dress his own
leather such as Squirel, Raccoon, Cat, Wolf or Dog
Skins; & also learned to make Whip Lashes: which
brought him some change at times; & was of considerable service in many ways.—At Six years old
John began to be quite a rambler in the wild new
country finding birds & Squirels, & sometimes a wild
Turkey's nest.   But about this period he was placed
in the school of *adversity:* which my young friend was
a most necessary part of his early training. You may
laugh when you come to read about it; but these were
sore trials to John: whose earthly treasures were very
few & small. These were the beginning of a severe
but *much needed course* of discipline which he afterwards was to pass through; & which it is to be hoped
has learned him before this time that the Heavenly
Father sees it best to take all the little things out of his
hands which he has ever placed in them. When John
was in his Sixth year a poor *Indian boy* gave him a
Yellow Marble the first he had ever seen. This he
thought a great deal of; & kept it a good while; but
at last *he lost it* beyond recovery. *It took years to heal
the wound;* & I *think* he cried at times about it. About
Five months after this he caught a young Squirrel

tearing off his tail in doing it; & getting severely bitten at the same time himself. He however held on *to the little bob tail* Squirrel; & finally got him perfectly tamed, so that he almost idolized his pet. *This too he lost;* by its wandering away; or by getting killed: & for a year or Two John was *in mourning;* and looking at all the Squirrels he could see to try & discover Bob tail, *if possible.* I must not neglect to tell you of a very *bad & foolish* habbit to which John was somewhat addicted. I mean *telling lies:* generally to screen himself from blame; or from punishment. He could not well endure to be reproached; & I now think had he been oftener encouraged to be entirely frank; *by making frankness a kind of atonement* for some of his faults; he would not have been so often guilty of this fault; nor have been obliged to struggle *so long* in after life with *so mean* a habit. John was *never quarelsome;* but was *excessively* fond of the *hardest & roughest* kind of plays; & could *never get enough* [of] them.

Indeed when for a short time he was sometimes sent to School the opportunity it afforded to wrestle & Snow ball & run & jump & knock off old seedy wool hats; offered to him almost the only compensation for the confinement, & restraints of school. I need not tell you that with such a feeling & but little chance of going to school *at all:* he did not become much of a schollar.* He would always choose to stay

* "He did not go to Harvard. He was not fed on the pap that is there furnished. As he phrased it, 'I know no more grammar than one of your calves' But he went to the University of the West, where he studied the science of Liberty; and, having taken his degrees, he finally commenced the public practice of humanity in Kansas. Such were his humanities — he would have left a Greek accent slanting the wrong way, and righted up a falling man." — HENRY D. THOREAU.

at home & work hard rather than be sent to school;
& during the warm season might generally be seen
barefooted & bareheaded: with Buck skin Breeches
suspended often with one leather strap over his shoulder
but sometimes with Two.   To be sent off through the
wilderness alone to very considerable distances was particularly his delight; & in this he was often indulged so
that by the time he was Twelve years old he was sent off
more than a Hundred Miles with companies of cattle;
& he would have thought his character much injured
had he been obliged to be helped in any such job.
This was a boyish kind of feeling but characteristic
however.*

At Eight years old John was left a Motherless
boy which loss was complete & permanent, for notwithstanding his Father again married to a sensible, inteligent, & on many accounts a very estimable woman: *yet he never addopted her in feeling:* but
continued to pine after his own Mother for years.   This
opperated very unfavourably uppon him; as he was

---

* A friend, referring to a later period, thus writes of John Brown's woodmanship:
"In his early manhood he had been a surveyor, and as such had traversed a large part
of Ohio and Pennsylvania and Western Virginia, and was thus in some degree familiar
with the locality where, it would seem, he intended to operate. This life in the woods,
to which he was trained from a boy, gave him the habits and the keen senses of a
hunter or an Indian. He told me he had been remarkably clear-sighted and quick of
ear, and that he had smelled the frying of doughnuts at five miles' distance; but this
was when extremely hungry. He knew all the devices of woodcraft; declared he
could make a dinner for forty men out of the hide of one ox, and thought he understood how to provide for an army's subsistence."

Last Spring, when in Boston, John Brown asked me where he could learn to "make
crackers in a rough way," in ovens, to be burrowed out in hill-sides; and where, also,
he could be taught how to manufacture beef-meal. He had often found it inconvenient, he said, to keep a herd of oxen, as they required too many men to tend them,
and could not always be concealed. He wanted to know how to boil a herd down into
a few barrels of beef-flour, so as to be ready for a speedy transportation, and to keep his
men employed when not engaged in other duties. I believe he learned the process
ere he left.

both naturally fond of females; & withall extremely
diffident; & deprived him of a suitable connecting
link between the different sexes; the want of which
might under some circumstances have proved his ruin.

When the war broke out *with England*,* his Father
soon commenced furnishing the troops with beef cattle,
the collecting & driving of which *afforded* him some .
opportunity for the chase (on foot) of wild steers &
other cattle through the woods. During this war he
had some chance to form his own boyish judgment of
men & measures : & to become somewhat familiarly
acquainted with some who have figured before the
country since that time.† The effect of what he saw
during the war was to so far disgust him with military
affairs that he would neither train, *or drill;* but paid
fines; & got along like a Quaker untill his age finally
has cleared him of Military duty.

During the war with England a circumstance occurred that in the end made him a most *determined
Abolitionist :* & led him to declare, *or Swear : Eternal war* with Slavery. He was staying for a short time

* "He accompanied his father to the camp, and assisted him in his employment, seeing considerable of military life, more, perhaps, than if he had been a soldier, for he
was often present at the councils of the officers. He learned by experience how
armies are supplied and maintained in the field. He saw enough of military life to
disgust him with it, and to excite in him a great abhorrence of it. Though tempted
by the offer of some petty office in the army, when about eighteen, he not only declined
to accept this, but refused to train, and was fined in consequence. He then resolved
that he would have nothing to do with any war unless it were a war for liberty." —
HENRY D. THOREAU.

† A friend, in his "Reminiscences of John Brown," thus writes of this period:
"As a boy he was present at Hull's surrender, in 1812, and overheard conversations
between Cass, McArthur, and other subordinate officers of that General, which, he said,
if he could have reported them to the proper persons at Washington, would have
branded them as mutineers. To their disorderly conduct he ascribed 'he surrender,
and thought great injustice had been done to Hull, who, though an old man, and unfit
for such a command, was brave and honest."

3 *

with a very gentlemanly landlord once a United States
Marshall who held a slave boy near his own age very
active, intelligent and good feeling; & to whom John
was under considerable obligation for numerous little
acts of kindness. *The master* made a great pet of
John: brought him to table with his first company;
& friends; called their attention to every little smart
thing he *said, or did:* & to the fact of his being more
than a hundred miles from home with a company of
cattle alone; while the *negro boy* (who was fully if
not more than his equal *) was badly clothed, poorly
fed; *& lodged in cold weather:* & beaten before his
eyes with Iron Shovels or any other thing that came
first to hand. This brought John to reflect on the
wretched; hopeless condition, of *Fatherless & Motherless* slave *children:* for such children have neither
Fathers nor Mothers to protect, & provide for them.
He sometimes would raise the question *is God their
Father ?*

At the age of Ten years an old friend induced him
to read a little history; & offered him the free use of
a good library; by; which he acquired some taste for
reading: which formed the principle part of his early
education: & diverted him in a great measure from
bad company. He by this means grew to be very fond
of the company, & conversation of old & intelligent
persons. He never attempted to dance in his life; nor
did he ever learn to know *one* of a pack of *cards* from
another. He learned nothing of Grammer; nor did

---

* This early fact is as characteristic of his modesty as humanity : both distinguishing traits of his old age.

he get at school so much knowledge of common Arithmetic as the Four ground rules. This will give you
some general idea of the first Fifteen years of his life;
during which time he became very strong & large of
his age & ambitious to perform the full labour of a
man; at almost any kind of hard work. By reading
the lives of great, wise & good men their sayings,
and writings; he grew to a dislike of vain & frivo-
lous *conversation & persons;* & was often greatly
obliged by the kind manner in which older & more
inteligent persons treated him at their houses; & in
conversation; which was a great relief on account of
his extreme bashfulness.*

He very early in life became ambitious to excel in
doing any thing he undertook to perform. This kind
of feeling I would recommend to all young persons
both *male & female :* as it will certainly tend to secure admission to the company of the more inteligent;
& better portion of every community. By all means
endeavor to excel in some laudable pursuit.

I had like to have forgotten to tell you of one of
John's misfortunes which set rather hard on him while
a young boy. He had by some means *perhaps* by gift
of his Father become the owner of a little Ewe Lamb
which did finely till it was about Two Thirds grown;
& then sickened & died. This brought another pro-

---

* "He told me," writes a distant relative of John Brown, "that when a lad, say of
fourteen, he had been at work on the road along with a man who should have been
above mere trifling and nonsense, but who talked nothing else. Returning home at
evening with the company in the ox-cart, as the convenient custom was, he dropped
some expression of contempt for this man. This led my paternal grandfather to take
special notice of him as a thoughtful boy, and to improve every opportunity to advise
and instruct him as he might."

tracted *mourning season:* not that he felt the pecuniary loss so much: for that was never his disposition: but so strong & earnest were his atachments.

John had been taught from earliest childhood to "fear God & keep his commandments;" & though quite skeptical he had always by turns felt much serious doubt as to his future well being; & about this time became to some extent a convert to Christianity & ever after a firm believer in the divine authenticity of the Bible.* With this book he became very familiar, & possessed a most unusual memory of its entire contents.

Now some of the things I have been *telling of;* were just such as I would recommend to you: & I w^d like to know that you had selected these out; & adopted them as part of your own plan of life; & I wish you to have *some definite plan.* Many seem to have none; & others never stick to any that they do form. This was not the case with John. He followed up with *tenacity* whatever he set about so long as it answered his general purpose: & hence he rarely failed in some good degree to effect the things he undertook. This was so much the case that he *habitually expected to succeed* in his undertakings. With this feeling *should be coupled;* the consciousness that our plans are right in themselves.

During the period I have named John had acquired a kind of ownership to certain animals of some little

---

* He joined the Congregational church in Hudson, Ohio, at the age of sixteen. Ten years later, on moving to Pennsylvania, he transferred his membership to the Presbyterian church, with which he remained connected till the day of his martyrdom.

value but as he had come to understand that the *title of minors* might be a little imperfect ; he had recourse to various means in order to secure a more *independant;* & perfect right of property. One of those means was to exchange with his Father for some thing of far less value. Another was by trading with other persons for something his Father had never owned. Older persons have some times found difficulty with *titles.*

From Fifteen to Twenty years old, he spent most of his time working at the Tanner & Currier's trade keeping Bachelors hall ; & he officiating as Cook ; & for most of the time as forman of the establishment under his Father. During this period he found much trouble with some of the bad habits I have mentioned & with some that I have not told you off: his concience urging him forward with great power in this matter : but his close attention to *business;* & success in its management; together with the way he got along with a company of men, & boys ; made him quite a favorite with the serious & more inteligent portion of older persons. This was so much the case ; & secured for him so many little notices from those he esteemed ; that his vanity was very much fed by it : & he came forward to manhood quite full of self-conceit ; & self-confident ; notwithstanding his *extreme* bashfulness. A younger brother used sometimes to remind him of this : & to repeat to him *this expression* which you may somewhere find, " A King against whom there is no rising up." The habit so early formed of being obeyed rendered him in after life too much disposed to speak in an imperious & dictating way. From Fifteen years &

upward he felt a good deal of anxiety to learn; but
could only read & studdy a little; both for want of
time; & on account of inflammation of the eyes.   He
however managed by the help of books to make himself
tolerably well acquainted with common arithmetic; &
Surveying: which he practiced more or less after he
was Twenty years old.

At a little past Twenty years led by his own incli-
nation *&· prompted also* by his Father, he married a
remarkably plain; but neat industrious & economical
girl; of excellent character; earnest piety; & good
practical common sense; about one year younger than
himself.   This woman by her mild, frank, & *more than
all* else: by her very consistent conduct; acquired &
ever while she lived maintained a most powerful; &
good influence over him.   Her plain but kind admoni-
tions generally had the right effect; without arousing
his haughty obstinate temper.   John began early in life
to discover a great liking to fine Cattle, Horses, Sheep,
& Swine: & as soon as circumstances would enable him
he began to be a practical *Shepherd: it being* a calling
for which *in early* life he had a kind of *enthusiastic
longing:* * together with the idea that as a business it
bid fair to afford him the means of carrying out his
greatest or principle object.   I have now given you a
kind of general idea of the early life of this boy; & if
I believed it would be worth the trouble: or afford

* A friend writes: " So keen was his observation, that, as was told me, he knew
when a strange sheep had got into his flock of two or three thousand head. He was a
great lover of good stock of all kinds — cattle, sheep, swine, and horses, and cared tenderly for all the beasts he owned or used."

much interest to any good feeling person : I might be tempted to tell you something of his course in after life; or manhood. I do not say that I *will do it.*

You will discover that in using up my *half sheets to save paper;* I have written Two pages, so that one does not follow the other as it should. I have no time to write it over; & but for unavoidable hindrances in traveling I can hardly say when I should have written what I have. With an honest desire for your best good, I subscribe myself,   Your Friend

J. Brown.

P. S.   I had like to have forgotten to acknowledge your contribution in aid of the cause in which I serve. God Allmighty *bless you;* my son.   J. B.

HE STUDIES FOR THE MINISTRY.

To this autobiographical sketch, there is one important incident of John Brown's early life to be added. "At the age of eighteen or twenty," writes a reliable authority, " he left Hudson, Ohio, and came East, with the design of acquiring a liberal education through some of our New England colleges. His ultimate design was the gospel ministry. In pursuance of this object he consulted and conferred with the Rev. Jeremiah Hallock, then clergyman at Canton, Connecticut, and in accordance with advice there obtained, proceeded to Plainfield, Massachusetts, where, under the instruction of the late Rev. Moses Hallock, he was fitted or nearly fitted for college."

The youngest brother of this clergyman thus describes John Brown :

" He was a tall, sedate, dignified young man. He had been a tanner, and relinquished a prosperous business for the purpose of intel-
lectual improvement, but with what ultimate end I do not now know.
He brought with him a piece of sole leather, about a foot square, which
he had himself tanned for seven years to resole his boots. He had
also a piece of sheepskin which he had tanned, and of which he cut some
strips about an eighth of an inch wide for other students to pull upon.
Father took one string, and, winding it around his fingers, said, 'I
shall *snap* it.' The very marked, yet kind unmovableness of the
young man's face on seeing father's defeat — father's own look, and the
position of the people and things in the old kitchen — somehow gave
me a fixed recollection of this little incident. How long John Brown
lived at our house, or at what period, I do not know. I think it must
have been in 1819 or 1820. I have the name John Brown on my list
of father's students. It is said that he was a relative of uncle Jeremiah Hallock's wife, and that uncle J. directed him to Plainfield."

" While pursuing his studies," says the first writer:

" He was attacked with inflammation of the eyes, which ultimately
became chronic, and precluded him from the possibility of the further
pursuit of his studies, when he returned to Ohio. Had not this inflammation supervened John Brown would not have died a Virginia
culprit on a Virginia gallows, but in all probability would have died
on a feather bed with D. D. affixed to his name."

God had higher work for this sedate, dignified young
man than to write and deliver sermons to a parish. He
was raising him up as a deliverer of captives . and a
teacher of righteousness to a nation ; as the conserver
of the light of true Christianity, when it was threatened
with extinction, under the rubbish of creeds and constitutions, and iniquities enacted into laws.

III.

THE MAN.

I DO NOT propose, in the present volume, to minutely trace the life of John Brown from the date of his
first marriage in 1821, up to the time of his removal to
Massachusetts, in 1846. Although this period embraces
twenty-five years, its incidents do not form an essential
part of his public career ; nor is a knowledge of them
requisite to correctly comprehend the illustrious actions of his later age. Every record of this quarter of
a century, let it suffice for me to state, exhibits to us
the same earnest, pious, and heroic character, which,
by its unusual manifestations during the last two
months, has thrilled the pulses of sixteen States. The
keeper of sheep, the humble farmer and tanner, appears, by the writings he has left behind him, and the
testimony of all who knew him, equally as courageous
and devout a personage as the Liberator of Kansas, the
Invader of Virginia, and the Prisoner of the Jail of
Charlestown.

The last chapter, indeed, is a prophecy of what his
future life would be, too faithful in its outline, and too
minute in its details, to render any record of its fulfil-

ment, in every varying phase of his business career, essential to a just conception of his character. It would be easy and safe enough to pass over these twenty-five years, without looking at a solitary incident of them, and yet to know that he would, and how he would, pour them full to the brim of the living waters of earnest deeds. Given: a stern inflexibility of purpose, and an earnestness of nature so intense that it did not seem to exist, — as wheels that revolve with the velocity of lightning, hardly seem to the looker-on to be moving at all; adding to them an infinite faith in God, and man, and freedom, growing out of a soul of the utmost integrity, self-reliance, modesty, and almost child-like simplicity, transfused with the teachings of Jesus Christ, and inspired by the examples of the Old Testament: putting this rare creation into the walks of lowly life, at the head of a loyal and patriarchal household, and in a nation which, in its eager hunt after gold, too often extinguishes the Holy Lamp placed by the hand of Deity in the human soul; and one can readily foresee how, wherever it shall move, common men at times must stand aghast at it — smiling sometimes in derision — oftener speaking in a pity begotten of involuntary admiration for the poor " monomaniac," who is so erratic as to follow his Heaven-implanted instincts, " no matter how ridiculous" in the eyes of fools they may be, " or how inconvenient to himself;" and " without the intellect to comprehend the necessities, the nature, and the obligations arising out of civil society."* To understand John Brown, the

---

* These phrases are quoted from conservative Republican journals. I spare the editors the misfortune of their names.

first thing needed is, to know what earnest sincerity
means. Do you believe in God? Do you believe the
Bible? John Brown believed in Jehovah and His Word.
Sincerely, for nothing was permitted to stand between
the commandments of Jehovah and his obedience to
them; sincerely, for while our scribes and pharisees
derided him, he translated his belief into earnest deeds,
and thereby proved how vain and false were their loud
professions. He was the last of the old Puritan type
of Christians. Gideon to him, and Joshua, and Moses,
were not interesting historic characters merely, — as,
judging from their acts, modern Christians regard
them, but holy examples set before us, by Deity himself, for our imitation and our guidance. Is the Bible
true? Yes, say many modern Christians, never doubting their own sincerity, and then denounce any forcible emancipation of God's enslaved poor. If the Bible
is the true Word, it follows that it is right to slay
God's enemies, if it be necessary thus to deliver God's
persecuted people. In John Brown's eyes, what Joshua did, and Jehovah sanctioned, could not be wrong.
And so with every doctrine. Between the command
of the Lord of Hosts and implicit obedience to it, he
permitted neither Creed nor Platform, Constitution nor
Law, to intervene. Did the Fathers of the Republic
intend to tolerate slavery? He might admit the historic fact; but still would he obey the divine command
— and interfere with slavery. Most men have a Third
Heaven of Abstract Theories, while their civil actions
form the pillars of a Hell. John Brown's acts were
in harmony with his God-inspired creed.

It was thus in every relation of his private life, during this long period of twenty-five years, over which we will now hurriedly pass, in order that we may the sooner come to those gigantic cameras — Harper's Ferry, and the Jail of Charlestown — in which, for forty days, every line and lineament of the old Puritan's noble soul were drawn with the unvarying fidelity of Nature.

THE FAMILY RECORD.

John Brown was married to his first wife, Dianthe Lusk, June 21, 1820, at Hudson, in Ohio. In order to make no interruptions in the narrative, or confusion of dates, I subjoin here the family record as it stood at John Brown's death.

By his first wife, John Brown had seven children :

JOHN BROWN, junior, July 25, 1821, at Hudson, Ohio; married Wealthy C. Hotchkiss, July, 1847. He now lives in Ashtabula County, Ohio; now fully recovered from his once dangerous malady.

JASON BROWN, January 19, 1823, Hudson, Ohio; married Ellen Sherboudy, July, 1847.

OWEN BROWN, November 4, 1824, Hudson, Ohio; he escaped from Harper's Ferry.

FREDERICK BROWN, (1st,) January 9, 1827, Richmond, Pennsylvania; died March 31, 1831.

RUTH BROWN, February 18, 1829, Richmond, Pennsylvania; married Henry Thompson, September 26, 1850.

FREDERICK BROWN, (2d,) December 21, 1830, Richmond, Pennsylvania; murdered at Osawatomie by Rev. Martin White, August 30, 1856.

An INFANT SON, born August 7, 1832, was buried with his mother three days after his birth.

By his second wife, Mary A. Day, to whom he was married at Meadville, Pennsylvania, (while he was living at Richmond, in Crawford County,) he had thirteen children :

SARAH BROWN, born May 11, 1834, at Richmond, Pennsylvania; died September 23, 1843.

WATSON BROWN, October 7, 1835, Franklin, Ohio; married Isa-oella M. Thompson, September, 1856; wounded at Harper's Ferry, October 17, while bearing a flag of truce; died October 19, 1859.

SALMON BROWN, October 2, 1836, Hudson, Ohio; married Abbie C. Hinckley, October 15, 1856; lives at North Elba.

CHARLES BROWN, November 3, 1837, Hudson, Ohio; died September 11, 1843.

OLIVER BROWN, March 9, 1839, Franklin, Ohio; married Martha E. Brewster, April 17, 1858; killed at Harper's Ferry, October 17, 1859.

PETER BROWN, December 7, 1840, Hudson, Ohio; died September 22, 1843.

AUSTIN BROWN, September 14, 1842, Richfield, Ohio; died September 27, 1843.

ANNE BROWN, December 23, 1843, Richfield, Ohio.

AMELIA BROWN, June 22, 1845, Akron, Ohio; died October 30, 1846.

SARAH BROWN, (2d,) September 11, 1846, Akron, Ohio.

ELLEN BROWN, (1st,) May 20, 1848, Springfield, Massachusetts; died April 30, 1849.

INFANT SON, April 26, 1852, Akron, Ohio; died May 17, aged 21 days.

ELLEN BROWN, (2d,) September 25, 1854, Akron, Ohio.

Thus, eight children now survive ; four by each wife.

THE YOUNG TANNER.

From his twenty-first to his twenty-sixth year, John Brown was engaged in the tanning business, and as a farmer, in Ohio.

In 1826, he went to Richmond, Richland township, Crawford County, Pennsylvania, where he carried on the old business till 1835. One of his apprentices at this period informs us that he was characterized for singular probity of life, and by his strong and " eccentric" benevolent impulses. He would refuse to sell leather until the last drop of moisture had been dried from it, " *lest he should sell his customers water, and reap the gain.*"

4*

"He is said to have caused a man to be arrested, or rearrested, for some small offence, not easily substantiated to a jury, or who had already passed a preliminary examination without effect, although he had sustained no personal injury, but simply because he thought the crime should be punished; and his benevolence induced him to supply the wants of the offender out of his private means, and to provide for the family until the trial."*

That stern old English sense of justice; that grand Puritan spirit of inflexible integrity — how beautifully do they bloom out, thus early, in the life of this illustrious man!. Evidently, in honor of this bright trait, history will place John Brown, in her American Pantheon, not among Virginia's culprits, but as high, at least, as Virginia's greatest chief, whose best sayings and achievements that young man just, was afterwards to be slaughtered by Washington's native State, for attempting to carry out to their legitimate results.

CHANGES OF RESIDENCE.

In 1835, he removed to Franklin Mills, Portage County, Ohio, where, until 1841, he was engaged in the tanning trade, and speculating in real estate. He made several unfortunate investments, and lost a considerable amount of money.

In March, 1839, he started from Ohio for Connecticut, with a drove of cattle. He returned in July of the same year, and brought back with him a few sheep, his first purchases in that business, in which he afterwards was so largely interested.

* This incident is related by a citizen of Warren, Pennsylvania, who knew him well, and regarded him at that time as an exemplary and highly Christian man.

In 1840, he went to Hudson, Ohio, and engaged in the wool business with Mr. Oviatt, of Richfield; to which place, in 1842, John Brown removed, and remained two years, when he entered into a partnership with Colonel Perkins. During his residence in Richfield, he lost four children, all of them within eleven days; and three were carried out together and interred in the same grave. "From boyhood," writes Mr. Oviatt, "I have known him through manhood; and through life he has been distinguished for his truthfulness and integrity; he has ever been esteemed, by those who have known him, as a very conscientious man."

It was in 1839 that he conceived the idea of becoming a Liberator of the Southern slaves. He had seen, during the twenty-five years that had elapsed since he became an Abolitionist, every right of human nature, and of the Northern States, ruthlessly trodden under the feet of the tyrannical Slave Power. He saw it blighting and blasting the manhood of the nation; and he listened to "the voice of the poor that cried." He heard Lafayette loudly praised; but he saw no helper of the bondman. He saw the people building the sepulchres of the fathers of '76, but lynching and murdering the prophets that were sent unto them. He believed that,

"Who would be free, themselves must strike the blow."

But the slaves, scattered; closely watched; prevented from assembling to conspire; without arms; apparently overpowered; at the mercy of every traitor; knowing the white man only as their foe; seeing, every where and always, that (as the Haytian proverb pithily ex-

presses it,) *"Zie blanc, bouille negues"* — the eyes of
the whites burn up the negroes — in order to arise and
strike a blow for liberty, needed a positive sign that
they had friends among the dominant race, who sympathized with them, believed in their right to freedom,
and were ready to aid them in their attempt to obtain
it. John Brown determined to let them know that
they had friends, and prepared himself to lead them to
liberty. From the moment that he formed this resolution, he engaged in no commercial speculations, which
he could not, without loss to his friends and family,
wind up in fourteen days. He waited patiently.
" LEARN TO WAIT : I have waited twenty years," he
often said to the young men of principle and talent,
who loved and flocked around him when in Kansas.

In 1844, John Brown removed to Akron, Ohio ; in
1846, he went to Springfield, Massachusetts ; where,
in the following year, his family joined him.

A few life notes now are all that can be given here.

JOHN BROWN'S FAVORITE BOOKS, TEXTS, AND HYMNS.

" My dear father's favorite books, of an historical character," writes a daughter, " were Rollin's Ancient History, Josephus's Works, Napoleon and his Marshals, and
the Life of Oliver Cromwell. Of religious books : Bax-
ter's Saints' Rest, (in speaking of this work, at one time,
he said he could not see how any person could read it
through carefully without becoming a Christian,) the
Pilgrim's Progress, Henry on Meekness ; but above all
others, the BIBLE was his favorite volume, and he had
such a perfect knowledge of it, that when any person was
reading it, he would correct the least mistake. His favorite passages were these, as nearly as I can remember :

" 'Remember them that are in bonds as bound with them.

" 'Whoso stoppeth his ear at the cry of the poor, he also shall cry himself, but shall not be heard.

" 'He that hath a bountiful eye shall be blessed; for he giveth his bread to the poor.

" 'A good name is rather to be chosen than great riches, and loving favor rather than silver and gold.

" 'Whoso mocketh the poor reproacheth his Maker, and he that is glad at calamities shall not be unpunished.

" 'He that hath pity upon the poor lendeth unto the Lord, and that which he hath given will he pay him again.

" 'Give to him that asketh of thee, and from him that would borrow of thee turn not thou away.

" 'A righteous man regardeth the life of his beast; but the tender mercies of the wicked are cruel.

" 'Withhold not good from them to whom it is due, when it is in the power of thine hand to do it.

" 'Except the Lord build the house, they labor in vain that build it; except the Lord keep the city, the watchman walketh in vain.

" 'I hate vain thoughts, but thy law do I love.'

"The last chapter of Ecclesiasticus was a favorite one, and on Fast days and Thanksgivings he used very often to read the fifty-eighth chapter of Isaiah.

"When he would come home at night, tired out with labor, he would, before going to bed, ask some of the family to read chapters, (as was his usual course night and morning,) and would most always say, Read one of David's Psalms.

"His favorite hymns (Watts's) were these — I give the first lines only :

" 'Blow ye the trumpet, blow.'
" 'Sweet is Thy work, my God, my King.'
" 'I'll praise my Maker with my breath.'
" 'O, happy is the man who hears.'
" 'Why should we start, and fear to die.'
" 'With songs and honors sounding loud.'
" 'Ah, lovely appearance of death.' "

He was a great admirer of Oliver Cromwell. Of

colored heroes, Nat Turner and Cinques stood first in
his esteem. "How often," writes a daughter, "have I
heard him speak in admiration of Cinques' character
and management in carrying his points with so little
bloodshed!" Of American writings, he chiefly admired
the sayings of Franklin, and the Farewell Address of
Washington.

I do not see how any one could draw the character
of John Brown better than by referring the reader to
his favorite books. The Bible, first and above all other
volumes, inspired every action of his life. He searched
it continually to find there the words of eternal life.
Nay, years hence, Christendom will recognize in John
Brown a translation of the Old Testament, not into
English words, but American flesh and blood.

As a father he was tenderly austere; as a husband
devotedly faithful and kind.

He brought up his family as the Hebrew patriarchs
reared their children. The law of God was their earliest and most constant study; unbounded and willing
obedience to it, their first and chief lesson. They
bended their knees every morning and evening at God's
altar; daily read the sacred volume, and sung psalms
and hymns, and spiritual songs. Grace before and after
meat sanctified their board. The patriarchal principle
of filial reverence was in this family a distinguishing
trait. Self-sacrifice was their idea of earthly life.

"The Puritan idea,"—here it was out-lived; nowhere else was the grandest thing brought over in
the Mayflower so sacredly preserved. Some descend-
ants of the passengers in that classic ship have chairs,

and tables, and other material evidences of her voyage
to America ; but this great family had the Idea that she
personifies, not pompously displayed in parlors or muse-
ums, but módestly, unconsciously, in their daily lives.

The sayings of Franklin, as will be seen in another
chapter, were exhibited in daily life in the household of
John Brown. And the Declaration of Independence
—-we will see how it was incarnated when we find the
old man and his sons in Kansas and Virginia.

" One of his favorite verses was," says a daughter,

> " Count that day lost whose low-descending sun
> Views from thy hand no worthy action done."

Here, although in advance of the time, two incidents
may be related, which show how the ideas of the Bible
interpenetrated his whole being.

" I asked him," says a child, " how he felt when he
left the eleven slaves, taken from Missouri, safe in Canada ? His answer was, ' " Lord, permit now thy servant to depart in peace, for mine eyes have seen thy
salvation." I could not brook the idea that any ill
should befall them, or they be taken back to slavery.
The arm of Jehovah protected us.' "

The next anecdote, related since the old man's cap
tivity, by a distinguished citizen of Pennsylvania, is no
less characteristic :

'He has elements of character, which, under circumstances favorable to their proper development and right direction, would have made
him one of the great men of the world. Napoleon himself had no
more blind and trusting confidence in his own destiny and resources;
his iron will and unbending purpose were equal to that of any man,
living or dead; his religious enthusiasm and sense of duty (exaggerated and false though it was) were yet earnest and sincere, and not
excelled by that of Oliver Cromwell or any of his followers; while no

danger could for a moment-alarm or disturb him. Though doubtless his whole nature was subject to, and almost constantly, for the last three or four years, pervaded by the deepest excitement, his exterior was always calm and cool. His manner, though conveying the idea of a stern and self-sustaining man, was yet gentle and courteous, and marked by frequent and decided manifestations of kindness; and it can probably be said of him, with truth, that, amid all his provocations, he never perpetrated an act of wanton or unnecessary cruelty. He was scrupulously honest, moral, and temperate, and never gave utterance to a boast. Upon one occasion, when one of the ex-Governors of Kansas said to him that he was a marked man, and that the Missourians were determined, sooner or later, to take his scalp, the old man straightened himself up, with a glance of enthusiasm and defiance in his gray eye, ' Sir,' said he, ' *the angel of the Lord will camp round about me.*' "

His self-sacrificing spirit, his devotion to the American idea, — in its spirit " which giveth life," not in its letter " which is death," — may be clearly seen in a single sentence from one of his family :

" On leaving us the first time that he went to Kansas, he said, ' If it is so painful for us to part, with the hope of meeting again, how dreadful must be the separation for life of hundreds of poor slaves ! ' "

He inspired every one of his family with this heroic Christianity. His sons were all young fathers ; John Browns, junior, every one. His son-in-law, also, was touched with the holy fire from the altar of the old man's soul.

" When William Thompson," * writes a sister-in-law, " talked of going to Harper's Ferry, his wife begged of him not to go, telling him that she was afraid he would be murdered : he said, ' O Mary, you do not think of any thing but self ! What is my life in comparison to thousands of poor slaves in bondage ? ' "

* He whom the " party of Virginia gentlemen " murdered in cold blood.

For John Brown's habits a few words will suffice. He was a very early riser, and a very hard worker. His dress was extremely plain ; never in the fashion, and never made of fine cloth. But he was always scrupulously clean and tidy in his personal appearance. When first I saw him in his camp at Kansas, although his clothing was patched and old, and he was almost barefooted, he was as tidy, both in person and dress, as any gentleman of Boston. He was noted for his orderly and methodic business habits. His account books and correspondence (which have been sacredly preserved) are models of systematic arrangement. Even to the day of his death, he regularly filed his letters, writing the name of the correspondent, and the word " Answered," or " Not time to read," or " No answer needed," on every one of them. His food was always plain and simple. He never used tobacco in any form, or wine or spirits on any pretence whatever. When at home, he drank milk, or water only. It was not till within a few years before his death, that he ever tasted tea or coffee. He relinquished this habit only from the desire to give no trouble to others ; for he found that in travelling, it sometimes annoyed good people to see their guests drink water instead of tea. He never ate cheese or butter. " When a little boy, ten years of age, he was sent of an errand, where a lady gave him a piece of bread and butter. He was so bashful, that he did not dare to tell her he never ate butter ; and as soon as he got out of the house, he ran as fast as he could for a long distance, and then threw the gift out of sight."

5

Mr. Doolittle, of Ohio, Mr. Weeks and Mr. Hallock, of Connecticut, were his favorite pastors. Although a rigid Puritan, he loved Theodore Parker. "I am free to say," he once told me, "that I do not agree with Mr. Parker in religious matters ; I think he is mistaken in most of his views ; but I like him, sir ; he is a good man."

"Captain Brown," writes a friend, "was extremely fond of music. I once saw him sit listening with the most rapt attention to Schubert's Serenade, played by a mutual friend, and, when the music ceased, tears were in the old man's eyes. He was indeed most tender-hearted — fond of children and pet creatures, and always enlisted on the weaker side. The last time I saw him in Boston, he had been greatly annoyed by overhearing in the street some rude language addressed to a black girl, who, he said, would never have been insulted if she had been white. To him might well be applied the words of the old Scotch ballad:

"'O Douglas, Douglas, tender and true.'"

Of the different members of John Brown's family I cannot write now ; but, on another occasion, I shall try to do justice to the old hero as a father. I think, from what I know of him, that John Brown by his wife's chair and the cradle of his children, was even a greater man than John Brown at Osawatomie, and on the scaffold of Charlestown.

Mrs. Brown, the present widow, was a fit mate for her husband. Is it necessary to say more ? If it be, I cannot write it. His first wife's character he himself has drawn, and the reader has seen the portrait.

I have a few testimonials of John Brown's character
during this long period, from men who knew him well.
Mr. Baldwin, of Ohio, who has known him from 1814,
" considered him a man of rigid integrity and of ardent
temperament." Mr. George Leech, who knew him from
early boyhood, says that he "always appeared strictly
conscientious and honest, but of strong impulses and
strong religious feelings." Mr. William S. C. Otis writes,
" I became acquainted with John Brown about the year
1836 ; soon after my removal to Akron, he became a
client of mine ; subsequently a resident of the township in which the town of Akron is situated ; and, during a portion of the latter time, a member of a Bible
class taught by me. In these relations which I sustained to Mr. Brown, I had a good opportunity to become acquainted with his mental, moral, and religious
character. I always regarded him as a man of more
than ordinary mental capacity, of very ardent and
excitable temperament, of unblemished moral character ; a kind neighbor, a good Christian, deeply imbued
with religious feelings and sympathies. In a business
point of view, his ardent and excitable temperament
led him into pecuniary difficulties ; but I never knew
his integrity questioned by any person whatever."

Since the foregoing chapter was stereotyped, I have found among
the North Elba manuscripts the following "Phrenological Description of John Brown, as given by O. S. Fowler." It is dated New
York, February 27, 1847 :

JOHN BROWN PHRENOLOGICALLY DESCRIBED.

" You have a brain of good size, and a physical organization of much more than
ordinary strength to sustain it. I should judge that you were from a long-lived ancestry, and that you yourself have inherited such a constitution as would enable you,
under ordinary circumstances, to live to a good old age. Your mind did not mature

as early as the majority of persons, but it is of the kind that is continually expanding and improving, and will continue to augment in power to a more advanced age than that of most persons. You are very active, both physically and mentally — are positive in your likes and dislikes, 'go the whole figure or nothing,' and want others to do the same. Your first ideas and impressions are your best; and, as a general thing, you will find them a more safe guide than your after deliberations. You have the faculty to take in all the various conditions of a thing at once, and hence the reason for the correctness of your first impressions. You are quick and clear in your perceptions, have good judgment of the quality and value of property, are a great observer, and want to *see*. You are more known for your practical off-hand talent than for depth and profundity of comprehension — have a discriminating mind, are quick to draw inferences, and are quite disposed to criticise. You reason more by analogy than from abstract principles, and are more practical than theoretical. You have a remarkable memory of faces and places, but poor of names and dates. You can measure well by your eye, and are annoyed if you see any thing out of proportion, or not exactly plumb — have an excellent memory of shape, outline, and size of whatever you see — are a systematic, methodical man : like to have a place for things, and things in their places. Your ability to reckon figures mentally is naturally good — you have a great deal of mechanical ingenuity, are just the man to set others at work, to make bargains, and do up the out-door business. You have a pretty good opinion of yourself — would rather lead than be led — have great sense of honor, and would scorn to do any thing mean or disgraceful. In making up your mind you are careful and judicious, but are firm as the hills when once decided. You might be persuaded, but to drive you would be impossible. You like to have your own way, and to think and act for yourself — are quite independent and dignified, yet candid, open, and plain ; say just what you think, and most heartily despise hypocrisy and artificiality ; yet you value the good opinion of others, though you would not stoop to gain applause. You are quite cautious and prudent, and generally look out for breakers ahead, and realize quite as much as you expect. It would be an advantage to you if you had a little more hope, and would allow yourself to look more on the bright side of things. As a religious man, you would be more inclined to deal justly and love mercy than to pay much regard to forms and ceremonies. You have not enough devotional feeling, nor of what we term spirituality of mind, to give harmony and balance to the moral sentiments. They should be cultivated. You believe what can be incontestably proved, and nothing else. You like to do business on a large scale, and can make money better than save it — you want it for its uses, in one form or another, rather than for its own sake. Your ability to read the characters of others is excellent, but you have little tact in adapting yourself to them. You are too blunt and free-spoken — you often find that your motives are not understood, and that you give offence when you do not intend to. When you criticise, you are apt to do it in such a plain, pointed manner that it does not produce so good an effect as it would if you should do it in a more bland and affable way. You have strong domestic feelings, are very fond of children, home, and friends ; you may be irritable, but are not contentious. You do not like to plod over one subject for a length of time ; but, on the contrary, like variety and change. Your thoughts and feelings are more rapid and lasting. In your character and actions you are more original than imitative, and have more taste for the useful than the beautiful and ornamental."

IV.

PERKINS AND BROWN, WOOL FACTORS.

JOHN BROWN went to Springfield, Massachusetts, in 1846. The following extract from a private letter by an eminent citizen of that place, to whom, when in prison, he wrote for legal assistance, will show the estimation in which he was held by the conservative men with whom he came in contact in his business relations there.

JOHN BROWN IN SPRINGFIELD.

"Your letter asking for such information as I am able to give you respecting John Brown is received, and in order to enable me to answer it more fully than I could otherwise have done, I have called upon a man who was his bookkeeper when he lived here. This person informs me that he came here from Akron, Ohio, in the spring of 1846, and engaged in the business of wool-dealing. He was afterwards associated in business with a Mr. Perkins, of Ohio, and their firm was Perkins and Brown. They sold large quantities of wool on commission; most of it was for farmers living in Western Pennsylvania. Mr. Brown left here in 1850 or 1851, and removed with his family to North Elba, Essex County, New York. This person says Gerritt Smith gave him a large tract of land there. He says he knows it because he saw the deed. . . . Mr. Brown's integrity was never doubted, and he was honorable in all his dealings, but peculiar in many of his notions, and adhering to them with great obstinacy. Mr. Brown was a quiet and peaceable citizen, and a religious man. Rev. Mr. Conklin, who was settled here in the North Congregational Church, and who separated himself in a great measure from other min-

5 *   (53)

isters because he thought them culpably indifferent to the sin of
slavery, was intimate with Mr. Brown, and they sympathized in their
anti-slavery ideas. Mr. Brown used to talk much on the subject, and
had the reputation of being quite ultra. His bookkeeper tells me
that he and his eldest son used to discuss slavery by the hour in his
counting room, and that he used to say that it was right for slaves to
kill their masters and escape, and thought slaveholders were guilty of
a very great wickedness. He says Brown had lived in .Ohio forty
years, and had been out there from Connecticut several times on foot;
that he was familiar with the region about Harper's Ferry, and knew
the wool growers in all that part of the country.

"Since Brown went to Kansas he has been in town several times.
I have seen him repeatedly. Once he called on me to inquire whether
the Emigrant Aid Company would assist him to purchase arms for the
protection of himself and his neighbors. I told him he could get no
aid from them. I understood he afterwards solicited subscriptions
from individuals. I never knew how he succeeded. He was here
again last summer, and called on me, and told me what he had been
doing in Kansas. His story was such that I told him I did not think
he had done wrong. He professed to have acted solely for the protection of himself and his neighbors, and said he went to Missouri to help
the slaves escape, merely to frighten the Missourians, and keep them
from going to Kansas to disturb the people, and that he was successful
in it. I cannot learn that he spoke to any one in this region of his
Harper's Ferry enterprise, and do not believe that he did. A lady
here asked him if he was not going to lead a quiet life hereafter, and
he replied that he should *unless he had a call from the Lord*."

A local journalist thus writes of John Brown's char-
acter in Springfield:

"While a resident of this city Brown was respected by all who
knew him for his perfect integrity of character. . . . He is so constituted that when he gets possessed of an idea he carries it out with
unflinching fidelity to all its logical consequences, as they seem to him,
hesitating at no absurdity, and deterred by no unpleasant consequences
to himself.* . . Brown was here about a year ago, and spent several days.
He talked freely with his friends in respect to his running off slaves from
Missouri. He seemed to feel that he had a special mission in respect
to slavery, and he justified the running off of slaves, not on the ground
of personal vengeance for the bitter wrongs he had received, but as an

---

* This statement was advanced as a proof that John Brown was a monomaniac! I
think it is the bitterest satire on the age that I have ever read — an unconscious and
unintentional, but no less resplendent eulogium on the character of my friend.

effective mode of operation against the institution itself. His theory was then, and it was the secret of his Harper's Ferry movement, that his mission was to make the institution insecure, to increase the general feeling of its insecurity at the South, and thus to act upon the fear and prudence of the slaveholders. In all this he was deliberate, calm, and conscientious. Doubtless his personal wrongs had contributed to the establishment of this fixed purpose of his life; but his vengeance was directed not against slaveholders, but against the institution itself. It was a matter of religion with him. He is a Presbyterian in his faith, and feels that it is for this very purpose that God raised him up."*

HIS FAILURE IN WOOL SPECULATIONS.

There are conflicting accounts of the reasons that induced John Brown to remove to Springfield. The best authenticated records, thus far produced, go to show it was the result of that same spirit of resistance to organized wrong which had distinguished itself in his own history and the history of his ancestry. A half-friendly writer says:

"John Brown initiated the system of grading wools — a system at this day universally adopted, and with perfect success; *but the New England manufacturers combined against him.* He had at Springfield, Massachusetts, a large deposit of graded Western wools, and he warred against the combination of New England manufacturers, who, having

---

* A correspondent who visited Springfield in 1847, and saw John Brown there, thus records an incident illustrative of his great strength of memory :

'In the summer of 1847, it happened to me that I spent a Sunday at the American House, in Springfield, Mass. A stranger who had seen my name on the register of the hotel, came to my room and claimed acquaintance with me. He was a plain man, intelligent in his appearance, with something of that independent air which so naturally characterizes Western men, his head beginning to be whitened, (if I remember correctly,) but his upright frame still perfectly firm and sinewy. As I was quite unable to recognize him, he told me he was John Brown, and made me remember, at last, that we were schoolfellows more than fifty years before, when I was one of the least of the pupils in the little log-cabin school at Hudson. I cannot recollect distinctly what he told me about his residence, his occupation, or his history; but I remember clearly the impression that he was an earnestly religious man, with somewhat more of the old Puritan sternness than is common in these days, and with some tendency to that eccentricity of opinion and of action which in modern phrase is called 'ultraism.' I am not sure that slavery was spoken of between us; but it was evident that his mental and moral idiosyncrasy would place him among men to whom extreme opinions on such a subject are most natural."

had the wool buying all their own way, did not fancy that a party should step in between them and the producers to show the latter what was for their interest, and to prevent the practice of imposition upon them. The combination was successful, and Brown, impetuous and indignant, shipped his wools to England, to find out that the price in Massachusetts was better than in Europe."

Another writer says:

"In 1848 we find him in a large woollen warehouse in Springfield, Massachusetts, where he was known as a quiet, modest man, of unswerving integrity. Indeed, hundreds of wool-growers in Northern Ohio consigned their stock to him to be sold at discretion. A combination of Eastern manufacturers, who wished to have no such stern and unflinching man between themselves and the wool-growers, formed in league against him, and forced him to send his wool to Europe for a market, which resulted in a second disaster, and Brown was again reduced to poverty."

The amount thus taken to Europe was two hundred thousand pounds, which was sold in London for half its value, and then reshipped to Boston.

JOHN BROWN IN EUROPE.

Of John Brown's travels in Europe, the only record in existence, as far as the writer can ascertain, is the following extract from reminiscences of conversations with him (already quoted) by a noted friend of freedom in Massachusetts:

"I heard from him an account of his travels in Europe, and his experience as a wool-grower. He had chiefly noticed in Europe the agricultural and military equipment of the several countries he visited. He watched reviews of the French, English, and German armies, and made his own comments on their military systems. He thought a standing army the greatest curse to a country, because it drained off the best of the young men and left farming and the industrial arts to be managed by inferior men. The German armies he thought slow and unwieldy; the German farming was bad husbandry, because there the farmers did not live on their land, but in towns, and so wasted the natural manures which should go back to the soil. England he thought the best cultivated country he had ever seen, but the seats of the English gentry he thought inferior to those of the wealthy among us. He visited several of the famous battle grounds of Napoleon, whose career he had followed with great interest; but he thought him

·vrong in several points of strategy, particularly in his choice of
;round for a strong position ; which Captain Brown maintained should
`ie a ravine rather than a hill top.   In riding with him in an adjoining
county, he pointed out several such ravines, which, he said, could be
]ield by a few men against a large force, adding that he had acted on
this principle in Kansas, and never suffered from it.   He ascribed his
·vinning the battle of Black Jack to his choice of ground.*   He thought
no American could visit Europe without coming home more in love
·vith our own country, for which he had a most ardent affection, while
].e so cordially hated its greatest curse — SLAVERY.

"He was noted for his skill in testing and recognizing different
qualities of wool.   Give him two samples of wool, one grown in Ohio
and the other in Vermont, and he would distinguish each of them in
the dark.   I have heard this story told of him while in England, where
]e went to consult wool-merchants and wool-growers.   One evening,
i company with several of these persons, each of whom had brought
samples of wool in his pocket, Captain Brown was giving his opinion
i s to the best use to be made of certain varieties of wool, when one of
the party, wishing to play a trick on the Yankee farmer, handed him
c sample, and asked him what he would do with such wool as that?
]Iis eyes and fingers were then so good, that he had only to touch it
to know that it had not the minute hooks by which the fibres of wool
cre attached to each other.   'Gentlemen,' said he, 'if you have any
rachinery that will work up dog's hair, I would advise you to put this
i ito it.'   The jocose Briton had sheared a poodle and brought the hair
i his pocket, but the laugh went against him ; and Captain Brown, in
spite of some peculiarities of dress and manner, soon won the respect
of all whom he met."

When in England at this time, John Brown di-
vulged his plan of liberation to several prominent
anti-slavery men ; but there, as elsewhere, while they
felt and professed an unbounded sympathy for the
slave, they neither countenanced nor approved of the
very earnest scheme of this dreadfully-in-earnest abolitionist.   The Peters had but little sympathy with
the Richards — the Heralds of Freedom, although an
earnest people, looked with suspicion and distrust on
the equally earnest Crusaders.   Singular, that the

---

* John Brown had undoubtedly great skill in choosing his ground and in erecting
field fortifications. Many of them still exist in Southern Kansas.

preachers of the word should only half welcome the
actors of it! Both are noble, and needed, and God-
commissioned; but the greatest of the Heralds, I
think, was not worthy to untie the latchet of John
Brown's shoes.

JOHN BROWN AND ANTHONY BURNS.

In the course of the partnership of Perkins and
Brown, a lawsuit arose, which is thus described by a
correspondent at Vernon, near Utica:

"During the years 1852, '3, and '4, Mr. Brown was one of the
firm of Perkins & Brown, doing a large wool trade, buying and selling,
in Ohio, New York, and Massachusetts. The sale of a large quantity
of wool to parties in Troy, N. Y., brought on a lawsuit between
Perkins & Brown and those parties. Mr. Brown's counsel resided in
Vernon, and he was here many times during those years. He prosecuted that suit with all the vigor and pertinacity which he is said to
have since displayed in other matters. He obtained a verdict in his
favor, just before the Anthony Burns affair in Boston — I think in
1853. The Trojans appealed from their verdict, and Brown then
spent some weeks here in looking over the testimony with his counsel,
and preparing an answer.

"The morning after the news of the Burns affair reached here,
Brown went at his work immediately after breakfast; but in a few
minutes started up from his chair, walked rapidly across the room
several times, then suddenly turned to his counsel, and said, 'I am
going to Boston.' 'Going to Boston!' said the astonished lawyer.
'Why do you want to go to Boston?' Old Brown continued walking vigorously, and replied, 'Anthony Burns must be released, or I
will die in the attempt.' The counsel dropped his pen in consterna-
tion. Then he began to remonstrate; told him the suit had been in
progress a long time, and a verdict just gained. It was appealed from,
and that appeal must be answered in so many days, or the whole labor
would be lost; and no one was sufficiently familiar with the whole
case except himself. I took a long and earnest talk with Old Brown
to persuade him to remain. His memory and acuteness in that long
and tedious lawsuit — not yet ended, I am told — often astonished his
counsel. While here he wore an entire suit of snuff-colored cloth,
the coat of a decidedly Quakerish cut in collar and skirt. He wore
no beard, and was a clean-shaven, scrupulously neat, well-dressed,
quiet old gentleman. He was, however, notably resolute in all that
he did."

V.

NORTH ELBA.

JOHN BROWN and his family removed to North Elba, in Essex County, New York, in 1849. It was about this time that Mr. Gerritt Smith, the eminent philanthropist, offered to colored settlers his wild lands in that district of the Adirondack wilderness. Many of them accepted the offer, and went there to make the experiment.

"At this period," writes a friend, "John Brown appeared one day at Peterboro', and said to Mr. Smith: 'I see, by the newspapers, that you have offered so many acres of wild land to each of the colored men, on condition that they cultivate them. Now, they are mostly inexperienced in this kind of work, and unused to the climate, while I am familiar with both. I propose, therefore, to take a farm there myself, clear it and plant it, showing the negroes how such work should be done. I will also employ some of them on my land, and will look after them in all ways, and will be a kind of father to them.' Mr. Smith accepted the generous proposal, gave John Brown the land, and allowed him to make the experiment, although he had never before seen him."

So far as the negroes were concerned, this proved a failure, but through no fault of John Brown's. He did his part faithfully by them.

"Captain Brown had a higher notion of the capacity of the negro race than most white men. I have often heard him dwell on this subject, and mention instances of their fitness to take care of themselves,

(59)

saying, in his quaint way, that ' they behaved so much like *folks* that he almost thought they were so.'   *He thought that perhaps a forcible separation of the connection between master and slave was necessary to educate the blacks for self-government;* * but this he threw out as a suggestion merely."

The home of John Brown, and the romantic region around it, have been visited by a scholar worthy of the original, whose translation of their grandeur, physical and moral, into the English language, makes the journey henceforward unnecessary, — save only for "instruction in godliness."   We see both the glory of the mountains, and the grandeur of the faith that animates its greatest family, in the vivid and touching description of a visit to the home of John Brown, herewith subjoined, — from the true and worthy pen of Thomas Wentworth Higginson.   No woman can read it without being deeply moved; and if there be a man who can do so — God pity him.

THE ROUTE TO NORTH ELBA.

"The traveller into the enchanted land of the Adirondack has his choice of two routes from Keeseville to the Lower Saranac Lake, where his out-door life is to begin.   The one least frequented and most difficult should be selected, for it has the grandest mountain pass that the Northern States can show.   After driving twenty-two miles of mountain road from Keeseville, past wild summits bristling with stumps, and through villages where every other man is black from the iron foundery, and every alternate one black from the charcoal pit, your pathway makes a turn at the little hamlet of Wilmington, and you soon find yourself facing a wall of mountain, with only glimpses of one wild gap through which you must penetrate.   In two miles more you have passed the last house this side the Notch, and you then drive on over a rugged way, constantly ascending, with no companion but the stream which ripples and roars below.   Soon the last charcoal clearing is past, and thick woods of cedar and birch

---

* There is a terrible truth wrapped up in this suggestion.   To obtain a recognition of their equality in countries where negro slavery has existed, the blacks must either fight the whites *and defeat them,* or seek to establish a separate nationality elsewhere.

close around you—the high mountain on your right comes nearer and nearer, and close beside, upon your left, are glimpses of a wall, black and bare as iron, rising sheer for four hundred feet above your head. Coming from the soft marble country of Vermont, and from the pale granite of Massachusetts, there seems something weird and forbidding in this utter blackness. On your left the giant wall now appears nearer—now retreats again; on your right foams the merry stream, breaking into graceful cascades—and across it the great mountain Whiteface, seamed with slides. Now the woods upon your left are displaced by the iron wall, almost touching the road-side; against its steep abruptness scarcely a shrub can cling, scarcely a fern flutter; it takes your breath away; but five miles of perilous driving conduct you through it; and beyond this stern passway, this cave of iron, lie the lovely lakes and mountains of the Adirondack, and the homestead of JOHN BROWN.

THE HOMESTEAD AND ITS ORNAMENTS.

"The Notch seems beyond the world, North Elba and its half dozen houses are beyond the Notch, and there is a wilder little mountain road which rises beyond North Elba. But the house we seek is not even on that road, but behind it and beyond it; you ride a mile or two, then take down a pair of bars; beyond the bars, faith takes you across a half-cleared field, through the most difficult of wood-paths, and after half a mile of forest you come out upon a clearing. There is a little frame house, unpainted, set in a girdle of black stumps, and with all leaven about it for a wider girdle; on a high hill-side, forests on north and west,—the glorious line of the Adirondacks on the east, and on the south one slender road leading off to Westport, a road so straight that you could sight a United States marshal for five miles.

"There stands the little house, with no ornament nor relief about it—it needs none with the setting of mountain horizon. Yes, there is one decoration which at once takes the eye, and which, stern and misplaced as it would seem elsewhere, seems appropriate here. It is a strange thing to see any thing so old, where all the works of man are new! but it is an old, mossy, time worn *tombstone*—not marking any grave, not set in the ground—but resting against the house as if its time were either past or not yet come. Both are true—it has a past duty and a future one. It bears the name of Captain John Brown, who died during the Revolution, eighty-three years ago; it was his tombstone brought hither by his grandson bearing the same name and title; the latter caused to be inscribed upon it, also, the name of his son Frederick, 'murdered at Osawatomie for his adherence to the cause of freedom,' (so reads the inscription;) and he himself has said, for years, that no other tombstone should mark his grave.

"For two years, now, that stone has stood there — no oath has been taken upon it, no curses been invoked upon it — it marks the abode of a race who do not curse. But morning and noon, as the sons have gone out to their work on that upland farm, they have passed by it; the early light over the Adirondacks has gilded it, the red reflection of sunset has glowed back upon it; its silent appeal has perpetually strengthened and sanctified that home — and as the two lately wedded sons went forth joyfully on their father's call to keep their last pledge at Harper's Ferry, they issued from that doorway between their weeping wives on the one side and that ancestral stone upon the other.

THE FARM, AND WHY JOHN BROWN BOUGHT IT.

"The farm is a wild place; cold and bleak. It is too cold to raise corn there; they can scarcely, in the most favorable seasons, obtain a few ears for roasting. Stock must be wintered there nearly six months in every year. I was there on the first of November; the ground was snowy, and winter had apparently begun — and it would last till the middle of May. They never raise any thing to sell off that farm, except sometimes a few fleeces. It was well, they said, if they raised their own provisions, and could spin their own wool for clothing.

"Do you ask why they lived in such a bleak spot? With John Brown and his family there is a reason for every thing, and it is always the same reason. Strike into their lives any where, and you find the same firm purpose at bottom, and to the widest questioning the same prompt answer comes ringing back, — the very motto of the tombstone — 'For adherence to the cause of freedom.' The same purpose, nay, the selfsame project that sent John Brown to Harper's Ferry, sent him to the Adirondack.

"Twenty years ago, John Brown made up his mind that there was an irrepressible conflict between Freedom and Slavery, and that in that conflict he must take his share. He saw at a glance, moreover, what the rest of us are only beginning to see, even now — that Slavery must be met, first or last, on its own ground. The time has come to tell the whole truth now — that John Brown's whole Kansas life was the result of this self-imposed mission, not the cause of it. Let us do this man justice; he was not a vindictive guerilla, nor a maddened Indian: nor was he of so shallow a nature that it took the death of a son to convince him that right was right, and wrong was wrong. He had long before made up his mind to sacrifice every son he ever had, if necessary, in fighting Slavery. If it was John Brown against the world, no matter; for, as his friend Frederick Douglass had truly said, "In the right, *one* is a majority." On this conviction, therefore, ne deliberately determined, twenty years ago this summer, that at some future period he would organize an armed party, go into a Slave State, and liberate a large number of slaves. Soon after, surveying professionally in the mountains of Virginia, he chose the very ground for his purpose. Visiting Europe afterwards, he studied military strategy for this purpose, even making designs (which I have seen) for a new style of forest fortification, simple and ingenious, to be used by parties of fugitive slaves when brought to bay. He knew the ground, he knew his plans, he knew himself; but where should he find his men? He came to the Adirondack to look for them.

"Ten years ago, Gerritt Smith gave to a number of colored men tracts of ground in the Adirondack Mountains. The emigrants were grossly defrauded by a cheating surveyor, who, being in advance of his age, practically anticipated Judge Taney's opinion, that black men have no rights which white men are bound to respect. By his villainy the colony was almost ruined in advance; nor did it ever recover itself; though some of the best farms which I have seen in that region are still in the hands of colored men. John Brown heard of this; he himself was a surveyor, and he would have gone to the Adirondack, or any where else, merely to right this wrong. But he had another object; he thought that among these men he should find coadjutors in his cherished plan. He was not wholly wrong, and yet he afterwards learned something more. Such men as he needed are not to be *found* ordinarily; they must be *reared*. John Brown did not merely look for men, therefore; he reared them in his sons. During long years of waiting and postponement, he found others; but his sons and their friends (the Thompsons) formed the nucleus of his force in all his enterprises. What services the females of his family may have rendered, it is not yet time to tell; but it is a satisfaction to think that he was repaid for his early friendship to these New York colored men, by some valuable aid from freed slaves and fugitive slaves at Harper's Ferry; especially from Dangerfield Newby, who, poor fellow! had a slave wife and nine slave children to fight for, all within thirty miles of that town.

"To appreciate the character of the family, it is necessary to know these things; to understand that they have all been trained from childhood on this one principle, and for this one special project; taught to believe in it as they believed in their God or their father. It has given them a wider perspective than the Adirondacks. Five years before, when they first went to Kansas, the father and sons had a plan of going to Louisiana, trying this same project, and then retreating into Texas with the liberated slaves. Nurtured on it so long, for years sacrificing to it all the other objects of life, the thought of its failure never crossed their minds; and it is an extraordinary fact that when the disastrous news first came to North Elba, the family utterly refused to believe it, and were saved from suffering by that incredulity till the arrival of the next weekly mail."

A PAUSE AT THE THRESHOLD.

"I had left the world outside, to raise the latch of this humble door amid the mountains; and now my pen falters on the threshold, as my steps did then. This house is a home of sacred sorrow. How shall we enter it? Its inmates are bereft and ruined men and women, as the world reckons; what can we say to them? Do not shrink; you are not near the world; you are near John Brown's household. 'In the world ye shall have tribulation; but be of good cheer: *they* have overcome the world.'

"It had been my privilege to live in the best society all my life—namely, that of abolitionists and fugitive slaves. I had seen the most eminent persons of the age: several men on whose heads tens of thousands of dollars had been set; a black woman, who, after escaping from slavery herself, had gone back secretly eight times into the jaws of death to bring out persons whom she had never seen; and a white man, who, after assisting away fugitives by the thousand, had twice been stripped of every dollar of his property in fines, and when taunted by the Court, had mildly said, 'Friend, if thee knows any poor fugitive in need of a breakfast, send him to Thomas Garrett's door.' I had known these, and such as these; but I had not known the Browns. Nothing short of knowing them can be called a liberal education. Lord Byron could not help clinging to Shelley, because he said he was the only person in whom he saw any thing like disinterested benevolence. He really believed that that man would give his life for another. Poor Byron! he might well have exchanged his wealth, his peerage, and his genius for a brief training at North Elba.

"Let me pause a moment, and enumerate the members of the family. John Brown was born in 1800, and his wife in 1816, though both might have been supposed older than the ages thus indicated. He has had in all twenty children—seven being the offspring of his first wife, thirteen of his second. Four of each race are living—eight in all. The elder division of the surviving family are John and Jason, both married, and living in Ohio; Owen, unmarried, who escaped from Harper's Ferry, and Ruth, the wife of Henry Thompson, who lives on an adjoining farm at North Elba, an intelligent and noble woman. The younger division consists of Salmon, aged twenty-three, who resides with his young wife in his mother's house, and three unmarried daughters, Anne, (sixteen,) Sarah, (thirteen,) and Ellen, (five.)

In the same house dwell also the widows of the two slain sons — young girls, aged but sixteen and twenty. The latter is the sister of Henry Thompson, and of the two Thompsons who were killed at Harper's Ferry; they also lived in the same vicinity, and one of them also has left a widow. Thus complicated and intertangled is this genealogy of sorrow.

"All these young men went deliberately from North Elba for no other purpose than to join in this enterprise. 'They could not,' they told their mother and their wives, '*live for themselves alone;.*' and so they went. One young wife, less submissive than the others, prevailed on her husband to remain; and this is the only reason why Salmon Brown survives. . Oliver Brown, the youngest son, only twenty, wrote back to his wife from Harper's Ferry in a sort of premonition of what was coming, 'If I can do a single good action, my life will not have been all a failure.'"

THE FAMILY OF JOHN BROWN.

" Having had the honor of Captain Brown's acquaintance for some years, I was admitted into the confidence of the family, though I could see them observing me somewhat suspiciously as I approached the door. Every thing that was said of the absent father and husband bore testimony to the same simple, upright character. Though they had been much separated from him for the last few years, they all felt it to be a necessary absence, and had not only no complaint to make, but cordially approved it. Mrs. Brown had been always the sharer of his plans. 'Her husband always believed,' she said, 'that he was to be an instrument in the hands of Providence, and she believed it too.' 'This plan had occupied his thoughts and prayers for twenty years.' 'Many a night he had lain awake, and prayed concerning it.' 'Even now,' she did not doubt, 'he felt satisfied, because he thought it would be overruled by Providence for the best.' 'For herself,' she said, 'she had always prayed that her husband might be killed in fight rather than fall alive into the hands of slaveholders; but she could not regret it now, in view of the noble words of freedom which it had been his privilege to utter.' When, the next day, on the railway, I was compelled to put into her hands the newspaper containing the death warrant of her husband, I felt no fears of her exposing herself to observation by any undue excitement. She read it, and then the tall, strong woman bent her head for a few minutes on the seat before us; then she raised it, and spoke calmly as before.

"I thought that I had learned the lesson once for all in Kansas, which no one ever learns from books of history alone, of the readiness with which danger and death fit into the ordinary grooves of daily life, so that on the day of a battle, for instance, all may go on as

6 *

usual; breakfast and dinner are provided, children cared for, and all external existence has the same smoothness that one observes at Niagara, just above the American Fall; but it impressed me anew on visiting this household at this time. Here was a family out of which four noble young men had, within a fortnight, been killed. I say nothing of a father under sentence of death, and a brother fleeing for his life, but only speak of those killed. Now that word *killed* is a word which one hardly cares to mention in a mourning household circle, even under all mitigating circumstances, when sad unavailing kisses and tender funeral rites have softened the last memories; how much less here, then, where it suggested not merely wounds, and terror, and agony, but also coffinless graves in a hostile land, and the last ignominy of the dissecting room.

"Yet there was not one of that family who could not pronounce that awful word with perfect quietness; never, of course, lightly, but always quietly. For instance, as I sat that evening, with the women busily sewing around me, preparing the mother for her sudden departure with me on the morrow, some daguerreotypes were brought out to show me, and some one said, 'This is Oliver, one of those who were killed at Harper's Ferry.' I glanced up sidelong at the young, fair-haired girl, who sat near me by the little table — a wife at fifteen, a widow at sixteen; and this was her husband, and he was KILLED. As the words were spoken in her hearing, not a muscle quivered, and her finger did not tremble as she drew the thread. For her life had become too real to leave room for wincing at mere words. She had lived through, beyond the word, to the sterner fact, and having confronted *that*, language was an empty shell. To the Browns, killing means simply dying — nothing more; one gate into heaven, and that one a good deal frequented by their family; that is all.

"There was no hardness about all this, no mere stoicism of will; only God had inured them to the realities of things. They were not supported by any notions of worldly honor or applause, nor by that chilly reflection of it, the hope of future fame. In conversing with the different members of this family, I cannot recall a single instance of any heroics of that description. There, in that secluded home among the mountains, what have they to do with the world's opinion, even now, still less next century? You remember Carlyle and his Frenchman, to whom he was endeavoring to expound the Scottish Covenanters. 'These poor, persecuted people,' said Carlyle, — 'they made their appeal.' 'Yes,' interrupted the Frenchman, 'they appealed to posterity, no doubt.' 'Not a bit of it,' quoth Carlyle; 'they appealed to the Eternal God!' So with these whom I visited. I was the first person who had penetrated their solitude from the outer

world since the thunderbolt had fallen. Do not imagine that they
asked, What is the world saying of us? Will justice be done to the
memory of our martyrs? Will men build the tombs of the prophets?
Will the great thinkers of the age affirm that our father 'makes the
ga lows glorious, like the cross'? * Not at all; they asked but one
question after I had told them how little hope there was of acquittal
or rescue. *Does it seem as if freedom were to gain or lose by this?*
That was all. Their mother spoke the spirit of them all to me, next
day, when she said, 'I have had thirteen children, and only four are
left; but if I am to see the ruin of my house, I cannot but hope that
Providence may bring out of it some benefit to the poor slaves.'

"No; this family work for a higher price than fame. You know
it is said that in all Wellington's despatches you never meet with the
word Glory; it is always DUTY. In Napoleon's you never meet with
the word Duty; it is always Glory. The race of John Brown is of
the Wellington type. *Principle* is the word I brought away with me
as most familiar in their vocabulary. That is their standard of classi-
fication. A man may be brave, ardent, generous; no matter — if he is
not all this from *principle*, it is nothing. The daughters, who knew
all the Harper's Ferry men, had no confidence in Cook, because 'he
was not a man of principle.' They would trust Stevens round the
world, because 'he was a man of principle.' 'He tries the hardest to
be good,' said Annie Brown, in her simple way, ' of any man I ever
saw.'

"It is pleasant to add that this same brave-hearted girl, who had-
known most of her father's associates, recognized them *all* but Cook
as being men of principle. 'People are surprised,' she said, 'at
father's daring to invade Virginia with only twenty-three men ; but I
think if they knew what sort of men they were, there would be less
surprise. *I* never saw such men.' †

"And it pleases me to remember that since this visit, on the day of
execution, while our Worcester bells were tolling their melancholy
refrain, I took from the post office a letter from this same young girl,
expressing pity and sorrow for the recreant Cook, and uttering the
hope that allowances might be made for his conduct, 'though she
could not justify it.' And on the same day I read that infuriated letter of Mrs. Mahala Doyle — a letter which common charity bids us

---

It was Emerson who uttered this truth of John Brown's death. J. R.

It was so in Kansas "I never saw such men" *outside* of John Brown's camp as
I saw when in it. When the old hero was last in Boston, I said of Cook : " He is brave,
generous, but too talkative, and without discretion; he has no moral foundation for his
bravery." " You've hit the nail, exactly, sir," he said. "That's just my opinion of
him." J. R.

suppose a forgery, uttering fiendish revenge in regard to a man, against whom, by her own showing, there is not one particle of evidence to identify him with her wrongs. Nothing impressed me more in my visit to the Brown family, and in subsequent correspondence with them, than the utter absence of the slightest vindictive spirit, even in words."

JOHN BROWN AMONG HIS CHILDREN.

"The children spoke of their father as a person of absolute rectitude, thoughtful kindness, unfailing foresight, and inexhaustible activity. On his flying visits to the farm, every moment was used; he was 'up at three, A. M., seeing to every thing himself,' providing for every thing, and giving heed to the minutest points. It was evident that some of the older ones had stood a little in awe of him in their childish years. 'We boys felt a little pleased sometimes, after all,' said the son, 'when father left the farm for a few days.' 'We girls *never* did,' said the married daughter, reproachfully, the tears gushing to her eyes. 'Well,' said the brother, repenting, 'we were always glad to see the old man come back again; for if we *did* get more holidays in his absence, we always missed him.'

"Those dramatic points of character in him, which will of course make him the favorite hero of all American romance hereafter, are nowhere appreciated more fully than in his own family. In the midst of all their sorrow, their strong and healthy hearts could enjoy the record of his conversations with the Virginians, and applaud the keen, wise, simple answers which I read to them, selecting here and there from the ample file of newspapers I carried with me. When, for instance, I read the inquiry, 'Did you go out under the auspices of the Emigrant Aid Society?' and the answer, 'No, sir; I went out under the auspices of John Brown,' three voices eagerly burst in with, 'That's true,' and 'That's so.' And when it was related that the young Virginia volunteer taxed him with want of military foresight in bringing so small a party to conquer Virginia, and the veteran imperturbably informed the young man that probably their views on military matters would materially differ, there was a general delighted chorus of, 'That sounds just like father.' And his sublimer expressions of faith and self-devotion produced no excitement or surprise among them — since they knew in advance all which we now know of him — and these things only elicited, at times, a half-stifled sigh as they reflected that they might never hear that beloved voice again.

"References to their father were constant. This book he brought them; the one sitting room had been plastered with the last money he sent; that desk, that gun, were his; this was his daguerreotype; and at last the rosy little Ellen brought me, with reverend hands, her prime t easure. It was a morocco case, enclosing a small Bible; and in the beginning, written in the plain, legible hand I knew so well, the following inscription, which would alone (in its touching simplicity) have been worthy the pilgrimage to North Elba to see.

" 'This Bible, presented to my dearly beloved daughter Ellen Brown, is not intended for common use, but to be carefully preserved *for her* and *by her*, in remembrance of her father, (of whose care and attentions she was deprived in her infancy,) he being absent in the Territory of Kansas from the summer of 1855.

" 'May the Holy Spirit of God incline your heart, *in earliest childhood*, "to receive the truth in the love of it," and to form your thoughts, words, and actions by its wise and holy precepts, is *my best wish* and *most earnest* prayer to Him in whose care I leave you. Amen.   From your affectionate father,

   " 'April 2, 1857.   JOHN BROWN.'

"This is dated two years ago; but the principles which dictated it were permanent. Almost on the eve of his last battle, October 1, 1859, he wrote home to his daughter Anne, in a letter which I saw, '.Anne, I want you first of all to become a sincere, humble, and consistent Christian — and then [this is characteristic] to acquire good and efficient business habits. Save this, to remember your father by, Anne. God Almighty bless and save you all.' "

JOHN BROWN'S ORTHODOXY.

"John Brown is almost the only radical abolitionist I have ever known who was not more or less radical in religious matters also. His theology was Puritan, like his practice; and accustomed as we now are to see Puritan doctrines and Puritan virtues separately exhibited, it seems quite strange to behold them combined in one person again. He and his wife were regular communicants of the Presbyterian church; but it tried his soul to see the juvenile clerical gentlemen who came into the pulpits up that way, and dared to call themselves Presbyterians— preachers of the gospel with all the hard applications left out. Since they had lived in North Elba, his wife said but twice had the slave been mentioned in the Sunday services, and she had great doubts about the propriety of taking part in such worship as that. But when the head of the family made his visits home from Kansas, *he* commonly held a Sunday meeting in the little church, ' under the auspices of John Brown,' and the Lord heard the slave mentioned pretty freely then.

"In speaking of religious opinions, Mrs. Brown mentioned two preachers whose sermons her sons liked to read, and 'whose anti-slavery principles she enjoyed, though she could not agree with all their doctrines.' She seemed to regard their positions as essentially the same. I need not say who the two are — the thunders of Brook-lyn and of Boston acquire much the same sound as they roll up among the echoes of the Adirondacks."

POLITICS.

"In respect to politics, Mrs. Brown told me that her husband had taken little interest in them since the election of Jackson, because he thought that politics merely *followed* the condition of public sentiment on the slavery question, and that this public sentiment was mainly created by actual collisions between slavery and freedom. Such, at least, was the view which I was led to attribute to him, by combining this fact which she mentioned with my own personal knowledge of his opinions. He had an almost exaggerated aversion to words and speeches, and a profound conviction of the importance of bringing all questions to a direct issue, and subjecting every theory to the test of practical application."

THE CHARGE OF INSANITY.

"I did not, of course, insult Mrs. Brown by any reference to that most shallow charge of insanity against her husband, which some even of his friends have, with what seems most cruel kindness, encouraged, — thereby doing their best to degrade one of the age's prime heroes into a mere monomaniac, — but it may be well to record that she spoke of it with surprise, and said that if her husband were insane, he had been consistent in his insanity from the first moment she knew him."

PECUNIARY CONDITION OF THE FAMILY.

"Now that all is over, and we appear to have decided, for the present, not to employ any carnal weapons, such as steel or iron, for the rescue of John Brown, but only to use the safer metals of gold and silver for the aid of his family, it may be natural for those who read this narra-tive to ask, What is the pecuniary condition of this household? It is hard to answer, because the whole standard is different, as to such matters, in North Elba and in Massachusetts. The ordinary condition of the Brown family may be stated as follows: They own the farm, such as it is, without incumbrance, except so far as unfelled forest constitutes one. They have ordinarily enough to eat of what the farm yields, namely, bread and potatoes, pork and mutton — not any great abundance of these, but ordinarily enough. They have ordinarily enough to wear, at least of woollen clothing, spun by themselves.

A: d they have *no* money. When I say this I do not merely mean th: t they have no superfluous cash to go shopping with, but I mean al: 10st literally that they have *none*. For nearly a whole winter, Mrs. Bi own said, they had no money with which to pay postage, except a tin y treasury which the younger girls had earned for that express ob, ect, during the previous summer, by picking berries for a neighbor th: ce miles off.

'The reason of these privations simply was, that it cost money to live in Kansas in 'adherence to the cause of freedom,' (see the tombstone in: cription again,) but not so much to live at North Elba; and there-foi e the women must stint themselves that the men might continue th ir Kansas work. But when the father came upon his visits, he ne 'er came empty-handed, but brought a little money, some plain ho 1sehold stores, flour, sugar, rice, salt fish; tea and coffee they do no : use. But what their standard of expense is may be seen from th : fact that Mrs. Brown seemed to speak as if her youngest widowed da 1ghter were not totally and absolutely destitute, because her hus-ba 1d had left a property of five sheep, which would belong to her. Tl ese sheep, I found on inquiry, were worth, at that place and season, tw > dollars apiece: a child of sixteen, left a widow in the world, with an est ate amounting to ten dollars! The immediate financial anxieties of M: s. Brown herself seemed chiefly to relate to a certain formidable tax bil !, due at New Year's time; if they could only weather *that*, all was cle ar for the immediate future. How much was it, I asked, rather sur-pr sed that that wild country should produce a high rate of taxation. It was from eight to ten dollars, she gravely said; and she had put by tei dollars for the purpose, but had had occasion to lend most of it to a po >r black woman, with no great hope of repayment. And one of the fir :t things done by her husband, on recovering his money in Virginia, wt 3 to send her, through me, fifteen dollars, to make sure of that ta: bill.

'I see, on looking back, how bare and inexpressive this hasty narra-tiv : is; but I could not bear to suffer such a privilege as this visit to pa s away unrecorded. I spent but one night at the house, and drove aw ay with Mrs. Brown, in the early frosty morning, from that breezy m(untain home, which her husband loved (as one of them told me) 'b cause he seemed to think there was something romantic in that ki d of scenery.' There was, indeed, always a sort of thrill in John Bi)wn's voice when he spoke of mountains. I never shall forget the qt ct way in which he once told me that 'God had established the A' .eghany Mountains from the foundation of the world that they m ;ht one day be a refuge for fugitive slaves.' I did not then know th .t his own home was among the Adirondacks.

"Just before we went, I remember, I said something or ther to Salmon Brown about the sacrifices of their family; and he looked up in a quiet, manly way, which I shall never forget, and said briefly, 'I sometimes think that is what we came into the world for — to make sacrifices.' And I know that the murmuring echo of those words went with me all that day, as we came down from the mountains, and out through the iron gorge; and it seemed to me that any one must be very unworthy the society which I had been permitted to enter who did not come forth from it a wiser and a better man."

From the family we learn that:

"In 1851 John Brown and his family returned to Akron, Ohio, where he managed Mr. Perkins's farm, and carried on the wool business. In 1855, on starting for Kansas, he again moved his household to North Elba, where they still reside, and where his body lies buried."

———

At the Agricultural Fair of Essex County, for 1850, a great sensation was created by the unlooked-for appearance on the grounds of a beautiful herd of Devon cattle. They were the first that had been exhibited at the county festival, and every one was surprised and delighted at the incident. The inquiry was universal, Whose are these cattle, and from whence do they come? The surprise and excitement were not diminished when it was understood that a certain John Brown was the owner, and that he resided in the town of North Elba. The report of the society for that year contains the following reference to that event: "The appearance upon the grounds of a number of very choice and beautiful Devons, from the herd of Mr. John Brown, residing in one of our most remote and secluded towns, attracted great attention, and added much to the interest of the fair. The interest and admiration they excited have attracted public attention to the subject, and have already resulted in the introduction of several choice animals into this region. We have no doubt that this influence upon the character of the stock of our county will be permanent and decisive." (Trans. 1850, page 229.)

The writer of this article soon after opened a correspondence with Brown in relation to these cattle. His reply is now before me. The letter is written in a strong and vigorous hand, and by its orthography, accurate punctuation, and careful arrangement of paragraphs, evinces far more than ordinary taste and scholarship. I consider it remarkable, not only for the force and precision of the language, for a business letter, and for the distinctness of its statements, but equally for its sound sense and honesty of representation. I think I am not wrong in the impression that an extract will interest your readers, as illustrating the former habits and pursuits of a man who has impressed an ill-omened episode upon our national history.

"Your favor of the 30th of September came on seasonably; but it was during my absence in Ohio, so that I could not reply sooner. In the first place, none of my cattle are pure Devons, but are a mixture of that and a particular favorite stock from Connecticut, a cross of which I much prefer to any pure English cattle after many years' experience of different breeds of imported cattle. * * * I was several months in England last season, and saw no one stock on any farm that would average better than my own, and would like to have you see them all together." — *Correspondence of the New York Observer.*

Book Second.

GOLIATH'S CHALLENGE ACCEPTED.

7

26. And David spake to the men that stood by him, saying, . . . Who is this uncircumcised Philistine, that he should defy the armies of the living God?

32. And David said to Saul, Let no man's heart fail because of him; thy servant will go and fight with this Philistine.

42. And when the Philistine looked about and saw David, he disdained him.

43. And the Philistine cursed David by his gods.

44. And the Philistine said to David, Come to me and I will give thy flesh unto the fowls of the air and to the beasts of the field.

45. Then said David to the Philistine, Thou comest to me with a sword, and with a spear, and with a shield; but I come to thee in the name of the Lord of Hosts, the God of the armies of Israel, whom thou hast defied.

46. This day will the Lord deliver thee into my hands: and I will smite thee, and take thine head from thee; and I will give the carcasses of the host of the Philistines this day unto the fowls of the air and to the wild beasts of the earth, that all the earth may know that there is a God in Israel.

50. Thereupon David ran and stood upon the Philistine, and took his sword, and drew it out of the sheath thereof, and slew him, and cut off his head therewith. And when the Philistines saw their champion was dead, they fled. — *I Samuel*, Chapter xvii.

I.

The Lord's First Call.

THE 25th day of May, 1854, was a day of great
sorrow, and of the wildest exultation at Washington. An infamous statute had been still more
infamously repealed. Thirty-four years before this
the passage of the Kansas-Nebraska act, — the representatives of the nation, in Congress assembled, for
the first time in our history, and in defiance of the
moral sentiment of Christendom, as well as in opposition to the noblest instincts of human nature, and,
resting on them, the spirit of the Federal Constitution,
solemnly — as they phrased it — and forever prohibited
the existence of slavery "in all that territory which
lies north of thirty-six degrees and thirty minutes;"
but, by the same law, as a "compromise" with the
South, established and legalized her organized and
distinguishing crime in that portion of the Union now
known as Missouri. Triumphant crime is never satisfied with temporary advantages. Missouri now secured, the South coveted Kansas, the most fertile portion of the remaining territory. By the pliancy of
Northern politicians, the compromise was repealed, and

75

Kansas and Nebraska thrown open for settlement. The vital and moral question of the extension of slavery, it was pretended, in justice to "the people," should be settled solely, and could only constitutionally be determined by the first inhabitants themselves. This atrocious doctrine, so revolting to every Christian or manly heart, was euphoniously designated, in the act of repeal and organization, the right to "form their domestic institutions in their own way, subject only to the constitution of the United States." Thus the nation solemnly repudiated the validity of the will of God, disregarded the principles of the Revolutionary Fathers, and ignored the venerated maxim of the common law, that all immoral statutes are void. The enslaving of God's poor children; the traffic in human souls and bodies; the forced, frequent, and final separation of families; the violation of all marital obligations — all the crimes of which slavery is the source, and by which it is supported: the expansion and perpetuation of the sum of all villanies, were questions, this instrument declared, which should be settled by the squatters alone, "subject only to the constitution of the United States." For, that the authors of the bill intended nothing else or more, was admitted in all their subsequent discussions; by the President in his message; and by the South and the Government, in all their actions. Non-intervention was the order of the day. Great and undisguised was the rejoicing at the South; for they thought that Kansas was now secured to them forever.

But, in the North, the indignation of the people,

thus treacherously defrauded of the territorial bribe that had been tendered long ago for the surrender of Missouri, was organized into societies for the encouragement of emigration, and it was every where determined, that, if the pioneers or first denizens of Kansas should pronounce the doom of slavery there, the Free States should have a voice and a vote in the solemn and momentous decision.

Emigration flowed rapidly into Kansas, both from the North and South. But, for a long time, all the advantages were on the side of slavery. Missouri, — her borders on Kansas peopled with semi-barbarous ruffians, — was the jealous guardian of the interests, and a fit representative of the Southern States. Every obstacle was soon thrown in the way of the Northern emigrants. They were driven back; they were tarred and feathered; their claims were seized; their cabins were burned down; they were often ordered, by committees of Southern emigrants, or the Missouri rabble, to leave the Territory at once, under penalty of death. A single paragraph from a single speech by one of the acknowledged champions of the South, will better illustrate their early career in Kansas, than even an extended account of their outrages. It is from a speech delivered at St. Joseph, Missouri, in 1854, by General Stringfellow,* a prominent citizen of that vandal state :

"I tell you to mark every scoundrel among you who is the least tainted with abolitionism, or free soilism, and exterminate him. Neither give nor take quarter from the d—d rascals. To those who have

---

* This is an assumed title; he had no right to it; he proved himself a great coward.

qualms of conscience as to violating laws, state or national, say, the time has come when such impositions must be disregarded, as your rights and property are in danger. I advise you, one and all, to enter every election district in Kansas, in defiance of Reeder and his myrmidons, and vote at the point of the bowie knife and revolver. Neither take nor give quarter, as the cause demands it. It is enough that the slaveholding interest wills it, from which there is no appeal."

This advice, reiterated by every paper and politician in the Platte Purchase, — which was preëminently the border ruffian region, — was translated into action on the 29th of November, 1854, at the first election ever held in Kansas for a delegate to Congress. Seventeen hundred men from Missouri marched over the border and voted in the Territory for the pro-slavery candidate.

The news of this crime against republican institutions excited the renewed indignation of the North. Liberty-loving hearts were every where moved by it. Instead of deterring, it incited emigration. Among the brave pulses thus stirred were those of the family of old John Brown.

"In 1854, the four eldest sons of John Brown,* named John, Jr., Jason, Owen, and Frederick, all children by a first wife, then living in Ohio, determined to remove to Kansas. John, Jr., sold his place, a very desirable little property near Akron, in Summit County. The other two sons held no landed property, but both were possessed of some valuable stock, (as were also the two first named,) derived from that of their father, which had been often noticed by liberal premiums, both in the State of New York and also of Ohio.

---

* This is a quotation from a manuscript in John Brown's handwriting, found at his house near Harper's Ferry.

"Jason Brown had a very valuable collection of grape vines, and also of choice fruit trees, which he took up and shipped in boxes at a heavy cost. The two first named, John and Jason, had both families. Owen had none. Frederick was engaged to be married, and was to return with his wife. In consequence of an extreme dearth in 1854, the crops in Northern Ohio were almost an entire failure, and it was decided by the four brothers that the two youngest should take the teams and entire stock, cattle and horses, and move them to South-Western Illinois to winter, and to have them on early in the spring of 1855. This was done at very considerable expense, and with some loss of stock to John, Jr., some of his best stock having been stolen on the way.

"The wintering of the animals was attended with great expense, and with no little suffering to the two youngest brothers, one of whom, Owen, being to some extent a cripple from childhood, by an injury of the right arm, and Frederick, though a very stout man, was subject to periodical sickness for many years, attended with insanity. It has been publicly stated that he was idiotic; nothing could be more false. He had subjected himself to a most dreadful surgical operation but a short time before starting for Kansas, which had well nigh cost him his life; and was but just through with his confinement when he started on his journey, pale and weak. They were obliged to husk corn all winter, out of doors, in order to obtain fodder for their animals.

"Solomon Brown, a very strong minor son of the

family, eighteen years of age, was sent forward early
in 1855, to assist the two last named, and all three
arrived in Kansas early in the spring. During this
slow journey with their stock across the entire width
of Missouri, they heard much from her people of the
stores of wrath and vengeance which were then and
there gathering for the free state men and abolitionists
gone or going to Kansas, and were themselves often
admonished, in no very mild language, to stop ere it
should be ' too late.' "

They settled near the Pottawattomie, a little stream
in Southern Kansas, in Lykins County, about eight
miles distant from the site of Ossawattomie, which
their father subsequently converted into classic ground.
Of the hardships they endured, and the outrages inflicted on them by the champions of slavery, their
father, in the paper above quoted, gave a detailed
account; but as to have published it would have dam-
aged the democratic party in the elections then pending, we are told that " a portion of the manuscript was
lost," and that " the history was of considerable length,
but did not further possess special interest."

"The brothers," writes a friend of the family,
" were all free state men in opinion; but, removing
thither with the intention of settling there, went without arms. They were harassed, plundered, threatened, and insulted by gangs of marauding border ruffians, with whom the prime object was plunder; and
noisy pro-slavery partizanship was equivalent to a free
charter to do so with impunity. The sons wrote to
their father, requesting him to procure such arms as

might enable them, in some degree, to protect themselves, and personally to bring them to Kansas."

It was not in the nature of John Brown to resist this
petition. He undoubtedly regarded it as a call from
the Almighty to gird up his loins and go forth to do
battle "as the warrior of the Lord," as " the warrior
of the Lord against the mighty," in behalf of His despised poor and His downtrodden people. The moment
long waited for had at length arrived; the sign he had
patiently expected had been given; and the brave old
soldier of the God of Battles prepared at once to obey
the summons.

A meeting of abolitionists was held in a county
adjoining Essex, New York, in the summer of 1855.
" When in session, John Brown appeared in that convention, and made a very fiery speech, during which
he said he had four sons in Kansas, and had three
others who were desirous of going there, to aid in
fighting the battles of freedom. He could not consent
to go unless he could go armed, and he would like to
arm all his sons; but his poverty prevented him from
doing so. Funds were contributed on the spot; principally by Gerritt Smith."

He had only two objects in going to Kansas: first,
to begin the work for which, as he believed, he had
been set apart, by so acting as to acquire the confidence
of the friends of freedom, who might thereby subsequently aid him; and, secondly, because, to use his
own language, " with the exposure, privations, hardships, and wants of pioneer life, he was familiar, and
thought he could benefit his children, and the new

beginners from the older parts of the country, and
help them to shift and contrive in their new home."

John Brown did *not* go to Kansas to settle there.
Already, elsewhere, I have made this statement; and
have seen it doubted by men who are friendly to him
— not from knowledge of his motives, but the dictates
of policy — because democratic journals and pro-slavery
politicians have sought to create a prejudice against
him for having voluntarily gone to Kansas, and *solely*
to fight the battles of freedom : as if it had been a
crime or a disgrace, instead of an illustrious, patriotic,
and Christian act for a Northern man to defend Northern rights; for an anti-slavery champion to oppose by
the sword the armed propagandists of slavery; for a
believer in the Bible to emulate the examples of Moses,
Joshua, and Gideon, and obey the solemn utterances
of the Most High God.   Believing God to be a Being
infallible and unchangeable; believing that He once
had ordered His enemies to be smitten hip and thigh;
believing that the Ever Just had commanded liberty
to be proclaimed " throughout all the land, unto all
the inhabitants thereof; " John Brown did not dare
to remain tending sheep at North Elba when the
American Goliath and his hosts were in the field,
defying the little armies of the living Lord, and sowing
desolation and great sorrow on the soil set apart
for his chosen people.   Either Freedom has no rights,
and the Bible is a lie, or John Brown, in thus acting,
was a patriot and a consistent Christian.

II.

The Work Begun.

BEFORE John Brown reached Kansas, the South had thrown off its flimsy disguises. Its hypocritical pretence of enabling the people to determine the nature of "their own domestic institutions" — that is to say, in honest English, to establish or prohibit the cowardly crime of American slavery — was finally abandoned in the month, and on the fourth, of March, 1856 ; when, instead of permitting the inhabitants of the Territory "freely" to vote for the members of their legislature, four thousand nine hundred and eight non-residents, citizens of Missouri, invaded Kansas, and controlled the elections at every precinct save one.* They elected several men who did not live in Kansas ; who never intended to settle there ; who are citizens of Missouri still. The writer was present at the first session of the legislature thus chosen, and saw it pass laws establishing human slavery, and punishing

---

* Manhattan. It was distant a hundred miles, and more, from Missouri ; and the company elected to control it remained at home, in order to watch the movements of Colonel Park, until it was too late to go to their appointed post.

83

"offences" against it — such as liberating negroes — with the penalty of death; prohibiting, by incarceration in the penitentiary, the exercise of the rights of free speech and a free press; excluding Northern (if anti-slavery) men from the bar, the bench, the ballot box, and the jury chamber; and many other statutes, transcribed from Southern codes, of equal moral atrocity and despotic character.

The Free State men declared that they would never recognize the code thus compiled, or obey the executive officers, whom, by an unprecedented usurpation, this legislature had chosen to enforce its statutes.

During the last week of November, 1855, an incident occurred to test the sincerity of the Free State men. A cowardly murder was committed by a person named Coleman, a pro-slavery settler, on Mr. Dow, a quiet New England emigrant. The authorities, instead of arresting the assassin, leagued themselves with him; and seized an innocent Free State squatter, in order to have him rescued in Lawrence — the Boston of the prairies — that, thereby, they might have a plausible excuse for calling on Missouri to destroy the town, under the pretence of enforcing the territorial laws. The prisoner was unexpectedly rescued several miles from Lawrence; but, despite of this accident, the "territorial militia" — as the rabble from Missouri was officially styled — were called to arms; and, in December, Lawrence was invested by a force of fifteen hundred armed men.

Not more than seventy-five, at any time, were residents of Kansas "Missouri," confessed Governor

Shannon, " sent not only her young men, but her gray-haired citizens were there; the man of seventy winters stood shoulder to shoulder with the youth of sixteen."

The writer and three companions were taken prisoners at this period, a few miles from Lawrence, by a company of eighteen men, who were presently joined by a still larger number; and *not one* of them, as their leader confessed, was, or had ever been, a resident of Kansas, or had any social or pecuniary interest in its present or future prosperity.

To Lawrence at once repaired the fighting men from every district of the Territory. Five hundred Free State men were soon gathered there, drilled daily, and prepared to defend the town to a "bloody issue." The Southern invaders, although three to one, and armed with United States muskets,—although furnished with heavy artillery, and having horsemen in great numbers, were afraid to attack the free men of the North in Lawrence assembled. Governor Shannon, alarmed at the tempest he had raised but could not control, hastened up from the Shawnee Mission to effect a compromise with the leaders of the rebels. He saw hundreds of ruffians around Lawrence armed with guns, which they acknowledged to have stolen from a United States arsenal in Missouri; yet he never complained of them, and none of them have ever been indicted or arrested, although the affidavits attesting the fact of the robbery are in the archives of Government, and the perpetrators of it are well-known persons, men of influence and position in the border districts.

8

This army encamped around Lawrence nearly two weeks. The Free State boys were impatient for a fight. But it was the policy of the leaders to avoid a collision, if possible; or, at least, to compel the enemy to commence the conflict.

"When the siege was pending," writes an eye witness, "the old man, John Brown, and his four sons, arrived in Lawrence. The balance he reported sick. As they drove up in front of the Free State hotel, they were all standing in a small lumber wagon. To each of their persons was strapped a short, heavy broadsword. Each was supplied with a goodly number of fire-arms and navy revolvers, and poles were standing endwise around the wagon box, with fixed bayonets pointing upwards. They looked really formidable, and were received with great eclat. A small military company was organized at once, and the command was given to Old Brown. From that moment, he commenced fomenting difficulties in camp, disregarding the command of superior officers, and trying to induce the men to go down to Franklin, and make an attack upon the pro-slavery forces encamped there. The Committee of Public Safety were called upon several times to head off his wild adventure, as the people of Lawrence had planted themselves on the law, claiming that they had not been guilty of its infraction, and that no armed body of men should enter the town for any purpose whatever, and that they would not go out of town to attack any such body. Peace was established, and Old Brown retired in disgust."

I have quoted this passage rather to contrast it

with the ideas of John Brown than for the facts that it contains, and to show the timid spirit of politicians as compared with the undaunted bearing of earnest, truth-devoted men. The Free State party, when it first met, resolved unanimously and with unbounded enthusiasm to resist the enforcement of the invader's code: if need be — "to a bloody issue." Now that the test came, the people were armed and ready to translate their resolution into revolution; to repeat their acclamations of that brave determination through the muzzles of their rifles and with the edges of their swords. But the politicians quibbled; sought other grounds to stand on; "planted themselves on the law;" restrained the ardor of the people which sought to drive the ruffians homeward or to the grave; saw the good Thomas Barber murdered in the open day for the crime of having visited their town; and yet, with hundreds of invaders of their soil within sight, who were sacking their cabins and robbing and imprisoning their citizens, they calmly "urged them not to allow the daily outrages to drive them to commence hostilities!" *

The leading military man made frequent fierce speeches; but, as the Kansas phrase is, "they all fizzled out" — in urging inaction. He loved to have the citizens under arms, for in tumults he was king; while the leading politician dreaded war for the sake of the republican party.

John Brown was not of this spirit. Slavery to him was a heinous crime, and its propagandists the enemies

* See Conquest of Kansas, by William Phillips, p. 214.

of his God; and with hosts of such men embattled and in view, who added to their championship of slavery the additional crime of invading the soil set apart for freedom, he did not hesitate to express his contempt for the "Committee of Safety"—most of them ox-intellects, vainly striving to fill an office fit for lion-hearts only—and to denounce the political preachers of peace as recreant to their recent and loudly-vaunted resolutions. He went out once with a dozen men to meet the Missouri invaders—"to draw a little blood," as he styled it—but, at the earnest entreaties of General Lane, he returned to the town without doing it.

Lane sent for him to attend a council of war. The reply was characteristic of the brave old man, who despised all manner of assumptions with no fact behind them to give them vitality and a title to respect.

"Tell the General," he said, "that when he wants me to fight, to say so: but that is the only order I will ever obey." *

Governor Shannon soon arrived in Lawrence, and was duly made drunk by the sagacious Free State leaders. While in this condition, or approaching it, he

---

* To better understand John Brown's reasons for despising the commands of these so-called "superior officers," it may be necessary for some minds to know his opinions of the two chief leaders:

"I am sorry for friend Lane," he remarked, as we were speaking of his blustering style of oratory; "I am afraid he does not respect himself.".

Of the other prominent leader, Dr. Robinson, as some radicals were speaking of his subsequent conservatism, he said, "What a pity it is, that men when they begin life, should not get hold of some fixed principles—make up their minds that they are right, and then hold on to them! He did not do that. That is his fault."

made a treaty with General Lane and Dr. Robinson, in
behalf of the "abolition rebels;" and, after guaran-
teeing that he would disperse the Missourians, or
take from them, at least, the cover of legality, he authorized these gentlemen to "take such measures, and
use the enrolled force under their command in such
manner, for the preservation of the peace, and protection of the persons and property of the people of Lawrence and vicinity, as, in their judgment, should best
secure that end." *

This negotiation undoubtedly exhibited both diplo-
matic tact and Yankee ingenuity; but John Brown, a
prophet by virtue of his purity of life and devotion to
ideas, foresaw that it was in fact a coming victory to
the South. For what was this enrolment of the Free
State men but a tacit acknowledgment of Southern
usurpation?

Governor Shannon, on recovering from his drunken-
ness, made a speech to the people assembled in Lawrence. He said, —

"There was a part of the people of this Territory, who denied the
validity of the laws of the Territorial Legislature. He was not there
to urge that validity, but these laws should be submitted to until a
legal tribunal set them aside. He did not see how there was any
course but such submission to them, and it certainly was not his part,
as an executive officer, to set them aside or disregard them. He was
happy to announce that, after having an interview with the officers of
their Committee of Safety, he had induced them thus far to respect
those laws, they being willing to see them enforced, provided they had
the reserved right of testing and escaping from them legally. He

* Kansas, Its Interior and Exterior Life, &c., by Mrs. Sara T. L.
Robinson, p. 154.

8*

was happy to announce that all difficulties were settled. (Faint cheers.) There was a perfect understanding between the Executive and the Committee."

Lane uttered a few fiery sentences, "which were cheered heartily," when Dr. Robinson was called for; who is reported as having "nothing to say but that they had taken an honorable position."

I now quote the book of Mr. William Phillips, the most trustworthy historian of Kansas as to facts: "There was an evident suspicion among the people that the negotiations had been closed too easily, and that their leaders had concealed something.

"CAPTAIN BROWN got up to address the people; *but a desire was manifested to prevent his speaking*. Amid some little disturbance, he demanded to know what the terms were. If he understood Governor Shannon's speech, something had been conceded, and he conveyed the idea that the Territorial laws were to be observed. Those laws they denounced and spit upon, and would never obey — no!

"Here the speaker was interrupted by the almost universal cry, No, no! Down with the bogus laws. Lead us down to fight first!

"Seeing a young revolution on the tapis, the influential men assured the people that *there had been no concession*. They had yielded nothing. They had surrendered nothing to the usurping Legislature. With these assurances the people were satisfied and withdrew. *At that time it was determined to keep the treaty secret*, but before many days it was sufficiently public."

The politicians feared the old man, knowing that neither cunning nor duplicity would please him. Hence their desire to prevent his speaking; hence their determination to keep the Treaty secret; hence their unblushing announcement that nothing had been conceded.

This Treaty, when published, justified the old man's suspicions. By an adroit but dishonest use of the phrases, "legal process" and "the laws," the Treaty was susceptible of a double interpretation; the most obvious and honest one, construing them to refer to Territorial enactments and Territorial legal instruments; while the other, or the Free State translation, rendered it Federal laws and Federal processes only.

John Brown ever afterwards regretted that he returned at General Lane's request, and maintained that this Treaty, and the policy which led to it, only served to postpone the inevitable conflict then rapidly approaching, and to demoralize the spirit of the Free State party. It occasioned, he thought, the death of many Northern men, whom, encouraged by this compromising action, the marauders, on their return, murdered in cold blood or in desultory warfare.

"I have often heard him lament," says an able correspondent of the New York Tribune, "the loss of this chance, with the most earnest sincerity. The odds of five to one he accounted as nothing. 'What are five to one?' said he, 'when our men would be fighting for their wives, their children, their homes and their liberties against a party, one half of whom were mercenary vagabonds, who enlisted for a mere frolic, lured on by the whiskey and the bacon, and a large portion of the others had gone under the compulsion of opinion and proscription, and because they feared being denounced as abolitionists if they refused ?' "

The politicians * called John Brown an "impracticable man," but their own subsequent history, and the history of Lawrence, afford an ample vindication of his conduct at this crisis. His predictions, in less than a year, were historical facts.

* The following amusing paragraph occurs in a Life of John Brown, written by a Republican politician, and published in the New York Herald. To spare an old acquaintance from ridicule, I omit a few words only.

"In December, 1855, during the 'Shannon war,' Brown first made his appearance among the Free State men at Lawrence. His entrance into the place at once attracted the attention of the people towards him. He brought a wagon load of cavalry sabres, and was accompanied by twelve men, seven of whom were his own sons. He first exhibited his qualities at the time the Free State and pro-slavery parties, under the lead of Governor Robinson on one side, and Governor Shannon on the other, met to make a treaty of peace. After Governor Robinson had stated to the people who were gathered around the hotel the terms of the peace, Brown took the stand uninvited, and opposed the terms of the treaty. He was in favor of ignoring all treaties, and such leading men as Robinson, Lane, &c., and, proceeding at once against the border ruffian invaders, drive them from the soil, or hang them if taken. The chairman of the Committee of Safety ordered Brown under arrest. The latter made no physical resistance, *but it was soon discovered that he was altogether too combustible a person to retain as a prisoner,* and a compromise was made with him by the Free State men, and he was released. He was informed by the leaders of that party that his remarks were intended to undo what they were trying to accomplish by means of the treaty; that he was a stranger in Lawrence and Kansas, and ought not, by his rash remarks, to compromise the people of Lawrence, until he had known them longer and knew them better."

III.

"SOUTHERN RIGHTS TO ALL."

THE siege of Lawrence raised, the ruffians, on re turning homeward, on the 15th of December, 1855, destroyed the Free State ballot box at Leavenworth; and, on the 20th, threw the press and types of the *Territorial Register*, the political organ of the author of t ie Kansas-Nebraska act, into the muddy streets of the l ttle town, and the still muddier bed of the Missouri J iver. The leaders of the riot did the writer of this volume the honor to say that the outrage was occas oned by an offensive paragraph emanating from his pen, and expressed themselves exceedingly solicitous to s :e him dangling in the air—for daring "freely" to e xercise the rights of a free press! This was my first public honor; a good beginning, I hoped, for a friend c f the slave; and one which, ever since, I have striven t) deserve.

The election, thus riotously interrupted by the ruf f ans at Leavenworth, was held under the auspices of a voluntary political organization; and the question suh i itted was — Shall the Topeka Constitution be re- j :cted or sustained?

93

The Topeka Constitution, ever intrinsically valueless, but sacred as the rallying standard of the Free State men, was an instrument which originated in the ostensible and vaunted principles of the Organic Act — the right of a people, inhabiting a Territory, to form their own domestic institutions in their own way; among which, if there had been any honesty in the framers of the Bill, or the advocates of the doctrine, the right of choosing a Governor, Judges, Legislators, Executive State officers and municipal functionaries must inevitably have been included. Assuming the good faith of the framers of the Act, the Free State men proceeded to carry out its principles — first, by repudiating the code of enactments compiled by the invaders, and denying the authority of the officers they had elected and appointed to execute them; and, secondly, by calling on the pioneers to choose representatives to a Convention to be held at Topeka, for the purpose of forming a *State* Constitution. The squatters did so; the Topeka Constitution was adopted; and, on the 15th of January, 1856, an election under it, for State officers and legislators, was held throughout the Territory.

The pro-slavery Mayor at Leavenworth forbade an election being held there. But there was one man, — Captain R. P. Brown, — as brave a hero as his venerable namesake — who determined to resist this tyranny; and, on the adjournment of the polls to a neighboring town, went out there with a few friends to defend the rights of free men. The Kickapoo Rangers, a ruffianly gang of Southern desperadoes, marched out there also; a skirmish ensued; they were successfully resisted and ᴄriven back; but Captain Brown, on the following day, in returning home, was surrounded by an overwhelming force; and, at the earnest entreaty of his companions, although against his own judgment, surrendered under a promise that their persons should be safe.

"But the moment this was complied with," writes Mr. Phillips, whose every statement I know to be correct,

"The terms were violated. One young man was knocked down, and a ruffian was going to cut him with his hatchet, (the Kickapoo Rangers carried hatchets,) but was prevented by the Captain of the Company. The prisoners were taken back to Easton; but Brown was separated from them, and put in an adjoining building. A rope was purchased at the store, and was shown to the prisoners, with the intimation that they should be hanged with it. . . . It was fiercely discussed for hours what should be done with them; and meanwhile liquor was drank pretty freely; and they who were brutal enough without any thing to make them more so, became ungovernably fierce. Unwilling that all of these men should be murdered, the Captain allowed the other prisoners to escape. One of them hastened to Fort Leavenworth, in hopes of getting some troops to go and rescue Brown; but it was a vain attempt — such protection was refused. Then followed a scene of atrocity and horror. Captain Brown had surrendered his arms, and was helpless. His enemies, who dared not face him the night before, though they had a superior force, now crowded round him. When they began to strike him, he rose to his feet, and asked to be permitted to fight any one of them. He challenged them to pit him against their best man — he would fight for his life; but not one of the cowards dared thus to give the prisoners a chance. Then he volunteered to fight two, and then three; but it was in vain. . . . These men, or rather demons, rushed around Brown, and literally hacked him to death with their hatchets. One of the rangers, a large, coarse-looking wretch named Gibson, inflicted the fatal blow — a large hatchet gash in the side of the head, which penetrated the skull and brain many inches. The gallant Brown fell, and his remorseless enemies jumped on him, while thus prostrate, or kicked him. Desperately wounded though he was, he still lived; and, as they kicked him, he said, 'Don't abuse me; it is useless; I am dying.' It was a vain appeal. One of the wretches [*since a United States Deputy Marshal*] stooped over the prostrate man, and, with a refinement of cruelty exceeding the rudest savage, spit tobacco juice in his eyes. Satiated brutality at last went back to its carousals, and it was then that a few of their number, whom a little spark of conscience or a fear of punishment had animated, raised the dying man, still groaning, and, placing him in a wagon, his gaping wounds but poorly sheltered from the bitter cold of that winter's day, drove him to the grocery, where they went through the farce of dressing his wounds; but, seeing the hopelessness of his case, took him home to his wife. . . . The pulse of life was ebbing out. She asked him what was the matter, and how he came thus. 'I have been murdered by a gang of cowards, in cold blood, without any cause!' he said. And, as the poor wife stooped over the body of her gallant husband, he expired."

And, as she thus stooped, with a fiendishness truly Southern, one of the ruffians dared to offer her an insult.

No notice has ever been taken of this atrocious murder by the powers that be; never once did they interfere to preserve the purity of the ballot box or the right of free speech. The polls were not permitted to be opened either at Kickapoo, or Atchison, or the other pro-slavery villages; and a clergyman, who, at Atchison, said in a private conversation, that he was a Free State man, was tarred and feathered, and sent down the river on a raft — Federal officeholders leading and encouraging the rioters.

John Brown, Junior, was elected a member of the Topeka Legislature.

In the month of February, the President, in an official proclamation, denounced the Topeka Legislature as an illegal assembly; endorsed the code of the invaders as the laws of Kansas; and ordered the Federal troops to aid the Territorial officers in the execution of these infamous enactments. With the opening of navigation on the river came hordes of Southern highwaymen from Georgia, the Carolinas, and Alabama, with the avowed intention of exterminating or banishing the Free State men. Organizing into guerilla companies, they soon scattered desolation throughout the Territory; but first were enrolled as Territorial militia, by Governor Shannon, and armed with United States muskets, the more effectually to enable them to carry out their purpose. An excuse was needed to march against Lawrence, in order to destroy it; for while it stood, they could hardly hope to succeed in their nefarious mission. A pretext was soon afforded. Sham writs were issued for the arrest of its citizens; United States troops entered Lawrence to enforce them. To Federal authority no opposition was made; for the sentiment of devotion to the Union, notwithstanding that to Kansas the Union was a curse, was in almost every breast an uneradicable prejudice. The Sheriff, thus protected and unopposed, in order to incite the people to resist him, encamped with his prisoners in Lawrence over night, and, in coarse and filthy language, abused the Northern citizens and his captives. Tired of the cowardice of the politicians, and exasperated by the outrages daily committed by the Southern marauders, one brave but wayward boy, on hearing the abusive language of the Sheriff, swore that he would bring matters to a crisis forthwith; and, in the evening, he and two companions, half drunk, and wholly incensed, fired at

9

and wounded the insolent officeholder as he stood at the entrance of his tent.

He was not dangerously wounded ; but, to subserve the interests of the South, it was reported that he was dead. Missouri, again appealed to, invaded the Territory ; the far Southern marauders assembled at Lecompton ; and now, in order that they might march together on devoted Lawrence, "under the shadow of the wings of the Federal eagle," it was determined to arrest Governor Reeder, then the leader of the party, under the pretence of needing him as a witness at Tecumseh. Mr. Reeder, dismissed from his office as Federal Governor, in consequence of his refusal to be the passive instrument of the ruffians, was elected as the Free State delegate to Washington, and was now in Kansas, with the Congressional Committee of Investigation, collecting evidence to sustain his claim to a seat in the National House of Representatives.

Governor Reeder, of course, refused to go, — for to have gone would have interrupted his duties, and have forfeited his life. He knew nothing of the case, in which, it was pretended, he was needed as a witness. This refusal was instantly made the pretext for marching on Lawrence, under the authority of a United States Marshal.

The news spread rapidly, that Lawrence was to be destroyed.

John Brown, Junior, at the head of sixty men, or more,* marched from Ossawattomic, and offered to

---

* My personal recollection is, that there were one hundred and twenty men in his company ; but, as I cannot recall my authority, I give the lowest number stated by others.

defend the town ; but the Committee of Safety, now so odious that it was ironically styled the Safety Valve, while valiantly declaring that " they would fight first," rather than submit to ignominious terms, and receiving from Governor Shannon the very courteous and patriotic answer, " Then war it is, by God ! " — took no efficient measures for defence, and determined to offer no resistance. John Brown, Junior, marched back to Ossawattomie ; but ere he reached it and disbanded, his father, with a company of seven men, left his camp, and began in right earnest the war of liberty.

Meanwhile, Messrs. Reeder, Robinson, and others, urged to it by the Congressional Committee, had fled ; but, excepting Reeder, were overtaken, arrested, and imprisoned on a charge of high treason. Their crime consisted in accepting office under the Free State Constitution ; save one, an editor, whose offence was the publication of a Free State journal.*

On the 5th of May, the two Free State papers in Lawrence, and a hotel erected by the Emigrant Aid Company ; as, also, a bridge over a stream to the south of Lawrence, which had been built by a Free State man ; were each indicted by a jury, under the instructions of the Federal Judge, Lecompte, *as a public nuisance*, and orders for their destruction were issued by the Court.

On the 11th of the same month, the United States Marshal issued a proclamation assembling the " militia ; " and from that time, as the writer personally

---

* He subsequently sold himself to the Federal Administration.

knows, till the 20th instant, in the words of a demo-cratic author,* "preparations were going forward, and vigorously prosecuted, for the sacking of Lawrence. The pro-slavery people were to wipe out this ill-fated town, under authority of law. They had received the countenance of the President, the approbation of the Chief Justice, the favorable presentment of the Grand Jury, the concurrence of the Governor, the order of the Marshal, and were prepared to consummate their pur-pose with the arms of the Government, in the hands of a militia force gathered from the remotest sections of the Union. They concentrated their troops in large numbers around the doomed city, stealing, or, as they termed it, 'pressing into the service' all the horses they could find belonging to Free State men; whose cattle were also slaughtered, without remuneration, to feed the Marshal's forces; and their stores and dwell-ings broken open and robbed of arms, provisions, blankets, and clothing. And all this under the pre-tence of 'law and order,' and in the name and under the sanction of the government of the United States."

These, and worse outrages, the murdering of the young boys Stewart and Jones, and the ravishing of a mother and a daughter among them, were speedy and infallible illustrations of the spirit of the South; convincing proofs to every man who would look with his own eyes, instead of using the false mirror of a con-servative education, that the American Union is not a Nation, but an unnatural joining of two hostile

* Gihon.

peoples — of a free, progressive, tolerant, enlightened,
law-loving race, on the one hand; and, on the other,
of lawless organized bands of despots, with able but
unprincipled leaders, and with a lower class only slightly in advance of our barbarous semi-civilized Indian
tribes of the West.

On the 20th of May, the United States Marshal, at
the head of eight hundred men, entered the town of
Lawrence, and made arrests; and then, with an ingenuity worthy of the South, or Austria, or any other
power satanic, dismissed his immense force *within the
limits of the corporation.* Had the army then committed any lawless act, how could the Democracy have
been held responsible? The *posse comitatus* was now
a mob. But the shot Sheriff, who so lately had been
lamented as dead, stepped forward at this juncture;
reorganized the force as his official staff; and then,
filing the streets with these Southern marauders, destroyed the presses and offices of the two Northern
papers, battered at with cannon, and finally burned
down, the recently finished and splendid hotel. In the
eyes of the Government, they were " public nuisances."
This mob was headed by an ex-Senator and ex-Vice
President of the United States!

Among the brave young men who saw these out
rages committed, were Charley Lenhart and John E.
Cook. Next day they left the town, to commence
reprisals. Nearly two hundred thousand dollars worth
of property had been stolen or destroyed, without reck-
oning, in this amount, nearly two hundred horses that
had been " pressed into the service " of the South.

9 *

North of the Kansas River, the conquest of the Territory was complete ; and, south of it, several Free State
districts had submitted to the power of the invaders.
All the towns on the Missouri River were in their
hands ; Lawrence had been sacked, its prosperity
checked, and its prestige broken ; while Tecumseh,
and Lecompton, Fort Scott, and the far Southern region, had always been faithful to the traffic in human
souls. On a flag that waved in the ranks of the lawless
sheriff's southern force, on that memorable 20th of
May, was printed the Goliath-like boast of the embattled
propagandists of oppression :

> " You Yankees tremble, and Abolitionists fall ;
> Our motto is, Southern Rights to All."

The cause of God, and his servants, and despised
poor, looked gloomy ; but there were many hearts,
fully conscious that, armed with justice and Sharpe's
rifles, the right would come uppermost ere long.   And
among them, encamped in the woods of Southern Kansas, was a stern old man, whose cold blue eye lighted
up with a holy lustre, as he read in the Sacred Book,
written by the finger of his God and Father :

> " Be strong and courageous ; be not afraid nor dismayed for the
> king of Assyria, nor for all the multitude that is with him : for there
> be more with us than with him ;
> " With him is an arm of flesh ; but with us is the Lord our God, to
> help us, and to fight our battles."

IV.

In Caucus and Camp.

IN CAUCUS.

THE first time that I heard of Old Brown was in connection with a caucus at the town of Ossawattomie.*. It was shortly after his arrival in the Territory. The politicians of the neighborhood were carefully pruning resolutions so as to suit every variety of anti-slavery extensionists; and more especially that class of persons whose opposition to slavery was founded on expediency — the selfishness of race, and caste, and interest: men who were desirous that Kansas should be consecrated to free *white* labor only, not to FREEDOM for all and above all. The resolution that aroused the old man's anger declared that Kansas should be a free *white* State, thereby favoring the exclusion of negroes and mulattoes, whether slave or free. He rose to speak, and soon alarmed and disgusted the politicians by asserting the manhood of the negro race, and expressing his earnest, anti-slavery convictions with a force and vehemence little likely to suit the hybrids

* I had no personal knowledge of his opposition to the Treaty o Peace.

103

then known as Free State Democrats. There were a number of emigrants from Indiana, I was told, whom his speech so shocked that they went over and remained in the pro-slavery party. This was John Brown's first and last appearance in a public meeting in Kansas. Like most men of action, he underrated discussion. He secretly despised even the ablest anti-slavery orators. He could see "no use in this talking," he said. "Talk is a national institution, but it does no manner of good to the slave." He thought it an excuse very well adapted for weak men, with tender consciences. Many abolitionists, too cowardly to fight, and yet too honest to be silent, deceived themselves with the belief that they faithfully discharged their duties to the slave by fiercely denouncing his oppressors. His ideas of duty were far different. The slaves, in his eyes, were prisoners of war; their tyrants, he held, had taken the sword, and must perish by it.

HIS POLITICAL CREED.

Here let me speak of his political affinities. It has been asserted that he was a member of the Republican party. It is false. He despised the Republican party. It is true that, like every abolitionist, he was opposed to the extension of slavery; and, like the majority of anti-slavery men, in favor, also, of organized political action against it. But he was too earnest a *man*, and too devout a Christian, to rest satisfied with the only action against slavery consistent with one's duty as a *citizen*, according to the usual Republican interpretation of the Federal Constitution. It teaches us that we must content ourselves with resisting the extension of

slavery. Where the Republicans said, Halt! John
Brown shouted, Forward! to the rescue! He was an
abolitionist of the Bunker Hill school. He followed
neither Garrison nor Seward, Gerritt Smith nor Wendell Phillips : but the Golden Rule, and the Declara-
ion of Independence, in the spirit of the Hebrew war-
iors, and in the God-applauded mode that they
adopted. "The Bible story of Gideon," records a
man who betrayed him, "had manifestly a great influence on his actions." He believed in human
brotherhood and in the God of Battles; he admired
Nat Turner, the negro patriot, equally with George
Washington, the white American deliverer. He could
not see that it was heroic to fight against a petty tax
on tea, and war seven long years for a political principle ;. yet wrong to restore, by force of arms, to an
outraged race, the rights with which their Maker
had endowed them, but of which the South, for two
centuries, had robbed them. The old man distrusted
the republican leaders. He thought that their success,
in 1860, would be a serious check to the anti-slavery
cause.* His reason was, that the people had confidence
in those leaders, and would believe that by their action
in Congress they would peacefully and speedily abolish
slavery. That the people would be deceived; that the
Republicans would become as conservative of slavery as
the Democrats themselves, he sincerely and prophetically
believed. Apathy to the welfare of the slave would

---

* "The Republicans of 1858 will be the Democrats of 1860" — a
pithy prophecy found among the manuscripts at Harper's Ferry, — is
a brief and clear statement of John Brown's ideas.

follow; and hence, to avert this moral and national calamity, he hurried on to Harper's Ferry.

He was no politician. He despised that class with all the energy of his earnest and determined nature. He was too large a man to stand on any party platform. He planted his feet on the Rock of Ages — the Eternal Truth — and was therefore never shaken in his policy or principles.

MY FIRST JOURNEY SOUTH.

A few days after the sacking of Lawrence, a startling rumor reached us. A messenger from Lecompton stated that a Southern squatter from Pottawattomie had arrived there with despatches for the Governor, which announced that five pro-slavery settlers had been murdered, at midnight, and their bodies shockingly disfigured and mutilated, by a party of Free State men. He brought a request for a body of troops to protect the pro-slavery people there; who, up to this time, had ruled that region with a rod of iron. This fact caused every one to doubt the truth of the report. It was regarded as a pretext for hurrying down the troops to arrest Captain John Brown, Junior, and the Free State force that he commanded. While the people of Lawrence were discussing the news, a body of troops from Lecompton passed the town, and it was discovered that they were destined for Osawatomie. Not a moment was to be lost if John Brown, the younger, and his boys, were to be warned of their coming and design. I was urged to go down and inform him of the approach of the troops. A horse was hired for me, and I started on the mission at once. Already the troops were several miles ahead, and I was not

familiar with the road; for this was my first journey
to the country south of the Wakarusa.

My first object was to overtake the troops; the second, to pass them, and defeat their design. Of every
one whom I met I inquired if, and where, they had
seen the soldiery. Just at twilight I rode up a hill;
and, on the opposite side of the brush, heard the noise
of the tramp of horses. I rode through it, and found
myself in camp. The dragoons were preparing to dismount and remain there for the night. There were
two or three civilians of the ruffian-breed along with
them, who, after eyeing me with fierce looks, went and
spoke to the captain. He, like the majority of the
army officers in Kansas, was an ultra pro-slavery man.
He looked steadily at me, and I returned the stare;
but, knowing his character, I did not salute him.
Without speaking to any one, I rode out of camp. In
five minutes, it was already dark; and I had not gone
half a mile ere I heard two men riding up behind me. -
I stopped my horse at once; turned off the road; and,
with my pistol ready for service, halted till they came
up to me. They also were heavily armed; but their
pistols were in their belts. I inquired of them the
way to Prairie City; one, in giving directions, tried to
ride outside of me. It was no time, I felt, for too tender a regard for the forms of etiquette; so I rode still
further out, slightly raising my pistol as I did so. We
understood each other at once. I rode with them a
little distance; and then, they having separated, I
halted until both were out of sight. Prairie City
according to their directions, was to be reached by an

Indian trail, which, difficult enough to trace in the daylight, it was impossible for a stranger to find or follow at night. I rode on to a hamlet of half a dozen log houses, dignified with the name of the City of Palmyra; and there, at the cabin of a moderate pro-slavery man, rested till the following morning, when I found that my horse had been stolen, and that my host had suffered with me in the loss of an Indian pony. H. Clay Pate and his friend Coleman, the murderer, were supposed to be encamped in the neighborhood, and were with reason suspected of having committed this theft. After the battle of Black Jack, and not till then, the horses were discovered and returned.

I walked over to Prairie City, — a municipality which consisted of two log cabins and a well, — and from there, having told my errand, a messenger was instantly despatched to inform John Brown, Junior, of the approach and supposed design of the Federal troops. I remained in Prairie City several days, to ascertain and describe the condition of the country.

I found that, in this region, when men went out to plough, they always took their rifles with them, and always tilled in companies of from five to ten; for, whenever they attempted to perform their work separately, the Georgia and Alabama bandits, who were constantly hovering about, were sure to make a sudden descent on them, and carry off their horses and oxen. Every man went armed to the teeth. Guard was kept night and day. Whenever two men approached each other, they came up, pistol in hand, and the first salutation invariably was: Free State or Pro-Slave? or its

equivalent in intent: Whar ye from? It not unfre-
quently happened that the next sound was the report
of a pistol. People who wished to travel without such
collisions, avoided the necessity of meeting any one, by
making a circuit or running away on the first indication of pursuit.

And why this condition of things? Because the
North had consented to compromise with the deadly
crime of Southern slavery; because it had been taught
that this stupendous and organized iniquity *could* have
any other right than to be crushed under the feet of
Christian freemen.

ARREST AS A HORSE THIEF.

On the afternoon of my first day at Prairie City, I
was sitting reading a book at the door of the cabin,
when, unexpectedly, I saw a company of the dragoons
approaching. They were riding, in double file, up to
where I sat; but I did not look at them again until
the horse of the captain was about to tread on me. I
knew that it was designed, in revenge for my indifference, on the captain's part; and to anger him still
more, as soon as I stepped aside, instead of saluting
him or looking at his men, I reopened my book and re-
commenced my reading.

In a voice of stifled anger, he asked me if my name
was Redpath?

I told him that it was.

"Then, sir, you are my prisoner!" he said.

"Indeed!" I responded. "Why? Where is your
warrant?"

"I have none," he answered angrily.

"Then how can you arrest me? This is said to be a country of law."

"We won't discuss that, sir," he said, savagely; "but you must go with me to my camp. If you are not guilty, you need have nothing to fear."

"I don't fear, Captain," I interrupted; "I know enough of law to know that Federal troops dare not punish citizens."

His eyes snapped. I had been trying to provoke him, without giving him an excuse for violence, and I saw that I had thus far been successful in hitting the most sensitive part of dragoon pride — the superiority of the civil Bench over the military Saddle.

"But what is my offence?" I asked.

"You are suspected of stealing horses! You came into our camp last night, acted very strangely, never spoke to any one, and, half an hour after you were gone, two of our best horses were missing."

I angered the vain dragoon still more by laughing heartily at the accusation, and explaining my reason for sympathizing with him, as well as my willingness to go to his camp, if only to have so good a chance to write an amusing letter. This intimation did not restore him to good humor.

"Well, sir, I hope you are innocent," he said, and then put his men into marching order.

I found that the strongest evidence against me was the fact they had discovered, that, on the previous evening, I had anxiously asked of every one where the soldiers were! Such is circumstantial evidence!

Returning in less than half an hour from the camp

of the soldiery, to which the horses, traced by a squatter, had been returned, I sat down and wrote a description of the adventure, which I entitled the Confessions of a Horse Thief. Now, how to send it? The mails were not safe; the country was covered with guerillas; Leavenworth was in the hands of the ruffians; to send it from Lawrence was impossible. I heard of an old preacher, who lived a few miles off, and who was going to Kansas City in Missouri. I went to find him. His house was situated on the southern side of a creek, which is two or three miles from Prairie City. I was advised to seek the cabin of Captain Carpenter; and there, where armed men were constantly on guard, they would lead me to "Old Moore, the minister."

IN CAMP.

The creeks of Kansas are all fringed with wood. I lost my way, or got off the path that crosses the creek above alluded to, when, suddenly, thirty paces before me, I saw a wild-looking man, of fine proportions, with half a dozen pistols of various sizes stuck in his belt, and a large Arkansas bowie-knife prominent among them. His head was uncovered; his hair was uncombed; his face had not been shaved for many months. We were similarly dressed — with red-topped boots worn over the pantaloons, a coarse blue shirt, and a pistol belt. This was the usual fashion of the times.

"Hullo!" he cried, "you're in our camp!"

He had nothing in his right hand — he carried a water-pail in his left; but, before he could speak again, I had drawn and cocked my eight-inch Colt.

I only answered, in emphatic tones, "Halt! or I'll fire!"

He stopped, and said that he knew me; that he had seen me in Lawrence, and that I was true; that he was Frederick Brown, the son of old John Brown; and that I was now within the limits of their camp. After a parley of a few minutes, I was satisfied that I was among my friends, put up my pistol, and shook hands with Frederick.

He talked wildly, as he walked before me, turning round every minute, as he spoke of the then recent affair of Pottawattomie. His family, he said, had been accused of it; he denied it indignantly, with the wild air of a maniac. His excitement was so great that he repeatedly recrossed the creek, until, getting anxious to reach the camp, I refused to listen to him until he took me to his father. He then quietly filled his pail with water; and, after many strange turnings, led me into camp. As we approached it, we were twice challenged by sentries, who suddenly appeared before trees, and as suddenly disappeared behind them.

I shall not soon forget the scene that here opened to my view. Near the edge of the creek a dozen horses were tied, all ready saddled for a ride for life, or a hunt after Southern invaders. A dozen rifles and sabres were stacked against the trees. In an open space, amid the shady and lofty woods, there was a great blazing fire with a pot on it; a woman, bare-headed, with an honest, sun-burnt face, was picking blackberries from the bushes; three or four armed men were lying on red and blue blankets on the grass; and two fine-looking youths were standing, leaning on their arms, on guard near by. One of them was the youngest son of Old Brown, and the other was "Charley," the brave Hungarian, who was subsequently murdered at Ossawatomie. Old Brown himself stood near the fire, with his shirt-sleeves rolled up, and a large piece of pork in his hand. He was cooking a pig. He was poorly clad, and his toes protruded from his boots. The old man received me with great cordiality, and the little band gathered about me. But it was for a moment only; for the Captain ordered them to renew their work. He respectfully but firmly forbade conversation on the Pottawattomie affair; and said that, if I desired any information from the company in relation to their conduct or intentions, he, as their Captain, would answer for them whatever it was proper to communicate.

In this camp no manner of profane language was permitted; no man of immoral character was allowed to stay, excepting as a prisoner of war. He made prayers in which all the company united, every morning and evening; and no food was ever tasted by his men until the Divine blessing had been asked on it. After every meal, thanks were returned to the Bountiful Giver. Often, I was told, the old man would retire to the densest solitudes, to wrestle with his God in secret prayer. One of his company subsequently informed me that, after these retirings, he would say that the Lord had directed him in visions what to do; that, for himself, he did not love warfare, but peace, — only acting in obedience to the will of the Lord, and fighting God's battles for His children's sake.

10 *

It was at this time that the old man said to me: "I would rather have the small-pox, yellow fever, and cholera all together in my camp, than a man without principles. It's a mistake, sir," he continued, "that our people make, when they think that bullies are the best fighters, or that they are the men fit to oppose these Southerners. Give me men of good principles; God-fearing men; men who respect themselves; and, with a dozen of them, I will oppose any hundred such men as these Buford ruffians."

I remained in the camp about an hour. Never before had I met such a band of men. They were not earnest, but earnestness incarnate. Six of them were John Brown's sons.

I left this sacred spot with a far higher respect for the Great Struggle than ever I had felt before, and with a renewed and increased faith in noble and disinterested champions of the right; of whose existence — since I had seen so much of paltry jealousy, selfishness, and unprincipled ambition among the Free State politicians — I was beginning to doubt, and to regard as a pleasant illusion of my youth. I went away, thoughtful, and hopeful for the cause; for I had seen, for the first time, the spirit of the Ironsides armed and encamped. And I said, also, and thought, that I had seen the predestined leader of the second and the holier American Revolution.

V.

POTTAWATTOMIE.

I HAVE spoken of the rumors of midnight murder in the Pottawattomie region, and stated that Captain Brown was accused by the invaders of having done the deed. The charge is false. It was first made by his enemies, who feared him, and desired to drive him out of the district, and subsequently repeated by a recreant Free State journalist, who sold himself to the Federal Administration for the paltry bribe of the public printing.

The killing of the ruffians of Pottawattomie was one of those stern acts of summary justice with which the history of the West and of every civil war abounds. Lynch law is one of the early necessities of far-western communities; and the terrors of it form the *only* efficient guarantee of the peaceful citizen from the ruffianism which distinguishes and curses every new Territory. The true story of Pottawattomie is briefly told.

In all that region, ever since the opening of the Territory for settlement, the pro-slavery party had been brutally tyrannical. Free State men were daily robbed, beaten, and killed; their property was stolen, openly, before their eyes; and yet they did not dare to resist the outrages. One or two families alone were occasionally exempted, by their character for desperate courage, from these daring and unwarrantable assaults. Among them were the sons and son-in-law of Old John Brown; and even they had repeatedly suffered from the conduct of the ruffians, until the arrival of their father in the autumn, with arms. Then, until the months of April and May, a season of peace was allowed them. But when, in fulfilment of the plan of the Missouri secret lodges, the Territory was to be conquered for slavery, it at once became a question of life, death, or immediate banishment to the settlers in Southern Kansas how they should act against the invading pro-slavery party and their allies among the squatters. Men who have passed their lives in the quiet of New England's valleys, or in Eastern cities, can never know what it is to be in earnest on what is seemingly a mere question of political right or constitutional interpretation. Hence this chapter may shock them; but it is my duty, nevertheless, to write it.

The pro-slavery party, in all the region around Pottawattomie, renewed their system of aggressions on the Free State men. John Brown began to stir himself and prepare for the defence of his neighborhood. With two sons or friends he went out into the prairies where a number of invaders were encamped, and, pretending to survey the country, drove his imaginary lines through the middle of their camp. All the Government officers in Kansas, from the Governor down to the humblest workmen, were at this time, and for long afterwards, ultra pro-slavery men; many of them pro-

fessed Secessionists who publicly cursed the Union as a
burden to the South. John Brown frequently adopted
this plan of entering the camp of the invading forces,
and not only never was suspected, but was never asked
what his political opinions were. Never doubting that
he was a Government surveyor, the Southrons never
doubted his political orthodoxy.

The men in this camp freely told him their plans.
There was an old man of the name of Brown, they
said, who had several sons here, whom it was necessary
to get out of the way, as, if they were driven out or
killed, the other settlers would be afraid to offer any
further resistance. They told him how Wilkinson, the
Doyles, and a Dutchman named Sherman had recently
been in Missouri, and succeeded in securing forces to
drive out the Browns, and that it was determined to
kill them in the latter part of May. They mentioned
several other prominent Free State men who were to
share this fate.

John Brown left their camp, and at once notified the
settlers who had been marked out for destruction, of
the murderous designs of the Missourians. A meeting
of the intended victims was held; and it was determined that on the first indication of the massacre, the
Doyles, — a father and two sons, — Wilkinson, and Sherman should be seized, tried by Lynch law, and sum-
marily killed.

On the 23d of May, John Brown left the camp of his
son, at Osawatomie, with seven or eight men, and
from that moment began his guerilla warfare in Southern Kansas. He ordered them to the vicinity of his

home, to be ready for the Missourians when they came. He himself went in a different direction, for the purpose of obtaining further aid.

On the night of the 25th of May, the Doyles, Wilkinson, and Sherman were seized, tried, and slain. This act was precipitated by a brutal assault committed during the forenoon on a Free State man at the store of Sherman, in which the Doyles were the principal and most ruffianly participators. These wretches, on the same day, called at the houses of the Browns; and, both in words and by acts, offered the grossest indignities to a daughter and daughter-in-law of the old man. As they went away, they said, " Tell your men that if they don't leave right off, we'll come back to-morrow and kill them." They added, in language too gross for publication, that the women would then suffer still worse indignities.

What redress could the husbands of these women have received, had they asked the protection of the law? They would have been obliged to seek it from Wilkinson, one of these ruffians, who was the magistrate of the Pottawattomie District! This instance had hundreds of parallels.

I do not know whether New England people will be able to vindicate the summary punishment inflicted on these wretches; but I do know that nearly every Free State man then in Kansas, when he came to know the cause, privately endorsed it as a righteous act, although many of them, " to save the party," publicly repudiated and condemned it.

These facts I derived from two squatters who aided

in the execution, and who were not ashamed of the part
they took in it. Neither of them was a son of John
Brown. They were settlers in the neighborhood.

John Brown himself subsequently corroborated their
statements, without knowing that they had made them,
by his account of the affair and denial of any participa-
tion in it. "But, remember," he added, "I do not say
this to exculpate myself; for, although I took no hand
in it, I would have advised it had I known the circumstances; and I endorsed it as it was."

"Time and the honest verdict of posterity," he said,
in his Virginia cell, "will approve of every act of
mine." I think it will also endorse all the acts that
I o endorsed; and among them this righteous slaughter
cf the ruffians at Pottawattomie. John Brown did not
know that these men were killed until the following
day; for, with one of his sons, he was twenty-five miles
distant at the time. He was at Middle Creek. This
fact can be proved by living witnesses. It is false, also,
that the ruffians were cruelly killed. They were tried,
made confession, allowed time to pray, and then slain
in a second.

The effect of this act was highly beneficial to the
security of the Free State men. It gave, indeed, to a
preconcerted invasion, an excuse for entering the Territory; but, by the terror which it inspired, by teaching the Missourians that the sword of civil war had a
double edge, it saved the lives of hundreds who otherwise would have fallen the victims of Southern aggression. Every one in Kansas at the time admitted that
fact, although many of them deny it now.

VI.

H. Clay Pate.

AMONG the unhappy men whom Old John Brown has dragged into an exceedingly undesirable immortality is H. Clay Pate, author, journalist, and warrior, alike unfortunate in each of these capacities, and in every thing that he has tried and lied and done or hoped for. A man-butterfly, whom no one would have ever thought of disturbing, with the vanity of the fabled frog he aspired to equal John Brown, and flew against his soul of fire — but only to be scorched for his pains, and pinned to a page of history by the stern old Puritan, and then placed, as a curious study, in the cabinet of human imbecilities forevermore.

By way of a contrast, if for no other reason, he deserves a separate chapter here — does H. Clay Pate, of Black Jack and Virginia.

Pate, by birth a Virginian, first sought to find fame and fortune in the city of Cincinnati. He published "a thin volume of collegiate sketches," and "several pointless, bombastically written stories," which, we are told, "was embellished with the author's portrait and autograph." He failed to get readers or even favorable

ieviewers, altnough he sought to make genial critics by
entering into sanctums "armed with a cowhide and
1 evolver." Not even by his next effort, "a large en-
graved portrait of himself," could the hungerer after
1 terary reputation find satisfaction.

He then sought fame as a journalist, and again was
preeminently unsuccessful. As the parasite of the Prot-
estant demagogue, Gavazzi, he gained in pocket, but
1 e lost in caste; and what he earned in purse he again
squandered in publication—in a new and equally fruit-
less effort to win a literary reputation without the intellect to found it on, or the moral character to dignify
and support it. "He had a signboard on his door,
iuscribed, H. Clay Pate, Author;" but as Heaven had
rot written this inscription on his forehead, the sign in
due time disappeared, and "the author" with it.

He hurried to the borders to' seek notoriety as a
champion of the South. He determined at first to be
distinguished by his pen; but, surpassed on every hand
as a journalist and writer, he next sought the ever-
flying phantom of fame with sword in hand, and in
the tented field.

At Lawrence, when the town was sacked, we are informed, "he distinguished himself chiefly by riding
about on a fine horse, he being decorated with ribbons."

What a contrast was this vain Virginian to the stern
old Puritan, who always dressed in the plainest clothing, regarding the purchase of fine apparel as a robbery
of the poor—who, only to gratify his most intimate
acquaintances, would consent, and then unwillingly, to
sit for a daguerreotype; and who, when an admiring

11

friend, without his permission, inscribed a volume to
him, regretted it, lest it should seem to be courting
notoriety, which he said, with simple honesty, is " not
in my way."

The vain, shallow, boasting pro-slavery propagàndist,
and the modest, thoughtful, humble warrior of the
Lord, were destined soon to meet as foes.

Mr. Pate set out from Westport, Missouri, about the
end of May, with the avowed intention of arresting Old
Brown, whom the pro-slavery men had charged with the
slaughter of the ruffians of Pottawattomie, and for
whom already they had a salutary and daily increasing
dread. His only fear, he said, was, that he might not
find him !

Captain Pate's achievements, from the day he left
Westport until " Old Moore, the minister," started for
Missouri, with my letters from Prairie City, are thus
narrated by my friend, Mr. Phillips, in his Conquest of
Kansas : —

" While near Osawatomie, he contrived to seize two of the old
man's sons — Captain John Brown, Jr., and Mr. Jason Brown. These
were taken while quietly engaged in their avocations. Captain Brown,
Jr., had been up with his company at Lawrence, immediately after the
sacking of the place, and at the time the men at Pottawattomie were
killed. He had returned home when he saw he could not aid Lawrence, and quietly went to work. He and his brother Jason were
taken by Pate, charged with murder, kept in irons in their camp, and
treated with the greatest indignity and inhumanity. While Pate was
thus taking people prisoners without any legal authority or writs, he
was joined by Captain Wood's company of Dragoons, who, so far
from putting a stop to his violent career, aided him in it, and took
from him, at his desire, the two prisoners, keeping them under guard
in their camp, heavily ironed and harshly treated. While these companies were thus travelling close to each other, Captain Pate's company burned the store of a man named Winer, a German ; the home

of John Brown, Jr., in which, amongst a variety of household articles, a valuable library was consumed; and also the house of another of he Browns—for the old man had six grown sons; and also searched houses, men, and Free State settlers, and acted in a violent and lawless manner generally. Not being able to find Captain Brown, senior, at Osawatamie, Pate's company and the troops started back for the Santa Fé road. In the long march that intervened, under a hot sun, the two Browns, now in charge of the Dragoons, and held without even the pretence of bogus law, were driven before the Dragoons, chained like beasts. For twenty-five miles they thus suffered under this outrageous inhumanity. Nor was this all. John Brown, Jr., who had been excited by the wild stories of murder told against his father, by their enemies, and who was of a sensitive mind, was unable to bear up against this and his treatment during the march, and afterwards, while confined in camp, startled his remorseless captors by the wild ravings of a maniac, while he lashed his chains in fury till the dull iron shone like polished steel.* To rescue his two sons from their captors became the determination of Captain Brown. Like a wolf robbed of its young, he stealthily but resolutely watched for his foes, while he skirted through the thickets of the Marais des Cygnes and Ottawa Creeks. Perhaps it was a lurking dread of Captain Brown's rescuing the prisoners, that made Captain Pate deliver them to the United States Dragoons. The Dragoons, with their prisoners, encamped on Middle Ottawa Creek, while Pate went on with his men to the Santa Fé road, near Hickory Point. On the evening of Saturday, the 31st of May, he encamped on the head of a small branch or ravine, called Black Jack, from the kind of timber growing there."

* Mrs. Robinson, whose husband was detained at Lecompton on a charge of high treason, thus describes the arrival of John Brown, Jr., in their camp:—"On the 23d June, the prisoners received an accession to their numbers in the persons of Captain John Brown, Jr., and H. H. Williams, likewise dignified with the name of traitors. The former was still insane from the ill-treatment received while in charge of the troops. . . . Captain Brown had a rope tied around his arms so tightly, and drawn behind him, that he will for years bear the marks of the ropes where they wore into his flesh. He was then obliged to hold one end of a rope, the other end being carried by one of the Dragoons; and for eight miles, in a burning sun, he was driven before them, compelled to go fast enough to keep from being trampled on by the horses. On being taken to Tecumseh, they were chained two and two, with a common trace chain, and padlock at each end. It was so fixed as to clasp tightly around the ankle. One day they were driven thirty miles, with no food from early morning until night. The journey, in a hot June day, was most torturing to them. Their chains wore upon their ankles until one of them, unable to go farther, was placed upon a horse." This son was detained in camp till the 10th September, although he was never even indicted!

As soon as Captain Pate had reached the ground that was destined to witness his failure as a military man, and, at the same time, with a humor almost puritanic in its grimness, to satisfy his longings for extended fame — although, possibly, not the kind of it he most desired — his friend Mr. Coleman, the murderer, and others of his company, marched on Palmyra, sacked a free state store there, and then blew it up with a keg of gunpowder. I heard of this robbery and outrage, and wrote an account of it; which, with my "Confessions," and a note to a lady, I handed to "Old Moore, the minister." I advised him, if he were pursued, to destroy the large letters, which were intended for publication; but to preserve the other, the note, as there was nothing in it that could implicate him with pro-slavery men.

He had not gone many miles before he was seen, and pursued by Clay Pate's scouts. In his excitement he forgot my directions — preserved the "incendiary documents," and destroyed the harmless *billet-doux!* He was captured, and brought to the camp of the marauders. Pate ordered the letters to be opened, as soon as he learned that they were mine, and appointed Coleman, the murderer whom I had denounced, to read my productions to his men!

First, came my humorous "Confessions of a Horse Thief." Captain Wood, the United States officer who arrested me, was spared the ridicule I had endeavored to throw on him; for Pate threw the letter into the fire!

Next, came my description of the sacking of Palmyra, and the Saxon names for Pate and his company. Old Moore declared afterwards, that he felt uneasy for his safety when he saw the rage which my letters aroused. It was universally admitted that I ought to be hanged; and they swore that they would do it, too — when the cat was belled. Pate's revenge was characteristic. He wrote to the *Missouri Republican* an account of the arrest of Mr. Moore, by his company, and stated that a number of my incendiary documents had been found on this person. This Redpath, he added, as if parenthetically, was arrested a few days ago by Captain Wood, of the United States army, on a charge of horse stealing; and was not released until the horses were produced! This was strictly and literally true, and yet, in its inference, such a splendid lie, that I should have admired the highwayman for his ingenuity, and given him credit for it, if he had not shown, by the sentence following, that the construction of the words was accidental only: "He was only released," he added, "because Captain Wood could not find a magistrate to indict him!"

This was his revenge on me; on Mr. Moore it was more brutal and cowardly, and still more characteristic. Some of Pate's company had known the old man in Missouri, and knew that he was strictly temperate in his habits and his principles. They therefore seized him, and, putting a tin funnel in his mouth, poured liquor down his throat — the ruffians swearing that they would make the old minister drunk.

These were the men whom John Brown was following to fight.

11 *

VII.

BATTLE OF BLACK JACK.

A FEW days after I left the camp of Old Brown, and returned to my post at Lawrence, he had his long-looked-for fight with Captain Pate's marauders. A friend has so faithfully narrated this action, that I prefer to transcribe his account of it, rather than describe the fight from my own recollections of the event. I make a few additions and corrections only.

A SABBATH GATHERING.

After dinner on Sunday, Pate's men wanted to go over to Prairie City and plunder it. Fancying that it would be easily taken, and that no resistance would be offered, six of Pate's men started on the expedition. At the time this party approached Prairie City, the people of that place and vicinity were congregated in the house of Dr. Graham to hear preaching, the doctor himself being a prisoner in the camp at Black Jack. They could watch as well as pray, however. There were some twenty men present, and most of them, after the old Revolutionary pattern, had gone to church with their guns on their shoulders. It was one of those primitive meetings, which may often be found in the

126

West, with the slight addition of its military aspects :
simple and unostentatious garb ; easy and primitive
manners ; a log house, the ribbed timbers of which
gave a rough-cast look to the simple scene, with here
and there the heavy octagon barrel of a long Western
rifle, or the smooth barrel of a shot gun, were visible
where they leaned against the wall, ready for action.
The worshippers were nearly through their devotions,
and the closing psalm was echoing through the timbers
of that log house to one of those quaint old melodies
to be found in the Missouri Harmony, when the sacred
strain was snapped by another Missouri harmony. A
watcher entered, saying,

" *The Missourians !   They are coming !* "

Never was a congregation dismissed on shorter no-
ice. The holy man forgot the benediction in remembering his rifle. The six ruffians had galloped up ;
when the congregation, suddenly rushing out, surrounded them. Two of the number, who were a little
back, wheeled their horses and galloped off, more than
one bullet going whizzing after them ; but, thanks to
their fleet steeds, or their enemy's hurried shooting,
they got off scathless, and got back to tell a frightful
story to Pate about the other men being killed — horribly ! &c. Their less lucky companions were merely
taken prisoners of war. One of them, however, had
some very near getting his quietus. A son of Dr.
Graham, a boy of about eleven years, seized his father's
double-barrelled gun at the first alarm, and hurried out
to the fence, the Missourians, who were all thus taken
aback, being immediately outside of it. The daring

boy, with his Kansas blood up, went within three rods of him, and, poking his gun over the fence, took deliberate aim at one of the men, and would have fired the next moment, — for "Bub" was not enlightened in the mysterious "articles of war," — when a Free State man put aside his gun, and said,

"Bub, what are you doing?"

"Going to shoot that fellow."

"You must n't."

Bub shook his head, and began to put up his gun again, muttering,

"He's on pap's horse." *

A SEARCH FOR PATE.

Through the whole of that Sunday night did Captain Brown and Shore's united company hunt for Captain Pate ; but their search was unsuccessful. As the gray dawn of Monday morning, June 2d, glimmered in, they had returned to Prairie City, when two scouts brought the tidings that the enemy was encamped on Black Jack, some four or five miles off. A small party was left to guard the four prisoners, and the remainder immediately took up their line of march for the enemy. Of those who thus left Prairie City, Captain Shore's company numbered twenty men, himself included ; and Captain Brown had nine men besides himself. They rode towards the Black Jack.

---

* A similar incident, illustrating the warlike spirit of the children, during the Kansas conflict, came under my own notice at the same house, a few days only before this occurrence. A scout came in and said that a pro-slavery guerilla band was approaching.

"O," shouted a little girl of five summers, ' don't I wish I could shoot one of them !"

Arrived within a mile of it, they left their horses, and two of their men to guard them. They despatched two other messengers to distant points for additional assistance, if it should be needed. The remainder, — twenty-six men, all told, — in two divisions, each captain having his own men, marched quietly forward on the enemy.

On Sunday night, there were sixty men in the pro-slavery camp on the Black Jack. Three or four wagons had been drawn up in a line, as a sort of breastwork, several rods out on the prairie from the ravine, and one of the tents was there. Such was the state of affairs when the outer picket-guard, about seven o'clock in the morning, galloped in and reported, " The abolitionists are coming ! " " Where — how many ? " There was a hurrying to and fro, and seizing of arms. " Across the prairie — there's a hundred of them," cried the frightened border ruffians, whose fears had multiplied the approaching force by four, and who probably had never stopped to examine carefully or to count, but had galloped off as soon as he caught the first glimpse of them.

PATE FOUND AND FOUGHT.

Captain Pate's position at Black Jack was a very strong one. It afforded shelter for his men, and, except by a force coming up the ravine or stream from the timber at Hickory Point, had to be approached over an open prairie, sloping up from the place where the Missourians were posted. When the alarm was sounded, Captain Pate drew up his men in line behind the breastwork of wagons.

When they neared the enemy's position, Captain Brown wished Shore to go to the left and get into the ravine below them, while he, with his force, would get into the upper or prairie part of the ravine, in the bottom of which was long grass. As the ravine made a bend, they would thus have got in range of the enemy on both sides, and had them in cross fire, without being in their own fire. Captain Brown, with his nine men, accordingly went to the right. Captain Shore, with more bravery than military skill, approached the foe over the hill, to the west of their camp, marching over the prairie up within good range, fully exposed, and with no means of shelter near them.

"Who comes there? What do you want?" cried Captain Pate.

"When I get my men in line, I'll show you," cried the gallant Captain Shore; and, true to his word, without waiting for or wanting any humbug parley, the gallant band poured in a volley on the Missourians, who were drawn up behind the wagons: the latter instantly returning it.

Volley after volley pealed through the air, and echoed through the ravine at Black Jack, away up to the dense timber of Hickory Point.

Meanwhile, Captain Brown had hurried into the ravine on the right of Captain Shore; and posting his men well, began to discourse the music of the spheres from that quarter.

"We're whipped! we're whipped!" yelled the Missourians, before the battle had lasted ten minutes; and, breaking from the wagon, they retreated to the ravine,

and concealed themselves there, some seven or eight of
them being wounded. One was shot through the
mouth by a Sharpe's rifle bullet. He had been squat-
ed behind the wagon wheel; the ball hit one of the
spokes, shivering it, and the border ruffian, in trying
the juggler's feat of catching it in his mouth, got it
lodged somewhere away about the root of the tongue
or the back of his neck. Another, was shot in the
upper part of the breast, or the lower part of his neck,
the bullet descending and lodging in his back. Another, a citizen of Westport, as he was galloping off,
received a very severe wound in the groin. He,
with several others, who were also wounded, left their
camp by the eastern side and escaped.

After Pate's men retreated to the ravine, he endeavored to rally them, and a fire was kept up from the
spot where they lay concealed, although the bullets
were whistling over their heads at a fearful rate. And
soon the position of Captain Shore was found to be
hazardous and critical: fully exposed to an enemy who
could shoot at his men almost without running risk,
they began to give way; and soon they had nearly all
retreated some two hundred yards up the slope, to the
high ground, where they were out of range. Captain
Shore, however, and two or three of his men, went
over and joined Brown, where the force lay in the long
grass, firing down the ravine. While this firing was
going on, to little purpose on either side, Captain
Brown went after the boys on the hill. Some few of
them had gone off after ammunition; one or two
of them were sitting in the grass, fixing their guns.

Finding that they could not be brought up again to a charge, he led them rather nearer the enemy, and induced them to shoot at their horses, which were over the ravine, at long shot. This he did to get up their spirits — as most of them were mere boys — and to intimidate the enemy. He returned to the ravine; the firing was still kept up. It is proper to state that Brown and Shore's men had but four guns of long range; there were only three or four Sharpe's rifles in both companies.

PATE'S PRISONERS AND THE WOUNDED.

While the firing was going on, one of Pate's men got up and swore he would see to the prisoners. A guard had been stationed to watch the three Free State prisoners, the tent in which they were being the most exposed of the camp. This guard was in great trepidation. The prisoners had thrown themselves on the ground, and the trembling guard also lay down, taking care to get the person of Dr. Graham between his own precious carcass and the enemy. So matters were, when the ruffian to whom I have alluded went to the tent with fierce oaths. Dr. Graham saw him approach with ferocious expression, and, just at that moment, the ruffian raised his pistol, aiming at the Doctor, who gave a spring just as the piece went off, the ball hitting him in the side, and inflicting a flesh wound. Graham sprang into the ditch of the ravine; and, as he did so, received another ball in his hip. He broke from the camp and fled, fifteen pistol shots being fired after him by the person who first attacked him, assisted by the guard. He got off without further injury, and joined his friends on the hill.

The firing had lasted three hours. Only two Free State men were wounded. One of them was shot in the arm, in the early part of the engagement. The other, a young man, with a great exuberance of spirits, kept springing up in the grass, shouting and firing his gun, when, on one of these occasions, he was struck by a ball in the side. Luckily it glanced off the ribs, or it would have killed him; as it was, it inflicted a severe wound, and two of his friends had to take him off the field. There were now only nine Free State men in the ravine keeping up a fire; and about as many more on the hill, three hundred yards from the enemy, who kept firing at the horses and occasionally making a sally, but never near enough to do much mischief.

CAPTAIN PATE CAPTURED.

At this juncture, Frederick Brown, who had been left in charge of the horses, becoming excited by the prolonged firing on both sides, suddenly appeared on the top of the hill, midway between the two divisions of the Free State force, and in full view of the enemy; and, brandishing a sword, shouting, " Come on — come on; I have cut off all communication: the sword of the Lord and of Gideon! " and other wild expressions, struck the ranks of the marauders with panic.

The Missourians in the ravine were getting discouraged; they did not dare to venture out of their shelter; and the bullets of the Free State men were making it a decidedly uncomfortable shelter. They began to drop off, one by one, by gliding down the ravine till they were out of range, running to where their horses were tied, and then galloping away. As the Free State men had no cavalry force in the field, and no men to spare, this prudential policy was very successful.

At last Captain Pate sent out his lieutenant and a prisoner with a flag of truce. They walked up the slope together to where the Free State men were; who, seeing them and their flag, ceased their fire. When they reached Captain Brown, he demanded of the Lieutenant whether he was the Captain of the Company?

"No," said the Lieutenant.

"Then," said the old man, "you stay here with me, and let your companion go and bring him out. I will talk with him."

Thus summoned, Captain Pate came out; and as he approached Captain Brown, began to say that he was an officer under the United States Marshal, and that he wanted to explain this fact; as, he supposed, the Free State men would not continue to fight against him, if they were aware of that circumstance. He was running on in this way, when the old man cut him short:

"Captain, I understand exactly what you are; and do not want to hear more about it. Have you a proposition to make to me?"

"Well, no — that is —

"Very well, Captain," interrupted the old man, "*I have one to make to you:* your unconditional surrender."

There was no evading this demand, and just as little chance to deceive Old Brown; who, pistol in hand, returned with Pate and his Lieutenant to their camp in the ravine, where he repeated his demand for the unconditional surrender of the whole company. They surrendered forthwith; although there were only nine Free State men in the ravine, or in sight, when the demand was made; and four of them, by Brown's orders, had remained where they were stationed. Five heroes, therefore, of whom John Brown was one, received the surrender of the arms and persons of twenty-one men, exclusive, too, of the wounded marauders. A large number of arms were obtained, many of which had been taken from Lawrence and Palmyra; twenty-three horses and mules, many of them recently stolen from the Northern squatters; a portion of the goods plundered at the sacking of the Free State store, two days before; as well as wagons, ammunition, camp-equipage, and provisions for the men. The wagons were all injured by the bullets.

The prisoners, being now disarmed, were ranged in file by the slender band of captors. The boys on the hill were induced to come in, thereby swelling the Free State force to sixteen persons. Captain Brown marched with the prisoners and a large portion of the spoils to his own camp. The wounded men were carefully cared for; and, on their recovery, admonished to do better in the future, and sent home to Missouri.

VIII.

The Conquest of Kansas Complete.

WHEN the news of the defeat of Clay Paté reached Missouri, a force of twenty-one hundred mounted men, not one of them a citizen of Kansas, set out from the border village of Westport, *under the lead of the Territorial delegate to Congress,* with the triple purpose of rescuing their brother-highwaymen, seizing Old Brown, and completing the conquest of the disputed land.

A few days before this invasion they had sent on supplies of provisions to the town of Franklin, with cannon and ammunition for their coming forces; and there the Georgians began to concentrate, and committed robberies and other outrages on the persons and property of the Free State men. To defeat the design of the Missourians, we marched upon Franklin on the night of the 2d of June, — only a few days after the fight at Black Jack, — and, after two or three hours of firing, chiefly in the dark, drove the ruffians out and captured their provisions. We then retired to Hickory Point, and there concentrated to oppose the invading force; which, although doubling us in numbers, we

136

saw with great delight, on the 5th of June, in battle array on the prairies near Palmyra. Every one in our camp was exultant at the prospect of obliterating and avenging the disgrace of Lawrence. But the Federal troops hastened down, and *induced* the Missourians to retire; which, knowing our readiness to fight, they willingly consented to do; but not until, in cold blood, they had murdered seven Free State men, not one of whom was armed, when they were taken prisoners by the invading forces. Mr. Cantroll was murdered by a ruffian named Forman, one of Captain Pate's men, who was wounded at Black Jack, carefully nursed at Prairie City, and dismissed by his captors uninjured. Of such were the Southern companies.

The Captain of the dragoons, when near Prairie City, heard that Old John Brown was in the neighborhood, and sent a messenger to him, requesting to have an interview. The old man came in response to the call, and voluntarily offered to give up his prisoners, in order that they might be tried for their highway robberies. But the dragoons insisted that they should be unconditionally surrendered; as, whatever their offences might be, there was no warrant out against them; and to receive them as prisoners, as the old man proposed, would be tacitly to admit that civil war existed, which, as a Federal officer, he could not acknowledge.

John Brown had voluntarily entered the camp of the dragoons, who never could have discovered or cared to penetrate his hiding place; for, as a Kansas author has truly said, "so carefully could he conceal his quarters, that when you wished to find him, when

he does not wish it, you might as well hunt for a needle in a haystack. He was astonished and indignant
when the Federal officer informed him that he must
consider himself a prisoner, as a civil functionary, who
accompanied the troops, had a warrant out for him
which he was there to serve. "Take my advice," said
the officer, "and make no resistance." Captain Brown
answered that if any territorial official dared to serve a
writ on him, he would shoot him dead on the spot;
and, fixing his stern glance on the Marshal, convinced
that trembling official that the presence of a company
of soldiers would not save him from the fate, the old
man threatened.

PATE LIBERATED.

"Colonel S—— ordered him to stand by his stirrup and lead him
into camp. Under these circumstances, the dragoons went into the
camp of Old Brown. So rapidly and unexpectedly did the thing
occur, that there was no opportunity to secure the arms and horses
taken at Black Jack. Only fifteen of Brown's men were in the camp
at the moment they entered it; * but that camp, Colonel S——, who
was astonished at it, afterwards said, a small garrison could have held
against a thousand men, as, from the peculiar nature of the ground,
artillery could not be brought to bear on it. It is not wonderful that
both Colonel S—— and the Deputy Sheriff should come to the conclusion that the handful of Free State men they saw, with nearly
twice their own number of prisoners, were only a part of Brown's
force. They believed that a hundred riflemen must be concealed in
the thickets around it; consequently the tone of these gallant officers
and gentlemen grew more urbane and polite. Colonel S—— asked
the Deputy Sheriff if he had not some writs of arrest. Deputy looked
carefully around him, fixed his timid, irresolute eyes on the prisoners,
and the small band Captain Brown had with him, and at the dense and
mysterious looking thickets around him, and said, in a hesitating
voice,

"'Well, I believe I don't see any body *here* against whom I have
any writ.'

* Among them was John E. Cook, who, a few days before, after Lenhart's camp was
broken up by the Dragoons, went and joined Old Brown for a time.

"'You don't!' said Colonel S——, indignantly. 'What did you tell me you had for ? What did you mean by getting my help to make arrests, if you have none ?'

"'Well,' faltered the hesitating Deputy, 'I don't think there is any body here I *want* to arrest !'

"Colonel S——, who is rather blunt and off-handed, and not much of a believer in humbug, gave the Deputy an objurgatory piece of his mind, which I need not inflict on the reader. He then liberated Captain Pate and the other prisoners. These men had been treated exceedingly well by Captain. Brown. They were allowed to use their own blankets and camp equipage, which were much better than any thing Brown had ; they also were fed, while thus held captive, much better than Brown was able to feed his own soldiers. Not only did the prisoners get their liberty, but their horses, arms, equipage, and stores ; nearly all that had been taken, and all except what Brown had given to those who came the day of the battle to help, or was in the hands of some others who had been there, and who were not now here. The guns these men had were United States arms.

"'Where did you get these arms ?' asked Colonel S—— of Captain Pate.

"'We got them from a friend,' was the reply.*

"'A friend !' growled S——. 'What friend had a right, or could give you United States arms ?'

"In this dilemma, Captain Pate did as many a wise man has done before him — evaded the question when he did not feel it advisable to answer it. The arms in question were the public Territorial arms, given in charge of the Federal officers of the Territory, for the use of the Territory, and by them given to the Missourians. This not being exactly a fit story to tell, Pate entered into a disquisition on the general subject of his imprisonment, and told S—— that he he was acting under orders of Governor Shannon ; and that his being taken prisoner was an outrage.

"'That is false, sir !' said Colonel S——, sternly ; 'I had a conversation with Governor Shannon about your particular case, and he declared that you had no authority for going about the country with an armed force.'

"There was no replying to this ; and the enraged and silenced Pate bit his lip. Colonel S—— went on and denounced him for his conduct in language more pointed and succinct than complimentary. He wound up his remarks, however, by allowing Pate to take every

---

* A more truthful answer was never given by man. The Government of the United States was the friend of every Missouri highwayman and far-Southern assassin, horse-thief, or burglar, who at this period infested Kansas.

thing his company had — even the public arms. Captain Brown and his company were then ordered to disperse." *

This was the first instance in which the Missourians were officially reprimanded ; and for this rebuke, Colonel Sumner, a relative of the distinguished Massachusetts Senator, was immediately superseded in command !

SACKING OF OSAWATOMIE.

The force under Whitfield, although they had given their word of honor to disperse, committed numerous and brutal depredations and outrages ; and on the 7th of June, one division of it entered the town of Osawatomie without resistance. Lest I should be supposed to be a partisan historian, I will transcribe an account of their proceedings there, as written by a National Democrat, then a Federal officeholder :

"On the 7th, Reid, with one hundred and seventy men, marched into Osawatomie, and, without resistance, entered each house, robbing it of every thing of value. There were but few men in the town, and the women and children were treated with the utmost brutality. Stores and dwellings were alike entered and pillaged. Trunks, boxes, and desks were broken open, and their contents appropriated or destroyed. Even rings were rudely pulled from the ears and fingers of the women, and some of the apparel from their persons. The liquor found was freely drank, and served to incite the plunderers to increased violence in the prosecution of their mischievous work. Having completely stripped the town, they set fire to several houses, and then beat a rapid retreat, carrying off a number of horses, and loudly urging each other to greater haste, as 'the d—d abolitionists were coming !' There are hundreds of well-authenticated accounts of the cruelties practised by this horde of ruffians ; some of them too shocking and disgusting to relate, or to be accredited if told. The tears and shrieks of terrified women, folded in their foul embrace, failed to touch a chord of mercy in their brutal hearts ; and the mutilated

* Mr. Phillips, to whom I am indebted for this narrative, received the facts from Captain Brown, Cook, and other witnesses of the scene.

t odies of murdered men, hanging upon the trees, or left to rot upon the prairies, or in the deep ravines, or furnish food for vultures and vild beasts, told frightful stories of brutal ferocity, from which the wildest savages might have shrunk with horror." *

And why? Because the North had consented to league and compromise with the hideous crime of Southern slavery.

THE SOUTH TRIUMPHANT.

Every movement made by the Free State men to defeat and punish the crimes of these organized marauders, was thwarted by the Federal troops, who, in an official proclamation, were ordered to disperse "all persons belonging to military companies, unauthorized by law;" in which were not included the banded Southern invaders, for they, as soon as they crossed over the border, were organized into Territorial militia. The face of Freedom was gloomy; every where the South was triumphant, or *had* conquered; only one additional indignity remained to be inflicted. Topeka had hitherto escaped the ravages of the ruffians. There, Colonel Aaron C. Stevens, a man afterwards destined to be immortally associated in fame with John Brown, had a company of Free State boys, who were ever on the alert to defeat the designs of the invaders, and always ready, at call, to march out against them.

Up to this time, also, the Free State Constitution had preserved its vitality. On the 4th of July, 1856, the crowning victory of the South was gained — not by their own cowardly forces, whom Black Jack, Frankli, and a series of successful guerilla fights had in-

* Geary in Kansas. By John H. Gihon, p. 91.

spired with a salutary aversion to battles, but by companies of artillery and dragoons of the United States
army, led on by a Federal officer. On that day, when,
elsewhere, Americans were celebrating the birth-day
of their liberty, the Free State Legislature was broken
up by force, and by the command of the Federal
Executive.

This was the last drop of bitterness in the Free State
cup; and this was, also, the culmination of Southern
success; the date, at once, of the death and the resurrection of Freedom in Kansas.

The Missouri River was closed against Northern emigration; "the roads were literally strewed with dead
bodies;"* the entire Free State population of Leavenworth had been driven from their homes; almost
every part of Kansas was in the power of the invaders;
the army, and the Government, Federal and Territorial, the Bench and the Jury box were in the hands of
the oppressor; and our State Organization had been
destroyed by the Dragoons; but this assemblage of eight
hundred men at Topeka, on the 4th of July, inspired a
feeling of unity and power never known before; and,
slowly coming to the Territory, with a little army, but
a mightier influence of inspiring rude men with furious passions, was General "Jim Lane;" while, in the
woods near the town, lay John Brown encamped, who
did not despair, but was ready to release the prisoners
at Lecompton, or attack the Dragoons if the party
would advise it. They did not; and he left the town.

* Declaration of Governor Shannon.

IX.

BATTLE OF OSAWATOMIE.

CAPTAIN BROWN, after the fourth of July, returned to Lawrence. Early in the month of
August, General Lane entered Kansas by the way of
Nebraska Territory. The confidence that the fighting
men felt in his military ability, made his return an
event of historical importance. Several revolting
atrocities — the mutilation of Major Hoyt, for example, the scalping of Mr. Hopps, and a dastardly outrage on a Northern lady * — aroused once more the
military ardor of the Free State men. Aggressive hostilities began. The cowardice that the Southerners,
now vigorously assailed, displayed at every point, has
never probably been equalled in American history :

"On the following morning, a young lady of Bloomington was
dragged from her home by a party of merciless wretches, and carried a
mile or two into the country, when her tongue was pulled as far as
possible from her mouth, and tied with a cord. Her arms were then
securely pinioned, and, despite her violent and convulsive struggles —
But let the reader imagine, if possible, the savage brutality that followed. She had been guilty of the terrible offence of speaking
adversely of the institution of slavery." — *Gilson's Geary in Kan-*
sas p. 98.

excepting recently, indeed, in the very valiant and venerable State of Virginia.

Hitherto, the Republican leaders in the East, by every mail and numerous messengers, had earnestly and successfully counselled peace — urging the Free State men, for party purposes, to submit to outrage rather than strike an offensive blow. The insult of the Fourth of July, followed up, on the 13th of August, by the Governor's proclamation, — which practically called on the Missourians to make a new invasion, — exhausted the patience of the Northern settlers, and, in a rapid series of surprises, they soon, and with unexampled precipitation, drove the Southern invaders from all their inland strongholds.

Let us follow John Brown during this eventful period. From the 4th of July till the 30th of August, he was neither idle nor inactive. With a wounded son-in-law, who had been shot at the battle of Black Jack, he left Topeka about the end of July; and, on the 5th of August, entered the camp of the organized Northern companies, then known as Jim Lane's army, at a place four miles from the northern boundary line, which the emigrants had named Plymouth, in honor of the Puritans, — who had crossed the sea for the same purpose that they were now crossing the prairie:

> " To make the West as they the East,
> The Homestead of the Free."

A brother of John Brown's wounded son-in-law, on learning of the casualties of Black Jack, at once left North Elba, and joined the second Massachusetts Company at Buffalo. The old man rode into camp, and inquired if Wm. Thompson * was there. He found him, and they left the camp together. The Captain was riding a splendid horse, and was dressed in plain white summer clothing. He wore a large straw hat, and was closely shaven; every thing about him was scrupulously clean. He made a great impression, by his appearance, on several of the company; who, without knowing him, at once declared that he must be a "remarkable man" in disguise. The old hero and his party then proceeded to Nebraska City, or Tabor, in Iowa, and left the wounded man and his brother there.

General Lane was not with his army, but came down with a few friends, — among them Captain Brown, — reached Topeka on the night of the 10th of August; and at once took command of the Free State forces. He immediately started for Lawrence, and, on arriving there, found that the Northern boys were preparing to attack the Georgians, then at Franklin. He and Captain Brown were both present at that skirmish. They proceeded on the same night to Rock Creek, for the purpose of seizing the murderers of Major Hoyt; and Captain Brown there assumed the command of a small company of cavalry. They encamped near Rock Creek; the disfigured body of Major Hoyt was discovered, and decently buried; and, in the morning, they started for Fort Sanders, on Washington Creek, to find that the Missourians had fled. It is probable that the old man was also at the capture of Fort Titus; and it is certain that, on the 26th of August, his company was at Middle Creek, at a point now called Battle

* He fell at Harper's Ferry.

13

Mound, eight miles from Osawatomie, where there was a camp of one hundred and sixty Southern invaders. The Free State forces, consisting of sixty men, — the united companies of John Brown, Captain Shore, and Preacher Steward,* — surprised and attacked these marauders at noon, and utterly routed them in a few minutes, killing two of them, and capturing thirteen prisoners, and twenty-nine horses, three wagon loads of provisions, and one hundred stand of arms.

On the same night, a detachment of this Free State force travelled to a point on the Sugar Creek, fifteen miles distant, and captured over sixty head of cattle, which the Southern marauders had brought into the Territory, or stolen from the settlers.

A NEW INVASION.

On the 17th of August, the Missourians, alarmed at the threatening aspect of affairs in the Territory, issued, at Lexington, an inflammatory appeal for another grand and overwhelming expedition against the Northern men in Kansas. It is so characteristic of the times and the spirit of the Slave States, and indicates so clearly the terror which Old Brown had inspired in Missouri, that I subjoin it with a few rhetorical omissions only :

To THE CITIZENS OF LAFAYETTE COUNTY :

It becomes our painful duty to inform you that civil war has again commenced in Kansas. Four hundred abolitionists, under Lane, have actually come into the Territory, and commenced a war of extermination upon the pro-slavery settlers.

---

* This gentleman was even more expert with the sword of Gideon than with the sword of the Spirit. He has been in more fights and liberated more slaves than any other man now in Kansas. He has won the honorable title of the Fighting Preacher. He "still lives."

On the 6th of August, the notorious Brown, with a party of three hundred abolitionists, made an attack upon a colony of Georgians, numbering about two hundred and twenty-five souls, one hundred and seventy-five of whom were women, children, and slaves. Their houses were burned to the ground, all their property stolen, — horses, cattle, clothing, money, provisions, all taken away from them, — and their ploughs burned to ashes. This colony came from Georgia to settle peaceably in Kansas, and were quietly cultivating the soil, and disturbing no one. They did not even have arms for defence. They are now driven from the territory, with nothing left but their clothes on their backs — indeed, they even took the boots off the men's feet, and put them on their own. Captain Cook, who has charge of the colony, is now here asking for arms and men to aid his colony to settle again in the Territory.*

August 12. — At night three hundred abolitionists, under this same Brown, attacked the town of Franklin, robbed, plundered, and burnt, took all the arms in town, broke open and destroyed the post office, carried away the old cannon " Sacramento," which our gallant Missourians captured in Mexico, and are now turning its mouth against our friends. Six men were killed, and Mrs. Crane knocked down by an abolitionist. [All false.]

The same day a Mr. Williams, a settler near St. Bernard, was shot by an abolitionist, who sneaked upon him while he was quietly mauling rails on his claim.†

August 13. — About fifty abolitionists attacked the house of Mr. White,‡ in Lykins County, robbed him of every thing, and drove him

---

* This "peaceable colony of Georgia men, women, children, and slaves," was really composed of about one hundred and sixty of Buford's Southron invaders, the Georgia contingent of that marauding force. About the beginning of July, they camped near Pottersville, a village of the Wea Indians, on the Reserve belonging to that nation. This place is about eight miles south-east of Osawatomie. They made no improvements, or took any steps toward a settlement, the fact of camping on the Wea lands being sufficient proof that they had no such intention, for they were not open to settlement. They lived there in tents, sold whiskey to the Weas and Miamis, with whom they pretended to form some sort of treaty, and plundered and annoyed the Free State settlers. About the second of August, they took prisoner Preacher Stewart, robbed him of his horse, and stated that they intended to hang him. Preparatory to the execution of this murderous threat, he was left in charge of two drunken Miami Indians. Stewart, not being desirous of a "suspension," made his escape, and reached Lawrence as speedily as possible. He immediately raised a company of ninety Free State men, and started for the Southern camp. They heard of his approach, and left in haste. When the Lawrence " boys " arrived at Battersville, they found some whiskey and a broken wagon. Captain Brown was on the northern boundary line at the time. Preacher Stewart and Captain Cutler were in command of the Free State men.

† Mr. Williams was a quiet, peaceable man. He was murdered by a pro-slavery ruffian named McBride, for the crime of being a Missourian and Free State.

‡ Preacher White, the murderer of Frederick Brown. This statement also is false.

into Missouri. He is a Free State man, but sustains the laws of the Territory.

August 15. — Brown, with four hundred abolitionists, mostly Lane's men, *mounted* and *armed*, attacked Treadwell's settlement, in Douglass County, numbering about thirty men.

They planted the old cannon "Sacramento" towards the colony, and surrounded them. They, being so largely overpowered, attempted to escape; but as they were on foot, it is feared they have all been taken and murdered.

* * * *

Meet at Lexington on WEDNESDAY, August 20, at 12 o'clock. BRING YOUR HORSES, YOUR GUNS, AND YOUR CLOTHING — all ready to go on to Kansas. Let every man who can possibly leave home, go now to save the lives of our friends. Let those who cannot go hitch up their wagons and throw in a few provisions, and get more as they come along by their neighbors, and bring them to Lexington on Wednesday. Let others bring horses and mules, and saddles and guns, — all to come in on Wednesday. We must go *immediately*. There is no time to spare, *and no one must hold back*. Let us all do a little, and the job will be light. We want two hundred to three hundred men from this county. Jackson, Johnson, Platte, Clay, Ray, Saline, Carroll, and other counties are now acting in this matter. All of them will send up a company of men, and there will be a concert of action. NEW SANTA FE, Jackson County, will be the place of rendezvous for the whole crowd, and our motto this time *will be*, "No quarter." Come up, then, on Wednesday, and let us have concert of action. Let no one stay away. *We need the old men to advise, the young men to execute.* We confidently look for eight hundred to one thousand citizens to be present.

At the same time a similar address, more general in its character, was issued from Westport, and dated August 16. It was signed by David R. Atchison, W. H. Russell, A. G. Boone, and B. F. Stringfellow.

Thus appealed to, a force of two thousand men assembled at the village of Santa Fé, on the border; and, after entering the Territory, divided into two forces — one division, led by Senator Atchison, marching to Bull Creek, and the other wing, under General Reid, advancing to Osawatomie.

The force under Atchison fled precipitately on the morning of August 31, on the approach of General Lane, and after a slight skirmish between the advance guards of the Northern and Southern " armies," which occurred about sunset on the previous evening. They fled in company with the division that had just returned from Osawatomie.

The reception of this force at Osawatomie by Captain John Brown is one of the most brilliant episodes of Kansas history. They were between four and five hundred strong, — armed with United States muskets, bayonets, and revolvers, with several pieces of cannon and a large supply of ammunition. When John Brown saw them coming, he resolved, to use his own modest phrase, to " annoy them."

This is his own account of the way in which he did it:

CAPTAIN BROWN'S ACCOUNT OF THE BATTLE.

" Early in the morning of the 30th of August, the enemy's scouts approached to within one mile and a half of the western boundary of the town of Osawatomie. At this place my son Frederick K. (who was not attached to my force) had lodged, with some four other young men from Lawrence, and a young man named Garrison, from Middle Creek.

" The scouts, led by a pro-slavery preacher named White, shot my son dead in the road, whilst he — as I have since ascertained — supposed them to be friendly. At the same time they butchered Mr. Garrison, and badly mangled one of the young men from Lawrence, who came with my son, leaving him for dead.

13 *

"This was not far from sunrise. I had stopped during the night about two and one half miles from them,
and nearly one mile from Osawatomie. I had no
organized force, but only some twelve or fifteen new
recruits, who were ordered to leave their preparations
for breakfast, and follow me into the town as soon as
this news was brought to me.

"As I had no means of learning correctly the force
of the enemy, I placed twelve of the recruits in a log
house, hoping we might be able to defend the town. I
then gathered some fifteen more men together, whom
we armed with guns; and we started in the direction
of the enemy. After going a few rods, we could see
them approaching the town in line of battle, about one
half a mile off, upon a hill west of the village. I then
gave up all idea of doing more than to annoy, from the
timber near the town, into which we were all retreated,
and which was filled with a thick growth of under-
brush, but had no time to recall the twelve men in the
log house, and so lost their assistance in the fight.

"At the point above named, I met with Captain
Cline, a very active young man, who had with him
some twelve or fifteen mounted men, and persuaded
him to go with us into the timber, on the southern
shore of the Osage, or Marais-des-Cygnes, a little to the
north-west from the village. Here the men, numbering
not more than thirty in all, were directed to scatter
and secrete themselves as well as they could, and await
the approach of the enemy. This was done in full
view of them, (who must have seen the whole movement,) and had to be done in the utmost haste. I

believe Captain Cline and some of his men were not even dismounted in the fight, but cannot assert posi-tively. When the left wing of the enemy had ap-proached to within common rifle shot, we commenced firing; and very soon threw the northern branch of the enemy's line into disorder. This continued some fifteen or twenty minutes, which gave us an uncom-mon opportunity to annoy them. Captain Cline and his men soon got out of ammunition, and retired across the river.

"After the enemy rallied, we kept up our fire; until, by the leaving of one and another, we had but six or seven left. We then retired across the river.

"We had one man killed — a Mr. Powers, from Captain Cline's company — in the•fight. One of my men — a Mr. Partridge — was shot in crossing the river. Two or three of the party, who took part in the fight, are yet missing, and may be lost or taken prisoners. Two were wounded, viz., Dr. Updegraff and a Mr. Collis.

"I cannot speak in too high terms of them, and of many others I have not now time to mention.

"One of my best men, together with myself, was struck with a partially spent ball from the enemy, in the commencement of the fight, but we were only bruised. The loss I refer to is one of my missing men. The loss of the enemy, as we learn by the different state-ments of our own, as well as their people, was some thirty-one or two killed, and from forty to fifty wounded. After burning the town to ashes, and killing a Mr. Williams they had taken, whom neither party claimed,

they took a hasty leave, carrying their dead and
wounded with them. They did not attempt to cross
the river, nor to search for us, and have not since
returned to look over their work.

"I give this in great haste, in the midst of constant
interruptions. My second son was with me in the
fight, and escaped unharmed. This I mention for the
benefit of his friends.

" *Old preacher White*, I hear, *boasts of having killed
my son.   Of course he is a lion.*

"JOHN BROWN.

"LAWRENCE, KANSAS, September 7, 1856."

The brilliancy of this exploit can only faintly be
traced in the old hero's modest and characteristic account of it. Nearly five hundred men, as the Missourians subsequently admitted, — and all of them
heavily armed, — were arrested in their march of desolation by a little band of sixteen heroes, imperfectly
equipped ; for the company of Captain Cline, after
firing a few shots, retired from the conflict, in consequence of being out of ammunition ; and there was
only one Sharpe's rifle in Captain Brown's command.
The old man stood near a " sapling," which is still
pointed out, during the whole of this memorable engagement, quietly giving directions to his men, and
"annoying the enemy" with his own steady rifle,
indifferent to the grape shots and balls which whizzed
around him, and hewed down the limbs, scattered the
foliage, and peeled off the bark from the trees on every
side. When the writer visited the site, many months
after this event, the wood still bore the marks of that

glorious conflict. The General of the invading army afterwards admitted that if Brown had been provided with Sharpe's rifles, nothing could have prevented his men from making an ignominious retreat.

The fearful slaughter was occasioned by the lawless character of the invading force. Alarmed at being fired at, they refused to obey orders, and foolishly huddled around the dead and wounded, instead of standing in their ranks and "closing up." Into these panic-stricken groups Old Brown poured a deadly fire; and, before the officers of the enemy could restore order in their companies, thirty-two men lay dead, and more than fifty wounded. The brave band of Captain Brown saw the whites of the enemy's eyes, ere the old man gave the order to retreat.

The invaders, true to the Southern instinct, murdered a wounded prisoner who fell into their hands, arrested and killed a Mr. Williams, who was "claimed by neither party," and who took no part in this or any other conflict; and, on the following morning, offered "Charley," the Hungarian, a chance for his life, if he should escape their fire — a cowardly excuse, as the fearless boy told them, for riddling him with balls. They fired a volley into him, as he faced them defiantly.

Erroneously supposing that they had shot Captain Brown, they returned to Missouri, and boasted of their success; but the large number of corpses and wounded men whom they brought from Osawatomie, and a knowledge of the insignificant force of abolitionists that had opposed them, created a feeling of terror in

the State, from which the Missourians never fully recovered. They never afterwards thought, and seldom
said, that the Yankees would not fight. Captain Brown
first created a dread of the NORTH and her men in the
minds of the Missourians; which, more than any other
terror, prevented them from proceeding vigorously with
the project of re-conquering Kansas. For General
Lane, in the North, with hardly any loss of life, had
done what Captain Brown, with this salutary slaughter,
had effected in the South of Kansas — made it necessary
to effect a re-subjugation of the Territory, or to give it
up to freedom. Lane frightened the Southern invaders; but Brown struck terror into the centre of
their souls.

"OLD PREACHER WHITE."

. Old Preacher White, who shot Frederick Brown
through the heart, — although his victim was quietly
walking along on the road unsuspecting and unarmed,
— and afterwards, as the corpse lay stiff and bloody on
the ground, discharged a loaded pistol into its open
mouth, was a "National" Divine, of "the Church
South," of course, whose fate deserves a passing notice
here.

In order to make capital against the Northern cor-
respondents in the Territory, by throwing discredit on
their statements of Southern outrage, a pro-slavery man
of Westport, Missouri, wrote an account of the recent
murder of a person whom he called "Poor Martin
White, a Free State preacher of the Gospel." It
served its purpose — for it was originally published in
a Republican paper and widely copied; when — as had

been arranged — Martin White re-appeared, denied the story of his death, and ridiculed the Republicans for believing such stories. For a long time afterwards, the pro-slavery papers, whenever an outrage was recorded, would sneeringly allude to " Poor Martin White."

For his services in furthering this stratagem, and as a reward for the murder of Frederick Brown, " Poor Martin White" was elected a member of the Territorial Legislature which assembled at Lecompton. During the course of the session he gave a graphic account of the killing of Frederick; laughingly described how, when shot, he " toppled over " — the honorable members roared at this Southern-Christian phrase — and amused my friend Phillips, author of " The Conquest of Kansas," for having spoken of the act as a murder; when, said the assassin-preacher, calmly, " I was acting as a part of the law and order militia."

Poor Martin White, when the session was finished, proceeded to his home. But he never reached it. " He went to his own place," indeed; for his corpse was found stiff and cold on the prairie — with a rifle ball in it. Poor Martin White!

BROWN'S ADDRESS TO HIS MEN.

They are coming — men, make ready;
See their ensigns — hear their drum;
See them march with steps unsteady :
Onward to their graves they come.

God of Freedom ! ere to-morrow,
Slavers' corpses Thou shalt see;
Georgia maids shall wail in sorrow,
For my sacrifice to Thee!

Philistines shall fall — the river
　That meanders through this wood
Shall be red with blood that never
　Throbbed for outraged womanhood ;

Blood of men, who, when their brothers
　Traffic human flesh for gold,
Laugh, like arch fiends, as poor mothers'
　Heartstrings break for daughters sold ;

Men who scoff at higher statutes
　Than their codes of legal wrong ;
Men whom only tyrant-rule suits ;
　Men whom Hell would blush to own :

.I will lay them as on altars,
　Prairies ! on your grasses green :
Curséd be the man who falters —
　Better had he never been.

Brothers ! we are God-appointed
　Soldiers in these holy wars ;
Set apart, sealed and anointed
　Children of a Heavenly Mars !

Weakness we need not dissemble —
　But Jehovah leads us on :
Who is he that dares to tremble,
　Led by God of Gideon ?

Let them laugh in mad derision
　At our little feeble band —
God has told me in a vision
　We shall liberate the land.

Rise, then, brothers ; do not doubt me ;
　I can feel his presence now,
Feel his promises about me,
　Like a helmet on my brow.

We must conquer, we must slaughter ;
　We are God's rod, and his ire
Wills their blood shall flow like water :
　In Jehovah's dread name — Fire !

A KANSAS POSTSCRIPT.

Since the foregoing chapter was stereotyped, an unfriendly Kansas paper has related the following incident of the Battle of Osawatomie:

"We have no disposition to extenuate the crimes recently committed by this noted man. But there is no reason why the acts of kindness and charity which he was wont to perform should be forgotten, now that he is about to suffer the doom of a felon.

"An instance of this sort fell under our personal observation. At the sacking of Osawatomie, one of the most bitter pro-slavery men in Lykins County was killed. His name was Ed. Timmons. Some time afterwards, Brown stopped at the log house where Timmons had lived. His widow and children were there, and in great destitution. He inquired into their wants, relieved their distresses, and supported them until her friends in Missouri, informed through Brown of the condition of Mrs. Timmons, had time to come to her aid carry her to her former home. Mrs. Timmons fully appreciated the great kindness thus shown her, but never learned that Captain John Brown was her benefactor."

14

X.

JOHN BROWN'S DEFENCE OF LAWRENCE.

WE next find our hero in the town of Lawrence, at the most perilous crisis of its history. His defence of it is still remembered with gratitude by all the brave men who witnessed and participated in it. The writer at that time was in Iowa, in charge of a train of provisions, clothing, and military supplies, furnished for the free state men by the patriotism and philanthropy of the generous North. He has, therefore, no personal knowledge of John Brown's conduct at that eventful period of the history of Lawrence; but from a friend who was an eye witness, and a brave actor in it under the command of "the mighty man of valor," he has been furnished with the following faithful and graphic narration. Brave like his captain, but, like the old man, modest also, we are not permitted to announce his name.

On the 13th day of September, 1856, Jim Lane, with an army of some seventy-five or eighty men, pursued a number of the "enemy," and compelled them to take shelter in some log houses at Hickory Point. These were so situated on a high, rolling prairie as to

command a view of the whole country about it; and
being well fortified in them, the besieged considered
themselves safe even from the destructive effects of
Sharpe's rifles; and knowing that the besiegers were
destitute of cannon, they ran up from the top of their
main building a black flag — "No Surrender." This
was too much for the besiegers, for they were the de-
scendants of those brave-hearted men who had once
intrusted their lives and their fortunes to the Mayflower and to their God. Immediately despatching a
messenger to Lawrence for reënforcements and a small
six-pound howitzer, with directions to come *via* Topeka,
Lane withdrew his men a few miles to the west, and
encamped for the night near a spring, where he found
a copy of the inaugural of Governor Geary, whose
arrival in the territory had been announced only a
few days before. Upon reading this document, Lane
at once became satisfied of the good intentions of
Geary towards the people of Kansas, and thereupon
disbanded his men; and after having sent another
messenger, also by the way of Topeka, to countermand
his previous order for reënforcements, he proceeded
in person to the north line of the territory. But
Colonel Harvey, to whom this message was sent, instead of going by Topeka, commenced his march
directly for Hickory Point, on Saturday night, about
ten o'clock, with about one hundred and fifty men, and
one piece of cannon. He arrived there about two
o'clock on Sunday afternoon; and being unable to
agree upon any terms with the besieged, immediately
commenced a cannonade upon their fortresses, and ere

the sun set on that Sabbath eve, that black flag was
taken down, and a white one run up in its place.
The vanquished came to terms, and agreed to leave
the territory if Colonel Harvey would graciously permit them to do so; which reasonable request, it is
hardly necessary to say, was granted.

But during this transaction, another scene in the
Kansas drama was enacted at Lawrence. Brown, who
had been up to Topeka, was on his way home, and
remained in Lawrence over Sunday. His little army
— which consisted of some eighteen or twenty men,
and probably never exceeded thirty at one time — was
at Osawattamie, where he lived. This was an independent company — so independent, indeed, that they
trusted alone for victory to their Sharpe's rifles and to
the God of battles. With these brave and resolute
men, six of whom were Brown's own sons, he carried
on a guerilla warfare ; and whatever may be said of
his movements at Harper's Ferry, whether they mili-
tate against his sanity or his loyalty to our government, his efforts in behalf of free Kansas will not
soon be forgotten by those who witnessed them.

I was up early on Sunday morning, and went down
to the river and bathed, and came back to my tent,
which was on the west side of Lawrence, and busied
myself in the forenoon in writing letters home, and in
writing in my journal the proceedings of the last
week, for I had been absent that length of time, and
my journal had necessarily been neglected. The number of men in town on that day was considerably less
than was usual ; for, besides those at Hickory Point and

Osawattamie, there were several other companies in different parts of the territory, leaving Lawrence unprotected by a single company. The number of available men — citizens, parts of companies, and strangers — that were in town that day, would not, when all told, amount to more than two hundred; so that it would not have been a very difficult job for a thousand well-armed and well-disciplined troops to have marched into the heart of the city, and burned it, as was partially done in the month of May previous, by federal authority. It was not, therefore, a very desirable piece of information, on this Sabbath morning, when the church bells should have been tolling the hour for the worship of Almighty God, an hour that is made holy by the long-remembered associations of aged pastors and Sabbath school teachers, whose frail forms are now fast fading from our view — the announcement that " twenty-eight hundred Missourians were marching down upon Lawrence, with drums beating, and with eagles upon their banners." Yet such was actually the case. Such an announcement was actually made, with the expectation that we would believe it. But we did not; for we considered it, as we had become accustomed to consider all of like character,· only rumors, and gave them no consideration until we should become convinced of their truth. We continued our several occupations, whatever they happened to be, whether reading, writing, cooking, moulding bullets, or cleaning guns, and paid but little attention to rumors, having found by experience that a large majority of them were false alarms. Yet, notwithstanding this seeming

14 *

indifference to danger, messenger after messenger
arrived in town during the day, each one bringing
additional news of the invading army, and corrob-
orating the statements of those who had preceded him,
viz., that Atchison and Reid were at the head of a
large force of Missourians, variously estimated at from
fifteen hundred to three thousand, and that Lawrence
would be the object of their attack that afternoon.

At about four o'clock in the afternoon of the same
day, we were compelled to give credence to these
rumors, for we had almost ocular demonstration of
their truth; for we saw the smoke of Franklin, a
little town five miles south-east of Lawrence, curling
up towards heaven, and mingling with the clouds.
There were dwellings, under whose roofs were clus-
tered many little ones; the domicile in whose sanctuary
are holily kept all the sacred household gods, that
receptacle for man's happiness here below, which, by
the principles of the great common law, is termed the
freeman's castle, was crumbling to ashes before his
eyes — the work of a horde of incendiaries, who are
urged on to their deeds of darkness and death by the
influence of that *missionary* system which a northern
contemporary gravely terms "a southern economical
interest of paramount magnitude." Then there was
"hurrying to and fro," but not in "hot haste," and
with "tremblings and tears of distress," but with the
cool and determined resolution to repel the invaders,
if there was enough virtue in powder to do so.

I believe it is the first impulse of an unorganized
populace, during the impending of such danger as now

threatened us, to desire a leader or commander, and to, obey his orders. At least, it was so in the present instance ; for it was very evident, that without a concert of action, and a combination of the different forces that were in town, there would be but little safety in that immediate vicinity. The inquiry was next, Who shall be that leader ? Who can so arrange the effective force of the place as to defend it to the best advantage ? It was no sooner known that Captain Brown was in town, than he was unanimously voted general-in-chief for the day. The principal portion of the people had assembled in Main Street, opposite the post office ; and Captain Brown, standing upon a dry-goods box in their midst, addressed them somewhat as follows : —

" Gentlemen, it is said there are twenty-five hundred Missourians down at Franklin, and that they will be here in two hours. You can see for yourselves the smoke they are making by setting fire to the houses in that town. Now is probably the last opportunity you will have of seeing a fight ; so that you had better do your best. If they should come up and attack us, don't yell and make a great noise, but remain perfectly silent and still. Wait till they get within twenty-five yards of you ; get a good object; be sure you see the hind sight of your gun : then fire. A great deal of powder and lead, and very precious time, is wasted by shooting too high. You had better aim at their legs than at their heads. In either case, be sure of the hind sights of your guns. It is from this reason that I myself have so many times escaped ; for, if all the bul-

lets which have ever been aimed at me had hit me, I
would have been as full of holes as a riddle."

Having thus taught them in the arts of war, he
commenced his preparations for defence. There were
several forts and breastworks, and also one or two unfinished churches in the south, south-west, and south-
east sides of the town : these were all manned with as
many soldiers as could be spared for them. On the
north of the town ran the Kansas River ; on the west was
a ravine ; and the enemy were looked for on the south.
As for myself, I occupied, with some fifteen or twenty
others, a breastwork thrown across the south end of
Massachusetts Street — a precaution which had been
found necessary in the early part of the season.

Captain Brown was always on the alert, visiting
every portion of the town, and all the fortifications, in
person, giving directions, and exhorting every man to
keep cool, and do his duty, and his reward would be
an approving conscience. Among other preparations
for a vigorous defence, a number of merchants went
into their stores and brought out a large lot of pitch-
forks ; and every man who was not provided with a
bayonet on his gun was furnished with a fork, which
certainly would be no mean weapon, if dexterously
handled.

In the mean time, the invading army had left Franklin, and were marching towards Lawrence ; and about
five o'clock in the afternoon, their advance guard, consisting of four hundred horsemen, crossed the Wake-
rusa, and presented themselves in sight of town, about
two miles off, when they halted, and arrayed them-

selves for battle, fearing, perhaps, to come within too close range of Sharpe's rifle balls. Brown's movement now was a little on the offensive order; for he ordered out all the Sharpe's riflemen from every part of town, — in all not more than forty or fifty, — marched them a half mile into the prairie, and arranged them three paces apart, in a line parallel with that of the enemy; and then they lay down upon their faces in the grass, awaiting the order to fire. While occupying this position, a gallant trooper from the enemy's side rode up about half a mile in advance of his comrades to reconnoitre; halting upon a little rise in the road, and while feasting his eyes with a sight of "Lane's Banditti," a full mile off, one of them, not having the fear of the Missourians before his eyes, drew a bead on him, and fired at him, waiting with breathless anxiety to see what came of it. In two or three seconds, the ball struck in the road, immediately at the horse's feet, and the rider, satisfied with this demonstration, immediately wheeled about, and putting spurs to his horse, was soon out of the reach of even Sharpe's rifle balls.

Brown now changed the position of his men to a rising piece of ground, about a quarter of a mile to the left, which overlooked a small cornfield of eight or ten acres, and there stationed them as before, with their faces to the ground. A simultaneous movement on the part of the enemy brought the two armies face to face, about half a mile apart, and with the cornfield between them.

It was now just approaching dusk. The shades of evening were fast settling upon all Kansas; and in-

stead of there being a Joshua there, to charter a little
more of the light of day, the sun, in anticipation of a
fratricidal strife, went rapidly down behind the mountains ; there was no light, even of the moon and stars,
for the intervening clouds; and Night — the good
angel that she was — came and spread her dark man-
tle over the earth, and concealed the further shedding
of blood from those who would weep at sight of it.
But during this cover, there were those among us who
were to depart and be no more with us forever.   They
were to

> " lie down
> With patriarchs of the infant world — with kings,
> The powerful of the earth,"

in that grand receptacle for the dead, "the distant
Aidenn," on the confines of whose shores there are
doubtless worthier and "better" soldiers, as well as
" elder."

The distance now between the contending armies
was such as to give to Sharpe's rifle balls, that were
fired with precision, a deadly effect ; as was evinced by
the fact that several horses were found riderless.   In a
few moments, the firing became general ; and in the
darkness, and otherwise stillness of the night, the continual flash, flash, flash of those engines of death along
that line of living fire, presented a scene the appearance of which was at once not only terrible, but sub-
limely beautiful.   For fear that the few men detailed
to meet the enemy would be surrounded in the darkness by the superior number of horsemen, and cut to
pieces, a twelve-pound brass piece, under guard of

twelve men, was sent to their assistance; but before it had arrived upon the ground, the foe had become panic-stricken and fled. The sons of chivalry and of the sunny South, four hundred strong, well armed and mounted, precipitately fled before thirty or forty footmen.

That night, T. and I took our blankets and lay down immediately within the breastwork before mentioned, with a stone for a pillow and the clouds for a covering. We had been here for a few moments only, when Captain Brown came along, and said, "With your permission, I will be the third one to aid in defending this fortification to-night." We readily granted his request, and he then lay down by our side, and told us of the trials and the wars he had passed through; that he had settled in Kansas with a large family, having with him six full-grown sons; that he had taken a claim in Lykins county, and was attending peacefully to the duties of husbandry, when the hordes of wild men came over from Missouri and took possession of all the ballot-boxes, destroyed his corn, stole his horses, and shot down his cattle, and sheep, and hogs, and repeatedly threatened to shoot him, hang him, or burn him, if he did not leave the territory; and as many times endeavored to put their threats in force, but were as often prevented by his "eternal vigilance," which he found to be the price of his life, and of those of his family; that they afterwards did kill and murder one of his sons, in cold blood, in his own hearing, and almost in his own sight; and all, forsooth, because he hated slavery! When he

told me that he held that promising son in his arms as
he drew his last breath, and thought of the resem-
blance he bore to his mother, I thought, in the indignation of the moment, that had that been my son, I
would have sworn, by the blood that crimsoned his
face, forever to raise my voice and my arm against the
measures and the men who had thus hunted him to an
untimely death.

Another eye witness and participator in this memorable action, who was posted with Major Bickerton
on Mount Oread, afterwards published a poetical
account of it; which, as the writer — Richard Realf —
had engaged to be at Harper's Ferry, but died on his
passage from England as he was coming over for that
purpose, I subjoin, as well as on account of its historical accuracy, literary merit, and an indication of the
range of intellect which the brave old hero gathered
around him.

THE DEFENCE OF LAWRENCE.

All night, upon the guarded hill,
  Until the stars were low,
Wrapped round as with Jehovah's will,
  We waited for the foe;
All night the silent sentinels
  Moved by like gliding ghosts;
All night the fancied warning bells
  Held·all men to their posts.

We heard the sleeping prairies breathe,
  The forest's human moans,
The hungry gnashing of the teeth
  Of wolves on bleaching bones;

We marked the roar of rushing fires,
  The neigh of frighted steeds,
And voices as of far-off lyres
  Among the river reeds.

We were but thirty-nine who lay
  Beside our rifles then;
We were but thirty-nine, and they
  Were twenty hundred men.
Our lean limbs shook and reeled about,
  Our feet were gashed and bare,
And all the breezes shredded out
  Our garments in the air.

Sick, sick, at all the woes which spring
  Where falls the Southron's rod,
Our very souls had learned to cling
  To Freedom as to God;
And so we never thought of fear,
  In all those stormy hours,
For every mother's son stood near
  The awful, unseen powers.

And twenty hundred men had met,
  And swore an oath of hell
That, ere the morrow's sun might set,
  Our smoking homes should tell
A tale of ruin and of wrath,
  And damning hate in store,
To bar the freeman's western path
  Against him evermore.

They came: the blessed Sabbath day,
  That soothed our swollen veins,
Like God's sweet benediction, lay
  On all the singing plains;
The valleys shouted to the sun,
  The great woods clapped their hands,

15

And joy and glory seemed to run
  Like rivers through the lands.

They came : our daughters and our wives,
  And men whose heads were white,
Rose sudden into kingly lives,
  And walked forth to the fight ;
And we drew aim along our guns,
  And calmed our quickening breath ;
Then, as is meet for Freedom's sons,
  Shook loving hands with Death.

And when three hundred of the foe
  Rode up in scorn and pride,
Whoso had watched us then might know
  That God was on our side ;
For all at once, a mighty thrill
  Of grandeur through us swept,
And strong and swiftly down the hill
  Like Gideons we leapt.

And all throughout that Sabbath day
  A wall of fire we stood,
And held the baffled foe at bay,
  And streaked the ground with blood ;
And when the sun was very low,
  They wheeled their stricken ranks,
And passed on, wearily and slow,
  Beyond the river banks.

Beneath the everlasting stars,
  We bended child-like knees,
And thanked God for the shining scars
  Of his large victories ;
And some, who lingered, said they heard
  Such wondrous music pass,
As though a seraph's voice had stirred
  The pulses of the grass.

XI.

A S soon as the Missourians retreated from Franklin, John Brown, with four sons, left Lawrence for the East, by the way of Nebraska Territory. When at Topeka he found a fugitive slave, whom, covering up in his wagon, he carried along with him.

He was sick, and travelled slowly. Northern squatters, at this time, were constantly leaving the Territory in large numbers. In coming down with a train of emigrants, in October, I met two or three hundred of these voluntary exiles — all of them having terrible stories of Southern cruelty to tell.

Not contented with having closed the Missouri River against Northern emigration, the South, through the Government, determined, also, to arrest the emigration from the Free States by the Nebraska route. It was intended to stop and disarm my train ; but a few forced marches defeated that design. It was known that another large party was coming in after me : this train several companies of cavalry and artillery marched northward to arrest. John Brown went up with them, and camped with them every night, although the Mar-

(171)

shal, who led the force, had a writ for his arrest! "He
was then acting in the capacity of a surveyor — or appeared as ·such to them. He had a light wagon and a
cow tied behind it. His surveyor's instruments were
in the wagon in full sight." *

As soon as the military supplies had been stored, I
left Topeka in company with a friend, and overtook the
troops a few miles from Lexington, a town site on the
prairie, thus named by the Massachusetts companies.
Passing them, and travelling twelve miles farther, I
found, lying sick in bed, at the solitary log hut at
Plymouth, the venerable hero of Osawatomie and Lawrence. My companion was a physician, who at once
prescribed remedies for his fever. I urged the old man
to move on, as the troops were approaching, not knowing that he had recently encamped with them. I told
him that they intended to remain at Plymouth until
the train should arrive there; and that, as many of the
people here knew his name, he might, without intentional treachery, be discovered and arrested.. He
thanked me for the advice, and promised to follow it.
Leaving the house he remained at, I saw the camp of
his little company — five men in all, and four of them
his sons. I urged on them, also, the importance of
moving on.

A few hours before we overtook the troops, a young
man joined us, ·and reported that he had recently
escaped from the ruffians at Leavenworth. Not suspecting or doubting his story, as we rode along I expressed, in enthusiastic terms, my admiration of the

* Letter from Joel Grover, of Lawrence.

character of Old Brown. Our new acquaintance suddenly pretended to be sick, and as he was, withal,
rather a bore to us, we advised him to return to Plymouth. He seemed to follow our advice, but rode back
to the dragoons, who had encamped for the night, and
informed them where Old Brown lay sick. A detachment of the soldiery was instantly sent on to arrest
him. Fortunately for the cause of the slave and
American honor, they arrived too late. The old man
had crossed the Nebraska line, and the officer in command did not dare to assume the responsibility of following him.

At Tabor, in Iowa, — a little village of true friends
of freedom, — the old man and his sons remained two
or three weeks. This village was a colony from Oberlin, in Ohio, and contributed more money and provisions, in proportion to its population, than any other
community in the Union.

About the end of November, John Brown reached
Chicago, and appeared before the National Kansas Committee, from whom, however, the only aid he obtained
was a suit of clothes, which, although of the plainest
cut and most common material, he did not like, because they were too fine, and not strong enough for a
man of his simple habits and tastes. In December he
was at Albany, urging on the leading friends of Kansas the necessity of more efficient action against the
Southern marauders.

When on his way to New York, he staid for a few
days at Cleveland. The Herald, of that city, recently
said of this visit:

15 *

"He was so demented as to suppose he could raise a regiment of. men in Ohio to march into Missouri to make reprisals against the Slave forces, and even asked a friend if the power of the State could not be enlisted in that matter. He was then told by many that he was a madman, and the poor man left sorrowing that there was no sympathy here for the oppressed."

How very demented! The whole North was shout-ing itself hoarse in execrating the Southern invaders of Kansas; and yet, when an earnest old man proposed to organize this resentment into an effective system of aggressive action, "he was told by many that he was a madman!"

His half brother, Jeremiah, seems to have been one of those unfortunate men with whom earnest heroism is synonymous with insanity. When the illustrious old man, who redeemed his name and family from the obscurity of an excessive familiarity,— and made the name of JOHN BROWN, hitherto a generic title for the Saxon race, mean the highest Christian military hero-ism, — this relative, under oath, declared:

"My brother John, from my earliest recollection, has been an hon-est, conscientious man; and this was his reputation among all who knew him in that section of the country. Since the trouble growing out of the settlement of Kansas Territory, I have observed a marked change in brother John. Previous to this, he devoted himself entirely to business; but since these troubles he has abandoned all business, and has become wholly absorbed by the subject of Slavery. He had property left him by his father, and of which I had the agency. He has never taken a dollar of it for the benefit of his family, but has called for a portion of it to be expended in what he called the Service. After his return to Kansas he called on me, and I urged him to go home to his family and attend to his private affairs; that I feared his course would prove his destruction and that of his boys. This was about two years ago. He replied that he was sorry that I did not sympathize with him; that he knew he was in the line of his duty, and he must pursue it, though it should destroy him and his family. He stated to me that he was satisfied that he was a chosen instrument in the hands of God to war against Slavery. From his manner and from his conversation at this time, I had no doubt he had become insane upon the subject of Slavery, and gave him to understand this was my opinion of him!"

With such insane men are the highest heavens peopled; and of such are the angels who minister at God's throne.

XII.

JOHN BROWN arrived in Boston in January, 1857. At that period there was an effort made, by the friends of freedom in the Commonwealth, to induce the legislature of Massachusetts to vote an appropriation of ten thousand dollars, for the purpose of protecting the interests of the North, and the rights of her citizens in Kansas, if the Territory should be again invaded by organized marauders from the Southern States.

A Joint Committee was appointed by the General Court to consider the petitions in favor of a State appropriation. It held its sittings publicly. Eminent champions of freedom in Massachusetts, and men who had distinguished themselves during the conflict in Kansas, were invited to address the Committee. Among the Kansas men was Captain John Brown, who, on the 18th of February, appeared at the capitol to make a statement of his views.

The writer was present at this sitting, and reported the old man's speech.

Captain Brown, as he stepped forward, was received

176

with applause. He said he intended to speak exclusively of matters of which he was personally cognizant; and, therefore, the committee must excuse him
if he should refer more particularly to himself and
family than he otherwise would do.

He then read the following statement in a clear,
ringing tone:

SPEECH TO THE LEGISLATURE.

" I saw, while in Missouri, in the fall of 1855, large
numbers of men going to Kansas *to vote*, and also
returning after they had so done : as they said.

" Later in the year, I, with four of my sons, was
called out, and travelled, mostly on foot and during
the night, to help defend Lawrence, a distance of
thirty-five miles ; where we were detained, with some
five hundred others, or thereabouts, from five to ten
days — say an average of ten days — at a cost of not
less than a dollar and a half per day, as wages ; to say
nothing of the actual loss and suffering occasioned to
many of them, by leaving their families sick, their
crops not secured, their houses unprepared for winter,
and many without houses at all. This was the case
with myself and sons, who could not get houses built
after returning. Wages alone would amount to seven
thousand five hundred dollars ; loss and suffering cannot be estimated.

" I saw, at that time, the body of the murdered Barber, and was present to witness his wife and other
friends brought in to see him with his clothes on, just
as he was when killed.*

---

* By a federal office-holder, who was *afterwards* promoted to a more
lucrative post,

" I, with six sons and a son-in-law, was called out, and travelled, most of the way on foot, to try and save Lawrence, May 20 and 21, and much of the way in the night. From that date, neither I nor my sons, nor my son-in-law, could do any work about our homes, but lost our whole time until we left, in October; except one of my sons, who had a few weeks to devote to the care of his own and his brother's family, who were then without a home.

" From about the 20th of May, hundreds of men, like ourselves, lost their whole time, and entirely failed of securing any kind of crop whatever. I believe it safe to say, that five hundred free state men lost each one hundred and twenty days, which, at one dollar and a half per day, would be — to say nothing of attendant losses — ninety thousand dollars.

" On or about the 30th of May, two of my sons, with several others, were imprisoned without other crime than opposition to bogus legislation, and most barbarously treated for a time, one being held about one month, and the other about four months. Both had their families on the ground. After this, both of them had their houses burned, and all their goods consumed by the Missourians. In this burning all the eight suffered. One had his oxen stolen, in addition."

The Captain, laying aside his paper, here said that he had now at his hotel, and would exhibit to the Committee, if they so desired, the chains which one of his sons had worn, when he was driven, beneath a burning sun, by federal troops, to a distant prison, on a charge of treason. The cruelties he there endured, added to the anxieties and sufferings incident to his position, had rendered him, the old man said, as his eye flashed and his voice grew sterner, "a maniac — yes, a MANIAC."

He paused a few seconds, wiped a tear from his eye, and continued his narration:

"At Black Jack, the invading Missourians wounded three free state men, one of them my son-in-law; and, a few days afterwards, one of my sons was so wounded that he will be a cripple for life.

"In August, I was present and saw the mangled and disfigured body of the murdered Hoyt, of Deerfield, Massachusetts, brought into our camp. I knew him well.

"I saw the ruins of many free state men's houses in different parts of the Territory, together with grain in the stack, burning, and wasted in other ways, to the amount, at least, of fifty thousand dollars.

"I saw several other free state men, besides those I have named, during the summer, who were badly wounded by the invaders of the Territory.

"I know that for much of the time during the summer, the travel over portions of the Territory was entirely cut off, and that none but bodies of armed men dared to move at all.

"I know that for a considerable time the mails on different routes were entirely stopped; and notwithstanding there were abundant troops in the Territory to escort the mails, I know that such escorts were not furnished, as they ought to have been.

"I saw while it was standing, and afterwards saw

the ruins, of a most valuable house, the property of a highly civilized, intelligent, and exemplary Christian Indian, which was burned to the ground by the ruffians, because its owner was suspected of favoring the free state men. He is known as Ottawa Jones, or John T. Jones.

"In September last, I visited a beautiful little free state town called Staunton, on the north side of the Osage, (or Marais-des-Cygnes, as it is sometimes called,) from which every inhabitant had fled for fear of their lives, even after having built a strong log house, or wooden fort, at a heavy expense, for their protection. Many of them had left their effects liable to be destroyed or carried off, not being able to remove them. This was to me a most gloomy scene, and like a visit to a sepulchre.

"Deserted houses and cornfields were to be found in almost every direction south of the Kansas River.

"I have not yet told all I saw in Kansas.

"I once saw three mangled bodies, two of which were dead, and one alive, but with twenty bullet and buck shot holes in him, after the two murdered men had lain on the ground, to be worked at by flies, for some eighteen hours. One of these young men was *my own son.*"

The stern old man faltered. He struggled long to suppress all exhibition of his feelings; and soon, but with a subdued, and in a faltering tone, continued:

"I saw Mr. Parker, whom I well know, all bruised about the head, and with his throat partly cut, after he had been dragged, sick, from the house of Ottawa

Jones, and thrown over the bank of the Ottawa Creek for dead.

" About the first of September, I, and five sick and wounded sons, and a son-in-law, were obliged to lie on the ground, without shelter, for a considerable time, and at times almost.in a state of starvation, and dependent on the charity of the Christian Indian I have before named, and his wife.

" I saw Dr. Graham, of Prairie City, who was a prisoner with the ruffians on the 2d of June, and was present when they wounded him, in an attempt to kill him, as he was trying to save himself from being murdered by them during the fight at Black Jack.

" I know that numerous other persons, whose names I cannot now remember, suffered like hardships and exposures to those I have mentioned.

. " I know well that on or about the 14th of September, 1856, a large force of Missourians and other ruffians, said by Governor Geary to be twenty-seven hundred in number, invaded the Territory, burned Franklin, and, while the smoke of that place was going up behind them, they, on the same day, made their appearance in full view of, and within about a mile of Lawrence ; and I know of no reason why they did not attack that place, except that about one hundred free state men volunteered to go out, and did go out on the open plain before the town, and give them the offer of a fight ; which, after getting scattering shots from our men, they declined, and retreated back towards Franklin. I saw that whole thing. The government troops, at this time, were at Lecompton, a distance of twelve

16

miles only from Lawrence, with Governor Geary; and yet, notwithstanding runners had been despatched to advise him, in good time, of the approach and setting out of the enemy, (who had to march some forty miles to reach Lawrence,) he did not, on that memorable occasion, get a single soldier on the ground until after the enemy had retreated to Franklin, and been gone for more than five hours. This is the way he saved Lawrence. (Laughter.) And it is just the kind of protection the free state men have received from the Administration from the first." '

These things the old man saw in Kansas.

He concluded his remarks by denouncing the traitors to freedom, who, when a question of this kind was raised, cried out, " Save the people's money ; the dear people's money ! " He made a detailed estimate of how much the National Government had expended in endeavoring to fasten Slavery on Kansas ; and asked why these politicians had never cried out, " Save the people's money ! " when it was expended to trample under the foot of the " peculiar " crime of the south, the rights, lives, and property of the Northern squatters. They were silent then." (Applause.)

THE CHAIRMAN — Captain Brown, I wish to ask you regarding Buford's men.* Did you ever mingle with them ? And if so, what did you see or hear ?

CAPTAIN BROWN replied, that he saw a great deal of

---

* Colonel Buford was the leader· of several companies of Georgia and Alabama bandits, who came to Kansas, in the spring of 1856, with the avowed intention of expelling or exterminating the emigrants from the North

them at first; that they spoke without hesitation before him, because he employed himself as a surveyor; and, as nearly all the surveyors were pro-slavery men, they probably thought he was "sound on the goose." * They told him all their plans; what they intended to do; how they were determined to drive off the free state men, and possess themselves of the Territory, and make it a Slave State at all hazards: cost what it might. They said that the Yankees could not be whipped, coaxed, nor driven into a fight, and that one pro-slavery man could whip a dozen abolitionists. They said that Kansas must be a Slave State to save Missouri from abolition; that both must stand or fall together. They did not hesitate to threaten that they would burn, kill, scalp, and drive out the entire free state population of the Territory, if it was necessary to do so to accomplish their object.

THE CHAIRMAN then asked who commanded the free state men at Lawrence?

His answer was characteristic of the man, whose courage was only equalled by his modesty and worth. He explained how bravely our boys acted — gave every one the credit but himself. When again asked who commanded them, he said — no one; that he was asked to take the command, but refused, and only acted as their *adviser!*

The Captain spoke, in conclusion, about the emigrants needed for Kansas.

"We want," he said, "good men, industrious men,

---

* Western phrase: equivalent to, a reliable friend of slavery.

men who respect themselves; who act only from the dictates of conscience; *men who fear God too much to fear any thing human.*"

THE CHAIRMAN — What is your opinion as to the probability of a renewal of hostilities in Kansas — of another invasion; and what do you think would be the effect, on the free state men, of an appropriation by Massachusetts?

CAPTAIN BROWN — Whenever we heard, out in Kansas, that the North was doing any thing for us, we were encouraged and strengthened to struggle on. As to the probability of another invasion, I do not know. We ought to be prepared for the worst. Things do not look one iota more encouraging now, than they did last year at this time. You ought to remember that, from the date of the Shannon treaty till May last, there was perfect quiet in Kansas; no fear of a renewal of hostilities; no violence offered to our citizens in Missouri. I frequently went there myself; was known there; yet treated with the greatest kindness."

Book Third.

THE SWORD OF GIDEON.

16 *

12. And the angel of the Lord appeared unto him and said, The Lord is with thee, thou mighty man of valor.

14. And the Lord looked upon him, and said, Go in this thy might, and thou shalt save Israel from the hands of the Midianites: have not I sent thee?

16. And the Lord said unto him, Surely I will be with thee, and thou shalt smite the Midianites as one man.

27. Then Gideon took ten men of his servants, and did as the Lord had said unto him: and so it was . . . that he did it by night.

28. And when the men of the city arose early in the morning, behold, the altar of Baal was cast down.

29. And they said one to another, Who hath done this thing? And when they inquired and asked, they said, Gideon the son of Joash hath done this thing. (Chapter vi.)

21. And all the host ran, and cried, and fled. — *Book of Judges,* Chapter vii.

I.

Whetting the Sword.

THUS far John Brown's action has been exclusively
defensive; even according to the usual but unjust
definition of the word. He had never struck a blow
but in defence of a threatened party. He had fought
against the invaders of Free Soil, but never yet invaded a slave country.

We are now to see him acting as an aggressor — if
we accept the popular interpretation of the phrase.
Rather, in truth, we are now to see him as a defender
of the faith delivered to the fathers. For error is
always an innovator — ever an aggression. It has
supplanted and fills the place that God intended for
the truth. Hence the radical reformer is the only
conservative; and the monomaniac is the man who sup-
ports any untrue thing, whether creed, party, church,
or civil institution.

The North says that slavery is a wrong. Why not,
then, destroy it? The Constitution, the Union, Federal laws, State rights, it answers; refusing to believe
that no real good can be gained by nourishing a gigantic wrong.

When John Brown walked, he neither turned to the right nor left. With a solemn, earnest countenance, he moved straight on, and every one he met made way for him. So in his ideas. He felt that he was sent here, into this earnest world of ours, not to eat, and sleep, and dress, and die merely, but for a divinely pre-appointed purpose — to see justice done, to help the defenceless, to clear God's earth of the Devil's lies, in the shortest time and at any cost.

He looked over the American field, and saw a huge embodied falsehood there; a magazine of all manner of ungodliness — the sum of all villanies. He heard people call it slavery, and regret its existence; others style it the peculiar institution, and hope that it might finally disappear. Others he heard loudly cursing it, but not one grappling with it. He was amazed at what he saw and heard; and, when he said so, people called him a monomaniac. He saw some afraid to assail it, because it was guarded by two lions in the way — called the Union, and the Constitution; while others, seeing the cotton that it belched from its mouth, were so pleased with that performance, that they would not look behind the bales. Some he saw bound with the chains of policy, and others with the manacles of non-resistance. But not one living, dreadfully-in-earnest foe among them all!

That is what he saw, or thought he saw. Perhaps, had he seen the hidden mines that some men were digging, he would have changed his opinion of the value of their labor; but even had he known it, as he was not a miner, but a fighter on the earth, he still would have acted as he did act. He marched straight ahead, trampling under foot the rotten stubble of unjust laws and constitutions, that stood between him and his foe. It is true that he finally fell among them; but not before he proved how very powerless they are to resist a MAN.

JOHN BROWN'S SCHEME.

John Brown returned to Kansas in the month of November, 1857.

What had he been doing since January, when we reported him in Boston? *Whetting his sword.* And how? In our free Republic, with its barbaric Southern rulers, it would not be here safe to say how. Only brief traces of his movements, therefore, can, in justice to his noble friends, be recorded at this time.

It should be stated, first, that at this period there was every prospect of renewed disturbances in Kansas. Our need of officers had been greatly felt in the recent conflict there. One hundred mounted men, well armed and officered, would at any time have swept the invaders from the Territory. John Brown fully appreciated his necessity, and the terror that his own name had inspired, arose from the dread, he modestly thought, of his military knowledge, as much as from the victories he had gained. Hence he desired to have funds to equip a sufficient force for the protection of the squatters, as well as to drill a select number of the young men of Kansas, who had proved themselves faithful to *principle.*

He well knew, from his power over men, that, should the Kansas difficulties cease, the youths thus drilled would follow him to Harper's Ferry, which, for many years, he had selected as the grand point of attack on slavery.

JOHN BROWN IN BOSTON.

I met John Brown in Boston in January, 1857 ; and many of the facts of this volume he told me at that period. To a gentleman of note in Massachusetts, who made his acquaintance at that time, I am indebted for the reminiscences that follow :

"He brought me a letter of introduction in January, 1857. His business was to raise money for the purpose of further protecting the Free State men of Kansas; and for this purpose he desired to equip one hundred mounted men. His son Owen accompanied him. He immediately impressed me as a person of no common order, and every day that I saw him strengthened this impression. . . . His brown coat of the fashion of ten years before, his waistcoat buttoning nearly to the throat, and his wide trousers, gave him the look of a well-to-do farmer in his Sunday dress; while his patent leather stock, gray surtout, and fur cap, added a military air to his figure. At this time he wore no beard.*

THE IDEALIST AMONG IDEALISTS.

"I found him frank and decided in his conversation; expressing his opinions of men and things with a modest firmness, but often in the most striking manner. I think it was in his second call on me that he used the language, '*I believe in the Golden Rule, sir, and the Declaration of Independence. I think they both mean the same thing; and it is better that a whole generation should pass off the face of the earth — men, women, and children — by a violent death, than that one jot of either should fail in this country.* I mean exactly so, sir.' I have twice or thrice heard him repeat this sentiment, which I particularly noticed at the time. He staid but a short time in Boston ; but returned in February, and soon after appeared before a committee of the Massachusetts Legislature. . . . In March he visited Concord, and spoke at a public meeting in the Town Hall, where, I am told, he exhibited the chain worn by his son John in Kansas, and, with a gesture and voice never to be forgotten by those who heard him, denounced the admin-

* The steel engraving which embellishes this volume is from a daguerreotype taken at that time, and presented to me by the old hero as a token of friendship.

istration and the South for their work in Kansas. He spent several days in Concord, and made the acquaintance of many of its citizens ; among others, of Ralph Waldo Emerson and Henry D. Thoreau, who have testified so clearly to his nobility of character.

"Near the end of March, 1857, being on my way to Washington, I met Capt. Brown in New York City, and spent a night with him at the Metropolitan Hotel. Capt. Brown objected to the show and extravagance of such an establishment, and said he preferred a plain tavern, where drovers and farmers lodged in a plain way. We went on to Philadelphia, and while there I was taken unwell, and could scarcely sit up. Capt. Brown nursed me as much as I had need of, and showed great skill and tenderness. In May he set out for Kansas, and I lost sight of him for nearly a year."

Emerson is reported at this time to have said that John Brown was the truest hero-man he had ever met. Theodore Parker, also, said to a friend of mine, who spoke of Captain Montgomery as a man of more harmonious and cultivated intellect than John Brown, "Do you know what you say, sir ? John Brown is one of the most extraordinary men of this age and nation." Henry D. Thoreau styled him a " true transcendentalist."

Mr. Stearns, an active and generous friend of Kansas, tells two incidents of John Brown's visit to Boston at this time, which are exceedingly characteristic of the old Puritan.

Shortly after his introduction to him, Mr. Stearns said, one day, half jestingly, "I suppose, Captain Brown, that if Judge Lecompte had fallen into your hands, he would have fared rather hard."

The old man turned round in his chair, and, in his most earnest tones, said, "If the Lord had delivered Judge Lecompte into my hands, I think it would have required the Lord to have taken him out again."

A meeting of prominent friends of freedom in Kansas, was to be held on the Sabbath, as no other day could a full attendance be obtained. Mr. Stearns, not knowing how the old Puritan might regard this use of the day of rest, — to him and to us a very holy use of it, — inquired if it would be consistent with his religious conviction to give his attendance.

"Mr. Stearns," said the old man, "I have a poor little ewe that has fallen into the ditch, and I think the Sabbath is as good a day as any to help her out. I will come."

TRAVELS IN THE EASTERN STATES.

The winter and spring of 1857 John Brown spent in travelling. He visited North Elba once. He spoke at different cities, and employed all his energies in collecting money. I believe that a large sum was voted for his use by the National Kansas Committee; but I know that — it is said through the dishonesty of an agent — he received only a very trifling portion of it. He published, also, the following appeal, which was widely copied by the press, and undoubtedly liberally responded to :

To the Friends of Freedom :

The undersigned, whose individual means were exceedingly limited when he first engaged in the struggle for liberty in Kansas, being now still more destitute, and no less anxious than in times past to continue his efforts to sustain that cause, is induced to make this earnest appeal to the friends of freedom throughout the United States, in the firm belief that his call will not go unheeded.

I ask all honest lovers of *liberty and human rights, both male and female*, to hold up my hands by contributions of pecuniary aid, either as counties, cities, towns, villages, societies, churches, or individuals.

I will endeavor to make a judicious and faithful application of all such means as I may be supplied with. Contributions may be sent, n drafts, to W. H. D. Calender, Cashier State Bank, Hartford, Conn. It is my intention to visit as many places *as I can* during my stay in he States, provided I am informed of the disposition of the inhab-tants to aid me in my efforts, as well as to receive my visit. Infor-mation may be communicated to me, (care of Massasoit House,) at Springfield, Mass. Will editors of newspapers, friendly to the cause, kindly second the measure, and also give this some half dozen inser-tions? Will either gentlemen or ladies, or both, volunteer to take up the business? It is with *no little sacrifice of personal feeling* I appear in this manner before the public.   JOHN BROWN.

In February, when in Collinsville, Connecticut, he ordered the manufacture of his pikes. I remember that, when in Boston, he spoke with great contempt of Sharpe's rifles as a weapon for inexperienced men, and said that with a pike, or bow and arrows, he could arm recruits more formidably than with patent guns. How he ordered the pikes is thus stated by the maker of them :

"In the latter part of February, or the early part of March, 1857, Old Brown, as he is familiarly called, came to Collinsville to visit his relatives, and by invitation addressed the inhabitants at a public meet-ing. At the close of it, or on the following day, he exhibited some weapons which he claimed to have taken from Capt. H. C. Pate, at the battle of Black Jack. Among others was a bowie knife or dirk, having a blade about eight inches long. Brown remarked that such an instrument, fixed to the end of a pole about six feet long, would be a capital weapon to place in the hands of the settlers in Kansas, to keep in their cabins to defend themselves against 'border ruffians or wild beasts,' and asked me what it would be worth to make one thousand. I replied that I would make them for one dollar each, not thinking that it would lead to a contract, or that such an instrument would ever be wanted or put to use in any way, if made ; but, to my surprise, he drew up a contract for one thousand, to be completed within three months, he agreeing to pay me. five hundred dollars in thirty days, and the balance within thirty days thereafter." *

* Having failed to raise the necessary money, the pikes were left unfinished at this time ; but, in the following year, in the month of June, John Brown was again in Collinsville, and completed the contract, and in August, under the name of J. Smith and Sons, ordered them to be forwarded to Chambersburg, Pennsylvania, upon which they were transported across the country to Harper's Ferry.

17

In March and April, Captain Brown made an agreement with a drill-master, named Hugh Forbes, an Englishman, and a Revolutionary exile, to instruct a number of young Kansas men in military science. Forbes engaged to be at Tabor, in Iowa, in June, to meet John Brown and his men there.

In May, John Brown set out for Kansas, but was delayed in the Central States for some time. Here is an incident of his travels, recently published to prove his insanity, by a citizen of Ohio:

"During the summer of 1857, I met John Brown in the cars between Cleveland and Columbus. He was about to return to Kansas. I sought to gather some information respecting the probable advantage of wool growing in that section; but found his mind was very restless on wool and sheep husbandry, and soon began to talk with great earnestness of the evil of Slavery, on which he soon became enthusiastic, and claimed that any course, whether stealing or coaxing niggers to run away from their masters, was honorable; at which I attempted to point out a more conservative course, remarking very kindly to him that Kentucky, in my opinion, would have been a free State ere this, had it not been for the excitement and prejudices engendered by ultra abolitionists of Ohio. At this remark, he rose to his feet with clinched fist, eyes rolling like an insane man, (as he most assuredly was,) and remarked that the South would become free within one year were it not that there were too many such scoundrels as myself to rivet the chains of Slavery. . . . I must, though, in justice to Mr. Brown, state that, when not under excitement or mental derangement, he has ever manifested to me a kind, benevolent, and humane disposition, as a man of strict integrity, moral and religious worth." *

Another person, who also met John Brown in the cars at this time, subsequently said that he regarded him as a monomaniac; and his chief reason was, that the old man " spoke of the Eastern people generally as criminally lukewarm on the subject and *sin* of slavery, and manifested a very great deal of warmth on the subject " !

That it is true that John Brown was not fully satisfied with the results of his trip to the east, may be seen

* Affidavit of S. N. Goodale, of Cleveland, Ohio.

by the following characteristic note, which was found in his own handwriting among the papers left at the homestead of North Elba. It is entitled:

OLD BROWN'S FAREWELL

To the Plymouth Rocks, Bunker Hill Monuments, Charter Oaks, and Uncle Thom's Cabbins.

He has left for Kansas. Has been trying since he came out of the Territory to secure an outfit, or in other words, *the means of arming and thoroughly equipping* his regular minuet men, who are mixed up *with the people of Kansas,* and *he leaves* the States, WITH A FEELING OF DEEPEST SADNESS: that after having exhausted *his own small means,* and with his *family and his* BRAVE MEN; suffered hunger, cold, naked-ness and *some* of them sickness, wounds, imprisonment *in Irons;* with extreme cruel treatment, and *others death:* that after lying on the ground for months in the most sickly, unwholesome, and uncom-fortable places; *some of the time with sick and wounded* destitute of any shelter; and hunted like wolves; sustained in part by Indians: that after all this; in order to sustain a cause which every citizen of this *"glorious Republic"* is under equal moral obligations to do: and *for the neglect of which, he will be held accountable by God:* a cause in which every man, women, and child; of the *entire human family* has a DEEP and AWFUL interest; that when *no wages* are asked; or expected; he cannot secure, amidst all the wealth, luxury and extravagance of this "Heaven exalted" people; even the necessary supplies of the common soldier. "How are the mighty fallen?"

Boston, April, A. D. 1857.

The diary of one of the old man's sons, which was found among the papers at the Kennedy Farm, gives an outline of his movements after starting for the Territory.

JOURNAL OF ONE OF BROWN'S SONS.

The journal, which opens on Tuesday, Aug. 25, 1857, is contained in an ordinary-sized account book, upon the fly-leaf of which is im-pressed a circular stamp, inscribed "Tabor, Fremont County, Iowa," and around the rim the name of "Jason Jones, Notary Public."

The first entry, of Aug. 25, states that the writer started at a certain late in June for Tabor, from Akron to Hudson; got goods at Hen-richs, &c.; harness; bought red mail stage at Jerries; next day went to Cleveland; shipped chest by express; staid at Bennett's Temper-ance House; next day went to church through the day and evening.

July 4, the entry is, "Father left for Iowa City," where he was joined by Jason, on the 5th, who records a meeting with Dr. Bowen, Mrs. Bowen, and Jessie and Eliza Horton.

The entries until the 10th record the purchases of wood for spears, staples, chains for mules, and canvas for wagon cover. A horse and buggy was swapped for two horses on the 13th; on the 14th tents and tent poles were carefully packed in the wagons, and additional blankets purchased.

July 15, the entry is, "The party crossed Iowa River," (Fort des Moines River at Red Rock, from which the autobiography is dated,) "stopped at noon on the stream beyond Six Mile House."

The entry of Aug. 9 records the "arrival of Col. Forbes," (at Tabor,) who from the frequent mention made of that work, the deference which the entries betray for the military judgment of the Colonel, and from the fact of the discovery of several copies of his work among the effects of Old Brown, we suppose to be Hugh Forbes, author of a Manual of the Patriotic Volunteer, the reading of which was the daily occupation of the writer, varied with the "cleaning of rifles and revolvers," and "fired twelve shots, drilled, cleaned guns and loaded, received letters from J. and G. Smith."

September 23, the record acknowledges the receipt of letters from Redpath and G. Smith; on the 30th the writer finishes "reading G. Smith's speech," and states that "efforts were made to raise a fund to send cannon and arms to Lane," but adds that they proved a failure. On the 1st of October the journalist visits Nebraska City with "Mr. Jones and Carpenter."

October 3d proves a lucky date to the writer, who records the receipt then of "seventy-two dollars from friend Sanborn." The succeeding day (Sunday) our journalist improves his leisure by perusing "speech of Judge Curtis, delivered before the students of Union College, New Jersey, and of Dartmouth College, and at the Normal School Convention, Westfield, Mass., and at Brown University, R. I.;" the entry of the same date continues, "Read of the awful disaster to the *Central America*, formerly the *George Law;* read answer of the Connecticut men to Buchanan, and had to shed a few tears over it."

On Nov. 4, the journalist rose at "ten minutes before four o'clock," elate with the remembrance that he is "thirty-three years old this day."

John Brown reached Tabor on the 7th of August, and Colonel Forbes, two days after him. They were obliged to remain there, inactive, till the 2d of November, in consequence of being out of funds.

"During this interval of suspense," writes Col. Forbes, "Captain Brown advocated the adoption of his plan, and I supported mine of stampedes. The conclusion arrived at was, that he renounced his Harper's Ferry project, and I consented to coöperate in stampedes in Virginia and Maryland instead of the part of the country I indicated as the most suitable. I perceived, however, that his mind constantly wandered back to Harper's Ferry, and it was not till it had been definitely settled that neither of us should do any thing unless under the direction or with the consent of a committee, that I felt easy in my mind respecting his curious notions of Harper's Ferry. He was very pious, and had been deeply impressed for many years with the *Bible Story of Gideon*, believing that he with a handful of men could strike down Slavery."

On the 2d of November, Colonel Forbes took steamer at Nebraska City for the East, and Captain Brown went down to Kansas by the emigrants' road, in a wagon driven by one of his sons. He left two others at Tabor.

Here Cook's Confession (which, although false in certain particulars, is mainly a correct statement of facts) becomes an authority of historical interest to the biographer of John Brown :

". . . I did not see him again until the fall of 1857, when I met him at the house of E. B. Whitman, about four miles from Lawrence, K. T., which, I think, was about the 1st of November following. I was told that he intended to organize a company for the purpose of putting a stop to the aggressions of the pro-slavery men. I agreed to join him, and was asked if I knew of any other young men, who were perfectly reliable, who, I thought, would join also. I recommended Richard Realf, L. F. Parsons, and R. J. Hinton. I received a note on the next Sunday morning, while at breakfast in the Whitney House, from Captain Brown, requesting me to come up that day, and to bring Realf, Parsons, and Hinton with me. Realf and Hinton were not in town, and therefore I could not extend to them the invitation. Parsons and myself went, and had a long talk with Captain Brown. A few days afterwards I received another note from Captain Brown, which read, as near as I can recollect, as follows:

DATE —— ——.

CAPTAIN COOK. Dear Sir: ' You will please get every thing ready to join me at Topeka by Monday night next. Come to Mrs. Sheridan's, two miles south of Topeka, and bring your arms, ammunition, clothing, and other articles you may require. Bring Parsons with you if he can get ready in time. Please keep very quiet about the matter. Yours, &c.,   JOHN BROWN.

"I made all my arrangements for starting at the time appointed. Parsons, Realf, and Hinton could not get ready. I left them at Lawrence, and started in a carriage for Topeka. Stopped at the hotel over night, and left early the next morning for Mrs. Sheridan's, to meet Captain Brown. Staid a day and a half at Mrs. Sheridan's — then left for Topeka, at which place we were joined by Stephens, Moffitt, and Cagt. Left Topeka for Nebraska City, and camped at night on the prairie north-east of Topeka. Here, for the first, I learned that we were to leave Kansas to attend a military school during the winter. It

17 *

was the intention of the party to go to Ashtabula County, Ohio Next morning I was sent back to Lawrence to get a draft of eighty dollars cashed, and to get Parsons, Realf, and Hinton to go back with me. I got the draft cashed. Captain Brown had given me orders to take boat to St. Joseph, Mo., and stage from there to Tabor, Iowa, where he would remain for a few days. I had to wait for Realf for three or four days; Hinton, could not leave at that time. I started with Realf and Parsons on a stage for Leavenworth. The boats had stopped running on account of the ice. Staid one day in Leavenworth, and then left for Westen, where we took stage for St. Joseph, and from thence to Tabor. I found C. P. Tidd and Leeman at Tabor. Our party now consisted of Captain John Brown, Owen Brown, A. D. Stephens, Charles Moffitt, C. P. Tidd, Richard Robertson, Col. Richard Realf, L. F. Parsons, William Leeman, and myself. *We stopped some days at Tabor, making preparations to start. Here we found that Captain Brown's ultimate destination was the State of Virginia.* Some warm words passed beween him and myself in regard to the plan, which I had supposed was to be confined entirely to Kansas and Missouri. Realf and Parsons were of the same opinion with me. After a good deal of wrangling we consented to go on, as we had not the means to return, and the rest of the party were so anxious that we should go with them. At Tabor we procured teams for the transportation of about two hundred Sharpe's rifles, which had been taken on as far as Tabor, one year before, at which place they had been left, awaiting the order of Captain Brown. There were, also, other stores, consisting of blankets, clothing, boots, ammunition, and about two hundred revolvers of the Massachusetts Arms patent, all of which we transported across the State of Iowa to Springdale, and from there to Liberty, at which place they were shipped for Ashtabula County, Ohio, where they remained till brought to Chambersburg, Pa., and were from there transported to a house in Washington County, Md., which Captain Brown had rented for six months, and which was situated about five miles from Harper's Ferry. It was the intention of Captain Brown to sell his teams in Springdale, and, with the proceeds, to go on with the rest of the company to some place in Ashtabula County, Ohio, where we were to have a good military instructor during the winter; but he was disappointed in the sale. As he could not get cash for the teams, it was decided we should remain in the neighborhood of Springdale, and that our instructor, Col. H. Forbes, should be sent on. We stopped in Pedee, Iowa, over winter, at Mr. Maxson's, where we pursued a course of military studies. Col. H. Forbes and Captain Brown had some words, and he (Col. F.) did not come on; consequently, A. D. Stephens was our drill-master. The people of the neighborhood did not know of our purpose. We remained at Pedee till about the middle of April, when we left for Chatham, Canada, via Chicago and Detroit."

In this extract there are two false statements; that "some warm words passed" between Cook and Brown; and that there was a "good deal of wrangling" between the Captain, and Parsons, and Realf.

II.

Some Shadows Before.

W E were at supper, on the 25th of June, 1858, at a hotel in Lawrence, Kansas. A stately old man, with a flowing white beard, entered the room and took a seat at the public table. I immediately recognized in the stranger, John Brown. Yet many persons who had previously known him did not penetrate his patriarchal disguise. A phrenologist, who was conversing with me, having noticed him, suddenly turned and asked if I knew that man? Such a head, such developments, he said, were infallible indications of "a most remarkable person."

I had several long conversations with the venerable hero, but do not deem it prudent to disclose their nature. Instead of relating, therefore, what I heard him say at this time, I subjoin some reminiscences by a friend, who was fully in his confidence, and fully worthy of it. These notes distinctly foreshadow the Liberator's plans; and, as they have been so grossly misrepresented, it is due to him, I think, that they should now be published, as far as prudence permits.

After premising that all the young men of principle

in Kansas, by the law of attraction or mental affinity, were the devoted friends and admirers of John Brown; and mentioning that, in November, 1857, Cook, Realf, and Kagi left the Territory for Tabor, in Iowa, in his company; and recording his arrival in Lawrence under the name of Captain Morgan, on the 25th of June, 1858, he thus continues:

A TALK WITH JOHN BROWN AND KAGI.

"On Sunday I held a very interesting conversation with Captain Brown, which lasted nearly the whole afternoon. The purport of it was, on his part, inquiries as to various public men in the Territory, and the condition of political affairs. He was very particular in his inquiries as to the movements and character of Captain Montgomery. The massacre of the Marais-des-Cygnes was then fresh in the minds of the people. I remember an expression which he used. Warmly giving utterance to my detestation of slavery and its minions, and impatiently wishing for some effectual means of injuring it, Captain Brown said, most impressively:

" ' *Young men must learn to wait. Patience is the hardest lesson to learn. I have waited for twenty years to accomplish my purpose.*'

"In the course of the conversation he reminded me of a message that I had sent him in 1857,* and said, ' he hoped I meant what I said, for he should ask the fulfilment of that promise, and that perhaps very soon ;' and further added, ' he wanted to caution me against rash promises. Young men were too apt to make them, and should be very careful. The promise given was of great importance, and I must be prepared to stand by it or disavow it now.' My answer need not be stated.

"In this conversation he gave me no definite idea of his plans, but seemed generally bent on ascertaining the opinions and characters of our men of anti-slavery reputations.

"Kagi, at the same time, gave me to understand that their visit to Kansas was caused by the betrayal of their plans, by a Colonel Forbes, to the Administration, and that they wished to give a different impression from what these disclosures had, by coming to the West. Both stated they intended to stay some time, and that night (Sunday)

---

* This message was an expression of regret, in a letter given to Richard Realf for John Brown, that the writer could not then join him, in consequence of other engagements; but promising, at any future time, to be ready to obey his call.

Captain Brown announced they should go South in the morning to
see Captain Montgomery, and visit his relatives. The Rev. Mr.
Adair's wife is the half-sister of Captain Brown. They live near
Osawatomie.

JOHN BROWN IN SOUTHERN KANSAS.

"Captain Brown started for Southern Kansas, on Monday morning,
June 26. I did not see him again until the middle of September, when
I met him at Mr. Adair's. Both the Captain and Kagi were sick with
the fever and ague, and had been for some time. In the interim, Captain Brown had been in Linn and Bourbon Counties, and also visited
other parts of Southern Kansas. One of his first acts, after arriving
South, was to negotiate with Synder, the blacksmith, upon whose
claim the terrible massacre of the Marais-des-Cygnes occurred, for its
purchase. This claim is situated about a half mile from the State line.
The buildings are located in an admirable position for defence. John
Brown saw both the moral and material advantages of the position,
and was desirous of obtaining possession. It will be remembered that
Synder successfully resisted Hamilton's gang on the day of the massacre. Captain Brown stated his object in wishing to obtain possession of the land, and Synder agreed to sell. But though a brave, he
was not specially an upright man, and, soon after making a bargain
with John Brown, having a better offer, he broke the contract. The
Captain had, in the interval, with the assistance of Kagi, Tidd,
Stephens, Leeman, and another member of his company, prepared a
very strong fortification, where they could have successfully resisted a
large force. In my journey through the Southern border counties, I
found that a general feeling of confidence prevailed among our friends,
because John Brown was near. Over the border the Missourians were
remarkably quiet from June until October, from the belief that the
old hero was in their vicinity. By the bad faith of Synder the farm
was abandoned, and Captain Brown and Kagi came to Mr. Adair's,
where I met them. The others were living in Linn and Anderson
Counties. I called at the house about ten in the morning, and remained until past three in the afternoon."

ANOTHER CONVERSATION.

"Captain Brown had been quite unwell, and was then somewhat
more impatient and nervous in his manner than I had before observed.
Soon after my arrival, he again engaged in conversation as to various
public men in the Territory. Captain Montgomery's name was introduced, and I inquired how Mr. Brown liked him. The Captain was
quite enthusiastic in praise of him, avowing a most perfect confidence in his integrity and purposes. 'Captain Montgomery,' he

said, 'is the only soldier I have met among the prominent Kansas men. He understands my system of warfare exactly. He is a natural chieftain, and knows how to lead.' The Captain spoke of General Lane, and alluded to the recent slaying of Gaius Jenkins. He said, 'he would not say one word against Lane in his misfortunes. His only comment was what he told the General himself — that he was his own worst enemy.' Of his own early treatment at the hands of ambitious 'leaders,' to which I had alluded in bitter terms, he said :

"'They acted up to their instincts. As politicians, they thought every man wanted to lead, and therefore supposed I might be in the way of their schemes. While they had this feeling, of course they opposed me. Many men did not like the manner in which I conducted warfare, and they too opposed me. Committees and councils could not control my movements, therefore they did not like me. But politicians and leaders soon found that I had different purposes, and forgot their jealousy. They have all been kind to me since.'

"Further conversation ensued relative to the Free State struggle, in which I, criticising the management of it from an anti-slavery point of view, pronounced it 'an abortion.' Captain Brown looked at me with a peculiar expression in the eyes, as if struck by the word, and in a musing manner remarked, '*Abortion !* — yes, that's the word.'

"He then spoke of Governor Robinson's actions as being of a 'weather-cock character,' and asked if it was true that Colonel Phillips had written his first two messages to the Topeka Legislature. I told him my reasons for believing the truth of the statement, among other things mentioning that the first draft of the message sent to the Legislature at Topeka, in June, 1857, as placed in the hands of the printers, was in Phillips' handwriting. At this John Brown grew angry — the only time I ever saw him so. He denounced the act severely, declaring it 'a deception to which no one should lend himself.' I replied that Phillips had done for the best without doubt; that the Free State men had placed Robinson in the position, and that they must sustain him in it.

"The Captain answered shortly, 'All nonsense. No man has a right to lend himself to a deception. Phillips had no business to write the messages. Robinson must be a perfect old woman. John Brown, sir, would, if he was Governor, write his own documents, if they contained but six lines.' Kagi interposed, and made some remarks, which calmed down the Captain, and the conversation became more general.

"The conviction was expressed that trouble would break out again in Southern Kansas. At this time I mentioned my intention of embarking in a newspaper enterprise. Captain Brown, in an impressive manner, reminded me of my promise to obey his call, and expressed a

wish that I should not enter into any entangling engagements, referring to my letter of 1857. He said 'that he thought all engagements
should be considered sacred, and liked my adhering to the one I had
at the time. That was the reason he had not sent to me; but now he
hoped I would keep myself free.' In this connection he used words
which I have often thought of since.

"'For twenty years,' he said, 'I have never made any business
arrangement which would prevent me at any time answering the
call of the Lord. I have kept my business in such condition, that in
two weeks I could always wind up my affairs, and be ready to obey
the call. I have permitted nothing to be in the way of my duty,
neither wife, children, nor worldly goods. Whenever the occasion
offered, I was ready. The hour is very near at hand, and all who are
willing to act should be ready.'

"I was not at this time aware of the precise plans, but had a general
conception of his purpose, which, as it dawned upon me, filled my
whole being with the radiance of its grandeur, as the July sunrise
filleth the heavens with glory. All through that conversation I had
the impression that those blue eyes, mild yet inflexible, and beaming
with the steady light of a holy purpose, were searching my soul, and
that my whole being was as transparent to him as the bosom of one
of his own Adirondack Lakes. I shall never forget the look or the
expression with which he said :

"'Young men should have a purpose in life, and adhere to it
through all trials. They would be sure to succeed if their purpose
s such as to deserve the blessing of God.'

KAGI UNFOLDS THE GREAT PLAN.

"After dinner, Kagi had some conversation with the Captain apart.
He then asked me if I would walk down to the Marais-des-Cygnes, ' as
he was going to fish.' I acquiesced, and we started. About half way
o the river we stopped, and sat on a fence. Kagi asked me what I
supposed was the plan of Captain Brown? My answer was, that I
thought it had reference to the Indian Territory and the South-
Western States. He shook his head, and gradually unfolded the
whole of their plans, a portion of which only has been elucidated in
he Harper's Ferry outbreak. I shall not, for obvious reasons, give
he full details. A full account of the convention in Canada was made,
s well as of the organization, its extent and objects, thereby effected. The mountains of Virginia were named as the place of refuge,
nd as a country admirably adapted in which to carry on a guerilla
warfare. In the course of the conversation, Harper's Ferry was
mentioned as a point to be seized, but not held, — on account of

the Arsenal. The white members of the company were to act as officers of different guerilla bands, which, under the general command
of John Brown, were to be composed of Canadian refugees, and the
Virginia slaves who would join them. A different time of the year
was mentioned for the commencement of the warfare from that which
has lately been chosen. It was not anticipated that the first movement
would have any other appearance to the masters than a slave stampede,
or local insurrection, at most. The planters would pursue their chattels and be defeated. The militia would then be called out, and
would also be defeated. It was not intended that the movement
should appear to be of large dimensions, but that, gradually increasing in magnitude, it should, as it opened, strike terror into the heart
of the Slave States by the amount of organization it would exhibit,
and the strength it gathered. They anticipated, after the first blow
had been struck, that, by the aid of the free and Canadian negroes who
would join them, they could inspire confidence in the slaves, and induce them to rally. No intention was expressed of gathering a large
body of slaves, and removing them to Canada. On the contrary,
Kagi clearly stated, in answer to my inquiries, that the design was to
make the fight in the mountains of Virginia, extending it to North
Carolina and Tennessee, and also to the swamps of South Carolina if
possible. *Their purpose was not the extradition of one or a thousand
slaves, but their liberation in the States wherein they were born, and were
now held in bondage.* ' The mountains and swamps of the South were
intended by the Almighty,' said John Brown to me afterwards, ' for a
refuge for the slave, and a defence against the oppressor.' Kagi spoke
of having marked out a chain of counties extending continuously
through South Carolina, Georgia, Alabama, and Mississippi. He had
travelled over a large portion of the region indicated, and from his
own personal knowledge, and with the assistance of Canadian negroes
who had escaped from those States, they had arranged a general plan
of attack. The counties he named were those which contained the
largest proportion of slaves, and would, therefore, be the best in
which to strike. The blow struck at Harper's Ferry was to be in
the Spring, when the planters were busy, and the slaves most needed.
The arms in the Arsenal were to be taken to the mountains, with such
slaves as joined. The telegraph wires were to be cut, and the railroad tracks torn up in all directions. As fast as possible other bands
besides the original ones were to be formed, and a continuous chain
of posts established in the mountains. They were to be supported by
provisions taken from the farms of the oppressors. They expected
to be speedily and constantly reënforced ; *first*, by the arrival of those
men, who, in Canada, were anxiously looking and praying for the time

of deliverance, and then by the slaves themselves. The intention was to hold the egress to the Free States as long as possible, in order to retreat when that was advisable. Kagi, however, expected to retreat *southward*, not in the contrary direction. The slaves were to be armed with pikes, scythes, muskets, shot guns, and other simple instruments of defence; the officers, white or black, and such of the men as were skilled and trustworthy, to have the use of the Sharpe's rifles and revolvers. They anticipated procuring provisions enough for subsistence by forage, as also arms, horses, and ammunition. Kagi said one of the reasons that induced him to go into the enterprise was a full conviction that at no very distant day forcible efforts for freedom would break out among the slaves, and that slavery might be more speedily abolished by such efforts than by any other means. He knew by observation in the South, that in no point was the system so vulnerable as in its fear of a slave-rising. Believing that such a blow would soon be struck, he wanted *to organize it so as to make it more effectual*, and also, by directing and controlling the negroes, to prevent some of the atrocities that would necessarily arise from the sudden upheaval of such a mass as the Southern slaves. The Constitution adopted at Chatham was intended as the framework of organization among the emancipationists, to enable the leaders to effect a more complete conrol of their forces. Ignorant men, in fact all men, were more easily managed by the *forms* of law and organization than without them. This was one of the purposes to be served by the Provisional Government. Another was to alarm the Oligarchy by discipline and the show of organization. In their terror they would imagine the whole North was upon them pell-mell, as well as all their slaves. Kagi said John Brown anticipated that by a system of forbearance to non-slaveholders many of them might be induced to join them."

My friend here explains at great length an admirably devised plan of an extended insurrection in the Southern States; but as its publication might prevent its successful execution — and of that, or an attempt to fulfil it, there is no doubt in my own mind — I deem it more prudent to suppress this portion of his narrative. He thus continues the report of his conversation with Mr. Kagi:

NO POLITICIANS TRUSTED.

"One thing I remember distinctly. In answer to an inquiry, Kagi stated that 'no politician, in the Republican or any other party,

18

knew of their plans, and but few of the abolitionists. It was no use talking,' he said, 'of Anti-slavery *action* to Non-resistant Agitators.' That there were men who knew of John Brown's general idea is most true ; but, *south of the Canadian Provinces* and of North Elba, there were but few who were cognizant of the *mode* by which he intended to mould those ideas into deeds."

JOHN BROWN ON INSURRECTION.

"After a long conversation, the substance of which I have given, we returned to the house. I had some further conversation with John Brown, mostly upon his movements, and the use of arms. The Captain expressed tersely his ideas of forcible emancipation. Of the terror inspired by the fear of slaves rising, he said :

"' Nat Turner, with fifty men, held Virginia five weeks. The same number, well organized and armed, can shake the system out of the State.'

"I remember also these sentences :

"' Give a slave a pike, and you make him a man. Deprive him of the means of resistance, and you keep him down.'

"' The land belongs to the bondman. He has enriched it, and been robbed of its fruits.'

"' Any resistance, however bloody, is better than the system which makes every seventh woman a concubine.'

"' I would not give Sharpe's rifles to more than ten men in a hundred, and then only when they have learned to use them. It is not every man who knows how to use a rifle. I had one man in my company who was the bravest man and worst marksman I ever knew.'

"' A ravine is better than a plain. Woods and mountain sides can be held by resolute men against ten times their force.'

"' A few men in the right, and knowing they are, can overturn a king. Twenty men in the Alleghanies could break Slavery to pieces in two years.'

"' When the bondmen stand like men, the nation will respect them. *It is necessary to teach them this.*'

"Much more was said which I cannot recall. The afternoon had more than half passed before I left for my destination. I rode over the prairies till sunset ; and in the glory of the grand scheme, which had been opened to me, it seemed as if the whole earth had become broader, and the heavens more vast. Since that day, when I stood in the light of those searching eyes, I have known what John Brown meant when he said :

"' Young men should have a purpose in life, and adhere to it in all trials. They will be sure to succeed if their purpose is such as to deserve the blessing of God.' "

III.

FLESHING THE SWORD.

IN order to understand the reason of John Brown's movements during this his third visit to the Terri-ory, it is first necessary briefly to review the history of Kansas from September, 1856, when the old man and his sons left Lawrence, up to the date when the reminiscences of my friend report him at the village of Osawatomie.

NORTHERN KANSAS.

In Northern Kansas there were no further disturb-nces or outrages committed from the date of the re-treat of the Twenty-Seven Hundred Invaders, under General Reid, who, on their return to Missouri, burned the village of Franklin, a Free State hotel, and a num-ber of private houses, stole four hundred head of cat-tle, and sacked, plundered and devastated the Free State settlements in every direction. Abandoning the agency of force in Northern Kansas, — for the immense migration of the spring of 1857 placed the pro-slavery party there in a hopeless minority, — the South and the Federal Administration directed their energies to the formation of a fraudulent Constitution, which, by va-

(207)

rious devices, — excluding, for example, by test oaths,
the majority of the people from voting, and using the
names of the Cincinnati Directory for the purpose
of increasing the vote in favor of slavery, — they pretended to adopt, and then carried up to Congress.
Its history there is well known. In August, 1858,
this Constitution, on being submitted to the vote of
the people of Kansas, was voted down by an unprecedented majority. From John Brown's defence of Lawrence, therefore, in the autumn of 1856, up to the
present hour, the history of Northern Kansas has
been a mere record of political intrigues and counter-
intrigues, and of a rapid progress in material wealth,
population, and civilization.

SOUTHERN KANSAS.

In Southern Kansas, also, there were no difficulties
until the winter of 1857–8 — until shortly after John
Brown paid his visit of three days to Lawrence for the
purpose of bringing out his young followers to drill
them.

In the summer of 1856, the entire Free State population of Lynn and Bourbon Counties had been driven
from the cabins and claims by organized marauders'
from Arkansas and the Indian Territory, under the
command of General Clarke, a Federal office-holder, and
the murderer of Robert Barber. The emigrants thus
expelled began to return to their homes in the spring,
summer, and autumn of 1857. They found their
houses and farms occupied by the Southern ruffians.
Instead of driving them out, or hanging them, as, in
strict justice, by the squatter code, they would have

been justified in doing, the Free State men built other cabins on their claims thus feloniously occupied, and avowed their willingness .to abide by the decision of the Land Office, of which the real chief was General Clarke, but from whose decision there was an appeal to Washington. Fort Scott, at this time, was the head-quarters of the ruffians in Southern Kansas; among them, the Hamiltons, the Littles, and Brockett, all of whom had been members of the Lecompton Constitu- · tional Convention; Brockett, the Hamiltons, and Clarke having attested their devotion to slavery by murdering Free State citizens in cold blood. In the expectation that the Lecompton Constitution would be passed by Congress, and enforced by the hireling legions of the United States, these leaders formed the plan of re-newing the disturbances in Southern Kansas, for the purpose of securing to their Missouri friends the farms and cabins they had stolen, facilitating the reconquest of the soil to slavery, and preventing the stream of Northern emigration from overflowing into the Indian Territory. In November this plan was carried into operation by organized bands of pro-slavery ruffians, who, issuing from Fort Scott, stole cattle, arrested men under false charges, and in other ways annoyed the Northern settlers. A Free State Squatter's Court was formed in November for the trial of these ruffians by the process of Lynch law. In order to inspire terror, the judge of this organization was called *Old Brown;* and, although the Captain was in Iowa at the time, the deception was not discovered for many months. It was at this time that Captain James Montgomery, called on

18 *

by the people, took the field. Little, one of the chief
ruffians, acting as a deputy United States Marshal, attempted, with a posse of eighty well-armed men, to
arrest this Court. Major Abbott,* with ten Sharpe's
riflemen, drove them back in disgrace to Fort Scott.
The United States forces marched to their rescue ; Jim
Lane went down to call out the Free State militia ; and
between these hostile fires the cause of the ruffians
fell temporarily to the ground. Neither force fought,
but Lane's men frightened ; and the Missourians staid at
home.   General Lane returned ; but the United States
troops remained, *and then joined the ruffians.* Many
of the soldiers, dressed in civilians' clothes, participated
in their midnight forays.   Montgomery organized a
force to resist them.   Brockett, in one of these nocturnal excursions, murdered two Free State men, and
wounded two others.† These events occurred in February and March, 1858.   The disturbances continued

---

* The Major was a spiritualist and peace man when he came to Kansas, but soon
took up carnal weapons, and did heroic service in the cause. He deserves honorable
mention in every history of Kansas.

† On the night of the 27th of March, 1858, the ruffians of the fort made a drive on the
Free State settlements on the Little Osage, being informed by their spies that the river
was unguarded. They first rode up to the house of a Mr. Denton, — an inoffensive Free
State man, — called him out, and after asking a few trifling questions, deliberately
shot him. Some five shots were fired at him, two of which took effect. He expired in
two hours. Before his death he charged his assassination to two men by the names of
Brockett and Hardwick. They then proceeded to the residence of a Mr. Davis, a
neighbor of Mr. Denton's, and demanded entrance. Suspecting them of being enemies,
Mr. Davis refused to open the door. The ruffians fired several times through the door ;
one of their shots took effect in his hand, but he was not seriously injured by any of
their discharges. The next place visited was the house of a Mr. Hedrick. They arrived there about two o'clock. Mr. Hedrick was up, waiting on his sick wife. The
attending physician was also present and up at the time. A call was made for admit-
tance, and as soon as Mr. Hedrick opened the door and stepped into the opening, he was
shot down, five buck shot entering his side just below the breast. He never spoke,
but fell dead upon the threshold of his dwelling. All these dark deeds were committed in one night. — WILLIAM TOMLINSON'S "*Kansas in Eighteen Hundred and
Fifty-eight.*"

with varying success until the month of April, when
Montgomery and his men were pursued by a force of
forty dragoons, who were acting with the ruffians of
Fort Scott. He had eight men only, but, posting them
in a good position, resisted the charge of the soldiery,
and drove them back — killing one man, wounding
four or five others, and leaving a number of horses
dead on the field. This was the first time in American
history that the Federal troops were resisted by citizens.
"Old Captain Brown," we are told by Montgomery's
biographer, "when he learned the particulars of the
engagement, said that the like had not happened before
in the Territory, and that the manner of his availing
himself of the strong position that offered, and the
skill with which he conducted the engagement, stamped
him as one of the first commanders of the age."

The news of this engagement exasperated Denver,
and he declared that Montgomery should be arrested.
At this time one of Montgomery's men stopped a messenger from Fort Scott, and found a letter on his person addressed to the Governor. Montgomery opened
t, found an account of the plans laid for his arrest, and
hen enclosed in it a note to Denver, in which he stated
hat if the Governor wanted him, he had only to do
ustice to the Free State men, and recall the troops
from Fort Scott. This double letter was then forwarded to Lecompton !

About this time Hamilton marched into the Territory at the head of twenty-five men, and committed the
hideous massacre of the Marais-des-Cygnes. This act
roused the most terrible passions. The whole Free

State population took up arms. It needed only a leader
and a provocation to create a revolution. The leader
was there — the troops were coming. But, alarmed by.
these symptoms of a rebellion, Governor Denver recalled
the soldiery; and, accompanied by a prominent Free
State politician, went down and made a treaty with
Montgomery. He agreed that all bygones should be
forgotten, and that the troops and obnoxious civil officers should be removed. This treaty restored peace.

ARRIVAL OF JOHN BROWN IN THE SOUTH.

Up to the middle of September, the movements of
John Brown have been given in the preceding chapter.
At this time it was reported that he had left the country, and the ruffians began to take courage. The volunteer militia company was dissolved. Now began a
new disturbance, created by the Free State democrats;
who, jealous of Montgomery's political influence, desired to annoy him by prosecutions until he should
leave the country. Up to this time, he had been
quietly working on his farm; but he was the real
Governor of all the Southern country, nevertheless.
On the 11th of October, a packed Grand Jury was impanelled at Fort Scott — the Marshal and Prosecuting Attorney being bitter personal enemies of Montgomery. On the 21st, learning that he and a number
of his men had been indicted, in violation of the treaty
with Governor Denver, Montgomery visited Fort Scott
with a small party, took the Court and Grand Jury
prisoners, quietly adjourned it, and made a bonfire of
the indictments! John Brown was not present at this
postponement, but "acted as an adviser." Several of

the men who fought at Harper's Ferry were there. This proceeding shocked the politicians in Northern Kansas, who were ever ready to indorse *any* wickedness if the words *Free State* preceded it. These men, who had sworn resistance "to a bloody issue" with the Usurpation, but, as soon as they got offices under it, indorsed and defended it, were naturally indignant at this translation of their Big Spring resolutions into Fort Scott actions.

Early in November, Montgomery's little cabin was surrounded and fired into by a party of marauders. The buck shot from their guns fell on the clothing of the bed in which Mrs. Montgomery was sleeping. She shouted, " O, we're going to have a fight!" The marauders heard her, and, supposing from the expression that a number of men were inside, turned about and led — fired at, as they ran, by Kagi, who had been ying in another bed.

During this period Captain Brown, expecting a renewal of disturbances, was busily engaged in building fortifications ; which may still be seen on the Little Osage and Little Sugar Creeks. One of them was a cabin near the Little Sugar Creek, in which the old man and his followers lived. They show great military ability.

In the month of November, the politicians began to exert themselves to incite a feeling of dissatisfaction among the people against Montgomery and Brown. On the 25th of that month, a meeting for this purpose was held at Mapleton ; but the friends of the two chieftains appeared in great force, and adjourned it to the 30th.

On the same day one of Montgomery's men was arrested, in violation of the treaty, taken to Fort Scott in chains, and imprisoned in a filthy cell.

ATTACK ON JOHN BROWN'S HOUSE.

On the 29th, Captain Brown left his house for Osawatomie, and Captain Montgomery for Osage City; and, at the same time, the Sheriff called out a posse of pro-slavery settlers, Missourians and Free State Democrats, for the purpose of arresting the old man and his boys. On the 30th, the posse assembled at Paris, one hundred strong, and marched to the cabin of John Brown, on the Little Sugar Creek. Stevens and Kagi were its only occupants. As soon as it was known that the posse was approaching, a messenger was sent for Montgomery, who arrived at midnight with thirteen men. They had previously been reënforced by thirteen neighbors. In the morning their number was still further increased, although they still numbered only thirty-four men. The Sheriff's posse approached within a quarter of a mile, about one hundred and twenty strong. Stevens and Kagi went out to meet the officer, who had ridden up within a few rods of the cabin.

They asked him what he wanted.

He replied, " To disarm them and demolish their fort."

Kagi told him to produce his authority.

" You are an illegal body, and it is my right to disperse you," said the Sheriff. " I have no writ, but I must disperse you, as you are more than five armed men ; and if I don't do it, I'll be covered with shame, and have to leave the country."

"We can't help that," retorted Kagi ; "it is no busi
ness of ours ; there is no use having any nonsense
about this ; if Paris * wants peace, the whole Treaty,
amnesty and all, must be observed ; if not, there must
be war."

At this time, the officer could not see more than five
armed persons, not knowing that there were thirteen
squatters in the cabin, or that Montgomery lay in.
ambush in a ravine close by, covering the whole wing
of the posse, with twenty-one picked men, who were
eager for the fight. He was so placed, that, in ten
minutes, he could have swept the entire posse from the
face of the earth.

"But you can't resist," said a politician, who accompanied the Sheriff ; "look at our force opposed
to you."

Stevens stretched his manly form to its full height,
and, raising his right arm, with a defiant glance, in a
ringing tone, gave a reply, every word of which the
followers of the Sheriff heard, and which evidently
made a great impression on them :

"But, believing we are right, before God, we *will*
resist if the whole Universe is against us !"

The posse retired without firing a shot ! On the same
day, the Sheriff and his companion were disarmed by
two men who fell at Harper's Ferry.

"Do you know who we are ?" asked the Sheriff.
' I am the High Sheriff of this county."

"To the devil with the High Sheriff of Lynn Coun
ty !" said Kagi. "Hand over that gun."

* The lesser head-quarters of the ruffians and Democrats.

John Brown returned from Osawatomie as soon as
he heard of the attack on his house. The pro-slavery
men, and Free State sycophants of the Federal Administration, had just again sent for United States
troops; for they now saw that it was impossible to
subdue the earnest Republican squatters, or with impunity break treaties made with anti-slavery men.
John Brown and James Montgomery, foreseeing further trouble, prepared for a formidable defence; being
resolutely determined to fight all comers, whether
troops, pro-slavery ruffians, invaders, or Free State
Democrats, who should endeavor to " crush out" the
defenders of freedom.   John Brown resolved to invade
Missouri, and stop at once the incursions from that
State, which were now the sole reliance of the friends
of Slavery in Kansas.

Montgomery marched on Fort Scott, on the 15th of
December, with one hundred and fifty men, officered
by John Brown's followers,—Kagi, among others, and
Anderson, — and rescued his friend whom the ruffians
had incarcerated.*

Governor Medary ordered down four companies of

---

* Among the prisoners taken were Epaphroditus Ransom, a very portly Federal official, who had been a Governor of Michigan, and was now a dignitary in the Land
Office. On hearing the noise, (it was early in the morning,) he came to the door in his
drawers and night dress; when a boy of seventeen years, carrying a musket longer
than himself, shouted, "Come out here; you're my prisoner." "What do you mean,
sir?" said Ransom; "I am a Federal officer, sir." "Federal officer, eh?" said the
boy; "who the devil cares? Come out here!" Ransom showed no willingness to do
so; whereupon the boy cocked his musket, and the "Federal officer" came out. He
ordered him to march to the middle of the square, obliging him to walk — dressed as
he was — at a sharp trot, in order to keep clear of the bayonet, which the boy held
in dangerous proximity to his body. The wiggling gait of the portly dignitary, and
the ludicrous contrast between captive and capturer, were long afterwards described by all who saw them, as one of the most ludicrous of Kansas incidents. When
Ransom reached the place appointed for him, "See what we sons of Freedom can do,
old fellow!" said the boy

United States dragoons; called out four bodies of militia, consisting chiefly of invaders and pro-slavery settlers; the Missourians began to assemble on the borders; every thing gave promise of a renewed civil war; when, unexpectedly, the aspect of affairs changed by the recall of the troops by order of the Cabinet, and the successful attack, on a Missouri force, by a party of Free State men, led by Captain Snyder, the blacksmith, whose name is inseparably associated with the history of the massacre of the Marais-des-Cygnes. This cabin was the head-quarters of these ruffians. When they saw the Free State men coming they offered· fight; a conflict ensued; they refused to surrender; the cabin was fired, and four of the murderers perished in its flames.

At this time John Brown and his men were at Bain's cabin, in Bourbon County, preparing for any emergency that might demand their aid. Two hundred Missourians had assembled at Fail's store, eight miles distant, in Missouri, for the purpose of invading the Territory; but, hearing that Old Brown was recruiting his forces to attack them, they withdrew fifteen miles farther from the borders.

While John Brown was stating his plan of following them, and, by invading Missouri and carrying off slaves, teaching the citizens of that State to attend to their own affairs, a negro man named Jim came over; and, stating that he and his family and a friend were about to be sold South, implored assistance and deliverance.

The poor that cried for deliverance from oppression never appealed in vain to the heart of John Brown,

19

IV.

Exodus.

JOHN BROWN, in January, 1859, wrote a letter in relation to his invasion of Missouri, which, of course, should precede all other accounts of it. It became a celebrated document, and was known as:

. JOHN BROWN'S PARALLELS.

TRADING POST, KANSAS, January, 1859.

Gentlemen: You will greatly oblige a humble friend by allowing the use of your columns while I briefly state two parallels, in my poor way.

Not one year ago, eleven quiet citizens of this neighborhood, viz.: William Robertson, William Colpetzer, Amos Hall, Austin Hall, John Campbell, Asa Snyder, Thomas Stilwell, William Hairgrove, Asa Hairgrove, Patrick Ross, and B. L. Reed, were gathered up from their work and their homes by an armed force under one Hamilton; and without trial or opportunity to speak in their own defence, were formed into line, and all but one shot — five killed and five wounded. One fell unharmed, pretending to be dead. All were left for dead. The only crime charged against them was that of being Free State men. Now, I inquire, what action has ever, since the occurrence in May last, been taken by either the President of the United States, the Governor of Missouri, the Governor of Kansas, or any of their tools, or by any pro-slavery or administration man, to ferret out and punish the perpetrators of this crime?

Now for the other parallel. On Sunday, December 19, a negro man called Jim came over to the Osage settlement, from Missouri, and stated that he, together with his wife, two children, and another negro man, was to be sold within a day or two, and begged for help to get

.(218)

away. On Monday (the following) night, two small companies were made up to go to Missouri and forcibly liberate the five slaves, together with other slaves. One of these companies I assumed to direct. We proceeded to the place, surrounded the buildings, liberated the slaves, and also took certain property supposed to belong to the estate.

We, however, learned, before leaving, that a portion of the articles we had taken belonged to a man living on the plantation, as a tenant, and who was supposed to have no interest in the estate. We promptly returned to him all we had taken. We then went to another plantation, where we found five more slaves, took some property and two white men. We moved all slowly away into the Territory for some distance, and then sent the white men back, telling them to follow us as soon as they chose to do so. The other company freed one female slave, took some property, and, as I am informed, killed one white man, (the master,) who fought against the liberation.

Now for a comparison. Eleven persons are forcibly restored to their natural and inalienable rights, with but one man killed, and all "hell is stirred from beneath." It is currently reported that the Governor of Missouri has made a requisition upon the Governor of Kansas for the delivery of all such as were concerned in the last-named "dreadful outrage." The Marshal of Kansas is said to be collecting a posse of Missouri (not Kansas men) at West Point, in Missouri, a little town about ten miles distant, to "enforce the laws." All pro-slavery, conservative free-state, and doughface men, and Administration tools, are filled with holy horror.

Consider the two cases, and the action of the Administration party.

Respectfully yours,

JOHN BROWN.

THE INVASION.

Of these two parties of liberators John Brown and Kagi were the Captains. The old man's force consisted of twelve men; Kagi's company of eight only. The slaves were to have been removed to Texas on the following day. Captain Brown went to the house of Hicklan, the master of Jim, and liberated that negro and four others. He then proceeded to the house of Isaac Jarné, another slaveholder, and released five more. Jarné was taken prisoner and carried into the Territory, to prevent an alarm being given.

John Brown was not merely an emancipationist, but
a reparationist. He believed, not only that the crime
of slavery should be abolished, but that reparation
should be made for the wrongs that had been done to
the slave. What he believed, he practised. On this
occasion, after telling the slaves that they were free, he
asked them how much their services had been worth,
and — having been answered — proceeded to take property to the amount thus due to the negroes.

Kagi went on the southern side of the Little Osage,
and called at several houses for the purpose of rescuing
slaves. But he failed to find one, until he reached the
residence of David Cruse. That robber of God's poor
children, on learning the purpose of the party, raised
his rifle to fire at it, but was shot dead before he pulled
the trigger. He had one slave only — who immediately
filled his place in the census of freemen.

The two parties soon reunited. Jarné was carried
several miles into the Territory. One of his late female
slaves attempted to console him; but, like Rachael
mourning for her children, he was not to be comforted;
upon which the sympathetic negress remarked:

" Gosh! massa's in a bad fix — hog no killed — corn
no gathered — nigger run away: laws-a-me! what'll
massa do?"

Jim, who was driving an ox team, " supposed to belong to the estate," asked one of the liberators, " How
far is it to Canada?"

" Twenty-five hundred miles."

" *Twenty-five hundred!* Laws-a-massa! Twenty-
five hundred miles! No get dar 'fore spring!" cried

Jim, as, raising his heavy whip and bringing it down on the ox's back, he shouted impatiently — " Whoa-ha, Buck, get up dar — g'lang, Bell ! "

A little boy of the party grasped his father by the leg and asked :

" Hows ye feel, fadder, when you's free ? " *

These liberated slaves constituted four families: one man, his wife, and two children ; a widowed mother, two daughters, and a son ; a young man, a boy, and a woman who had been separated from her husband. They were taken by one party several miles into Kansas, and there they remained for two or three weeks.

A FIGHT OR TWO.

Captain Brown and Kagi returned to their fortified position — known as Bain's Fort — on the Little Osage, in which fifty men could have resisted five hundred.

When the news of the invasion of Missouri spread, a wild panic went with it, which, in a few days, resulted in clearing Bates and Vernon Counties of their slaves. Large numbers were sold south ; many ran into the Territory and escaped ; the others were removed farther inland. When John Brown made his invasion there were five hundred slaves in that district where there are not fifty negroes now. For a short time a dead calm in the Territory followed this movement; the public seemed to hold their breath in anxious expectation for the next step. The Governor of Missouri, appealed to by the Borderers, offered a reward of three thousand dollars for the arrest of John Brown, to which the President added a further reward of two hundred and fifty

* These incidents were related by Kagi.

19 *

dollars. The politicians of Lawrence, of both parties, became alarmed at a movement which defied their pusillanimous policy — and men who had only hypocritically cursed when their territory was invaded, now worked in earnest to arrest the schemes of the brave retaliators. Some honest men, also, aided in this effort "to restore tranquillity;" but it owed its embodiment into a law to the Free State sycophants of the South. That embodiment was the Amnesty Act, which pardoned all "political offences" up to that time, and which the Federal Governor was *compelled*, by the fear of renewed disturbances, to approve, in order to induce Montgomery to disband his organization.

Montgomery, sent for by the politicians, reached the town of Lawrence while John Brown was on his journey to it, for the purpose of arranging to carry off his negroes. To save Montgomery from the odium that his enemies had attempted to cast on him, for his supposed implication in the invasion of Missouri, the old man wrote his parallels from the "Trading Post" in Lynn County.

During the absence of Montgomery and Brown, Kagi, who had been left in command, had two or three fights with the invaders.

BATTLE OF THE SPURS.

About the 20th of January, John Brown left Lawrence for Nebraska, with his emancipated slaves, who had been increased in number by the birth of a child at Osawatomie. It was named, *Captain John Brown.*

When at the third resting place of "Jim Lane's army," which had been named Concord, but which subsequent settlers called Holton, a party of thirty pro-slavery men, who had followed them from Lecompton, approached so near that it was necessary to halt and make a defence. The old man had at this time four white companions and three negro men. The whites were Stevens, Tidd, and Anderson, (who fought at Harper's Ferry,) and another Kansas boy. The Captain took possession of two log cabins in the wood, which the pursuers surrounded — at a distance, — while they sent to Atchison and Lecompton for further aid. From Atchison twelve men arrived; thus making a force of forty-two men opposed to eight only. They were preparing for the attack, when Captain Brown and his men issued from the woods for the purpose of offering fight. The Sheriff's Lecompton posse turned and fled! Not a shot was fired, not a drum was heard, as, putting spurs to their horses, they ran panic-stricken across the prairie. Only four men — ashamed of the conduct of their comrades — stood their ground; and they were made prisoners forthwith. This incident was ironically called the Battle of the Spurs, as those sharp instruments of torture were the only weapons used on the occasion.

The old man caused them to dismount, and put the negroes on their horses. They swore. He ordered them to be silent, as he would permit no blasphemy in his presence. They swore again.

"Kneel!" said the old man, as, with stern earnestness, he drew his pistol.

They knelt down, and he ordered them to pray.- He detained them for five days, and compelled them to pray night and morning. They never swore again in

.the old man's presence. They returned to Atchison, I
was told, and one of them indiscreetly related the story:
the ridicule that overwhelmed them compelled them to
leave the town.

THE OVERLAND JOURNEY.

Kagi, in the mean time, arrived at Topeka from
the South, and found the town in a great commotion.
News had just arrived that Old Brown was surrounded.
As soon as he appeared, all the fighting boys flocked
around him. At the head of forty mounted men, he
started at once to rescue his old Captain. He came up
just in time to see the last of the posse retreating across
the prairie. He advocated the hanging of the captured
slave-hunters, but the old man opposed it, and the kidnappers were saved.*

Seventeen of the "Topeka boys" escorted the party
of liberators to Nebraska City.

The kidnappers, on being released, asked the old man
to restore their horses and weapons.

"No," said John Brown, gravely; "your legs will
carry you as fast as you want to run; you won't find
any more Old Browns between this and Atchison."

The party reached Tabor in the first week of February, and travelled slowly across the State of Iowa.

As he was performing this journey, men panting for
the price of blood closely followed him; but the sight
of his well-armed company prevented an attack on the

---

* One of these men, since the capture of Captain Brown at Harper's Ferry, has
spoken of him with the greatest admiration; and said, that "although evidently
monomaniac on the subject of slavery," he was an honest and brave man. On being
jestingly advised to go into mourning for him, he said : he might go into black for many
a worse man. This testimony from a kidnapper is not without value.

band of liberators. He stopped at several villages, and was well received by the friends of freedom. From one of his hosts, we have the following letter, which was published at the time:

CAPTAIN BROWN IN IOWA.

"'Old Captain Brown of Kansas!' I have set my eyes on this old hero, feared by Missouri invaders, and loved by the legions of liberty in Kansas as a father. He had a company of twelve colored people, (who I only *guess* were once slaves,) *en route* for Canada, where I trust they are safe. To me he is an historic character. In the family, simple-hearted as a child, he narrates stirring scenes, placing himself in the background of the picture; while an eye of the most determined expression I ever saw at once supplies what the modesty of the narrator has withheld as personal. He is the impersonation of firmness. Among his company, white and black, with a long gray beard and a head frosted with sixty winters, he walks like a patriarch, if that early name implies leadership and devotion.

"Captain Brown avows his philosophy to be the showing of Border Ruffians that they have enough to do in taking care of slavery in Missouri, without making a foray on the people of Kansas to establish slavery there against the votes and wishes of the people. As God spares him, he says, he will 'deliver the poor that cry;' and does not conceal the fact that, in open day, he conducted out those who dreaded, next to death, a more Southern prison house. Two companies of slave-hunters, headed by a Marshal, looked upon them, but were not ready to lose their lives in a negro hunt. A reward of three thousand dollars by the Governor of Missouri, with the value of his company as chattels, has made him quite a lion through the State of Iowa. The 'dirt-eating' Democracy covet the reward, but keep at a good distance from the cold lead, and have no desire to be awed into silence and shame by one glance from the old hero, who feels that 'God will cover his head in the day of battle.' Stranger than fiction have been his escapes and exploits in Kansas. Combining the gentleness of a Christian, the love of a patriot, and the skill and boldness of a commander, whether ending his career in the quiet of home or in bloody strife, the freemen of Kansas will hallow his memory, and history will name him the Cromwell of our Border Wars.

"How unlike the Old Brown sketched by fiendish hate is the man at your fireside!—his mouth unpolluted with tobacco, strong drinks abjured, regimen plain, conversation grave, and occupied with pleasant memories of other days. He drops a tear of gratitude on the mention of the practical kindness of ——— to him in the hour of extremity. He recurs to the solid principles and hearty affection of Dr. Osgood, of Springfield, on whose ministry he attended for many years. He had a lucrative occupation as wool grower and dealer in Ohio, and gained a medal as exhibitor of wool at the World's Fair ; and now finds himself in the ' wool business ' still, in a land where men find more dreaded foes than the young Hebrew shepherd found in the beasts that took a lamb out of the flock. I am well informed that the people at Grinnell took care of the company for two days, furnishing them food for their journey, and, on Sabbath evening, took up a collection for them as well as on Saturday evening."

The same writer, in a letter published since the trial of John Brown, gives additional particulars of the old hero's talks when under his roof:

"Nothing seemed to so much excite him as an intimation that oppression aroused a spirit of revenge. As he spoke in public there was no boasting, nor a display of himself. The wrongs of Kansas, and the atrocities of slavery, he pictured in a clear style, declaring :

" *That it was 'nothing to die in a good cause, but an eternal disgrace to sit still in the presence of the barbarities of American slavery.'*

"His logic, with all who were captious as to his course, was like a chain shot argument; yet he courted no discussion, being then occupied with the safe escape of the eleven supposed chattels from Missouri.

" '*Providence,' said he, 'has made me an actor, and Slavery an outlaw.*

" '*A price is on my head, and what is life to me ?*

" '*An old man should have more care to end life well than to live long.*

" '*Duty is the voice of God, and a man is neither worthy of a good home here, or a heaven, that is not willing to be in peril for a good cause !*

" '*The loss of my family and the troubles in Kansas have shattered my constitution, and I am nothing to the world but to defend the right, and that, by God's help, I have done, and will do.'*

"This, in substance, and much more, was said in reply to a wish which I expressed that he would not return to Kansas, but seek that quiet with his family which his health demanded.

" *He scouted the idea of rest while he held ' a commission direct from God Almighty to act against slavery.'*

"He claimed to be responsible for the wise exercises of his powers only, and not for the quality of certain acts. In taking slaves out of Missouri, he said that he would teach those 'living in glass houses not to throw stones,' and they would have more than they could do to keep slavery in Missouri, without extending it against the will of

Kansas. The battle of 'Black Jack' and others, he was free to say, he thought had scared Missouri, and that was Gen. Lane's opinion. They did not report half the number killed, which they were ashamed to do, nor will it ever be known. I could repeat much that he said which showed a wonderful sagacity, and a bold, undaunted spirit. His whole demeanor was that of a well-bred gentleman, and his narratives were given with child-like simplicity. He feared nothing, for said he,

"'*Any who will try to take me and my company are cowards, and one man in the right, ready to die, will chase a thousand. Not less than thirty guns have been discharged at me, but they only touched my hair.*

"'*A man dies when his time comes, and a man who fears is born out of time.*'

". . . The nation was not worthy of him. Tyranny is relentless as the grave, and its tools want a victim. Cowardice will hang him, but humanity will stand appalled at the sacrifice of such a victim to the cruel Moloch."

When in Chicago, he sent his men in different directions, retaining Kagi and Stevens with him. A gentleman who conversed with him in that city thus writes to me:

"There is one thing he charged me to do when I last saw him. It was this:

"'Do not allow any one to say I acted from revenge.› I claim no man has a right to revenge myself. It is a feeling that does not enter into my heart. What I do, I do for the cause of human liberty, and because I regard it as necessary.'"

The party reached Detroit on the 12th of March, and immediately crossed over to Canada. There, free children of the God of the oppressed, the old warrior of the Lord left the people he had snatched from the earthly hell of American slavery. Eight months afterwards, when their deliverer lay in prison for endeavoring to free others of the same despised race, we hear the sobbings of this little group, intermingled with prayers for their benefactor's safety, as they waft across the Lakes to the Southern jail. A Canadian correspondent thus writes:

JOHN BROWN'S COLONY.

WINDSOR, UPPER CANADA, Nov, 6, 1859.

As every thing relative to "Old John Brown" is now interesting, I would inform your readers that I have spent a few hours in Windsor, Upper Canada, with seven of the twelve colored Missourians who are now residing in that place. The other five are living about nine miles in the country. These make the twelve persons taken by Brown last January into Canada. As various reports are afloat concerning them, I wish to inform all parties that those living here are very industrious. Two of the seven are men. They "team," saw wood, and "job round." One, a boy about twelve, helps around generally. Two of the women, who were field hands in Missouri last spring, on arriving at Windsor, hired, for four dollars, an acre of land, and with a spade each, they actually spaded it, planted it with corn and potatoes, and attended it well; this crop would challenge any crop I ever saw in Missouri, and not often beaten even in Kansas, where soil and climate are superior to most portions of this world; their potatoes are very fine — all dug and put up in a secure manner in the garden back of their house for winter; the corn, of which I brought some away, is beautiful. One of their houses has a small garden attached; they pay two dollars a month for this. In this little garden they have grown some very fine onions, carrots, parsnips, and some extraordinary cabbages; the cabbage are taken up, put together, and covered thick with fodder or straw, rather neatly packed. They have amply sufficient corn, potatoes, &c., for winter. As to meat, they do without, till they have some fit to kill. They have three hogs growing finely, which they paid one dollar each for, and feed them on what they collect in swill from neighbors, &c. As to clothing, they are neat, with well-patched articles. They say they have twenty dollars salted down. They informed me that, after being here a short time, they were burned out, losing all, or nearly all, of the useful articles given them by friends on their way, while escorted by that man whom they venerate. While I read aloud the sentence of Brown, with his speech, from the paper, to them, O, how affecting to see their tears and hear their sobs! Two women declared, if it could be, they would willingly die instead of their liberator. A woman among them remarked, if the Bible was true, John Brown practised most of it here; so he would be rewarded by "old Master," up higher, with greater happiness. The father, mother, and three children in the country, work a farm on shares; they have about sixteen acres of corn, potatoes, &c., part of which are theirs; and they are all anticipating the day when they can get a piece of land of their own.

V.

IN the Canadian Provinces there are thousands of fugitive slaves. They are the picked men of the Southern States. Many of them are intelligent and rich ; and all of them are deadly enemies of the South. Five hundred of them, at least, annually visit the Slave States, passing from Florida to Harper's Ferry, on heroic errands of mercy and deliverance. They have carried the Underground Railroad and the Underground Telegraph into nearly every Southern State. Here, obviously, is a power of great importance for a war of liberation.

Up to the period when the last chapter closes, John Brown, wherever he had lived, had acquired the reputation of a prudent man. In Kansas, although, by the Missourians, he was regarded as a reckless desperado, those who best knew him and his plans gave him credit for great caution and foresight. Nothing that he did or tried, however seemingly insane, but, when examined, gave proofs of his prudence no less than his courage. Recently, the nation saw him undertake the conquest of Virginia, with a band, seemingly, of twenty-one fol-

20   (229)

lowers only. People called the attempt an insane one; but they did not know that many hundreds of men, earnest haters of the Slavery whose terrors they had known, and drilled for the service, were eagerly awaiting, in the Canadian Provinces, for the signal to be given at Harper's Ferry, to hasten southward and join the army of Immediate Emancipation.

To conquer the South, a small band only is needed: but it must have backers in the North, who shall send down recruits from time to time. It is necessary, also, in order to prevent unnecessary bloodshed, for the liberated negroes to be held under strict control. John Brown knew all these facts. To inspire the Canadian fugitives with confidence in his plans, and, at the same time, to indicate his intentions in order to induce them to participate in it, he called a secret Convention of the friends of freedom at Chatham, in Canada.

At this time he intended to attack Virginia within a very few months. Cook, in his Confession, thus writes of the Convention:

"While we were in Chatham, he called a Convention, the purpose of which was to make a complete and thorough organization. He issued a written circular, which he sent to various persons in the United States and Canada. The circular, as near as I can recollect, reads as follows:

CHATHAM, May —, 1859.

Mr. ——. Dear Sir: We have issued a call for a very *quiet* Convention at this place, to which we shall be happy to see any *true* friends of freedom, and to which you are most earnestly invited to give your attendance.   Yours, respectfully,   JOHN BROWN.

"The names were left blank; but as they were directed by Captain Brown or J. H. Kagi, I do not know the parties to whom they were addressed. I do know, however, that they were sent to none save those whom Captain Brown knew to be radical Abolitionists. I think it was about ten days from the time the circulars were sent that the

· Convention met. The place of meeting was in one of the negro churches in Chatham. The Convention, I think, was called to order by J. II. Kagi. Its object was then stated, which was to complete a thorough organization and the formation of a Constitution. The first business was to elect a President and Secretary. Elder Monroe, a colored minister, was elected President, and J. H. Kagi, Secretary. The next business was to form a Constitution. Captain Brown had already drawn up one, which, on motion, was read by the Secretary. On motion it was ordered that each article of the Constitution be taken up, and separately amended and passed, which was done. On motion, the Constitution was then adopted as a whole. The next business was to nominate a Commander-in-Chief, Secretary of War, and Secretary of State. Captain John Brown was unanimously elected Commander-in-Chief, J. II. Kagi, Secretary of War, and Richard Realf, Secretary of State. Elder Monroe was to act as President until another was chosen. A. M. Chapman, I think, was to act as Vice-President. Dr. M. K. Delany was one of the Corresponding Secretaries of the Organization. There were some others from the United States, whose names I do not now remember. Most of the delegates to the Convention were from Canada. After the Constitution was adopted, the members took their oath to support it. It was then signed by all present. During the interval between the call for the Convention and its assembling, regular meetings were held at Barbour's Hotel, where we were stopping, by those who were known to be true to the cause, at which meetings plans were laid and discussed. There were no white men at the Convention, save the members of our company. *Men and money had both been promised from Chatham and other parts of Canada.* When the Convention broke up, news was received that Colonel H. Forbes, who had joined in the movement, had given information to the Government. This, of course, delayed the time of attack. A day or two afterwards most of our party took the boat to Cleveland — J. II. Kagi, Richard Realf, William II. Leeman, Richard Robertson, and Captain Brown remaining. Captain Brown, however, started in a day or two for the East. Kagi, I think, went to some other town in Canada to set up the type, and to get the Constitution printed, which he completed before he returned to Cleveland. We remained in Cleveland for some weeks, at which p.ace, for the time being, the company disbanded."

Another report, which was found among John Brown's papers at Harper's Ferry, gives some addi tional information respecting this assembly. The full reports, not only of this public Convention, but of many secret meetings, which are mentioned in Cook's Confession, and were written in phonography, and then translated into a secret cipher by Kagi, have happily not yet been discovered; or, it is probable that the scheme with which John Brown's name is now forever inseparably united, would have perished with his earthly life at Charlestown.

CHATHAM, CANADA WEST,
Saturday, *May* 8, 1858 — 10 A. M.

The Convention met in pursuance of a call of John Brown and others, and was called to order by Mr. Jackson, on whose motion Mr. Wm. C. Monroe was chosen President; when, on motion of Mr. Brown, Mr. J. H. Kagi was elected Secretary.

On motion of Mr. Delany, Mr. Brown then proceeded to state the object of the Convention at length, and then to explain the general features of the plan of action in execution of the project in view by the Convention. Mr. Delany and others spoke in favor of the project and plan, and both were agreed to by a general consent.

Mr. Brown then presented a plan of organization, entitled Provisional Constitution and Ordinances for the People of the United States, and moved the reading of the same.

Mr. Kinnard objected to the reading until an oath of secrecy be taken by each member of the Convention, whereupon Mr. Delany moved that the following parole of honor be taken by all members of the Convention:

"I solemnly affirm that I will not, in any way, divulge any of the secrets of this Convention, except to the persons entitled to know the same, on the pain of forfeiting the respect and protection of this organization."

Which motion was carried.

The President then proceeded to administer the obligation, after which the question was taken on reading of the plan proposed by Mr. Brown, and the same carried.

The plan was then read by the Secretary, after which, on motion of Mr. Whipple, it was ordered that it be now read by articles for consideration.

The articles from 1 to 45 were then read and adopted. On reading of the 46th, Mr. Reynolds moved to strike out the same. Reynolds spoke in favor, and Brown, Monroe, Owen Brown, Delany, Realf, Kennard, and Page against striking out. The question was then taken and lost, there being but one vote in the affirmative. The article was then adopted. The 47th and 48th articles, with the schedule, were then adopted in the same manner. It was then moved by Mr. Delany that the title and preamble stand as read. Carried.

On motion of Mr. Kagi, the Constitution, as a whole, was then unanimously adopted.

Mr. Whipple nominated John Brown for Commander-in-Chief, who was, on the seconding of Delany, elected by acclamation.

Mr. Realf nominated J. H. Kagi for Secretary of War, who was elected in the same manner. On motion of Mr. Brown, the Convention adjourned to nine P. M. of Monday, the 10th.

MONDAY, May 10th, 1859 — 9¼ P. M. — The Convention assembled and went into balloting for the election of Treasurer and Secretary of Treasury. Owen Brown was elected to the former office, and George B. Gill to the latter.

The following resolution was then introduced by Mr. Brown, and unanimously passed.

Resolved, That John Brown, J. H. Kagi, Richard Realf, L. F. Parsons, C. H. Tidd, C. Whipple, C. W. Moffit, John E. Cook, Owen Brown, Steward Taylor, Osborn Anderson, A. M. Ellsworth, Richard Richardson, W. H. Leeman, and John Lawrence, be, and are hereby, appointed a Committee, to whom is delegated the power of the Convention to fill by election all offices specially named in the Provisional Constitution, which may be vacant after the adjournment of the Convention. The Convention then adjourned *sine die.*   Signed,   J. KAGI, *Secretary of the Convention*

Names of the Members of the Convention, written by each Perton.

Wm. Charles Monroe, President of the Convention; G. J. Reynolds, J. C. Grant, A. J. Smith, James M. Jones, Geo. B. Gill, M. F. Bailey, Wm. Lambert, C. W. Moflitt, John J Jackson, J. Anderson. Alfred Whipple, James M. Bue, W. H. Leeman, Alfred M. Ellsworth, John E. Cook, Stewart Taylor, James W. Purnell, Geo. Akln. Stephen Dettin, Thos. Hickerson, John Cannct, Robinson Alexander, Richard Realf, Thomas F. Cary, Richard Richardson, I. T. Parsons, Thos. M. Kinnard, J. H. Delany, Robert Vanranker, Thomas M. Stringer, Charles H. Tidd, John A. Thomas, C. Whipple, J. D. Shadd, Robert Newman, Owen Brown, John Brown, J. H. Harris, Charles Smith, Simon Fislin, Isaac Holley, James Smith.

Signed,　　　　　　J. H. KAGI, *Secretary of the Convention.*

Memorandum — Offices filled.

Commander-in-Chief — John Brown. Secretary of War — J. H. Kagi. Members of Congress — Alfred M. Ellsworth, Osborn Anderson. Treasurer — Owen Brown. Secretary of Treasury — Geo. B. Gill. Secretary of State — Richard Realf.

Premising that the plan of the Liberators was not ex· *tradition* into the North, but *emancipation* in the South, — not to run off negroes to Canada, but to free them in Virginia, and to keep them there, — the Constitution adopted at this time is at once divested of the ridicule with which it has hitherto been clothed. Special attention should be paid, as indications of the design of the Liberators, to Article 1st, from 28 to 38, and from 43 to 46, of as much of the Constitution as Virginia permitted to be published. It will be seen that, even n this its fragmentary state, it organizes a Government eminently adapted to preserve order amongst insurgent slaves, and to prevent unnecessary suffering and devastation. They sought no offensive warfare against he South, but only to restore to the African Race its inherent rights, by enabling it to demand them of its oppressors, with the power to enforce and maintain the claim. Not revolution, but justice; not aggression, but defence; not negro supremacy, but citizenship; not var *against* society, but *for* freedom: such were the beneficent objects which they designed to effect.

The following document is the Constitution as mu ilated by the Virginians:

20 *

Provisional Constitution and Ordinances for the People of the United States.

PREAMBLE. — *Whereas,* Slavery, throughout its entire existence in the United States, is none other than the most barbarous, unprovoked, and unjustifiable war of one portion of its citizens against another portion, the only conditions of which are perpetual imprisonment and hopeless servitude. or absolute extermination, in utter disregard and violation of those eternal and self-evident truths set forth in our Declaration of Independence:

Therefore, We, the citizens of the United States, and the oppressed people, who, by a recent decision of the Supreme Court, are declared to have no rights which the white man is bound to respect. together with all the other people degraded by the laws thereof, do, for the time being, ordain and establish for ourselves the following Provisional Constitution and ordinances, the better to protect our people, property, lives, and liberties, and to govern our actions.

ARTICLE I.   *Qualifications of Membership.* — All persons of mature age, whether proscribed, oppressed, and enslaved citizens, or of proscribed and oppressed races of the United States, who shall agree to sustain and enforce the Provisional Constitution and ordinances, together with all minor children of such persons, shall be held to be fully entitled to protection under the same.

ART. II.   *Branches of Government.* — The Provisional Government of this organization shall consist of three branches, viz.: the Legislative, the Executive, and Judicial.

. ART. III.   *The Legislature.* — The Legislative Branch shall be a Congress or House of Representatives, composed of not less than five, nor more than ten members, who shall be elected by all the citizens of mature age and sound mind connected with this organization, and who shall remain in office for three years, unless sooner removed for misconduct, inability, or death.   A majority of such members shall constitute a quorum.

ART. IV.   *Executive.* — The Executive Branch of the organization shall consist of a President and Vice-President, who shall be chosen by the citizens or members of this organization, and each of whom shall hold his office for three years, unless sooner removed by death. or for inability, or for misconduct.

ART. V.   *Judicial.* — The Judicial Branch consists of one Chief Justice of the Supreme Court, and four Associate Judges of the said Court, each of them constituting a Circuit Court.   They shall each be chosen in the same manner as the President, and shall continue in office until their places have been filled in the same manner by an election of citizens.

ART. XIII. to XXV. provide for the trial of the President and other officers, and Members of Congress, the impeachment of Judges; the duties of the President and Vice-President, the punishment of crimes, Army appointments, salaries, &c., &c. These articles are not of special interest, and are therefore omitted.

ART. XXVI.   *Treaties of Peace.* — Before any treaty of peace shall take full effect, it shall be signed by the President, Vice-President, Commander-in-Chief, a majority of the House of Representatives, a majority of the Supreme Court, and a majority of the general officers of the army.

ART. XXVII.   *Duty of the Military.* — It shall be the duty of the Commander-in-Chief, and all the officers and soldiers of the army, to afford special protection, when needed, to Congress. or any member thereof. to the Supreme Court, or any member thereof, to the President, Vice-President, Treasurer, and Secretary of War, and to afford general protection to all civil officers, or other persons having a right to the same.

ART. XXVIII.   *Property.* — All captured or confiscated property, and all the property the product of the labor of those belonging to this organization, and of their families, shall be held as the property of the whole equally, without distinction, and may be used for the common benefit, or disposed of for the same object. And any person, officer or otherwise, who shall improperly retain, secrete, use, or needlessly destroy such property, or property found, captured, or confiscated, belonging to the enemy, or shall wilfully neglect to render a full and fair statement of such property by him so taken. or held, shall be guilty of a misdemeanor, and, on conviction, shall be punished accordingly.

ART. XXIX.   *Safety or Intelligence Fund.* — All money, plate, watches, or jewelry captured by honorable warfare, found, taken. or confiscated, belonging to the army, shall be held sacred, to constitute a liberal safety or intelligence fund ; and any person who shall improperly retain, dispose of, hide, use, or destroy such money or other article above named, contrary to the provisions and spirit of this article, shall be deemed guilty of theft, and. on conviction thereof, shall be punished accordingly. The Treasurer shall furnish the Commander-in-Chief at all times with a full statement of the condition of such fund, and its nature.

ART. XXX.   *The Commander-in-Chief and the Treasury.* — The Commander-in-Chief shall have power to draw from the Treasury the money and other property of the fund provided for in Art cle XXIX., but his orders shall be signed also by the Secretary of War, who shall keep a strict account of the same, subject to examination by any member of Congress or General Officer.

ART. XXXI. *Surplus of the Safety or Intelligence Fund.* — It shall be the duty of the Commander-in-Chief to advise the President of any surplus of the Safety or Intelligence Fund, and he shall have power to draw the same, his order being also signed by the Secretary of State, to enable him to carry on the provisions of Article XXII.

ART. XXXII. *Prisoners.* — No person, after having surrendered himself a prisoner, and who shall properly demean himself or herself as such, to any officer or private connected with this organization, shall afterwards be put to death, or be subjected to any corporeal punishment, without first having had the benefit of a fair and impartial trial; nor shall any prisoner be treated with any kind of cruelty, disrespect, insult, or needless severity; but it shall be the duty of all persons, male and female, connected herewith, at all times, and under all circumstances, to treat all such prisoners with every degree of respect and kindness that the nature of the circumstances will admit of, and insist on a like course of conduct from all others, as in fear of the Almighty God, to whose care and keeping we commit our cause.

ART. XXXIII. *Volunteers.* — All persons who may come forward, and shall voluntarily deliver up slaves, and have their names registered on the books of this organization, shall, so long as they continue at peace, be entitled to the fullest protection in person and property, though not connected with this organization, and shall be treated as friends, and not merely as persons neutral.

ART. XXXIV. *Neutrals.* — The persons and property of all non-slaveholders who shall remain absolutely neutral shall be respected so far as circumstances can allow of it, but they shall not be entitled to any active protection.

ART. XXXV. *No needless Waste.* — The needless waste or destruction of any useful property or article by fire, throwing open of fences, fields, buildings, or needless killing of animals, or injury of either, shall not be tolerated at any time or place, but shall be promptly and peremptorily punished.

ART. XXXVI. *Property confiscated.* — The entire personal and real property of all persons known to be acting, either directly or indirectly, with or for the enemy, or found in arms with them, or found wilfully holding slaves, shall be confiscated and taken whenever and wherever it may be found, in either Free or Slave States.

ART. XXXVII. *Desertion.* — Persons convicted, on impartial trial, of desertion to the enemy after becoming members, acting as spies, of treacherous surrender of property, arms, ammunition, provisions or supplies of any kind, roads, bridges, persons, or fortifications, shall be put to death, and their entire property confiscated.

ART. XXXVIII. *Violation of Parole of Honor.* — Persons proved to be guilty of taking up arms, after having been set at liberty on parole of honor, or after the same to have taken any active part with or for the enemy, direct or indirect, shall be put to death, and their entire property confiscated.

ARTS. XXXIX., XL., and XLI. require all labor for the general good, and prohibit immoral actions.

ART. XLII. *The Marriage Relation — Schools — The Sabbath.* — Marriage relations shall be at all times respected, and families shall be kept together as far as possible, and broken families encouraged to reunite, and intelligence offices shall be established for that purpose. Schools and churches shall be established as may be, for the purpose of religious and other instruction, and the first day of the week shall be regarded as a day of rest, and appropriated to moral and religious instruction and improvement, to the relief of the suffering, the instruction of the young and ignorant, and the encouragement of personal cleanliness; nor shall any person be required on that day to perform ordinary manual labor, unless in extremely urgent cases.

ART. XLIII. *To carry Arms openly.* — All persons known to be of good character, and of sound mind and suitable age, who are connected with this organization, whether male or female, shall be encouraged to carry arms openly.

ART. XLIV. *No Persons to carry concealed Weapons.* — No person within the limits of conquered territory, except regularly appointed policemen, express officers of army, mail carriers, or other fully accredited messengers of Congress, the President, Vice-President, members of the Supreme Court, or commissioned officers of the Army, and those under peculiar circumstances, shall be allowed at any time to carry concealed weapons; and any person not specially authorized so to do, who shall be found so doing, shall be deemed a suspicious person, and may at once be arrested by any officer, soldier, or citizen, without the formality of a complaint or warrant; and may at once be subjected to thorough search, and shall have his or her case thoroughly investigated, and be dealt with as circumstances on proof shall require.

ART. XLV. *Persons to be seized.* — Persons living within the limits of territory holden by this organization, and not connected with this organization, having arms at all, concealed or otherwise, shall be seized at once, or be taken in charge of by some vigilant officer, and their case thoroughly investigated; and it shall be the duty of all citizens and soldiers, as well as officers, to arrest such parties as are named in this and the preceding section or article, without formality of complaint or warrant; and they shall be placed in charge of some proper officer for examination, or for safe keeping.

ART. XLVI. *These Articles not for the Overthrow of Government.* — The foregoing articles shall not be construed so as in any way to encourage the overthrow of any State Government, or of the General Government of the United States, and look to no dissolution of the Union, but simply to amendment and repeal, and our flag shall be the same that our fathers fought under in the Revolution.

ART. XLVII. *No Plurality of Offices.* — No two offices specially provided for by this instrument shall be filled by the same person, at the same time.

. ART. XLVIII. *Oath.* — Every officer, civil or military, connected with this organization, shall, before entering upon the duties of office, make a solemn oath or affirmation to abide by and support the Provisional Constitution and these ordinances. Also, every citizen and soldier, before being recognized as such, shall do the same.

Schedule. — The President of this Convention shall convene, immediately on the adoption of this instrument, a Convention of all such persons as shall have given their adherence by signature to the Constitution, who shall proceed to fill by election all offices specially named in said Constitution — the President of this Convention presiding and issuing commissions to such officers elect; all such officers being hereafter elected in the manner provided in the body of this instrument.

There are many things, not yet clear to the public, and sometimes quoted as proofs of insanity, but, rightly understood, giving evidence of a comprehensive and penetrating intellect, which it is impossible, at this time, fully to explain, in justice to the Cause for which John Brown died, and to the noble friends by whom he was supported. Among these mysteries must be placed some parts of the Constitution; for, apart from the explanation already given, there are portions of it which still require a further elucidation. The organization behind the letter of the Constitution cannot now be described. To persons familiar with it there is neither insanity nor inconsistency in the instrument; but, on the contrary, every evidence of a judicious and humane statesmanship. The day will yet come when John Brown's name will stand first in the list of American statesmen.

Why John Brown did not at once proceed to Harper's Ferry, is thus stated by Cook in his Confession:

" We staid about two weeks in Chatham — some of the party staid six or seven weeks. We left Chatham for Cleveland, and remained there until late in June. In the mean time, Captain Brown went East

on business ; but, previous to his departure, he had learned that Colonel Forbes had betrayed his plans to some extent. This, together
with the scantiness of his funds, induced him to delay the commencement of his work, and was the means, for the time being, of disband-
ing the party. He had also received some information which called
for his immediate attention in Kansas. I wished to go with him ; but
he said that I was too well known there, and requested me and some
others to go to Harper's Ferry, Va., to see how things were there,
and to gain information.

"In his trip East, he did not realize the amount of money that he
expected. The money had been promised *bona fide;* but, owing to the
tightness of the money market, they failed to comply with his demands. The funds were necessary to the accomplishment of his
plans. I afterwards learned that there was a lack of confidence in the
success of his scheme. It was, therefore, necessary that a movement
he d be made in another direction, to demonstrate the practicability
of his plan. This he made about a year ago by his invasion of Mis-
ouri, and the taking of about a dozen slaves, together with horses,
cattle, &c., into Kansas, in defiance of the United States Marshal and
his posse."

The news of the massacre of the Marais-des-Cygnes
was the immediate cause of John Brown's return to
Kansas ; although it is also true, that the action of
Colonel Forbes rendered it imperatively necessary to
divert the attention of the Government from his original plan.

VI.

Making Ready.

FROM the 16th of March, when John Brown was in Canada, up to the 16th of October, when he conquered Virginia, — a period of eight months, — it would neither be prudent nor just to trace his movements too minutely; and I do not propose to do so now. From the 20th to the 30th of March, he was at Cleveland, with Kagi. An incident of this residence is thus related by Wendell Phillips:

"Prudence, skill, courage, thrift, knowledge of his time, knowledge of his opponents, undaunted daring in the face of the nation, — all these he had. He was the man who could leave Kansas and go into Missouri, and take eleven men and give them to liberty, and bring them off on the horses which he carried with him, and two which he took as tribute from their masters in order to facilitate escape. Then, when he had passed his human *protégés* from the vulture of the United States to the safe shelter of the English lion, — this is the brave, frank, and sublime truster in God's right and absolute justice, that entered his name, in the city of Cleveland, 'John Brown, of Kansas,' and advertised there two horses for sale, and stood in front of the auctioneer's stand, notifying all bidders of the defect in the title. But, he added, with *nonchalance*, when he told the story, 'They brought a very excellent price.'"

At this time there was great excitement in Cleveland, in consequence of the arrest and imprisonment of a number of prominent citizens of Oberlin, charged with the manly virtue of liberating a fugitive slave, which, by the laws of the United States, is an indictable and penitentiary offence. On Tuesday, the 22d of March, a large meeting was held at Cleveland, at which Kagi and John Brown were invited to speak. Kagi described the scenes I have endeavored to depict in the chapter entitled, Fleshing the Sword. John Brown was then called on, and made a speech; but the report preserved of it is exceedingly imperfect. Such as it is, here it is:

JOHN BROWN'S SPEECH.

"He prefaced his remarks by saying that he had called for an admission fee that he might use in place of money he had expended upon the slaves on their way to Canada. He remarked that since his last return to Kansas he had had no fight with the pro-slavery ruffians, although he had been threatened abundantly. He wished to say that he had never lifted a finger towards any one whom he did not know was a violent persecutor of the Free State men. He had never killed any body; although, on some occasions, he had shown the young men with him how some things might be done as well as others; and they had done the business. He had never destroyed the value of an ear of corn, and had never set fire to any pro-slavery man's house or property, and had never by his own action driven out pro-slavery men from the Territory; but if occasion demanded it, he would drive them into the ground, like a fence stake, where they would remain permanent settlers. Further, he had yet to learn of any pro-slavery men being arrested or punished [by the Territorial authorities] for any crime. He related the circumstance of the murder of his son at Osawatomie, who was shot down for the crime of being a Free State man. On the afternoon of the same day the Osawatomie fight occurred. Mr. Brown remarked that he was an outlaw, the Governor of Missouri having offered a reward of $3000, and James Buchanan $250 more, for him. He quietly remarked, parenthetically, that John Brown would give two dollars and fifty cents for the safe delivery of the body of James Buchanan in any jail of the Free States. He would never submit to an arrest, as he had nothing to gain from submission; but he should settle all questions on the spot if any attempt was made to take him. The liberation of those slaves was meant as a direct blow to slavery, and he laid down his platform that he considered it his duty to break the fetters from any slave when he had an opportunity. He was a thorough abolitionist. The remainder of his speech was a narration of Kansas affairs.

"At the close of his remarks, the audience, by resolution, indorsed and approved of his course in Kansas, for which he heartily thanked them."

In the beginning of April he was in Ashtabula County, sick of the ague. On the 16th, he was at Westport, Essex County, New York — near home. On his journey there, he staid over at Peterboro', the residence of Gerritt Smith, and at Rochester, where he delivered a public speech and met the brave negro, Shields Green, or Emperor. In May he was in Boston, New York City, and Rochester. At Boston he learned how to manufacture crackers and beef meal.

On the 3d of June he was at Collinsville, and concluded the contract for the pikes afterwards found on the Kennedy farm. On the 7th he was at Troy, from which he sent a draft of three hundred dollars to pay for the pikes. He then proceeded to Summit, Portage, and Ashtabula Counties, in Ohio. He went from Ohio to Chambersburg, stopping at Pittsburg City and Bedford. He remained at Chambersburg toward the close of June, for several days; and, on the 30th, with two sons and Captain Anderson, left for Hagerstown, in Maryland.

The next movements of the party are thus described by a resident of Hagerstown, a pro-slavery man, in a letter written after the arrest of Captain Brown at Harper's Ferry:

"John Brown, his two sons, and a Captain Anderson spent a night here, at the Washington House, in June, and were taken to Harper's Ferry next day in a hack. When here I was struck with the long beard of one of them, and called over to learn who they were and where they came from. Brown registered as 'Smith and two sons' from Western New York, and told Mr. Singling, the landlord, that they had got tired of farming in that region ; that the frosts had taken their crops for two or three years ; that they were going to Virginia to look out a location for raising sheep and growing wool, &c. After looking around Harper's Ferry a few days, and prowling through the mountains in search of minerals, as they said, they came across a large farm with three unoccupied houses — the owner, Dr. Booth Kennedy, having died in the spring. These houses they rented from the family till next March, and paid the rent in advance, and also purchased a lot of hogs from the family for cash, and agreed to take care of the stock until a sale could be had ; and they did attend most faithfully to them, and have it all in first-rate order ; were gentlemen, and kind to every body. After living there a few weeks, others joined them, until as many as twelve were in these three houses, and every few days a stranger would appear and disappear again without creating the least surprise."

A correspondent of a New York paper gives these additional particulars :

"About five or six miles distant from Harper's Ferry, on the Maryland side, is the Kennedy Farm, which John Brown hired in July at a rent of thirty-five dollars a year. . . . A short time afterwards the party was increased by the arrival of two women, said to be his wife and daughter ; and about three weeks ago three men arrived. The house is located in the midst of a thickly-settled neighborhood, five or six families living within hail, and the movements of the strangers were regarded with much curiosity. They seemed to have no settled purpose ; but a large number of boxes and packages were sent to them by railroad, which they carted home, and nearly every day one or more of them paid a visit to the village. They paid for every thing they wanted in hard cash, and were sociable and friendly towards their neighbors. A great deal of their time appeared to be passed in hunting in the mountains, although they never brought home any game.* On one occasion a neighbor remarked to Mr. Smith (as Old Brown was called) that he had observed twigs and branches bent down in a peculiar manner, which Smith explained by stating that it was the habit of the Indians, in travelling through a strange country, to mark their path in that way, so as to find their way back. He had no doubt, he said, that Indians passed over these mountains, unknown to the inhabitants."

* "We strike at higher and wickeder game," said Mr. Hunter — acted, Captain rown

21

These statements of conversations with John Brown must not be fully credited; but the accounts of the hiring of the farm are substantially correct. "The greater part of the men," according to Cook's Confession, "kept out of sight during the day, for fear of attracting attention. The arms, munitions, et cetera, were carted from Chambersburg to his rendezvous. The spear heads and guards came in strong boxes, and the shafts passed for fork handles. They were put together by our men at the house, where most of them were afterwards found."

"During his residence at the Kennedy Farm," writes one who lived with him, "the old man used often to take his Bible, sit down on a stool in the corner near the door, and read a chapter, and then make a prayer. He always did so in the morning. We never ate a meal at 'head-quarters,' until a blessing was asked on it."

During the period that elapsed from the hiring of his farm till his invasion of Virginia, John Brown had occasion to revisit the North. On the 14th of October he is supposed to have been in Baltimore; and on the 16th he took occasion to report himself at Harper's Ferry. The announcement was made so loudly, that it reached every home in the North, and penetrated every cabin of the Southern plantations.

VII.

The Blow Struck.

IT was the original intention of Captain Brown to seize the Arsenal at Harper's Ferry on the night of the 24th of October, and to take the arms there deposited to the neighboring mountains, with a number of the wealthier citizens of the vicinity, as hostages, until they should redeem themselves by liberating an equal number of their slaves. When at Baltimore, for satisfactory reasons, he determined to strike the blow that was to shake the Slave System to its foundations, on the night of the 17th. One of the men who fought at Harper's Ferry gave me as the chief reason for the precipitate movement, that there was a Judas whom they suspected in their midst. That the reasons were just and important, the prudence that John Brown had always hitherto manifested satisfactorily proves. But this decision, however necessary, was unfortunate; for the men from Canada, Kansas, New England, and the neighboring Free States, who had been told to be prepared for the event on the 24th of October, and were ready to do their duty at Harper's Ferry at that time, were unable to join their Captain at this earlier period.

Many, who started to join the Liberators, halted half way; for the blow had already been struck, and their Captain made a captive. Had there been no precipitation, the mountains of Virginia, to-day, would have been peopled with free blacks, properly officered and ready for field action.*

The negroes, also, in the neighboring counties, who had promised to be ready on the 24th of October, were confused by the precipitate attack; and, before they could act in concert — which they can only do by secret nocturnal meetings — were watched, overpowered, and deprived of every chance to join their heroic liberators.

Having sent off the women who lived at their cabins — Cook's wife and others — the neighbors began to talk about the singularity of the proceeding; and it became necessary, on that account also, to precipitate an attack on Harper's Ferry.

On Saturday, a meeting of the Liberators was held, and the plan of operations discussed. On Sunday evening, a council was again convened, and the programme of the Captain unanimously approved. "In closing," wrote Cook, "John Brown said:

"And now, gentlemen, let me press this one thing on your minds. You all know how dear life is to you, and how dear your lives are to your friends; and, in remembering that, consider that the lives of others are as dear to them as yours are to you. Do not, therefore, take the life of any one if you can possibly avoid it; but if it is necessary to take life in order to save your own, then make sure work of it."

---

* John Brown had engaged a competent military officer to take charge of the liberated slaves as soon as it became necessary to descend from the mountains, and meet the militia forces in the field.

HARPER'S FERRY.

" Fearful and Exciting Intelligence! Negro Insurrection at Harper's Ferry! Extensive Negro Conspiracy in Virginia and Maryland! Seizure of the United States Arsenal by the Insurrectionists! Arms taken and sent into the Interior! The Bridge fortified and defended by Cannon! Trains fired into and Stopped! Several Persons killed! Telegraph Wires cut! Contributions levied on the Citizens! Troops despatched against the Insurgents from Washington and Baltimore!"

Such were the headings of the first telegraphic reports of John Brown's brave blow at American Slavery.

Before briefly describing the events that they foreshadow, it is necessary to speak of the place where they occurred. The standard Virginia authority of the day thus writes :

"Harper's Ferry is situated in Jefferson County, Virginia, at the confluence of the Potomac and Shenandoah Rivers, on a point just opposite the gap through which the united streams pass the Blue Ridge on their way toward the ocean. The Ridge here is about twelve hundred feet in height, showing bare, precipitous cliffs on either side on the river, and exhibiting some of the most beautiful and imposing natural scenery to be found in the country. The town was originally built on two streets stretching along a narrow shelf between the base of the bluff and the rivers, meeting at the point at nearly a right angle, and named respectively Potomac and Shenandoah Streets. To accommodate its increasing population, the town has straggled up the steep bluff, and, in detached villages and scattered residences, occupies the level ground above — about four hundred feet above the streams.

"It has altogether a population of five thousand; is distant from Richmond one hundred and seventy-three miles ; from Washington City fifty-seven miles by turnpike road ; and from Baltimore eighty miles by rail. Here the Baltimore and Ohio Railroad crosses the Potomac by a magnificent covered bridge, nine hundred feet long, and passes along Potomac Street westward, its track lying forty feet above the river. The Winchester and Harper's Ferry Railroad, lying along Shenandoah Street, connects with the Baltimore and Ohio at the bridge. Potomac Street is entirely occupied by the workshops and offices of the National Armory, and its entrance is enclosed by a handsome gate and iron railing. Nearly at the angle of junction are the

21 *

old Arsenal buildings, where usually from one hundred thousand to two hundred thousand stand of arms are stored. The other buildings on the point, and nearer the bridge, are railroad offices, hotels, eating houses, stores, shops, &c. Shenandoah Street contains stores and dwelling houses for half a mile or more, when we come to Hall's rifle-works, situated on a small island in the Shenandoah River."

Harper's Ferry, by the admission of military men, was admirably chosen as the spot at which to begin a war of liberation. The neighboring mountains, with their inaccessible fastnesses, with every one of which, and every turning of their valleys, John Brown had been familiar for seventeen years, would afford to guerilla forces a protection the most favorable, and a thousand opportunities for a desperate defence or rapid retreats before overwhelming numbers of an enemy.

THE FIRST NIGHT.

The first movement of the Liberators was to extinguish the lights of the town, and take possession of the Armory buildings. This they did without opposition, or exciting alarm ; although they took the three watchmen prisoners, and locked them up in the Guard House. They were aided, it is believed, by friendly negroes. The number of Liberators in the town was twenty-two only, of whom seventeen were whites, and five blacks and mixed bloods. But, outside of the town, there were others, (who afterwards succeeded in escaping,) to whom were assigned the duty, which they successfully performed, of cutting down the telegraphic wires, and, after the train had passed, of tearing up the railroad track.

At half past ten, the watchman at the Potomac

Bridge was arrested and imprisoned. At midnight, his successor, who came down to take his place, was hailed by the sentinels placed there by Captain Brown; but, supposing that they were robbers, he refused to surrender, and ran off: one shot being fired at him from the bridge. He gave the alarm at the hotel near by, but it produced no immediate action. The train eastward-bound arrived at a quarter past one o'clock, and the conductor was made aware of the possession of the bridge by armed men. The officers of the train, accompanied by some passengers, attempted to walk across the bridge, but presently saw the muzzles of four rifles resting on a railing, and prudently turned back. One man, refusing to surrender, was shot in the back and died next morning. It was found that he was a negro porter. At this time there were several shots exchanged between a clerk of the hotel and one or two of the Liberators. The passengers in the train went into the hotel, and remained there, in great alarm, for four or five hours. The conductor, although permission was granted to him, at three o'clock, to pass over with his train, refused to do so till he could see for himself that all was safe.

"After taking the town," says Cook, "I was placed under Captain Stevens, who received orders to proceed to the house of Colonel Lewis Washington, and to take him prisoner, and to bring his slaves, horses, and arms ; and, as we came back, to take Mr. Alstadtt ar d his slaves, and to bring them all to Captain Brown at the Armory."

This party of six arrived at the house of Colonel Washington shortly after midnight, took him prisoner, seized his arms, horses, and carriage, and liberated his slaves. "It is remarkable," said Governor Wise, speaking of this event, "that the only thing of material value which they took, besides his slaves, was the sword of Frederick the Great, which was sent to General Washington. This was taken by Stevens to Brown, and the latter commanded his men with that sword in this fight against the peace and safety of Washington's native State!"

In returning to the Armory, Mr. Alstadtt and his son were taken prisoners, and the slaves on their estate were freed.

"On entering the Armory," said Washington, "I found some eight or ten persons, who recognized me. We were seated together and conversing, when the old man, whom we found by this time to be Brown, after asking our names, said, 'It is now too dark to write, but when it is sufficiently light, if you have not paper and pens, I will furnish you, and I require that you shall each write to your friends to send a negro man apiece as a ransom.'"

At daylight, every person who appeared in the street was taken prisoner, until they numbered between forty and fifty men. The train was also allowed to proceed, Captain Brown himself walking over the bridge with the conductor. Whenever the Virginians asked the object of their captors, the uniform answer was, "To free the slaves." One of the workmen, we are told, on seeing an armed guard at the gate, asked by what authority they had taken possession of the public premises. The guard replied, "By the authority of God Almighty."

VIII.

SWORD IN HAND.

THE train that left Harper's Ferry carried a panic to Virginia, Maryland, and Washington with it. The passengers, taking all the paper they could find, wrote accounts of the Insurrection, which they threw from the windows as the train rushed onward.

At daylight the news spread in Harper's Ferry that the town was in the hands of Abolitionists and the slaves. A terrible panic ensued. Report magnified the numbers of the Invaders forty-fold. The public buildings were already in the hands of the Liberators, and at the bridges, and the corners of the principal streets, armed sentinels, wrapped in blankets, were seen stationed, or walking up and down. Every man who appeared in the street was forthwith arrested and imprisoned in the Armory. Captain Brown and his sons Oliver and Watson, Stevens and two others, were stationed inside of the Armory grounds; Kagi, with Leeman, Stewart Taylor, Anderson, (black,) and Copeland, (colored,) held the lower part of the town and the rifle works; Cook, Owen Brown, Tidd, Merriam, and Barclay Coppoc were stationed at the cabins of the Kennedy Farm and the school house; while the remainder were posted as guards at the bridges and at the corners of the streets and the public buildings.

Early in the morning Captain Brown sent an order to the Wager House for breakfast for forty-five men — his hostages and company. By eight o'clock the number of Virginians thus held was over sixty persons.

The first firing after daybreak was by a person named Turner, who fired at the guards as they were ordering two citizens to halt. Mr. Boerley, a grocer, fired the second shot. A bullet from a Sharpe's rifle instantly killed him. A number of Virginians then obtained possession of a room overlooking the Armory gates, and fired at a party of the sentinels. One of the Liberators fell dead, and another — Watson Brown — retired mortally wounded.

The panic that these proceedings caused in the town is thus described by a Virginia panegyrist of the people:

"As the sun rose upon the scene, the reported outrages and the bodies of the murdered men showed that, from whatever source the movement came, it was of a serious nature. Sentinels, armed with rifles and pistols, were seen guarding all the public buildings, threatening death or firing at all who questioned or interfered with them; and the savage audacity with which they issued their orders gave assurance that the buildings were occupied by large bodies of men. Messages were despatched to all the neighboring towns for military assistance, while panic-stricken citizens seized such arms as they could find, and gathered in small bodies on the outskirts of the town, and at points remote from the works. All was confusion and mystery. Even the sight of several armed negroes among the strangers did not at once excite suspicion that it was an anti-slavery movement, and the report of one of the captured slaves, confirmatory of that fact, was received with doubt and incredulity. Indeed, so averse was the public mind to the acceptance of this belief, that the suggestion was every where received with derision, and every and any other explanation adopted in preference. Some supposed it was a strike among the discontented armorers, or the laborers on a government dam, who had taken this means to obtain redress for real or imaginary grievances.

Others argued that it was a band of robbers organized in some of the cities for the purpose of robbing the pay-master's strong box, known to contain some thousands of public money; that the armed negroes were whites in disguise; that the idea of inciting a servile insurrection was a ruse, put forth to distract the public mind, and enable them to escape with their booty."

During all the forenoon the Liberators had full possession of the town. There was a good deal of desultory firing, but no men were reported killed on either side. The prisoners were permitted frequently to visit their families, under guard, in order to quiet the apprehension of their wives and children. Had John Brown carried out his original plan, he would now have retreated to the mountains. He could have done so unopposed. But two reasons seem to have induced him to delay: first, to prove to the people that the prisoners would suffer no cruelty while in his hands; and, secondly — although this we infer only — the hope of being joined by the slaves when the night set in.

The delay was fatal to his plans. For, half an hour after midday, the first detachment of militia, one hundred strong, arrived at Harper's Ferry from Charlestown. Their movements are thus described by their Colonel in command:

"I proceeded on, with the few troops we had under arms, on foot to Harper's Ferry, where we arrived about twelve o'clock. I found the citizens in very great excitement. By this time the insurgents occupied all the lower part of the town, had their sentinels posted on all the different streets, and had shot one of our citizens and a negro man who had charge of the depot on the Baltimore and Ohio Railroad. I here formed two companies of the citizens, and placed them under the command of Captain Lawson Botts and Captain John Avis. Their forces were variously estimated from three hundred to five hundred strong, armed with Sharpe's rifles and revolvers.

"I detached the Jefferson Guards, under the command of Captain Rowan, and ordered them to cross the Potomac River in boats, about two miles above Harper's Ferry, and march down on the Maryland side, and take possession of the bridge, and permit no one to pass. This order was strictly executed. The command under Captain Botts was ordered to pass down the hill below Jefferson's Rock and take possession of the Shenandoah Bridge, to leave a strong guard at that point, and to march down to the Galt House, in rear of the Arsenal building, in which we supposed their men were lodged. Captain Avis's command was ordered to take possession of the houses directly in front of the Arsenal. Both of the above commands were promptly executed. By this movement we prevented any escape."

The first attack was made by the Charlestown Guards at the Shenandoah Bridge. William Thompson was taken prisoner, unwounded, having just previously returned from the school house. A companion was killed at the same time.

The rifle works were then attacked, and, as only five persons were stationed inside, the building was soon carried. Kagi and his men attempted to cross the river, and four of them succeeded in reaching the rock in the middle of it. As soon as they stood on the rock they renewed the fight, drawing on them the fire of two hundred Virginians, who shot at them from both sides of the river. Yet not one of these brave Liberators cried for quarter, or ceased to keep up the unequal conflict, until the corpse of Kagi, riddled with balls, floated down the river, followed by one of his faithful black comrades, and Leary lay mortally wounded. Copeland, the unwounded survivor, seeing that the fight was over, yielded himself a prisoner, and, with Leary, who lingered twelve hours in agony, was taken to the town and imprisoned.

About the same time, or just previous to the taking of the rifle works, William H. Leeman, having probably been despatched by Kagi with a message to Captain Brown, was seen, pursued, and attempted to escape by swimming the river. He was the youngest of the party — only twenty-two years of age. A dozen shots

were fired at him as he ran ; he partially fell, but rose
again, threw away his gun, drew his pistols and tried
to shoot, but both of them snapped. He then un-
sheathed his bowie-knife, cut off his accoutrements, and
plunged into the river. George Schoppart, one of the
Virginia militia, waded in after him. Leeman turned
round, threw up his hands, and said, "*Don't shoot!*"
Unheeding this cry of surrender, the cowardly Virginian fired his pistol in the young man's face, and blew
it into bloody fragments. He then cut off the coat-
skirts of the corpse, and found in the pockets a Captain's commission.*

While the fight at the rifle works was going on, Captain Avis and his company took possession of the houses
around the Armory buildings. As they were doing so,
Captain Turner, who had opened the fire in the morning, was shot dead while in the act of raising his rifle.
He was killed by a sentinel at the Arsenal gate. About
the same time, Dangerfield Newby, a man of color, and
a native of the neighborhood, who still had a wife and
nine children in slavery in the vicinity, fell dead as he
was bravely fighting for the freedom of his enslaved
little ones and their mother. His courage was warmly
eulogized by the Liberators who witnessed it. Jim,
one of Washington's negroes, was also slain at this
period — as he, also, was valiantly asserting his man-

* *Whereas*, W. H. Leeman has been nominated a Captain in the Army established
under the Provisional Constitution ; now, therefore, in pursuance of the authon.y
vested in me by said Constitution, we do hereby appoint and commission the said
W. H. Leeman, Captain.
    Given at the office of the Secretary of War, the 15th day of October, 1859.
                                            JOHN BROWN, *Commander-in-Chief.*
    J. H. KAGI, *Secretary of War.*

22

hood through the muzzle of a rifle.* A free negro, his
companion, who had lived on Washington's estate, was
shot for the same virtue at the same hour.

Shortly after the death of Captain Turner, a stray
shot killed Mr. Beckman, the Mayor of the town, who
foolishly came within range of the rifles, as the Liberators and Virginians were exchanging volleys. In the
course of this fight, Oliver Brown was shot, retreated
inside of the gate, " spoke no word, but yielded calmly
to his fate," and died in a few seconds after his
entrance.

At the request of Mr. Kitzmiller, one of John Brown's
hostages, Stevens went out of the Arsenal with him, in
order to enable him, if he could do so, to " accommodate matters " for the benefit of the prisoners. Stevens
carried a flag of truce ; but yet he was shot down, and
seized by the ruffianly militia.

Thompson was then ordered to prepare for death,
by a number of young Virginia gentlemen, whose conduct, on this occasion, is a vivid illustration of the
effects of slavery on the manners of men.

" In 1608, an Indian girl flung herself before her
father's tomahawk, on the bosom of an English gentleman, and the Indian refrained from touching the English traveller, whom his daughter's affection protected.
Pochahontas lives to-day, the ideal beauty of Virginia,
and her proudest names strive to trace their lineage to
the brave Indian girl. That was Pagan Virginia, two
centuries and a half ago." Far different is the Vir-

ginia of 1859. These Virginians tried to murder Mr.
Thompson in the parlor where he was detained a prisoner of war; and were only prevented from doing so
by a young lady throwing herself between their rifles
and his body. They then dragged him to the bridge,
where they killed him in cold blood. They shot him
off the bridge; shot him as he was falling the fearful
height of forty feet; and, some appearance of life still
remaining, riddled him with balls as he was seen crawl-
ing at the base of the pier. Contrast the Virginia
savages of the olden time with the Virginia gentlemen
of the present day. The contrast does not stop here.
Miss Foulke, the modern Pochahontas, when asked
why she shielded Mr. Thompson, replied, not that she
loathed a murder, but that she "didn't want to have
the carpet spoiled!"*

While these gallant young Virginians were murdering an unarmed prisoner, a party of men from Martinsburg arrived, and, led by a railroad conductor, attacked
the Armory buildings in the rear. Another detachment
of the same company attacked the buildings in front.
Seeing them approach on both sides in overwhelming
numbers, Captain Brown retreated to the engine house,
after exchanging volleys with the advancing forces.
The company that attacked the rear broke open sev-

* Wendell Phillips, in his great speech recently delivered at New York, in which he
so successfully subdued the satraps of Virginia who had assembled to put him down,
related another incident of the fight at Harper's Ferry, in which this Miss Foulke was
a participator:

"When, in the midst of the battle of Harper's Ferry, the Mayor's body lay within
range of the rifles of those northern boys, his friends wanted to bring it off, but none
of them would go. At last the porter of the hotel said to a lady, if you will stand between me and the rifles, I will go; and he went. He knew he could trust the gentle
sacredness of woman in the eyes of those brave northern boys. He went and placed
the body in a carriage, and, sheltered by her presence, carried it back in safety. That
is the difference between Northern blood and Southern."

eral windows, which enabled eighteen prisoners to escape. An attempt to carry the engine house was
repulsed with the loss of two men killed and six
wounded. The attacking party was fifty strong.

. During the day three trains had been detained outside of the town ; reënforcements were constantly arriving from the surrounding counties ; the telegraph
and railroad tracks were under repair ; and the Cabinet at Washington, the Governor of Virginia, and the
City of Baltimore, had ordered troops to hasten on to
subdue the Liberators.

The last militia force, under Captain Simms, from
Maryland, arrived at five o'clock in the afternoon ; and
with the other companies already there, completely
surrounded the Armory buildings. He arrived in time
to prevent another cowardly murder ; for the Virginia
gentlemen, afraid to attack the engine house, and fresh
from the murder of Thompson, were exhibiting the
nature of their valor by yelling for the blood of the
wounded Stevens.

The united forces were placed under the command
of Colonel Baylor. An offer made by Captain Brown
to liberate the hostages, if his men were permitted to
cross the bridge, was refused by him ; and by this time,
as the night had fallen, the firing ceased on both sides.

The result of the day's fight to the Liberators looked
extremely gloomy. In the rivers floated the corpses of
Kagi, Leeman, Stewart Taylor, and Wm. Thompson.
Imprisoned, and near to death, lay Lewis Leary and
Stevens. Copeland was a captive. On the street lay
the dead bodies of Hazlitt and Newby. In the engine

house were the remains of Oliver Brown, and Dauphin Thompson ; while Watson, the Captain's son, lay without hope of recovery. The only unwounded survivors of the Liberators in the engine house were Captain Brown, Jerry Anderson, Edwin Coppoc, and Shields Green, the negro. Eight Virginia hostages, and a small number of armed negroes, were with them.

Where were the others, and what had they been doing? John E. Cook, in his Confession, thus stated their position :

" When we returned from the capture of Washington, I staid a short time in the engine house to get warm, as I was chilled through. After I got warm, Captain Brown ordered me to go with C. P. Tidd, who was to take William H. Leeman, and I think four slaves with him, in Colonel Washington's large wagon across the river, and to take Terence Burns and his brother and their slaves prisoners. My orders were to hold Burns and brother as prisoners at their own house, while Tidd and the slaves who accompanied him were to go to Captain Brown's house, and to load in the arms and bring them down to the school house, stopping for the Burnses and their guard. William H. Leeman remained with me to guard the prisoners. On return of the wagon, in compliance with orders, we all started for the school house. When we got there, I was to remain, by Captain Brown's orders, with one of the slaves to guard the arms, while C. P. Tidd, with the other negroes, was to go back for the rest of the arms, and Burns was to be sent with William H. Leeman to Captain Brown at the Armory. It was at this time that William Thompson came up from the Ferry and reported that every thing was all right, and then hurried on to overtake William H. Leeman. A short time after the departure of Tidd, I heard a good deal of firing, and became anxious to know the cause ; but my orders were strict to remain at the school house and guard the arms, and I obeyed the orders to the letter. About four o'clock in the evening C. P. Tidd came with the second load. I then took one of the negroes with me and started for the Ferry. I met a negro woman a short distance below the school house, who informed me they were fighting hard at the Ferry. I hurried on till I came to the lock kept by George Hardy, about a mile above the bridge, where I saw his wife and Mrs. Elizabeth Read, who told me that our men were hemmed in, and that several of them had been shot. I expressed my intention to try to get to them, when Mrs. Hardy asked me to try to get her husband released from the engine house. I told her I would. Mrs. Read begged of me not to go down to the Ferry. She said I would be shot. I told her I must make an attempt to save my comrades, and passed on down the road. A short distance below the lock I met two boys whom I knew, and they told me that our men were all hemmed in by

22 *

troops from Charlestown, Martinsburg, Hagerstown, and Shepherds-
town. The negro who was with me had been very much frightened at
the first report we received, and as the boys told me the troops were
coming up the road after us soon, I sent him (the negro) back to inform Tidd, while I hastened down the road. After going down opposite the Ferry, I ascended the mountain in order to get a better view
of the position of our opponents.

"I saw that our party were completely surrounded, and as I saw a
body of men on High Street firing down upon them, — they were about
half a mile distant from me, — I thought I would draw their fire upon
myself; I therefore raised my rifle and took the best aim I could and
fired. It had the desired effect, for the very instant the party returned
it. Several shots were exchanged. The last one they fired at me cut
a small limb I had hold of just below my hand, and gave me a fall of
about fifteen feet, by which I was severely bruised, and my flesh
somewhat lacerated. I descended from the mountain and passed down
the road to the Crane on the back of the canal, about fifty yards from
Mr. W.'s store. I saw several heads behind the door-post looking at
me; I took a position behind the Crane, and cocking my rifle, beck-
oned to some of them to come to me. After some hesitation, one of
them approached, and then another, both of whom knew me. I asked
them if there were any armed men in the store. They pledged me
their word and honor that there were none. I then passed down to
the lock house, and went down the steps to the lock, where I saw
William McGreg, and questioned him in regard to the troops on the
other side. He told me that the bridge was filled by our opponents,
and that all of our party were dead but seven — that two of them
were shot while trying to escape across the river. He begged me to
leave immediately. After questioning him in regard to the position
and number of the troops, and from what sources he received his information, I bade him good night, and started up the road at a rapid
walk. I stopped at the house of an Irish family at the foot of the hill,
and got a cup of coffee and some eatables. I was informed by them
that Captain Brown was dead; that he had been shot about four o'clock
in the afternoon. At the time I believed this report to be true. I
went on up to the school house, and found the shutters and door
closed; called to Tidd and the boys, but received no answer; cocked
my rifle, and then opened the door; it was dark at the time. Some
of the goods had been placed in the middle of the floor, and, in the
dark, looked like men crouching. I uncocked my rifle, and drew my
revolver, and then struck a match; saw that there was no one in the
school house; went into the bushes back of the school house, and
called for the boys; receiving no answer, I went across the road into
some pines, and again called, but could find no one. I then started
up the road towards Captain Brown's house; I saw a party of men
coming down the road; when within about fifty yards, I ordered them
to halt; they recognized my voice, and called me. I found them to
be Charles P. Tidd, Owen Brown, Barclay Coppic, F. J. Merriam,
and a negro who belonged to Washington or Alstadtt. They asked
me the news, and I gave the information that I received at the canal lock
and on the road. It seemed that they thought it would be sheer mad-
ness in them to attempt a rescue of our comrades, and it was finally
determined to return to the house of Captain Brown. I found that Tidd,

before leaving the school house to go for Brown, Coppic, and Merriam, had stationed the negroes in a good position in the timber back of the school house. On his return, however, they could not be found. We therefore left for Captain Brown's house. Here we got a few articles which would be necessary, and then went over into the timber on the side of the mountain, a few yards beyond the house, where the spears were kept. Here we laid down and went to sleep. About three o'clock in the morning one of our party awakened, and found that the negro had left us. He immediately aroused the rest of the party, and we concluded to go to the top of the mountain before light. Here we remained for a few hours, and then passed over to the other side of the mountain, where we waited till dark, and then crossed the valley to the other range beyond."

The town was filled with militia forces, which guarded every street and approach to the Ferry. There were fifteen hundred men under arms. During the night, Colonel Lee, with ninety United States marines, and two pieces of artillery, arrived in the town, took possession of the Armory guard, in immediate proximity to the engine house.

The scene in the town is thus described by a correspondent of the Frederick Herald, a Maryland pro-slavery paper :

"The dead lay on the streets, and in the river, and were subjected to every indignity that a wild and madly excited people could heap upon them.

"Curses were freely uttered against them, and kicks and blows inflicted upon them. The huge mulatto that shot Mr. Turner was lying in the gutter in front of the Arsenal, with a terrible wound in his neck, and though dead and gory, vengeance was unsatisfied, and many, as they *ran sticks into his wound, or beat him with them*, wished that he had a thousand lives, that all of them might be forfeited in expiation and avengement of the foul deed he had committed.

"Leeman lay upon a rock in the river, and was made a target for the practice of those who had captured Sharpe's rifles in the fray. Shot after shot was fired at him, and when tired of this *sport*, a man waded out to where he lay, and *set him up, in grotesque attitudes*, and finally pushed him off, and he floated down the stream. His body and hat of Thompson, which was also in the water, were subsequently brought to shore, and were buried, as were all of them, except a few which were taken by some of the physicians. It may be thought that here was cruelty and barbarity in this ; but the state of the public mind had been frenzied by the outrages of these men ; and being outlaws, were regarded as food for carrion birds, and *not as human creatures*."

IX.

Fallen among Thieves.

UP to the close of Monday evening, John Brown
had successfully maintained his position against
the united forces of Virginia and Maryland. With
his three surviving followers he was now prepared to
oppose the Nation ; and, knowing no fear but the failure
to do his duty, he prepared to resist her forces also.

Hemmed in by an overwhelming force, with the
knowledge that, when the morrow's sun should rise,
he must fall before its physical superiority, he never
once faltered in his resolution, or exhibited the slightest sign of fear. During the live-long night, said one
of the hostages, the voice of Brown was heard continually repeating, Are you awake, men ? Are you
ready ? "And Colonel Washington said that he —
Brown — was the coolest man he ever saw in defying
death and danger. With one son dead by his side,
and another shot through, he felt the pulse of his
dying son with one hand, and held his rifle with the
other, and commanded his men with the utmost composure, encouraging them to be firm, and to sell their

(260)

"With one son dead by his side, and another dying, he felt the pulse of his dying son with one hand and held his rifle with the other."

lives as dearly as possible."* The old man, we are told, spoke freely with Colonel Washington, and referred to his sons. He said he had lost one in Kansas, and two here. He had not pressed them to join him in the expedition, but did not regret their loss — they had died in a good cause.

At seven o'clock the preparations for an assault began. Watson Brown lay writhing in agony on the ground, unable to assist in the defence ; but his undaunted comrades stood fearless and ready to defend their lives, and resist the hireling bands of the oppressor.

The correspondent of a Baltimore paper thus describes the closing scenes :

"Shortly after seven o'clock, Lieutenant E. B. Stuart, of the 1st C.valry, who was acting as aid for Colonel Lee, advanced to parley w th the besieged, Samuel Strider, Esq., an old and respectable citizen, bearing a flag of truce. They were received at the door by Captain Brown. Lieutenant Stuart demanded an unconditional surrender, only promising them protection from immediate violence, and a trial by law. Captain Brown refused all terms but those previously demanded, which were substantially, "That they should be permitted to march out with their men and arms, taking their prisoners with them ; that they should proceed unpursued to the second toll-gate, when they would free their prisoners; the soldiers would then be permitted to pursue them, and they would fight if they could not escape." Of course, this was refused, and Lieutenant Stuart pressed upon Brown his desperate position, and urged a surrender. The expostulation, though beyond earshot, was evidently very earnest. At this moment the interest of the scene was most intense. The volunteers were ranged all around the building, cutting off escape in every direction. The marines, divided in two squads, were ready for a dash at the door.

'Finally, Lieutenant Stuart, having failed to arrange terms with the determined Captain Brown, walked slowly from the door.

'Immediately the signal for attack was given, and the marines, headed by Major Russell and Lieutenant Green, advanced in two lines on each side of the door. Two powerful fellows sprung between the lines, and with heavy sledge hammers attempted to batter down the door. The door swung and swayed, but appeared to be secured with a rope, the spring of which deadened the effect of the blows. Failing thus, they took hold of a ladder, some forty feet long, and, advancing at a run, brought it with tremendous effect against the door. At the second blow it gave way, one leaf falling inward in a slanting

* Speech of Governor Wise, at Richmond, on his return from Harper's Ferry.

position. The marines immediately advanced to the breach, Major Russell and Lieutenant Green leading. A marine in front fell. The firing from the interior was rapid and sharp. They fired with deliberate aim, and for a moment the resistance was serious, and desperate enough to excite the spectators to something like a pitch of frenzy. The next moment the marines poured in, the firing ceased, and the work was done. In the assault a private of the marines received a ball in the stomach, and was believed to be fatally wounded. Another received a slight flesh wound."

One of the Liberators fell dead — Jerry Anderson — and only three shots were fired; Brown, Coppoc, and Green each discharging their rifles at the marines on their first assault.

Before the entrance of the troops, the Liberators ceased firing; and, therefore, by all the rules of honorable warfare, should now have been sacredly protected from violence. Offering no resistance, every civilized people would have taken them prisoners of war. But not so the assailants in Virginia.

Before the fight began, John Brown, according to the testimony of Colonel Washington, urged his hostages to seek places of safety — to keep themselves out of harm's way; while the crowd in the streets, judging the Liberators by their own standard of humanity, supposed that they were killing them in cold blood. How did the descendant of GEORGE WASHINGTON reciprocate this consideration? Let his friend and eulogist reply:

"Colonel Washington, who, through all these trying scenes, had borne himself with an intrepid coolness that excited the admiration of the brigand chief himself, now did important service. The moment the marines entered, he sprang upon one of the engines, told his fellow-prisoners to hold up their hands that they might be recognized as non-combatants, and *then rapidly pointed out the outlaws to the vengeance of the soldiers*. . . . A soldier, seeing Colonel Washington in an active and prominent position, mistook him for one of the outlaws, levelled his piece, and put his finger on the trigger; but, fortunately remembering the caution in regard to the prisoners, he desisted. Shields Green, *alias* Emperor, a negro M. C. under the future Provisional Government, sneaked among the slave prisoners, hoping thus to escape notice and detection; but, perceived by Colonel Washington, he was hauled forth to meet his doom."

Lieutenant Green, as soon as he saw John Brown, although he was unarmed, (according to the testimony of a Virginian,) struck him in the face with his sabre, which instantly knocked him down. Not content with his brutality, the Lieutenant repeated the blow several times, and then another soldier ran a bayonet twice into the prostrate body of the old man.*

The scenes that followed this assault are so discreditable to Virginia — nay, to human nature — that I dare not trust myself to describe them; but will content myself with quoting the accounts of two ultra pro-slavery journalists. This is the report of the Baltimore American :

"When the insurgents were brought out, some dead and others wounded, they were greeted with execrations, and only the precautions that had been taken saved them from immediate execution. The crowd, nearly every man of which carried a gun, swayed with tumultuous excitement, and cries of 'Shoot them! shoot them!' rang from every side. The appearance of the liberated prisoners, all of whom, through the steadiness of the marines, escaped injury, changed the current of feeling, and prolonged cheers took the place of howls and execrations.

"The lawn in front of the engine house, after the assault, presented a dreadful sight. Lying on it were two bodies of men killed on the previous day, and found inside the house ; three wounded men, one of them just at the last gasp of life, [Anderson;] and two others groaning in pain. One of the dead was Brown's son Oliver. The wounded father and his son Watson were lying on the grass, the old man presenting a gory spectacle. He had a severe bayonet wound in his side, and his face and hair were clotted with blood."

Porte-Crayon, a Virginia artist and author, and a fiendish historian of the holy Invasion, thus writes of the same infamous scene :

* In the trial of Copeland, the following dialogue occurred :

Mr. Sennott. You say that when Brown was down you struck him in the face with your sabre?
Lieut. Green. Yes, sir.
Mr. Sennott. This was after he was *down?*
Lieut. Green. Yes, sir, he was down.
Mr. Sennott. How many times, Lieut. Green, did you strike Brown in the face after he was down?
Lieut. Green. Why, sir, he was defending himself with his gun.
Mr Hunter. *I hope the counsel for the defence will not press such questions as these.*
Mr. Sennott. Very well, sir.

"The citizen captives, released from their long and trying confinement, hurried out to meet their friends with every demonstration of
joy; while the bloody carcasses of the dead and dying outlaws were
dragged into the lawn amidst the howls and execrations of the people.
It was a hideous and ghastly spectacle. Some, stark and stiff, with
staring eyes and fallen jaws, were the dead of yesterday; while others,
struck with death wounds, writhed and wallowed in their blood.
Two only were brought out unhurt, — Coppoc, and Green the negro,
— and they only escaped immediate death by accident, the soldiers not
at once distinguishing them from the captive citizens and slaves."

There is only one account of the conversation of
John Brown, as he lay wounded and bloody on the
lawn. It is thus narrated:

"A short time after Captain Brown was brought out, he revived,
and talked earnestly to those about him, defending his course, and
avowing that he had done only what was right. He replied to ques-
tions substantially as follows:
" 'Are you Captain Brown, of Kansas?'
" 'I am sometimes called so.'
" 'Are you Osawatomie Brown?'
" '*I tried to do my duty there.*' "

These two replies are eminently characteristic — so
manly and so modest. He never himself assumed the
title of Captain, even in Kansas, where titles were as
common as proper names. "I tried to do my duty
there," — the sentence was a key to his whole life.
Neither honor nor glory moved him; the voice of duty
was the only one he heard.

" 'What was your present object?'
" 'To free the slaves from bondage.'
" 'Were any other persons but those with you now connected with
the movement?'
" 'No.'
" 'Did you expect aid from the North?
" 'No; there was no one connected with the movement but those
who came with me.'
" 'Did you expect to kill people in order to carry your point?'
" 'I did not wish to do so, but you force us to it.'
"Various questions of this kind were put to Captain Brown, which
he answered clearly and freely, with seeming anxiety to vindicate
himself.
"He urged that he had the town at his mercy; that he could have
burned it, and murdered the inhabitants, but did not; he had treated
the prisoners with courtesy, and complained that he was hunted down
like a beast. He spoke of the killing of his son, which he alleged was
done while bearing a flag of truce, and seemed very anxious for the
safety of his wounded son. His conversation bore the impression of

the conviction that whatever he had done to free slaves was right, and that in the warfare in which he was engaged he was entitled to be treated with all the respect of a prisoner of war.

"He seemed fully convinced that he was badly treated, and had a right to complain. Although at first considered dying, an examination of his wounds proved that they were not necessarily fatal. He expressed a desire to live, and to be tried by his country. In his pockets nearly three hundred dollars were found in gold. Several important papers, found in his possession, were taken charge of by Colonel Lee, on behalf of the government. To another, Brown said it was no part of his purpose to seize the public arms. He had army and ammunition enough reshipped from Kansas. He only intended to make the first demonstration at this point, when he expected to receive a rapid increase of the allies from Abolitionists every where settled through Maryland and Virginia, sufficient to take possession of both States, with all of the negroes they could capture. He did not expect to encounter the Federal troops. He had only a general idea as to his course; it was to be a general south-west course through Virginia, varying as circumstances dictated or required. Mr. Washington reports that Brown was remarkably cool during the assault. He fell under two bayonet wounds — one in the groin, and one in the breast — and four sabre cuts on the head. During the fight he was supposed to be dead, or doubtless he would have been shot. He was not touched by a ball. The prisoners also state that Brown was courteous to them, and did not ill-use them, and made no abolition speech to them. Coppoc, one of the prisoners, said he did not want to join the expedition, but added, 'Ah, you gentlemen don't know Captain Brown; when he calls for us we never think of refusing to come.'" *

Captain Brown, after his pockets were rifled, was carried, with his dying son, to the Guard House, and Stevens was soon brought and laid down beside them on the floor. No beds were provided for the prisoners. Coppoc, the brave Iowa boy, thus described, in a letter to their mother, the death of John Brown's sons, and the accommodations provided for them by the Virginians:

"I was with your sons when they fell. Oliver lived but a very few moments after he was shot. He spoke no word, but yielded calmly to his fate. Watson was shot at ten o'clock on Monday morning, and died about three o'clock on Wednesday morning. He suffered much. Though mortally wounded at ten o'clock, yet at three o'clock Monday afternoon he fought bravely against the men who charged on us. When the enemy were repulsed, and the excitement of the charge was over, he began to sink rapidly. After we were taken prisoners, he was placed in the Guard House with me. He complained of the hardness of the bench on which he was lying. I begged hard for a bed for him, or even a blanket, but could obtain none for him. I took off my coat, and placed it under him, and held his head in my lap, in which position he died, without a groan or struggle."

* These statements are unworthy of belief.

23

X.

Spoils of War.

SOME time after the capture of the Liberators, a
negro, held in bondage by Colonel Washington,
reported that Captain Cook was in the mountains, only
three miles off. Scouting parties went out in search
of him, but all of them returned unsuccessful. From
this time until the day of John Brown's death, the whole
country around Harper's Ferry and Charlestown was
kept in a condition of perpetual alarm. Rumors of
invasion, and rescue, and murder — letters written by
lovers of fun in the North, for the purpose of fright-
ening the authorities — "mysterious Roman lights
seen shooting up at night among the mountains" —
and cows of bellicose propensities, who rebelliously refused to advance and give the countersign ; all aided to
exhibit the exceeding cowardice of Virginia, and how
dastardly a spirit her criminal institution has created
among a people once brave and chivalrous. The invasion of John Brown, if it had done no more than effect
this object, was an eminent success ; for, more effectually than ever all the pens and tongues of eloquent
champions of Freedom had done, it tore away the veil

of decency and courage which hither.o had hidden the enormities of Slavery.

All Virginia was in alarm. Her militia forces were every where called out, and all business for the time was suspended. They, who had boasted of the stability of slave society, now acknowledged that its foundations lay in fire, whose irruption they daily feared would overwhelm them with ruin.

COMPLICITY OF SLAVES.

At Washington City the military force was increased, and every precaution taken to keep the negroes down. A telegraphic despatch from the Capital, on the 18th — the day when John Brown was captured — thus portrays their fears and the reason for them:

"It appears from intelligence received here to-day from various portions of Virginia and Maryland, that a general stampede of slaves has taken place. There must have been an understanding of some nature among them in reference to this affair, for in numerous instances — so I am informed by the slaveholders since this insurrection — they have found it almost impossible to control them. The slaves were in many instances insolent to their masters, and even refused to work. It is believed by the slaveholders, since this insurrection, that the slaves were aware of it, but were afraid to coöperate. This view of the case is corroborated by Brown and other leaders."

Large numbers of negroes were also reported to have left the neighborhood of Hagerstown, Maryland, and Alexandria, Virginia. A reporter of a pro-slavery paper gives additional information with respect to the 'complicity" of the slaves:

"The inhabitants are not by any means easy in their minds, as to the temper of the slaves and free negroes among them. Col. Washington, who was one of Old Brown's hostages, does not spend his nights at home, and we are assured that many of the wealthy slave owners, whose residences lie at a distance from those of their neighbors, also regard it prudent to lodge elsewhere for the present; and yet the personal courage of these gentlemen cannot be questioned. It has been ascertained, reports to the contrary notwithstanding, that many negroes in the neighborhood, who had been tampered with by Cook and others of Brown's gang, had at least cognizance of the plans of the marauders, if they did not sympathize with them. On the night that Col. Washington was taken, a free negro, who has a wife on the Colonel's plantation, was spending the night there, and although he might in half an hour have raised an alarm at Charlestown, only two or three miles distant, he refrained from doing so, and the first news of the affair was brought to that village by citizens of Harper's Ferry the next day. There is no doubt that Washington's negro coachman Jim, who was chased into the river by citizens and drowned, had joined the rebels with a good will. A pistol was found on him, and he had his pockets filled with ball cartridges when he was fished out of the river. On Sunday evening, before the attack, a gentleman on the way to Harper's Ferry was stopped in a lonely place, three or four miles distant, by a white man, carrying a rifle, and two negroes, armed with axes, who told him there was something going on at Harper's Ferry, and he must turn back. He did so, and the men remained standing there until he was out of sight. Who these parties were, or what their connection with Brown's party, is still a mystery. It is certain that Brown's party was considerably larger when the attack was made than he had acknowledged, or was at first supposed. There must have been at least thirty men."

The *Richmond Examiner* found yet another trace of slave " conspiracy." It says :

"We are informed by a highly respectable gentleman of this city that he saw, yesterday morning, a letter which Mr. Samuel Gordon took from his negro, which was addressed to a negro from Baltimore, saying that he (the recipient of the letter) was expected in Baltimore by the 13th of this month, that a post had been assigned him, and that he was expected to be there by that time. The letter concluded in these words : ' And you know what will happen next day.' "

These few and faint indications of sympathy among the slaves struck terror to the hearts of the Virginians. What would they have done, had they known the terrible facts that now lie buried with the corpse of John Brown ? Not buried eternally, however ; for they will rise again — with the slaves.

CAPTURE OF THE ARMS.

The Independent Grays of Baltimore, who went out in search of Cook, — for the Virginians did not dare to venture beyond the parade ground, — returned in two hours with the arms and ammunition found in the school house. The brave exploit by which they captured these arms, which was the most courageous action of the sober militia forces, — for the company of the editor, Albertus, by their own confession, were intoxicated when they charged on the Armory buildings, — is thus described by a native historian, worthy of the heroes whose valor he extols :

FEARFUL CHARGE ON AN ARMED LOG CABIN.

"The gallant Grays proceeded at 'double-quick' time, along a constantly ascending and rocky road, to execute the order. About a mile from the Ferry, they arrived within sight of the school house, a cabin situated in a gloomy hollow, and, apparently, closely barricaded. Halting for a few moments, the Grays formed into platoons, under the respective commands of Lieuts. Simpson and Kerchner, and, at a given signal, dashing down the declivity of the road, and with the butt-ends of their muskets, battered in the doors and windows, through which they entered. *The cabin was entirely empty of occupants.* Against the front door were piled sixteen long and heavy boxes, one of which, upon being burst open, was found to contain ten newly-finished Sharpe's breech-loading rifles, evidently fresh from the hands of their maker. There was also discovered one large square box, exceedingly heavy, which was suffered to remain unopened: a large and heavy black trunk, a box filled with bayonets and sabres, and several boxes of rifle cartridges and ammunition. There were in all twenty-one boxes, several of which were filled with Maynard's large-sized patent revolvers, with powder flasks accompanying. The room was littered with Sharpe's rifles, revolvers, and pikes, evidently distributed with a view to their immediate use, either for the purpose of defence or an aggressive action. After satisfying themselves that the traitors had fled, the gallant Grays proceeded to possess themselves — each man — of a rifle and a pair of revolvers, the remainder being placed, together with a large number of pikes, &c., upon a large new wagon, (purchased a few days before, by Smith, or Capt. Brown, as he is now known,) to which the captors harnessed a pair of fine horses they caught grazing in the enclosure, and conveyed their valuable prize into town, where they were received with loud cheers by the citizens and military.

"The captured boxes were placed for safe keeping in the Arsenal of the United States, though the Grays asserted an exclusive right to their possession, as the lawful prize of the captors."

The stores found in this cabin, are thus classified :

102 Sharpe's Rifles.	1 Pair Linen Pants.
12 Mass. Arms Company's Pistols.	Canvas for Tent.
56 " " " Powder	1 Old Porte-monnaie.
4 Large Powder Flasks. [Flasks.	625 Envelopes.
10 Kegs Gunpowder.	1 Pocket Map of Kentucky.
3,000 Percussion Rifle Caps.	1 Pocket Map of Delaware.
1 0,000 Percussion Pistol Caps	3 Gross Steel Pens.
3,000 Sharpe's Rifle Cartridges, slightly	5 Inkstands.
damaged by water.	21 Lead Pencils.
160 Sharpe's Primers.	34 Pen Holders.
14 lbs. Lead Balls.	2 Boxes Wafers.
1 Old Percussion Pistol.	47 Small Blank Books.
1 Major General's Sword.	2 Papers Pins.
55 Old Bayonets.	5 Pocket Small Tooth Combs.*
12 Old Artillery Swords.	1 Ball Hemp Twine.
483 Pikes.	1 Ball Cotton Twine.
150 Broken Handles for Pikes.	50 Leather Water Caps.
16 Picks.	1 Emery.
40 Shovels.	2 Yards Cotton Flannel.
[The railroad way bill called for several	1 Roll Sticking Plaster for Wounds
dozen, showing that more were to come.]	12 Reams Cartridge Paper.
1 Tin Powder Case.	2 Bottles Medicine,
1 Sack Coat.	1 Large Trunk.
1 Pair Cloth Pants.	1 Horse Wagon.

The discovery of these "deadly" implements of domestic warfare, it has been argued, proved incontestably the intention of the Liberators to make war upon the "peculiar institutions" of Virginia.

23 *

JOHN BROWN'S CARPET BAG.

The next military movement must also be described in the glowing language of the friends of the fearless heroes who executed it :

"The excitement attending this clever exploit [the charge on the deserted school house] had scarcely subsided, when another alarm was given, that the notorious insurgent leader, Cook, had a few minutes before been seen upon the mountains on the Maryland shore. A scouting party, consisting of several members of the Grays, (the only foreign corps in the town, quite or nearly all of those present in the forenoon having left for their homes,) some score or more of volunteers, and about twenty United States marines, under command of Capt. J. E. B. Stewart, was instantly formed, and proceeded rapidly in pursuit. Following the same path which the Grays had pursued in making their discoveries, and which is known as the 'County Road,' leading into the heart of Washington Co., Md., the party continued their course for a distance of 4½ miles from the Ferry, until they reached the farm and house bought and occupied by Brown, under the name of John Smith. The dwelling — a log house, containing two unpaved basement rooms, used apparently for storage, and in which were several empty gun boxes; two rooms and a pantry upon the second floor; and one large attic room in which were six husk mattresses — was discovered to be unoccupied, save by a huge savage-looking mastiff, tied with a rope to the railing of a small piazza outside the house; but there was abundant evidence of its recent hurried vacation. The floors of all the rooms were littered with books, papers, documents, and wearing apparel of several persons, hastily snatched from eight or ten trunks and an equal number of valises and coarse carpet bags strewn around, the fastenings of all of which had been forcibly broken, as if their violators were too much pressed for time to adopt the tardier method of entrance by looking up keys. In the pantry, which appeared to have been used for kitchen purposes, besides an almost new cooking stove, and an abundance of tin utensils, were two barrels of flour, a large quantity of sausage meat and cured hams, together with several pounds of butter, lard, &c. The fire was yet smouldering in the stove, and the water in the boilers was quite hot at the time of the entrance. But the most valuable discovery was a trunk belonging to Captain Brown, containing a great number of highly important papers, documents, plans, and letters from private individuals throughout the Union — all revealing the existence of an extensive and thoroughly organized conspiracy.

"The telegraphic account of this 'clever exploit' stated that they found a large quantity of blankets, boots, shoes, clothes, tents, and 1500 pikes with large blades affixed. They also discovered a carpet bag, containing 'documents throwing much light on the affair, printed constitutions and by-laws of an organization showing or indicating ramifications in various States of the Union.'"

In this carpet bag were found various unimportant notes, from prominent persons in different States; letters to "J. Henrie," meaning Kagi; and "Friend Isaac," meaning Captain Brown — referring chiefly to the old man's Kansas work; brief entries, in journals, of subscriptions received, and journeys made, and hardships endured in Iowa, the Eastern States, and Canada;

copies of the Constitution, and of books of military tactics, with numerous receipts and bills for stock and provisions purchased for the war of liberation.

In the mean time, now that the fight was over, the valiant Virginians flocked to Harper's Ferry. Governor Wise came down by the midday train, and, after ridiculing the people, visited the prisoners. The interview lasted several hours. None but the bitterest enemies of the Liberators were present during this confronting of the representatives of the North and South. The most graphic narrative is written by a Virginia artist, who stands high in the estimation of her people, and is regarded as a true representative of her chivalry. The character of her gentry, therefore, may be judged from the spirit of his description :

"The midday train of Tuesday brought Governor Wise, accompanied by several hundred men from Richmond, Alexandria, Baltimore, and elsewhere. There was real disappointment to find that the fight was all over, and when the Governor was informed of the mere handful of men who had created all this bobbery, he boiled over. In his wrath he said some good things. Indeed it was universally seen and felt that Governor Wise was just the man for such an occasion.

"Accompanied by Andrew Hunter, Esq., a distinguished lawyer of Jefferson County, the Governor presently repaired to the guard room where the two wounded prisoners lay, and there had a protracted and interesting conversation with the chief of the outlaws. It had more the character of a conversation than a legal examination, for the Governor treated the wounded man with a stately courtesy that evidently surprised and affected him. Brown was lying upon the floor with his feet to the fire and his head propped upon pillows on the back of a chair. His hair was a mass of clotted gore, so that I could not distinguish the original color; his eye a pale blue or gray, nose Roman, and beard, originally sandy, was white and blood-stained. His speech was frequently interrupted by deep groans, not awakening sympathy like those of the young soldier dying in the adjacent office, but reminding one of the agonized growl of a ferocious beast.

"A few feet from the leader lay Stevens, a fine-looking fellow, quiet, not in pain apparently, and conversing in a voice as full and natural as if he were unhurt How ever, his hands lay folded upon his breast in a child-like, helpless way — a position that observed was assumed by all those who had died or were dying of their wounds Only those who were shot stone dead lay as they fell.

"Brown was frank and communicative, answering all questions without reserve, except such as might implicate his immediate associates not yet killed or taken. I append some extracts from notes taken during the conversation by Mr. Hunter:

"'Brown avers that the small pamphlet, many copies of which were found on the ersons of the slain, and entitled "Provisional Constitution and Ordinances for the 'ople of the United States," was prepared principally by himself, and adopted at a

convention of Abolitionists held about two years ago at Chatham, Canada West, where
it was printed. That under its provisions he was appointed "Commander-in-Chief."
His two sons and Stevens were each captains, and Coppoc a lieutenant. They each
had their commissions, issued by himself.

"'He avers that the whole number operating under this organization was but twenty-
two, each of whom had taken the oath required by Article XLVIII.; but he confidently expected large reënforcements from Virginia, Kentucky, Maryland, North and
South Carolina, and several other Slave States, besides the Free States — taking it for
granted that it was only necessary to seize the public arms and place them in the hands
of the negroes and non-slaveholders to recruit his forces indefinitely. In this calcula-
tion he reluctantly and indirectly admitted that he had been entirely disappointed.'

"Concluding that the prisoner must be seriously weakened by his vigils and his
wounds, the Governor ordered some refreshment to be given him, and appointing a
meeting on the following day, took his leave. As some of us lingered, the old man
recurred again to his sons, of whom he had spoken several times, asking if we were
sure they were both dead. He was assured that it was so.

"'How many bodies did you take from the engine house?' he asked.

"He was told three.

"'Then,' said he, quickly, 'they are not both dead; there were three dead bodies
there last night. Gentlemen, my son is doubtless living and in your power. I will
ask for him what I would not ask for myself; let him have kind treatment, for he is
as pure and noble-hearted a youth as ever breathed the breath of life.'

"There was some show of human feeling in the old felon at last, but his prayer was
vain. Both his boys lay stark and bloody by the Armory wall.

"I had observed Stevens holding a small packet in his folded hands, and feeling
some curiosity in regard to it, it was handed to me. It contained miniatures of his
sisters; one, a sweet girlish face of about fourteen, the other more mature, but pretty.
What strange reflections these incidents awakened! This old man craves a boon for his
noble boys which neither pain nor death can bring him to ask for himself. The other
clasps to his dying breast a remembrance of his gentle sisters and his father's elm-shaded
cottage far away in peaceful Connecticut. Is this pity that thus dims my eyes? a
rising sympathy that struggles in my heart? Away with pulling weakness. Has not
this hoary villain, that prates about his sons, been for months a deliberate plotter
against the lives and happiness of thousands? Did he not train these very boys to aid
him in his attempt to waste, with fire and sword, the fairest land under the cope of
heaven? And this bloody dupe — his follower — how many men's sisters did he propose to murder? how many social hearths to quench in blood? For what use were
those hundreds of deadly rifles, those loads of pikes, those bundles of incendiary
fagots? A felon's death! Almighty Providence! is man indeed so weak that he can
inflict no more?"

The man whom God had anointed, and the man
whom the people had appointed — both were too conscious of their earthly position, as they stood in the
guard house of Harper's Ferry, to feel that either
could do the other a favor. The assertion that John
Brown was affected by the conduct of Governor Wise,
is one that none but an unheroic pen could make.
Coarse brutality and stately courtesy were alike indif-

ferent to the venerable warrior. Conscious of having tried to do his duty, he serenely awaited his preappointed fate. What was it to him that he would be brutally accused of having sought to lay " waste, with fire and sword, the fairest land under the cope of Heaven ? " of having proposed to murder innocent women, or having conspired against the lives and happiness of thousands ? Knowing that he had obeyed the Divine behest only by listening to the poor that cried ; that he had done unto others as he would have desired that others should have done unto him ; he was neither to be awed into fear, nor softened into gratitude, to the enemies of his God : and thus he aroused, by the modest manliness of his demeanor, the astonishment — almost the veneration — of the able but distorted intellect who stood beside him. When Governor Wise, on his return to Richmond, appeared before the people, he thus spoke of the wounded Liberator :

"They are themselves mistaken who take him to be a madman. He is a bundle of the best nerves I ever saw, cut and thrust, and bleeding and in bonds. He is a man of clear head, of courage, fortitude, and simple ingenuousness. He is cool, collected, and indomitable, and it is but just to him to say, that he was humane to his prisoners, as attested to me by Col. Washington and Mr. Mills, and he inspired me with great trust in his integrity, as a man of truth. He is a fanatic, vain and garrulous, but firm, and truthful, and intelligent. His men, too, who survive,.except the free negroes with him, are like him. He professes to be a Christian, in communion with the Congregationali t Church of the North, and openly preaches his purpose of universal emancipation : and the negroes themselves were to be the agents, by means of arms, led on by white commanders. When Col. Washington was taken, his watch, and plate, and jewels, and money were demanded, to create what they call a 'safety fund,' to compensate the liberators for the trouble and expense of taking away his slaves. This, by a law, was to be done with all slaveholders. Washington, of course, refused to deliver up any thing; and it is remarkable, that the only thing of material value which they took, besides his slaves, was the sword of Frederick the Great, which was sent to General Washington. This was taken by Stevens to Brown, and the latter commanded his men with that sword in this fight against the peace and safety of Washington's native State! He promised Col. Washington to return it to him when it was done with it. And Col. Washington says that he, Brown, was the coolest and firmest man he ever saw in defying danger and death. With one son dead by his side, and another shot through, he felt the pulse of his dying son with one hand and held his rifle with the other, and commanded his men with the utmost composure, encouraging them to be firm, and to sell their lives as dearly as they could."

XI.

The Political Inquisitors.

A S soon as it was known that John Brown was not
dead, and that three of his followers had been
safely protected from the fury of the populace, four
political inquisitors hastened down to see him; to
extort, if possible, from the lips of the dying chief, or
the fears or hopes of the younger captives, confessions
that might criminally implicate the champions or friends
of the Republican party. From the South came Governor Wise and Senator Mason of Virginia; from the
North, a United States Marshal named Johnson, and
Mr. Vallandingham, a member of Congress from Ohio.

The result of these visits was one of John Brown's
greatest victories. From the three published reports
of it, carefully compared and corrected, we give the
conversation that ensued between the wounded insurrectionists and their cowardly political inquisitors.

Never before, in the United States, did a recorded
conversation produce so sudden and universal a change
of opinion. Before its publication, some, who subsequently eulogized John Brown, with fervor and sur-

(274)

passing eloquence, as well as the great body of the press
and people who knew not the man, lamented that he
should have gone insane, — never doubting that he was
a maniac; while, after it, from every corner of the
land came words of wonder, of praise rising to worship,
and of gratitude mingling with sincerest prayers for
the holy old hero. Enemies and friends were equally
amazed at the carriage and sayings of the wounded
warrior. " During his conversation," wrote a Southern
pro-slavery reporter to a Southern pro-slavery paper,
' no signs of weakness were exhibited. In the midst
of enemies whose home he had invaded; wounded and
a prisoner ; surrounded by a small army of officials and
a more desperate army of angry men ; with the gallows
staring him full in the face, Brown lay on the floor,
and, in reply to every question gave answers that
betokened the spirit that animated him. The language
of Governor Wise well expresses his boldness when he
said : ' He is the gamest man I ever saw.' I believe
he worthy Executive had hardly expected to see a
man so act in such a trying moment."

" Such a word as *insane*," said an eloquent speaker,
unconsciously uttering the opinion of the people of the
North, " is a mere trope with those who persist in using
it; and I have no doubt that many of them, in silence,
have already retracted their words. Read his admirable
answers to Mason and others. How they are dwarfed
and defeated by the contrast! On the one side, half-
brutish, half-timid questioning ; on the other, Truth,
clear as lightning, crashing into their obscene temples.
They are made to stand as Pilate or Gesler and the
Inquisition. Probably all the speeches of all the men

whom Massachusetts has sent to Congress for the last
few years do not match, for manly directness and force,
and for simple truth, the few casual remarks of John
Brown on the floor of the Harper's Ferry engine house
— that man whom you are about to send to the other
world; though not to represent *you* there. He is too
fair a specimen of a man to represent the like of us.
Who, then, were his constituents? Read his words,
understandingly, and you will find out. In his case
there is no idle eloquence. Truth is the inspirer and
earnestness the polisher of his sentences. He could
afford the loss of his Sharpe's rifles while he retained
the faculty of speech — a rifle of far straighter sight
and longer range."

It is seldom that men of views so opposite meet
together, either in the events themselves, or in their
subsequent views of those events, as met at Harper's
Ferry, when Captain John Brown and Senator Mason
— the abolitionist and the extraditionist — the slave
liberator in virtue of the higher law, and the slaveholding author of the fugitive slave law — gazed at
each other face to face; or when the Baltimore American and the hermit of Concord united to do honor to
the venerable invader of Virginia! The reader will
notice, also, how the two earnest men respected each
other; how Mason, the "fanatic," unlike his compromising compeer, was courteous to the old man, fearless
and almost reverential in his questionings.

THE CONVERSATION.

Senator Mason. Can you tell us, at least, who furnished money for
your expedition?

Capt. Brown. I furnished most of it myself. I cannot implicate
others. It is by my own folly that I have been taken. I could easily

have saved myself from it if I had exercised my own better judgment, rather than yielded to my feelings. I should have gone away, but I had thirty odd prisoners, whose wives and daughters were in tears for their safety, and I felt for them. Besides, I wanted to allay the fears of those who believed we came here to burn and kill. For this reason I allowed the train to pass the bridge, and gave them full liberty to pass on. I did it only to spare the feelings of those passengers and their families, and to allay the apprehension that you had got here in your vicinity a band of men who had no regard for life and property, nor any feeling of humanity.

Senator M. But you killed some people passing along the streets quietly.

Capt. B. Well, sir, if there was any thing of that kind done, it was without my knowledge. Your own citizens, who were my prisoners, will tell you that every possible means were taken to prevent it. I did not allow my men to fire, nor even to return a fire, when there was danger of killing those we regarded as innocent persons, if I could help it. They will tell you that we allowed ourselves to be fired at repeatedly, and did not return it.

A Bystander. That is not so. You killed an unarmed man at the corner of the house, over there, (at the water tank,) and another besides.

Capt. B. See here, my friend; it is useless to dispute or contradict the report of your own neighbors, who were my prisoners.

Senator M. If you would tell us who sent you here, — who provided the means, — that would be information of some value.

Capt. B. I will answer freely and faithfully about what concerns myself — I will answer any thing I can with honor, but not about others.

Mr. Vallandingham, (member of Congress from Ohio, who had just entered.) Mr. Brown, who sent you here?

Capt. B. No man sent me here; it was my own prompting and that of my Maker, or that of the devil whichever you please to ascribe it to. I acknowledge no master in human form.

Mr. V. Did you get up the expedition yourself?

Capt. B. I did.

Mr. V. Did you get up this document called a constitution?

Capt. B. I did. They are a constitution and ordinances of my own contriving and getting up.

Mr. V. How long have you been engaged in this business?

Capt. B. From the breaking out of the difficulties in Kansas. Four of my sons had gone there to settle, and they induced me to go. I did not go there to settle, but because of the difficulties.

Senator M. How many are engaged in this movement? I ask these questions for your own safety.

Capt. B. Any questions that I can honorably answer, I will; not otherwise. So far as I am myself concerned, I have told every thing truthfully. I value my word, sir.

Senator M. What was your object in coming?

Capt. B. We came to free the slaves, and only that.

A Young Man, (in the uniform of a volunteer company.) How many men in all had you?

Capt. B. I came to Virginia with eighteen men besides myself.

Volunteer. What in the world did you suppose you could do here in Virginia with that amount of men?

Capt. B. Young man, I don't wish to discuss that question here.

Volunteer. You could not do any thing.

Capt. B. Well, perhaps your ideas and mine, on military subjects, would differ materially.

Senator M. How do you justify your acts?

Capt. B. I think, my friend, you are guilty of a great wrong against God and humanity — I say it without wishing to be offensive — and it would be perfectly right for any one to interfere with you so far as to free those you wilfully and wickedly hold in bondage. I do not say this insultingly.

Senator M. I understand that.

Capt. B. I think I did right, and that others will do right who interfere with you, at any time, and all times. I hold that the golden rule — "Do unto others as you would that others should do unto you" — applies to all who would help others to gain their liberty.

Lieutenant Stuart. But you don't believe in the Bible?

Capt. B. Certainly I do.

Mr. V. Where did your men come from? Did some of them come from Ohio?

Capt. B. Some of them.

Mr. V. From the Western Reserve, of course! None came from Southern Ohio?

Capt. B. O, yes. I believe one came from Steubenville, down not far from Wheeling.

Mr. V. Have you been in Ohio this summer?

Capt. B. Yes, sir.

Mr. V. How lately?

Capt. B. I passed through to Pittsburg on my way, in June.

Mr. V. Were you at any county or state fair there?

Capt. B. I was not there since June.

Senator M. Did you consider this a military organization in this

paper? (Showing a copy of John Brown's constitution and ordinance.)
. have not yet read it.

Capt. B. I did in some measure. I wish you would give that paper your close attention.

Senator M. You considered yourself the commander-in-chief of this provisional military force?

Capt. B. I was chosen, agreeably to the ordinance of a certain document, commander-in-chief of that force.

Senator M. What wages did you offer?

Capt. B. None.

Lieut. S. "The wages of sin is death."

Capt. B. I would not have made such a remark to you, if you had been a prisoner and wounded, in my hands.

Bystander. Did you not promise a negro in Gettysburg twenty dollars a month?

Capt. B. I did not.

Bystander. He says you did.

Mr. V. Were you ever in Dayton, Ohio?

Capt. B. Yes, I must have been.

Mr. V. This summer?

Capt. B. No; a year or two since.

Senator M. Does this talking annoy you at all?

Capt. B. Not in the least.

Mr. V. Have you lived long in Ohio?

Capt. B. I went there in 1805. I lived in Summit County, which was then Trumbull County. My native place is York State.

Mr. V. Do you recollect a man in Ohio named Brown, a noted counterfeiter?

Capt. B. I do. I knew him from a boy. His father was Henry Brown, of Irish or Scotch descent. The family was very low.

Mr. V. Have you ever been in Portage County?

Capt. B. I was there in June last.

Mr. V. When in Cleveland, did you attend the Fugitive Slave Law Convention there?

Capt. B. No. I was there about the time of the sitting of the court to try the Oberlin rescuers. I spoke there, publicly, on that subject. I spoke on the fugitive slave law, and my own rescue. Of course, so far as I had any influence at all, I was disposed to justify the Oberlin people for rescuing the slave, because I have myself forcibly taken slaves from bondage. I was concerned in taking eleven slaves from Missouri to Canada, last winter. I think that I spoke in Cleveland before the Convention. I do not know that I had any conversation with any of the Oberlin rescuers. I was sick part of the time I was in Ohio. I had the ague. I was part of the time in Ashtabula county.

Mr. V. Did you see any thing of Joshua R. Giddings there?

Capt. B. I did meet him.

Mr. V. Did you converse with him?

Capt. B. I did. I would not tell you, of course, any thing that would implicate Mr. Giddings; but I certainly met with him, and had a conversation with him.

Mr. V. About that rescue case?

Capt. B. Yes, I did. I heard him express his opinion upon it very freely and frankly.

Mr. V. Justifying it?

Capt. B. Yes, sir. I do not compromise him, certainly, in saying that.

A Bystander. Did you go out to Kansas under the auspices of the Emigrant Aid Society?

Capt. B. No, sir; I went out under the auspices of John Brown, and nobody else.

Mr. V. Will you answer this? Did you talk to Giddings about your expedition here?

Capt. B. No, sir! I won't answer that, because a denial of it I would not make; and to make an affidavit of it, I should be a great dunce.

Mr. V. Have you had any correspondence with parties at the North on the subject of this movement?

Capt. B. I have had no correspondence.*

Bystander. Do you consider this a religious movement?

Capt. B. It is, in my opinion, the greatest service a man can render to his God.

Bystander. Do you consider yourself an instrument in the hands of Providence?

Capt. B. I do.

Bystander. Upon what principle do you justify your acts?

Capt. B. Upon the golden rule. I pity the poor in bondage that have none to help them. That is why I am here; it is not to gratify any personal animosity, or feeling of revenge, or vindictive spirit. It is my sympathy with the oppressed and the wronged, that are as good as you, and as precious in the sight of God.

Bystander. Certainly. But why take the slaves against their will?

Capt. B. I never did.

Bystander. You did in one instance, at least.

Stevens. (To the inquirer, interrupting Brown.) You are right, sir; in one case — (a groan from the wounded man) — in one case, I

---

* One report reads thus: the other omits the word "no."

know the negro wanted to go back. — (To Brown.)   Captain, the gentleman is right.

Bystander.   (To Stevens.)   Where did you come from?

Stevens.   I lived in Ashtabula County, Ohio.

Mr. B.   How recently did you leave Ashtabula County?

Stevens.   Some months ago.   I never resided there any length of time.   I have often been through there.

Mr. V.   How far did you live from Jefferson?

Capt. B.   (To Stevens.)   Be very cautious, Stevens, about an answer to that; it might commit some friend.   I would not answer it
at all.

Stevens, who had been groaning considerably, as if the exer-
tion necessary to conversation seriously affected him, seemed content
to abide by the captain's advice.   He turned partially over, with a
groan of pain, and was silent.

Mr. V.   (To Capt. Brown.)   Who are your advisers in this movement?

Capt. B.   I cannot answer that.   I have numerous sympathizers
throughout the entire North.

Mr. V.   In Northern Ohio?

Capt. B.   No more there than any where else — in all the Free States.

Mr. V.   But are you not personally acquainted in Southern Ohio?

Capt. B.   Not very much.

Mr. V.   (To Stevens.)   Were you at the convention last June?

Stevens.   I was.

Mr. V.   (To Capt. Brown.)   You made a speech there?

Capt. B.   I did, sir.

Bystander.   Did you ever live in Washington city?

Capt. B.   I did not.   I want you to understand, gentlemen, that I
respect the rights of the poorest and weakest of the colored people,
oppressed by the slave system, just as much as I do those of the most
wealthy and powerful.   That is the idea that has moved me, and that
alone.   We expected no reward except the satisfaction of endeavoring
to do for those in distress — the greatly oppressed — as we would be
done by.   The cry of distress, of the oppressed, is my reason, and the
only thing that prompted me to come here.

Bystander.   Why did you do it secretly?

Capt. B.   Because I thought that necessary to success, and for no
other reason.

Bystander.   And you think that honorable, do you?   Have you
read Gerrit Smith's last letter?

Capt. B.   What letter do you mean?

Bystander.   The New York *Herald* of yesterday, in speaking of this

24 *

affair, mentions a letter in which he says, "that it is folly to attempt to strike the shackles off the slave by the force of moral suasion or legal agitation," and predicts that the next movement made in the direction of negro emancipation will be an insurrection in the South.

Capt. B. I have not seen a New York *Herald* for some days past; but I presume, from your remarks about the gist of the letter, that I should concur with it. I agree with Mr. Smith, that moral suasion is hopeless. I don't think the people of the Slave States will ever consider the subject of slavery in its true light until some other argument is resorted to than moral suasion.

Mr. V. Did you expect a general rising of the slaves in case of your success?

Capt. B. No, sir; nor did I wish it. I expected to gather strength from time to time; then I could set them free.

Mr. V. Did you expect to hold possession here till then?

Capt. B. Well, probably I had quite a different idea. I do not know that I ought to reveal my plans. I am here a prisoner, and wounded, because I foolishly allowed myself to be so. You overrate your strength when you suppose I could have been taken if I had not allowed it. I was too tardy, after commencing the open attack, in delaying my movements through Monday night, and up to the time I was attacked by the government troops. It was all occasioned by my desire to spare the feelings of my prisoners and their families, and the community at large.

Mr. V. Did you not shoot a negro on the bridge, or did not some of your party?

Capt. B. I knew nothing of the shooting of the negro, (Heywood.)

Mr. V. What time did you commence your organization over in Canada?

Capt. B. It occurred about two years ago. If I remember right, it was, I think, in 1858.

Mr. V. Who was the secretary?

Capt. B. That I would not tell if I recollected; but I do not remember. I think the officers were elected in May, 1858. I may answer incorrectly, but not intentionally. My head is a little confused by wounds, and my memory of dates and such like is somewhat confused.

Dr. Biggs. Were you in the party at Dr. Kennedy's house?

Capt. B. I was the head of that party. I occupied the house to mature my plans. I would state here that I have not been in Baltimore to purchase percussion caps.

Dr. B. What was the number of men at Kennedy's?

Capt. B. I decline to answer that.

Dr. B. Who lanced that woman's neck on the hill?

Capt. B. I did. I have sometimes practised in surgery, when I thought it a matter of humanity or of necessity — when there was no one else to do it; but I have not studied surgery.

Dr. B. (To the persons around.) It was done very well and scientifically. These men have been very clever to the neighbors, I have been told, and we had no reason to suspect them, except that we could not understand their movements. They were represented as eight or nine persons; on Friday there were thirteen.

Capt. B. There were more than thirteen.

Questions were now put in by almost every one in the room.

Q. Where did you get arms to obtain possession of the armory?

Capt. B. I bought them.

Q. In what state?

Capt. B. That I would not state.

Q. How many guns?

Capt. B. Two hundred Sharpe's rifles, and two hundred revolvers — what is called the Massachusetts Arms Company's revolvers — a little under the navy size.

Q. Why did you not take that swivel you left in the house?

Capt. B. I had no occasion for it. It was given to me a year or two ago.

A Reporter. I do not wish to annoy you; but if you have any hing else you would like to say, I will report it.

Capt. B. I do not wish to converse any more; I have nothing to ay. I will only remark to these reporting gentlemen, that I claim to e here in carrying out a measure I believe to be perfectly justifiable, nd not to act the part of an incendiary or ruffian; but, on the conrary, to aid those suffering under a great wrong. I wish to say, furhermore, that you had better — all you people of the South — preare yourselves for a settlement of this question. It must come up for ettlement sooner than you are prepared for it, and the sooner you ommence that preparation the better for you. You may dispose of : ie very easily. I am nearly disposed of now; but this question is : till to be settled — this negro question, I mean. The end of that is) ot yet. These wounds were inflicted upon me, — both the sabre cut ι n my head, and the bayonet stabs in the different parts of my body, · - some minutes after I had ceased fighting, and had consented to sur·) ender for the benefit of others, and not for my own benefit.

(Several persons vehemently denied this statement. Without no- ι cing the interruption, the old man continued:)

I believe the Major here (pointing to Lieut. Stuart) would not have been alive but for me. I might have killed him just as easy as I could kill a mosquito, when he came in ; but I supposed that he came in only to receive our surrender. There had been long and loud calls of surrender from us, — as loud as men could yell, — but in the confusion and excitement I suppose we were not heard. I do not believe the major, or any one else, wanted to butcher us after we had surrendered.

An officer present here stated that special orders had been given to the marines not to shoot any body ; but when they were fired upon by Brown's men, and one of them had been killed, and another wounded, they were obliged to return the compliment.

Captain Brown insisted, with some warmth, that the marines fired first.

An Officer. Why did you not surrender before the attack ?   .

Capt. B. I did not think it was my duty or interest to do so. We assured our prisoners that we did not wish to harm them, and that they should be set at liberty. I exercised my best judgment, not believing the people would wantonly sacrifice their own fellow-citizens. When we offered to let them go upon condition of being allowed to change our position about a quarter of a mile, the prisoners agreed by vote among themselves to pass across the bridge with us. We wanted them only as a sort of guarantee for our own safety — that we should not be fired into. We took them, in the first place, as hostages, and to keep them from doing any harm. We did kill some men when defending ourselves ; but I saw no one fire except directly in self-defence. Our orders were strict not to harm any one not in arms against us.

Q. Well, Brown, suppose you had every nigger in the United States, what would you do with them?   `

Capt. B. (In a loud tone, and with emphasis.) Set them free, sir !

Q. Your intention was to carry them off and free them ?

Capt. B. Not at all.

Bystander. To set them free would sacrifice the life of every man in this community.

Capt. B. I do not think so.   ,

Bystander. I know it. I think you are fanatical.

Capt. B. And I think you are fanatical. " Whom the gods would destroy, they first make mad ; " and you are mad.

Q. Was your only object to free the negroes?

Capt. B. Absolutely our only object.

Bystander. But you went and took Col. Washington's silver and watch.

Capt B. O, yes ; we intended freely to have appropriated the propcrty of slaveholders, to carry out our object. It was for that, and only that; and with no design to enrich ourselves with any plunder whatever.

Q. Did you know Sherrod in Kansas? I understand you killed him.

Capt. B. I killed no man except in fair fight. I fought at Black Jack, and at Osawatomie; and if I killed any body, it was at one of those places.

During this conversation, the wounded Liberators, we are told by pro-slavery writers, "lay stretched on miserable shake-downs." John Brown's "long gray hair was matted and tangled, and his hands and clothes all smooched and smeared with blood, and begrimed with dirt—the effect of continued exposure to the smoke of powder. His manner and conversation were courteous and affable, and he appeared to make a favorable impression upon his auditory."

Mr. Vallandingham, not ashamed of having attempted to extort political capital from the lips of a dying man—or having inquired if he knew one Brown, a noted counterfeiter, or having striven to bring dishonor on the people of Ohio, in the eyes of the South —returned to his native state, and, unconscious of the immortality of infamy he had gained, publicly and in writing declared that "I have only to regret now that I did not pursue the matter further, asking more questions, and making them more specific." Of the old hero he said :

'It is in vain to underrate either the man or the conspiracy. Cap. John Brown is as brave and resolute a man as ever headed an insurrection, and, in a good cause, and with a sufficient force, would have been a consummate partisan commander. He has coolness, daring, persistency, the stoic faith and patience, and a firmness of will and purpose unconquerable. He is the farthest possible remove from the ordinary ruffian, fanatic, or madman. Certainly it was one of the best planned and best executed conspiracies that ever failed."

XII.

Lodged in Jail.

AFTER a public exhibition of more than thirty hours, as they lay unattended and bloody on the floor of the guard house, interrogated by unmanly politicians and insulted by the brutal mob, the surviving Liberators, on Wednesday evening, October 19, were conveyed to the jail of Charlestown, under an escort of marines.

A United States Marshal from Ohio, after the political inquisitors had finished with the whites, endeavored to extort from the negroes, Copeland and Green, confessions to criminate the friends of freedom in his native State. He succeeded in procuring no confession whatever, but only a few brief answers to leading questions, which served to show at once his political purpose and his depravity of heart.

A Virginia journalist thus describes the journey to Charlestown :

" On Wednesday evening they were conveyed to the jail of Jefferson County, under an escort of marines. Stevens and Brown had to be taken in a wagon, but the negro Green and Coppoc, being unhurt, walked between a file of soldiers, followed by hundreds of excited men, exclaiming, 'Lynch them;' but Governor Wise, who was standing on the platform of the cars, said, 'O, it would be cowardly to do so

low;' and the crowd fell back, and the prisoners were safely placed
on the train. Stevens was placed in the bottom of the car, being
unable to sit up. Brown was propped up on a seat with pillows, and
Coppoc and Green seated in the middle of them; the former was evi-
lently much frightened, but looked calm, while the latter was the very
impersonation of fear. His nerves were twitching, his eyes wild and
almost bursting from their sockets, his whole manner indicating the
dreadful apprehensions that filled his mind. This fellow was a member of Congress, under the Provisional Government, had been very
daring while guarding the arsenal, and very impudent while in the
engine house, but when the marines entered it, he jumped back
among the imprisoned, and cried out that he was a prisoner; but Mr.
Washington thrust him forward, and informed the besiegers that he
was one of the guerillas, upon which a stab was made at him, but
missed him, and he still lives to expiate his guilt on the gallows."

These statements, with regard to the negroes, are in
all probability false. The Virginians, who had not
dared to fight them armed, mustered courage to insult
them when manacled.

On the same evening there was another panic at
Harper's Ferry: it was Cook, this time, who was murdering all the people at Sandy Hook! The marines
hastened out to protect the citizens, but found neither
Cook nor a broil there. When they returned to Harper's Ferry, the Virginia militia, who had been afraid
to follow, now valiantly offered to go out to defend
their fellow-citizens.

But the limits of this volume will not permit me to
recount how often and pusillanimously the Virginians
acted. From the arrest of the Liberators till the death
of their Chief, the shivering chivalry of the once gallant State of Virginia suffered from a chronic but
ludicrously painful fright.   ·

Governor Wise and Mr. Hunter accompanied the
prisoners to Charlestown, where they were lodged in
jail, and placed under the charge of Capt. John Avis.
Of the jail and jailer a trust-worthy writer says:

"Brown is as comfortably situated as any man can be in a jail. He has a pleasant room, which is shared by Stevens, whose recovery remains doubtful. He has opportunities of occupying himself by writing and reading. His jailer, Avis, was of the party who assisted in capturing him. Brown says, that Avis is one of the bravest men he ever saw, and that his treatment is precisely what he should expect from so brave a fellow. Avis is a just and humane man. He does all for his prisoners that his duty allows him to. I think he has a sincere respect for Brown's undaunted fortitude and fearlessness. Brown is permitted to receive such visitors as he desires to see. He states that he welcomes every one, and that he is preaching, even in jail, with great effect, upon the enormities of Slavery, and with arguments which every body fails to answer. His wounds, excepting one cut on the back of the head, have all now healed, without suppuration, and the scars are scarcely visible. He attributes his very rapid recovery to his strict abstemious habits through life. He is really a man of imposing appearance, and neither his tattered garments, the rents in which were caused by sword cuts, nor his scarred face, can detract from the manliness of his mien. He is always composed, and every trace of disquietude has left him."

On the following day — Thursday, October 20 — the body of Kagi was taken from the river, and the other corpses were buried in a large pit. The body of Watson Brown, however, was crammed into a box and carried off for medical dissection. The corpses of the negroes were horribly mutilated by the brutal populace. A. D. 1859 — VA., U. S. A.!

Book Fourth.

AMONG THE PHILISTINES

25

8. And he smote them hip and thigh, with great slaughter. (Chapter xv.)

21. But the Philistines took him and brought him down to Gaza.

23. Then the lords of the Philistines gathered them together for to offer a great sacrifice unto Dagon, their god, and to rejoice : for they said, Our god hath delivered Samson our enemy into our hand.

24. And when the people saw him, they praised their god : for they said, Our god hath delivered into our hands our enemy, and the destroyer of our country, which slew many of us.

30. The dead which he slew at his death were more than they which he slew in his life. — *Book of Judges*, Chapter xvi.

I.

The Preliminary Examination.

THE prisoners were formally committed to jail on the
20th of October, by a Justice of the Peace of
Charlestown, on the oaths of Henry A. Wise and two
others, " for feloniously conspiring with each other, and
other persons unknown, to make an abolition insurrection and open war against the Commonwealth of Virginia," and for the additional crimes of murder and
" conspiring with slaves to rebel and to make insurrection." On the same day a warrant was issued to the
Sheriff, commanding him to summon eight Justices of
the Peace to hold a Preliminary Court of Examination
on the 25th of October.

On the day thus appointed the Preliminary Court
assembled; a person named Colonel Davenport presiding. At half past ten o'clock in the forenoon, the
prisoners were conducted from the jail under a guard
of eighty armed men. Another military force was stationed around " the Court House, which was bristling
with bayonets on all sides."

John Brown and Coppie were manacled together.
" The prisoners, as brought into Court," writes a pro-

291)

slavery eye witness, "presented a pitiable sight, *Brown and Stevens being unable to stand without assistance.* Brown had three sword cuts in his body, and one sabre cut over the head. Stevens had three balls in his head and two in his breast, and one in his arm. He was also cut on the forehead with a rifle bullet, which glanced off, leaving a bad wound. Brown seemed weak and haggard, with eyes swollen from the effects of wounds on the head. Stevens seemed less injured than Brown, but looked haggard and depressed."

Never before, in our Christian country, or in any other civilized land, were men, thus suffering and disabled, dragged from their beds of sickness to a Court of Justice, to be tried for a capital offence. Judge Jeffreys, of England, never fully equalled this atrocity; it needed, for its perpetration, men brutalized by the influence of American slavery.

Charles B. Harding, attorney for the County of Jefferson, and Andrew Hunter, counsel for the State, appeared for the prosecution. The Sheriff read the commitment of the prisoners, and the Prosecuting Attorney asked the Court that counsel might be assigned them. The Presiding Magistrate then inquired if the prisoners had counsel.

John Brown replied:

FIRST SPEECH IN COURT.

"Virginians: I did not ask for any quarter at the time I was taken. I did not ask to have my life spared. The Governor of the State of Virginia tendered me his assurance that I should have a fair trial; but under no circumstances whatever, will I be able to attend to my trial. If you seek my blood, you can have it at any moment without this mockery of a trial.

"I have had no counsel. I have not been able to advise with any one. I know nothing about the feelings of my fellow-prisoners, and am utterly unable to attend in any way to my own defence. My memory don't serve me. My health is insufficient, although improving.

: If a fair trial is to be allowed us, there are mitigating circumstances, that I would urge in our favor. But, if we are to be forced with a mere form — a trial for execution — you might spare yourselves that trouble. I am ready for my fate. I do not ask a trial. I beg for no mockery of a trial — no insult — nothing but that which conscience gives or cowardice would drive you to practise.

"I ask again to be excused from the mockery of a trial. I do not know what the special design of this examination is. I do not know what is to be the benefit of it to the Commonwealth. I have now little further to ask, other than that I may be not foolishly insulted, only as cowardly barbarians insult those who fall into their power."

Without paying the slightest attention to this brave speech, calmly delivered in the midst of infuriated enemies, the Court assigned Charles J. Faulkner and Lawson Botts, both Virginians and pro-slavery men, as counsel for the defendants. Mr. Faulkner, after consultation with the prisoners, desired to decline the appointment, — because he doubted the authority of the Court to order him to defend them; because John Brown had declared that such a defence would be a mockery; and because, having been at the place of action, and having heard all the admissions of the defendants, it would be improper and inexpedient for him to be their counsel. But if the Court peremptorily ordered him, and the prisoners consented, he would see that full justice was done them. Mr. Botts accepted.

"*Mr. Harding* then asked John Brown if he was willing to accept these gentlemen as counsel.

John Brown replied: "I wish to say that I have sent for counsel. I did apply, through the advice of some persons here, to some persons whose names I do not now recollect, to act as counsel for me; and I have sent for other counsel, who have not had time to reach here, and have had no possible opportunity to see me. I wish for counsel, if I am to have a trial; but if I am to have nothing but the mockery of a

25 *

trial, as I said, I do not care any thing about counsel. It is unnecessary to trouble any gentleman with that duty."

Mr. Harding. "You are to have a fair trial."

John Brown. "There were certain men — I think Mr. Botts was one of them — who declined acting as counsel, but I am not positive about it; I cannot remember whether he was one, because I have heard so many names. I am a stranger here, and do not know the disposition or character of the gentlemen named. I have applied for counsel of my own, and doubtless could have them, if I am not, as I have said before, to be hurried to execution before they can reach here. But if that is the disposition that is to be made of me, all this trouble and expense can be saved."

Mr. Harding. "The question is, do you desire the aid of Messrs. Faulkner and Botts as your counsel? Please to answer yes or no."

John Brown. "I cannot regard this as an examination under any circumstances. I would prefer that they should exercise their own pleasure. I feel it as a matter of little account to me. If they had designed to assist me as counsel, I should have wanted an opportunity to consult with them at my leisure."

Mr. Harding. "Stevens, are you willing those gentlemen should act as your counsel?"

Stevens. "I am willing that gentleman shall," (pointing to Mr. Botts.)

Mr. Harding. "Do you object to Faulkner?"

Stevens. "No; I am willing to take both."

Mr. Harding then addressed each of the other prisoners separately, and each stated his willingness to be defended by the counsel named.

The Court then issued peremptory orders that the press should not publish detailed testimony, as it would render the getting of a jury before the Circuit Court impossible." *

Eight witnesses were then examined, who testified to the arrest of citizens, the occupation of the armory, the fight, the casualties of the conflict, and the self-avowed object of the liberators. Kitzmillar admitted that Stevens was fired at and shot while under a flag of truce, with which, accompanied by the witness, and at his request, he had left the armory, to permit him to try to "accommodate matters" for the safety of the citizens

---

* Telegraphic report of the Associated Press.

detained there; that Brown, while the Virginia prisoners were in his power, treated them with great courtesy and respect; and repeatedly stated that his only object was to liberate the negroes, and that, to accomplish it, he was willing to fight the pro-slavery men. The witnesses who were prisoners in the Armory also testified that during the conflict they were requested by the Liberators to keep themselves out of the fire of the marines. One thought that Coppic shot Beckman, and Brown the marine.

At one stage of the proceedings, Stevens, weak from his wounds, appeared to-be fainting, and a mattress was procured for him, on which he reposed during the remainder of the examination. What a scene for an American Court!

The prisoners were of course remanded to the Circuit Court for trial.

The telegraph, although entirely managed by the partisans of Slavery at this time, involuntarily told truths disgraceful to Virginia, and illustrative of the effect of her iniquitous institution on the character of her citizens of every rank, as well as of the danger that this criminal tenacity to Human Slavery creates to the stability of Southern society. Two paragraphs will suffice to sustain me.

'There is an evident intention to hurry the trial through, and execute the prisoners as soon as possible— FEARING *attempts to rescue them.* It s rumored that Brown is desirous of making a full statement of his motives and intentions through the press, but the Court has refused all access to reporters — FEARING *that he may put forth something calculated to influence the public mind, and to have a bad effect on the slaves.*"

The reason given for hurrying the trial is, that the people of the whole country are kept in a state of excitement, and a large armed force is required to prevent attempts at rescue."

II.

Judicial Alacrity.

HARDLY had the Preliminary Court adjourned, ere the Circuit Court assembled. At two o'clock the Grand Jury were called, and charged by Judge Richard Parker. By way of a contrast to the subsequent proceeding, the plausible yet Jesuitical address of the Judge, which promises and urges a fair trial, but, at the same time, so clearly indicates the spirit of Virginia, is deserving of a record here.

CHARGE TO THE GRAND JURY.

GENTLEMEN OF THE JURY: In the state of excitement into which our whole community has been thrown by the recent occurrences in this county, I feel that the charge which I usually deliver to a grand jury would be entirely out of place. These occurrences cannot but force themselves upon your attention. They must necessarily occupy a considerable portion of that time which you will devote to your public duties as a Grand Jury. However guilty the unfortunate men who are now in the hands of justice may prove to be, still they cannot be called upon to answer to the offended laws of our Commonwealth for any of the multifarious crimes with which they are charged, until a Grand Jury, after "dignified" inquiry, shall decide that for these offences they be put upon their trial. *I will not permit myself to give expression to any of those feelings which at once spring up in every breast when reflecting upon the enormity of the guilt in which those are involved who invade by force a peaceful, unsuspecting portion of our common coun-*

(296)

ry, raise the standard of insurrection amongst us, and shoot down without mercy Virginia citizens defending Virginia soil against their invasion. . must remember, gentlemen, that, as a minister of justice, bound to execute our laws faithfully, and in the very spirit of Justice herself, I must, as to every one accused of crime, hold, as the law holds, that he is innocent until he shall be proved guilty by an honest, an independent, and an impartial jury of his countrymen. And what is obligatory upon me is equally binding upon you, and upon every one who may be connected with the prosecution and trial of these offenders. In these cases, as in all others, you will be controlled by that oath which each of you has taken, and in which you have solemnly sworn that you will diligently inquire into all offences which may be brought to your knowledge, and that "you will present no one through ill-will," as well as "that you will leave no one unpresented through fear or favor, but in all your presentments you shall present the truth, the whole truth, and nothing but the truth." Do but this, gentlemen, and you will have fulfilled your whole duty. Go beyond this, and, in place of that diligent inquiry and calm investigation which you have sworn to make, act upon prejudice or from excitement of passion, and you will have done a wrong to that law in whose service you are engaged. As I before said, these men are now in the hands of justice. *They are to have a fair and an impartial trial.* We owe it to the cause of justice, as well a to our own characters, that such a trial should be afforded them. If guilty, they will be sure to pay the extreme penalty of their guilt, and the example of punishment, when thus inflicted by virtue of law, will be beyond all comparison more efficacious for our future protection than any torture to which mere passion could subject them. Whether, then, we be in public or private position, let each one of us remember that, as the law has charge of these alleged offenders, the law alone, through its recognized agents, must deal with them to the last. *It can tolerate no interference by others with duties it has assumed to itself.* If true to herself, — and true she will be, — our Commonwealth, through her courts of justice, will be as ready to punish the offence of such interference as she is to punish these grave and serious offences with which she is now about to deal — in case these offences be proved by legal testimony to have been perpetrated. Let us all, gentlemen, bear this in mind, and in patience await the result — confident that that result will be whatever strict and impartial justice shall determine to be necessary and proper. It would seem, gentlemen, — and yet I speak from no evidence, but upon vague rumors which have reached me, — that these men who have thrown themselves upon us confidently expected to be joined by our slaves and free negroes, and unfurled the banner of insurrection,

and invited this class of our citizens to rally under it.   And yet, I am
told, they are unable to obtain a single recruit.*

The Preliminary Court reported the result of their
examination, and the Grand Jury at once retired with
the witnesses. At five o'clock they returned, and asked
to be discharged for the day. They reassembled at ten
o'clock on the following forenoon, Wednesday, and, at
twelve o'clock, reported " a true bill " against each of
the prisoners : *First,* For conspiring with negroes to
produce insurrection ; *second,* For treason in the Commonwealth, and, *third,* For murder. The Grand Jury
was then discharged.

This is the indictment of the Grand Jury :

THE INDICTMENT.

Judicial Circuit of Virginia, Jefferson County, to wit. — The Jurors of the Commonwealth of Virginia, in and for the body of the County of Jefferson, duly impanelled,
and attending upon the Circuit Court of said county, upon their oaths do present that
John Brown, Aaron C. Stephens, alias Aaron D. Stephens and Edwin Coppic, white
men, and Shields Green and John Copeland, free negroes, together with divers other
evil-minded and traitorous persons to the Jurors unknown, not having the fear of God
before their eyes, but being moved and seduced by the false and malignant counsel of
other evil and traitorous persons, and the instigations of the devil, did, severally, on the
sixteenth, seventeenth, and eighteenth days of the month of October, in the year of our
Lord eighteen hundred and fifty-nine, and on divers other days before and after that
time, within the Commonwealth of Virginia, and the County of Jefferson aforesaid, and
within the jurisdiction of this Court, with other confederates to the Jurors unknown,
feloniously and traitorously make rebellion and levy war against the said Commonwealth
of Virginia, and to effect, carry out, and fulfil their said wicked and treasonable ends
and purposes did, then and there, as a band of organized soldiers, attack, seize, and hold
a certain part and place within the county and State aforesaid, and within the jurisdiction aforesaid, known and called by the name of Harper's Ferry, and then and there
did forcibly capture, make prisoners of, and detain divers good and loyal citizens of said
Commonwealth, to wit: Lewis W. Washington, John M. Allstadt, Archibald M. Kitzmiller, Benjamin J. Mills, John E. P. Dangerfield, Armistead Ball, John Donoho, and
did then and there slay and murder, by shooting with firearms, called Sharpe's rifles,
divers good and loyal citizens of said Commonwealth, to wit: Thomas Boerly, George
W. Turner, Fontaine Beckham, together with Luke Quinn, a soldier of the United States,
and Hayward Sheppard, a free negro, and did then and there, in manner aforesaid, wound
divers other good and loyal citizens of said Commonwealth, and did then and there feloniously and traitorously establish and set up, without authority of the Legislature of the
Commonwealth of Virginia, a government, separate from, and hostile to, the existing
Government of said Commonwealth; and did then and there hold and exercise divers
offices under said usurped Government, to wit: the said John Brown as Commander-in
Chief of the military forces, the said Aaron C. Stephens alias Aaron D. Stephens, as Captain; the said Edwin Coppic, as Lieutenant, and the said Shields Green and John Cope-

---

* It is true that the slaves did not join John Brown. But why? Because they had not time
to know his design, and to act, ere their heroic liberators were either killed or imprisoned. But
one negro, I know, — a slave of Washington, — whom Governor Wise pretended had probably
been killed by Captain Cook in endeavoring to return home, was shot in the river *as he was
fighting for freedom.* I know this fact from one of John Brown's men who saw him. I have
positive knowledge, also, of sixteen slaves who succeeded in escaping from Harper's Ferry.

land as soldiers; and did then and there require and compel obedience to said officers; and then and there did hold and profess allegiance and fidelity to said usurped Government; and under color of the usurped authority aforesaid, did then and there resist forcibly, and with warlike arms, the execution of the laws of the Commonwealth of Virginia, and with firearms did wound and maim divers other good and loyal citizens of said Commonwealth, to the Jurors unknown, when attempting, with lawful authority, to uphold and maintain said Constitution and laws of the Commonwealth of Virginia, and for the purpose, end, and aim of overthrowing and abolishing the Constitution and laws of said Commonwealth, and establishing, in the place thereof, another and different government, and constitution and laws hostile thereto, did then and there feloniously and traitorously, and in military array, join in open battle and deadly warfare with the civil officers and soldiers in the lawful service of the said Commonwealth of Virginia, and did then and there shoot and discharge divers guns and pistols, charged with gunpowder and leaden bullets, against and upon divers parties of the militia and volunteers embodied and acting under the command of Colonel Robert W. Baylor, and of Colonel John Thomas Gibson, and other officers of said Commonwealth, with lawful authority to quell and subdue the said John Brown, Aaron C. Stephens, alias Aaron D. Stephens, Edwin Coppic, Shields Green, and John Copeland, and other rebels and traitors assembled, organized, and acting with them, as aforesaid, to the evil example of all others in like case offending, and against the peace and dignity of the Commonwealth.

Second Count. — And the Jurors aforesaid, upon their oaths aforesaid, do further present that the said John Brown, Aaron C. Stephens, alias Aaron D. Stephens, Edwin Coppic, Shields Green, and John Copeland, severally, on the sixteenth, seventeenth, and eighteenth days of October, in the year of our Lord eighteen hundred and fifty-nine, in the said County of Jefferson, and Commonwealth of Virginia, and within the jurisdiction of this Court, not having the fear of God before their eyes, but moved and seduced by the false and malignant counsels of others, and the instigations of the devil, did each severally, maliciously, and feloniously conspire with each other, and with a certain John E. Cook, John Kagi, Charles Tidd, and others to the Jurors unknown, to induce certain slaves, to wit, Jim, Sam, Mason, and Catesby, ... the slaves and property of Lewis W. Washington, and Henry, Levi, Ben, Jerry, Phil, George, and Bill, the slaves and property of John H. Allstadt, and other slaves to the Jurors unknown, to rebel and make insurrection against their masters and owners, and against the Government and the Constitution and laws of the Commonwealth of Virginia: and then and there did maliciously and feloniously advise said slaves, and other slaves to the Jurors unknown, to rebel and make insurrection against their masters and owners, and against the Government, the Constitution and laws of the Commonwealth of Virginia, to the evil example of all others in like cases offending, and against the peace and dignity of the Commonwealth.

Third Count. — And the Jurors aforesaid, upon their oaths aforesaid, further present that the said John Brown, Aaron C. Stephens, alias Aaron D. Stephens, Edwin Coppic, Shields Green, and John Copeland, severally, on the sixteenth, seventeenth, and eighteenth days of October, in the year of our Lord one thousand eight hundred and fifty-nine, in the County of Jefferson and the Commonwealth of Virginia aforesaid, and within the jurisdiction aforesaid, in and upon the bodies of Thomas Boerly, George W. Turner, Fontaine Beckham, Luke Quinn, white persons, and Hayward Sheppard, a free negro, in the peace of the Commonwealth then and there being, feloniously, wilfully, and of their malice aforethought, did make an assault, and with firearms called harpe's rifles, and other deadly weapons to the Jurors unknown, then and there, charged with gunpowder and leaden bullets, did then and there feloniously, wilfully, and of their malice aforethought, shoot and discharge the same against the bodies sev erally and respectively of the said Thomas Boerly, George W. Turner, Fontaine Beckham, Luke Quinn, and Hayward Sheppard; and that the said John Brown, Aaron C. Stephens, alias Aaron D. Stephens, Edwin Coppic, Shields Green, and John Copeland, with the leaden bullets aforesaid, out of the firearms called Sharpe's rifles, aforesaid, shot and discharged as aforesaid, and with the other deadly weapons to the jurors unknown, as aforesaid, then and there feloniously, wilfully, and of their malice aforethought did strike, penetrate and wound the said Thomas Boerly, George W. Turner, Fontaine Beckham, Luke Quinn, Hayward Sheppard, each severally; to wit: the said Thomas Boerly in and upon the left side; the said George W. Turner in and upon the left shoulder; the said Fontaine Beckham in and upon the right breast; the said Luke Quinn in and upon the abdomen, and the said Hayward Sheppard in and upon the back and side, giving to the said Thomas Boerly, George W. Turner, Fontaine Beckham, Luke Quinn. Hayward Sheppard, then and there with the leaden bullets, so as aforesaid shot and discharged by them, severally and respectively out of the Sharpe's rifles aforesaid, and with the other deadly weapons to the Jurors unknown, as aforesaid, each one mortal wound, of which said mortal wounds they the said Thomas Boerly, George W. Turner, Fontaine Beckham, Luke Quinn, and Hayward Sheppard each died; and so the Jurors aforesaid, upon their oaths aforesaid, do say that the said John Brown, Aaron C. Stephens, alias Aaron D. Stephens, Edwin Coppic, Shields Green, and John Copland, then and there, them the said Thomas Boerly, George W. Turner, Fontaine Beckham, Luke Quinn, and Hayward Sheppard, in the manner aforesaid, and by the means aforesaid, feloniously, wilfully, and of their, and each of their malice aforethought, did kill and murder, against the peace and dignity of the Commonwealth.

Fourth Count. — And the Jurors aforesaid, upon their oaths aforesaid, further present that the said John Brown, Aaron C. Stephens, alias Aaron D. Stephens, and Edwin Coppic, and Shields Green, each severally on the seventeenth day of October, in the year of our Lord eighteen hundred and fifty-nine, in the County of Jefferson and Commonwealth of Virginia aforesaid, and within the jurisdiction of this Court, in and upon the bodies of certain Thomas Boerly, George W. Turner, and Fontaine Beckham, in the peace of the Commonwealth, then and there being feloniously, wilfully, and of their malice aforethought, did make an assault, and with guns called Sharpe's rifles, then and there charged with gunpowder and leaden bullets, did then and there feloniously, wilfully, and each of their malice aforethought, shoot and discharge the same against the bodies of the said Thomas Boerly, George W. Turner, and Fontaine Beckham, and that the said John Brown, Aaron C. Stephens, alias Aaron D. Stephens, Edward Coppic, and Shields Green, with leaden bullets aforesaid, shot out of the Sharpe's rifles aforesaid, then and there, feloniously, wilfully, and of their malice aforethought, did strike, penetrate, and wound the said Thomas Boerly, George W. Turner, and Fontaine Beckham, each severally, viz.: The said Thomas Boerly in and upon the left side; the said George W. Turner in and upon the left shoulder and breast, and the said Fontaine Beckham in and upon the right breast, giving to the said Thomas Boerly, George W. Turner, and Fontaine Beckham, then and there, with leaden bullets aforesaid, shot by them severally out of Sharpe's rifles aforesaid, each one mortal wound, of which said mortal wounds they the said Thomas Boerly, George W. Turner, and Fontaine Beckham then and there died; and that the said John Copland, then and there, feloniously, wilfully, and of his malice aforethought, was present, aiding, helping, abetting, comforting and assisting the said John Brown, Aaron C. Stephens, alias Aaron D. Stephens, Edwin Coppic, and Shields Green in the felony and murder aforesaid, in manner aforesaid to commit. And so the Jurors aforesaid, upon their oaths, do say that the said John Brown, Aaron C. Stephens, alias Aaron D. Stephens, Edwin Coppic, Shields Green, and John Copland, then and there them, the said Thomas Boerly, George W. Turner, and Fontaine Beckham, in the manner aforesaid, and by the means aforesaid, feloniously, wilfully, and of their and each of their malice aforethought, did kill and murder, against the peace and dignity of the Commonwealth of Virginia.

Lewis W. Washington, John H. Allstadt, John E. P. Dangerfield, Alexander Kelly, Emanuel Spangler, Armstead M. Ball, Joseph A. Brua, William Johnson, Lewis P. Starry, Archibald H. Kitzmiller, were sworn in open Court this 26th day of October, 1859, to give evidence to the Grand Jury upon this bill of indictment.

Teste: ROBERT T. BROWN, Clerk.

A true copy of said indictment.
Teste: ROBERT T. BROWN,
    Clerk of the Circuit Court of Jefferson County, in the State of Virginia.

Which bill of indictment the Grand Jury returned this 26th day of October.
A true bill.   THOMAS RUTHERFORD, Foreman.
October 26, 1859.

Before the indictment was read, as Mr. Faulkner had gone home, the Court requested a Mr. Green, a Virginian, to act as assistant counsel for the defendants. It was understood that all the prisoners were willing that this arrangement should be made.

APPEAL FOR A DECENT DELAY.

John Brown then rose and said :

I do not intend to detain the court, but barely wish to say, as I have been promised a fair trial, that I am not now in circumstances that enable me to attend a trial, owing to the state of my health. I have a severe wound in the back, or rather in one kidney, which enfeebles me very much. But I am doing well, and I only ask for a very short delay of my trial, and I think I may get able to listen to it; and I merely ask this, that, as the saying is, "the devil may have his due" — no more. I wish to say, further, that my hearing is impaired, and rendered indistinct, in consequence of wounds I have about my head. I cannot hear distinctly at all; I could not hear what the court has said this morning. I would be glad to hear what is said on my trial, and am now doing better than I could expect to be under the circumstances. A very short delay would be all I would ask. I do not presume to ask more than a very short delay, so that I may in some degree recover, and be able at least to listen to my trial, and hear what questions are asked of the citizens, and what their answers are. If that could be allowed me, I should be very much obliged.

Mr. Hunter said that the request was rather premature. The arraignment should be made, and this question could then be considered.

The Court ordered the indictment to be read, so that the prisoner could plead guilty or not guilty, and it would then consider Mr. Brown's request.

The indictment was now read, and each of the prisoners pleaded Not Guilty, and demanded to have separate trials. One incident of this scene is so revolting, that I must record it in the language of the enemies of the prisoners:

' The prisoners were brought into court, accompanied by a body of armed men. Cannon were stationed in front of the court house, and an armed guard were patrolling round the jail. Brown looked something better, and his eye was not so much swollen. Stevens had to be supported, and reclined on a mattress on the floor of the court room — *evidently unable to sit.* He has the appearance of a dying man, *breathing with great difficulty.* The prisoners were compelled to stand during the indictment, but it was with difficulty, *Stevens being held upright by two bailiffs.*"

As soon as the prisoners had responded to the arraignment, Mr. Hunter rose and said, "The State

26

elects to try John Brown first." A discussion and
decision, fit accompaniments to the scene above described, then ensued; which are thus reported by the
partisans of the State :

Mr. Botts said, I am instructed by Brown to say that he is mentally
and physically unable to proceed with his trial at this time. He has
heard to-day that counsel of his own choice will be here, whom he
will, of course, prefer. He only asks for a delay of two or three days.
It seems to be but a reasonable request, and I hope the Court will
grant it.

Mr. Hunter said, he did not think it the duty of the prosecutor for
the Commonwealth, or for one occupying the position, to oppose any
thing that justice required, nor to object to any thing that involved a
simple consideration of humanity, where it could be properly allowed;
yet, in regard to this proposition to delay the trial of John Brown two
or three days, they deemed it their duty that the Court, before deter-
mining matters, should be put in possession of facts and circumstances,
judicially, that they were aware of in the line of their duties as prosecutors. His own opinion was, that it was not proper to delay the
trial of this prisoner a single day, and that there was no necessity for
it. He alluded in general terms to the condition of things that surrounded them. They were such as rendered it dangerous to delay, *to
say nothing of the exceeding pressure upon the physical resources of the
community*, growing out of circumstances connected with affairs for
which the prisoners were to be tried. He said our laws, in making
provisions for allowing, in the discretion of the Court, briefer time than
usual, in cases of conviction, for such offenders, between the condemnation and execution, evidently indicates, indirectly, the necessity of
acting promptly and decisively, though always justly, in proceedings
of this kind. In reference to Brown's physical condition, he asked
the Court not to receive the unimportant statements of the prisoners
as sufficient ground for delay, but that the jailer and physicians be
examined. As to expecting counsel from abroad, he said that no im-
pediment had been thrown in the way of the prisoners' procuring such
counsel as they desired, but, on the contrary, every facility had been
afforded; able and intelligent counsel had been assigned them here, and
he apprehended that there was little reason to expect the attendance
of those gentlemen from the North who had been written for. *There
was also a public duty resting upon them to avoid as far as possible, within
the forms of law, and with reference to the great and never to be lost sight
of principle of giving of a fair and impartial trial to the prisoners, the*

ntroduction of any thing likely to weaken our present position, and give strength to our enemies abroad, whether it issues from the jury in time, or whether it comes from the mouths of the prisoners, or any other source. It was their position that had been imperilled and jeopardized, as they supposed, by enemies.

Mr. Harding concurred in the objection of Mr. Hunter, *on the ground of danger in delay,* and also because Brown was the leader of the insurrection, and his trial ought to be proceeded with *on account of the advantage thereby accruing in the trial of the others.*

Mr. Green remarked that he had had no opportunity of consulting with the prisoner, or preparing a defence. The letters for Northern counsel had been sent off, *but not sufficient time had been afforded to receive answers.* Under the circumstances, he thought a short delay desirable.

Mr. Botts added, that at present the excitement was so great as perhaps to deter Northern counsel from coming out; but now that it had been promised that the prisoners should have a fair and impartial trial, he presumed that they would come and take part in the case.

The *Court* stated that, if physical inability were shown, a reasonable delay must be granted. As to the expectation of other counsel, that did not constitute a sufficient cause for delay, as there was no certainty about their coming. Under the circumstances in which the prisoners were situated, it was rational that they should seek delay. *The brief period remaining before the close of the term of the Court rendered it necessary to proceed as expeditiously as practicable, and to be cautious about granting delays.* He would request the physician who had attended Brown to testify as to his condition.

Were ever before, in any civilized State, such reasons given for refusing the delay of a few days only to a wounded prisoner, charged with a capital offence, whose sole request was, that time might be allowed for honest counsel, whom he knew, to arrive and defend him? Even had the old man been unwounded, surrounded as he was by excited enemies, in a county and Commonwealth where a verdict of acquital was an impossible event, it would have been a very grave judicial outrage to have tried him until he could obtain proper counsel, or before considering a demand for a change of venue. Because the expense of a trial was great; because the

offences *charged* on the prisoner were dec.ared to be
grave ones — by the unjust Virginia code ; because the
arrival of Northern counsel might elicit facts unfavora-
ble to the reputation of the State, but that might tend to
exculpate the defendant — for this is what Mr. Hunter's
last orphic sentence meant ; because there might be
danger, if the request was granted, of a second conquest of Virginia by the friends of her first anti-
slavery invader ; and because — how and why is not yet
explained — a speedy trial of the leaders would result
in a benefit to his followers in jail : these were the reasons, as extraordinary as inhuman, advanced by the
prosecution why a wounded man's request should be
refused by a Court of *Justice ;* not one of them, by all
the rules of law, either pertinent or just, and one of
them the strongest argument why the case should be
protracted. The graver the crime, the more lenient
the law should be in granting opportunities of defence
to the accused. The Judge's reply ignores this salutary rule, and assumes that it was necessary to try the
prisoners at that particular term of the Court ! With
every faculty undimmed, with every legal facility
around him, with able lawyers and a Pardoning
Power unpledged against the exercise of his highest
prerogatives, the prisoner had a right to demand a postponement of the trial until the prejudices of the people
were less excited against him.

The physician was called, and swore, of course, that
the old man was able to go on with the trial, and did
not think that his wounds were such as to affect his
mind and recollection.

The Court, accordingly, refused to postpone the trial.

IMPANELLING A JURY.

The afternoon session, which lasted three hours, was occupied in obtaining a jury. At this time no Republican reporters were permitted to enter Charlestown, or had succeeded in obtaining entrance to the prison or Court. Hence, for the only accounts of the trial, we are obliged to accept the statements of John Brown's bitterest foes. This is their report of that afternoon's proceedings:

"The jailer was ordered to bring Brown into Court. He found him in bed, from which he declared himself unable to rise. *He was accordingly brought into Court on a cot, which was set down within the bar.* The prisoner lay most of the time with his eyes closed, and the counterpane drawn up close to his chin. The jury were then called and sworn. The Court excluded those who were present at Harper's Ferry during the insurrection and saw the prisoners perpetrating the act for which they were about to be tried. They were all from distant parts of the country, mostly farmers — some of them owning a few slaves, and others none. The examination was continued until twenty-four were decided by the Court and counsel to be competent jurors. Out of these twenty-four, the counsel for the prisoner had a right to strike off eight, and then twelve are drawn by ballot out of the remaining sixteen. The following were the questions put to the jurors: Were you at Harper's Ferry on Monday or Tuesday? How long did you remain there? Did you witness any of the proceedings for which this party is to be tried? Did you form or express any opinion, from what you saw there, with regard to the guilt or innocence of these people? Would that opinion disqualify you from giving these men a fair trial? Did you hear any of the evidence in this case before the Examining Court? What was your opinion based on? Was it a decided one, or was it one which would yield to evidence, if the evidence was different from what you supposed? Are you sure that you can try this case impartially from the evidence alone, without reference to any thing you have heard or seen of this transaction? Have you any conscientious scruples against convicting a party of an offence to which the law assigns the punishment of death, merely because that is the penalty assigned?"

26*

But these statements give no just notion of the manner of impanelling the juries in the trials of the Liberators. As they were all similarly conducted, it will
be proper here to quote, from the graphic sketches of
an eye witness, a description of the impanelling of the
jury who tried Edwin Coppie.

"Let me endeavor to represent to you how some of the jurors in
these cases are qualified.

A stolid and heavy man stands up before the judge to answer the
necessary questions. His countenance is lighted only by the hope of
getting a chance to give his voice against the wounded man upon the
ground. You can see this as plainly as if he told you.

Judge. Were you at Harper's Ferry, sir, during these proceedings?
Juror. No, sir.
Judge. You are a freeholder of this county?
Juror. Yes, sir.
Judge. Have you heard the evidence in the other cases?
Juror. (Eagerly.) Yes, sir.
Judge. I mean, if you have heard the evidence, and are likely to
be influenced by it, you are disqualified here. Have you heard much
of the evidence?
Juror. No, sir.
Judge. Have you expressed any opinion as to the guilt of these
parties?
Juror. Yes, sir, (eagerly again.)
Judge. Are you, then, capable of judging this case according to
the evidence, without reference to what you have before heard said?
Juror. Yes, sir.
Judge. Have you any conscientious scruples, which will prevent
you finding this man guilty, because the death penalty may be his
punishment?
Juror. Yes, sir, (promptly.)
Judge. I think you do not understand my question. I ask you if
you would hesitate to find this man guilty, because he would be hung
if you did?
Juror looks around puzzled, overcome by the abstract nature of the
proposition?
Judge. This man will be hung if you find him guilty. Will that
certainty of his being hung prevent you from finding him guilty, if
the evidence convinces you he is so?

Juror. (Catching the idea.) No, sir — no, sir.
Judge. Very well, sir; you can take your seat as a juror.''

Mr. Botts, who had solemnly promised to John Brown to defend him faithfully, did not fulfil this moral and professional obligation, for a jury was obtained without delay and without any objection on his part. The names of these unfortunate men * were announced, but they were not sworn till the following day.

At five o'clock " the prisoner was carried over to jail on his cot, and the Court adjourned till morning.''

* They were — Richard Timberlake, Joseph Myers, Thomas Watson, Jr., Isaac Dust, John G. McClure, William Rightsdale, Jacob J. Millar, Thomas Osborne, George W. Boyer, John C. Wiltshare, George W. Tapp, and William A. Martin.

III.

State Evidence.

O N Thursday morning, October 27, the trial began in earnest. John Brown was brought from jail, supported on either side — for he was too feeble to walk alone, — and laid down on his cot within the bar.* The author of the Fugitive Slave Law was present. Did he know that he was witnessing the beginning of the end of the rule of the wicked Power that he represents? Did he think that the wounded old man on the pallet was undermining, with his every groan and breath, the foundations of Human Slavery in America? As John Brown embodied the Northern religious anti-slavery idea, so Senator Mason, who now gazed at him, incarnated the Southern idolatrous principle of infidelity to man. Yet, seemingly, how reversed did their positions appear! The Slave Liberator with no earthly prospect but a speedy death on the gallows; and the Slave Extraditionist buoyed up with the hope of soon filling the Presidential Chair!

A PLEA OF INSANITY.

The plea of insanity — first advanced by political

---

* See the engraving.

monomaniacs in the Northern States, who could not understand a heroic action when they saw one, and yet,
admiring his spirit, were unwilling to denounce John
Brown — was brought forward, before the jury were
sworn, by the production of a telegraphic despatch from
Ohio. It asserted that insanity was hereditary in John
Brown's family; that his mother's sister died with it,
and her daughter was now in an insane asylum; and
that three of the children of his maternal uncle were
also mentally deranged.

" *Mr. Botts* said, that on receiving the above despatch, he went to the
jail with his associate, Mr. Green, and read it to Brown, and was desired by him to say that in his father's family there has never been any
insanity at all. On his mother's side there have been repeated instances
of it. He adds that his first wife showed symptoms of it, which were
also evident in his first and second sons by that wife. Some portions
of the statements in the despatch he knows to be correct, and of other
portions he is ignorant. He does not know whether his mother's sister died in the lunatic asylum; but he does believe that a daughter of
that sister has been two years in the asylum. He also believes that a
son and daughter of his mother's brother have been confined in an
asylum; but he is not apprised of the fact that another son of that
brother is now insane, and in close confinement. Brown also desires
his counsel to say that he does not put in the plea of insanity." *

John Brown then rose, and spurned the plea thus
sought to be introduced. He said:

"I will add, if the Court will allow me, that I look upon it as a
miserable artifice and pretext of those who ought to take a different
course in regard to me, if they took any at all, and I view it with contempt more than otherwise. Insane persons, so far as my experience
goes, have but little ability to judge of their own sanity; and if I am
insane, of course I should think I knew more than all the rest of the
world. But I do not think so. I am perfectly unconscious of insanity, and I reject, so far as I am capable, any attempts to interfere in my
behalf on that score."

* Report of Associated Press.

A DAY'S DELAY REFUSED.

"The course taken by Brown this morning," writes a pro-slavery correspondent, "makes it evident that he sought no postponement for the mere purpose of delay." And yet, although the prisoner again asked for a suspension of the proceedings for one day only, until a lawyer in Ohio, to whom he had written, and who had telegraphed a reply, should arrive in Charlestown, the Court again refused to grant the request, and ordered the examination to proceed! Mr. Hunter, in opposing the request, involuntarily showed that he regarded the trial as a form only, — a mockery of justice, — and expressed his belief that the old man was less solicitous for a fair trial than to give to his friends the time and opportunity to organize a rescue. Mr. Harding, with greater brutality, asserted that the prisoner was merely shamming sickness — although he could not stand unsupported for any length of time, and was covered with wounds, not one of which had healed!

The Jury were sworn, and the indictment read. The Court permitted the prisoner, while arraigned, to remain prostrate on his pallet. He did so. The indictment charged Insurrection, Treason, and Murder. John Brown pleaded Not Guilty.

ARGUMENTS OF THE COUNSEL.

Mr. Hunter then stated the facts that he designed to prove by the evidence for the prosecution, and reviewed the laws relating to the offences charged on the prisoner, and concluded by hypocritically

"Urging the jury to cast aside all prejudices, and give the prisoners a fair and impartial trial, and not to allow their hatred of Abolitionists to influence them against those who have raised the black flag on the soil of this Commonwealth."

Mr. Green responded, stating what should be proved, and how, to convict of the offences charged:

1. To establish the charge of treason it must be proven that the prisoner attempted to establish a separate and distinct government within the limits of Virginia, and the purpose also of any treasonable acts; and this, not by any confessions of his own, elsewhere made, but by two different witnesses for each and every act.

2. To establish the charge of a conspiracy with slaves,

"The jury must be satisfied that such conspiracy was done within the State of Virginia, and within the jurisdiction of this Court. If it was done in Maryland, this Court could not punish the act. If it was done within the limits of the Armory at Harper's Ferry, it was not done within the limits of this State, the Government of the United States holding exclusive jurisdiction within the said grounds. Attorney General Cushing had decided this point with regard to the Armory grounds at Harper's Ferry, which opinion was read to the jury, showing that persons residing within the limits of the Armory cannot even be taxed by Virginia, and that crimes committed within the said limits are punishable by Federal Courts."

3. Over murder, (he argued,) if committed within the limits of the Armory, the Court had no jurisdiction; and, in the case of Mr. Beckham, if he was killed on the railroad bridge, it was committed within the State of Maryland, which claims jurisdiction up to the Armory grounds.

Mr. Botts followed him, and supported these views. The only noteworthy thing he said was, that—

"It is due to the prisoner to state that he believed himself to be actuated by the highest and noblest feelings that ever coursed through human breast. They could prove by those gentlemen who were prisoners that they were treated with respect, and that they were kept in positions of safety, and that no violence was offered to them. These acts must be taken into consideration, and have their due weight with the jury."

Mr. Hunter replied. The State law of treason, he argued, was more full than that of the Federal Constitution.

"It includes within its definition of treason the establishing, without the authority of the Legislature, any Government within its limits separate from the existing Government, or the holding or executing, under such Government, of any office, professing allegiance or fidelity to it, or resisting the execution of law under the color of its authority; and it goes on to declare that such treason, if proved by the testimony of two witnesses to the same overt act, or by confession in Court, shall be punished with death. Any one of these acts constitutes treason against this Commonwealth; and he believed that the prisoner had been guilty of each and all these acts, which would be proven in the clearest manner, not by two, but by a dozen witnesses, unless limited by the lack of time. The prisoner had attempted to break down the existing Government of the Commonwealth, and establish on its ruins a new Government; he had usurped the office of Commander-in-chief of this new Government, and, together with his whole band, professed allegiance and fidelity to it; he represented not only the civil authorities of State, but our own military; he is doubly, trebly, and quadruply guilty of treason. Mr. Hunter proceeded again to the question of jurisdiction over the Armory grounds, and examined the authority, cited on the other side, of Attorney General Cushing. The latter was an able man; but he came from a region of country where opinions are very different from ours in relation to the power of the Federal Government as affecting State rights. Our Courts are decidedly adverse to Mr. Cushing's views. In all time past, the jurisdiction of this County of Jefferson in criminal offences committed at Harper's Ferry, has been uninterrupted and unchallenged, whether they were committed on the Government property or not. He cited an instance, twenty-nine years ago, where an atrocious murder was committed between the very shops in front of which these men fought their battles, and the criminal was tried here, convicted, and executed under our laws. There was a broad difference between the cession of jurisdiction by Virginia to the Federal Government and mere assent of the State that the Federal Government should become a landholder within its limits. The law of Virginia, by virtue of which the grounds at Harper's Ferry were purchased by the Federal Government, ceded no jurisdiction. Brown was also guilty, on his own notorious confession, in advising conspiracy. In regard to the charge of murder, the proof will be, that this man was not only actually engaged in murdering our citizens, but that he was the chief directer.

o:' the whole movement. No matter whether he was present on the
sp ot, or a mile off, he is equally guilty."

The examination of witnesses was commenced at the
a 'ternoon session. The conductor of the train was
fi st called, narrated the circumstances of its stoppage
o 1 the morning of Monday, October 17, and thus de-
sc ribed his interview with Captain Brown:

"I met a man whom I now recognize as Coppic, and asked what
th ·y meant. He replied, 'We don't want to injure you or detain
yc ur train. You could have gone at three o'clock: all we want is to free
th ? negroes.' I then asked if my train could now start, and went to
th ? guard at the gate, who said, 'There is Captain Smith; he can
te l you what you want to know.' I went to the engine house, and
th ? guard called Captain Smith. The prisoner at the bar came out,
a: d I asked him if he was captain of these men. He replied he was.
I asked him if I could cross the bridge, and he peremptorily re-
s] ·onded, 'No, sir.' I then asked him what he meant by stopping my
tr .in. He replied, 'Are you the conductor on that train?' I told
hi n I was, and he said, 'Why, I sent you word at three o'clock that you
cc uld pass.' I told him that, after being stopped by armed men on the
b1 .dge, I would not pass with my train. He replied, 'My head for it,
yc u will not be hurt;' and said he was very sorry. It was not his in-
te ition that any blood should be spilled; it was bad management on
th ? part of the men in charge of the bridge. I then asked him what
sc :urity I would have that my train would pass safely, and asked him
if he would walk over the bridge ahead of my train with me. He
ca led a large, stout man to accompany him, and one of my passen-
ge ·s, Mr. McByrne, asked to accompany me; but Brown ordered him
to get into the train, or he would take them all prisoners in five min-
ul ·s; but it was advice more than in the form of a threat. Brown
ac :ompanied me; both had rifles. As we crossed the bridge, the three
ar ned men were still in their places. When we got across, Brown
sa d to me, 'You, doubtless, wonder that a man of my age should be
he ·e with a band of armed men; but if you knew my past history,
yc 1 would not wonder at it so much.' My train was then through
th bridge, and I bade him good morning, jumped on my train, and
le t him."

He narrated the conversation between Captain Brown
ai d Governor Wise, when the Liberator was confined

27

in the guard house at Harper's Ferry, in which he said that the prisoner stated, in reply to a question, that he thought he *had* been betrayed to the Secretary of War, but had practised a ruse to prevent suspicion ; yet refused to inform them whom he believed to be the traitor, or how he had acted to avert the consequences of the betrayal.

John Brown thus alluded to Colonel Forbes and his own third visit to Kansas.

During the examination of this witness, a despatch arrived from Cleveland, announcing that Northern counsel would arrive in Charlestown that evening; whereupon the Virginia counsel for John Brown, in his name, asked that the cross-examination might be postponed till the following morning. It was already late in the evening, but the prosecuting attorney resisted the request, because :

"If the cases were not pushed on, the whole balance of the term would not be sufficient to try these men. He thought there was no reason for delay, *especially as it was uncertain whether the counsel could get here before* — to-morrow !"

The Court, as usual, ordered the case to proceed.

Colonel Washington described his arrest, and testified that Captain Brown permitted his prisoners to keep in a safe position ; that he never spoke rudely or insultingly to them ; that he allowed them to go out, to quiet their families, by assuring them of their personal safety ; that he heard him direct his men, on several occasions, never to fire on an unarmed citizen ; that he assured the captives that they should be treated well, and none of their property destroyed ; and that he overheard a conversation between Stevens and another person, on Southern Institutions, in the course of which that Liberator asked, "if he was in favor of slavery?" and, on receiving the reply, that, although a non-slaveholder, yet, "as a citizen of the South, he would sustain the cause," immediately answered, "Then you are the first man I would hang; you deserve it more than a man who is a slaveholder and sustains his interests." He could not swear whether the marines fired after they broke into the engine house; the noise, he said, was great, and several shouted from the inside that some one had surrendered among the prisoners.

This evidence ended the proceedings of the Court on Thursday. The official report closed with this extraordinary announcement: "*Orders have been given to the jailers to shoot all the prisoners if an attempt is made for their rescue.*"

When it is borne in mind that the only offence of these prisoners was an effort to fulfil two commands of Jesus, "Do unto others as ye would that others should do unto you," and "Remember those in bonds, as bound with them;" and that, by the laws of every free Commonwealth, the accused man, until convicted of a crime, is held to be guiltless, — what a fearful picture of the civilization and Christianity of Virginia does this barbarous and bloody order hold up to our view!

IV.

STATE EVIDENCE CLOSED.

THERE was great exultation in Charlestown on Friday, October 28. John E. Cook was brought in as a prisoner, by men who, in a Free State, betrayed and seized him, for the price of his blood, previously offered by Governor Wise. But until this record of the outrage called the trial of John Brown be completed, I will not divert the attention of the reader to the fears and hopes, the crimes and prayers which were agitating the world outside of the Court House and the Jail of Charlestown.

On Friday morning, Mr. Hoyt, a young Boston lawyer, arrived as a volunteer counsel for John Brown; and, although declining to act until he obtained a knowledge of the case, was qualified as a member of the bar.

The testimony for the prosecution was resumed. Colonel Washington, recalled, stated that he heard Captain Brown frequently complain of the bad faith of the people by firing on his men when under a flag of truce; "*but he heard him make no threat, nor utter any vindictiveness against them;*" and that, "during the

(316)

day, one of Brown's sons was shot in the breast, the ball passing around to the side; but he took his weapon again and fired repeatedly before his sufferings compelled him to retire."

Mr. Hunter then laid before the Jury the printed Constitution and Ordinance of the Provisional Government, and a large bundle of letters and papers. He asked that the Sheriff, who knew the handwriting of the prisoner, be brought to identify his handwriting.

John Brown. I will identify any of my handwriting, and save all that trouble. I am ready to face the music.

Mr. Hunter. I prefer to prove them by Mr. Campbell.

John Brown. Either way you please.

The bundle of letters was then opened; each was identified by Campbell, and then handed to the prisoner, who, in a firm tone, replied, "Yes — that is mine," as soon as he recognized his writing.

Mr. Hunter presented the form of Government established by the insurgents, and read a list of the members of the Convention. It is headed, "William Charles Morris, President of the Convention, and I. Kagi, Secretary of the Convention." On handing the list to Brown, he exclaimed, with a groan, "That is my signature."

Mr. Ball, master machinist of the Armory, one of the prisoners made by Captain Brown, testified as to his arrest, and stated that he was conducted to Captain Brown, who told me his object was to free the slaves, and not the making of war on the people; that my person and private property would be safe; that his war was against the accursed system of slavery; that he had power to do it, and would carry it out; it was no child's play he had undertaken. He then gave me permission to return to my family, to assure them of my safety and get my breakfast; started back home, and was accompanied by two armed men, who stopped at the door; breakfast not being ready, went back, and was allowed to return home again, under escort, at a later hour; on returning again, Captain Brown said it was his determination to seize the arms and munitions of the Government, to arm the blacks to defend themselves against their masters."

27 *

He testified, also, as to several incidents narrated in the account of the fight. He added, in his cross-examination, that —

"Brown repeatedly said that he would injure no one but in self-defence, and Coppic frequently urgèd us to seek places of safety; but Brown did not — he appeared to desire us to take care of ourselves. There were three or four slaves in the engine house; they had spears, but all seemed badly scared; Washington Phil was ordered by Brown to cut a port-hole through the brick wall; he continued until a brisk fire commenced outside, when he said, ' This is getting too hot for Phil,' and he squatted. Brown then took up the tools and finished the hole."

John Allstadt told how he was brought from his farm by a party of men who declared that their object was to " free the country from slavery; " described his detention at the engine house, and various incidents of the fight there ; said that " the negroes were placed in the watch house with spears in their hands, but showed no disposition to use them; that he saw Phil making port-holes by the Captain's order, but that the other negroes did nothing, and had dropped their weapons — some of them being asleep nearly all the time; that John Brown's rifle was always cocked, and that he believed, although he would not swear, that it was the old man himself who shot the marine.

Alexander Kelly described the manner of Thomas Boerley's death. He was armed with a gun when killed. George W. Turner, also, was killed as he was levelling his rifle.

Albert Grist described his arrest, by a man armed with a spear, on Sunday night, and his detention in the Armory until he was dismissed by Captain Brown, after delivering a message to the conductor of the train.

" Brown," he said, " declared that his object was to free
the slaves. I told him there were not many there.
He replied : ' The good Book says we are all free and
equal.' "

At the afternoon session of Friday, three additional
witnesses were produced for the State, but their testimony presented no new facts ; and Henry Hunter, who
is described as " a very intelligent young gentleman,
apparently about twenty-two years of age, the son of
Andrew Hunter, Esq., who conducts the prosecution,"
was examined as to the murder of Thompson.

Although, technically, the record of the evidence for
the prosecution should here close, it will be seen, by
the subsequent proceedings, that, in consequence of the
intentional negligence of the prisoner's Virginia counsel, it was not concluded till the adjournment of the
Court. The defence began on the following day. Yet,
in this Friday's proceedings, one incident of the conflict
at Harper's Ferry, as described by a witness first introduced by the State, is so characteristic of the spirit
engendered by slavery, — so faithful a mirror of modern
Southern chivalry, — that it deserves to be reported in
full, and preserved as a contrast to the conduct of the
Liberators.

THE MURDER OF THOMPSON.

Mr. Green stated to the Court that he desired to bring out testimony relative to the shooting of Thompson, one of the insurgents, on
he bridge ; but the State objected to it, unless Brown had a knowledge
of that shooting.

Mr. Hunter said there was a deal of testimony about Brown's for-
)earance and not shooting citizens, that had no more to do with this
:ase than the dead languages. If he understood the offer, it was to
how that one of those men, named Thompson, a prisoner, was de-

spatched after Beckham's death. The circumstances of the deed might be
such as he himself might not at all approve. He did not know how
that might be, but he desired to avoid any investigation that might be
used. Not that it was so designed by the respectable counsel employed
in the case, but because he thought the object of the prisoner in getting at it was for out-door effect and influence. He therefore said if
the defence could show that this prisoner was aware of these circumstances, and the manner in which that party was killed, and still
exerted forbearance, he would not object. But unless the knowledge
of it could be brought home to the prisoner and his after conduct, he
could not see its relevancy.

Mr. Green, counsel for defence, contended that they had a right to
infer that Brown had been made aware of it, as it was already proved
that communications passed between him and the citizens several times
after the killing of Thompson.

Judge Parker decided that the whole transaction of that day constituted a part of the *res gestæ*, and might be inquired into.

Henry Hunter called, — examined by counsel for defence.

Q. Did you witness the death of this man Thompson ? *

A. I witnessed the death of one whose name I have been informed
was Thompson.

Q. The one who was a prisoner ?

A. Yes, sir.

Q. Well, sir, what were the circumstances attending it ?

A. Do you wish my own connection with it, or simply a description
of the circumstances? Shall I mention the names?

Mr. Andrew Hunter. Every bit of it, Henry; state all you saw.

Witness. There was a prisoner confined in the parlor of the hotel,
and after Mr. Beckham's death he was shot down by a number of us
there belonging to this sharp-shooting band.

Mr. Andrew Hunter. Will you allow him to state, before proceeding
further, how he was connected with Mr. Beckham ?

Mr. Green. Certainly, sir.

Witness. He was my grand-uncle and my special friend — a man
I loved above all others. After he was killed, Mr. Chambers and
myself moved forward to the hotel for the purpose of taking the prisoner out and hanging him ; we were joined by a number of other
persons, who cheered us on in that work ; we went up into his room,
where he was bound, with the undoubted and undisguised purpose of
taking his life ; at the door we were stopped by persons guarding the
door, who remonstrated with us, and the excitement was so great that
persons who remonstrated with us at one moment would cheer us on
the next ; we burst into the room where he was, and found several

around him, but they offered only a feeble resistance; we brought our guns down to his head repeatedly, — myself and another person, — for the purpose of shooting him in the room.

There was a young lady there, the sister of Mr. Fouke, the hotel keeper, who sat in this man's lap, covered his face with her arms, and shielded him with her person whenever we brought our guns to bear ; she said to us, "For God's sake, wait and let the law take its course ; " my associate shouted to kill him ; "Let us shed his blood," were his words; all round were shouting, "Mr. Beckham's life was worth ten thousand of these vile abolitionists; " I was cool about it, and deliberate; my gun was pushed up by some one who seized the barrel, and I then moved to the back part of the room, still with purpose unchanged, but with a view to divert attention from me, in order to get an opportunity, at some moment when the crowd would be less dense, to shoot him; after a moment's thought, it occurred to me that that was not the proper place to kill him ; we then proposed to take him out and hang him ; some portion of our band then opened a way to him, and first pushing Miss Fouke aside, we slung him out of doors ; I gave him a push, and many others did the same ; we then shoved him along the platform and down to the trestle work of the bridge ; he begged for his life all the time, very piteously at first.

By-the-by, before we took him out of the room, I asked the question what he came here for : he said their only purpose was to free the slaves or die ; then he begged, "Don't take my life — a prisoner ; " but I put the gun to him, and he said, "You may kill me, but it will be revenged; there are eighty thousand persons sworn to carry out this work; " that was his last expression ; we bore him out on the bridge with the purpose then of hanging him ; we had no rope, and none could be found ; it was a moment of wild excitement; two of us raised our guns — which one was first I do not know — and pulled the trigger; before he had reached the ground, I suppose some five or six shots had been fired into his body ; he fell on the railroad track, his back down to the earth, and his face up ; we then went back for the purpose of getting another one, (Stevens;) but he was sick or wounded, and persons around him, and I persuaded them myself to let him alone ; I said, "Don't let us operate on him, but go around and get some more ; " we did this act with a purpose, thinking it right and justifiable under the circumstances, and fired and excited by the cowardly, savage manner in which Mr. Beckham's life had been taken.

Mr. Andrew Hunter. Is that all, gentlemen ?

Mr. Botts. Yes, sir.

Mr. Andrew Hunter. (To the witness.) Stand aside.

This sworn statement of a cold-blooded murder, by one of the perpetrators of it, elicited *not one word of condemnation from any journal published in the Southern States.*

Wm. M. Williams, the watchman, stated the particulars of his arrest and confinement in the watch house. Capt. Brown told the prisoners to hide themselves, or they would be shot by the people outside; he said he would not hurt any of them. He told Mr. Grist to tell the people to cease firing, or he would burn the town; but if they didn't molest him, he wouldn't molest them; heard two shots on the bridge about the time the express train arrived, but did not see Hayward killed.

Capt. Brown. State what was said by myself, and not about his being shot.

Williams. I think you said that if he had taken care of himself, he would not have suffered.

Reason Cross. I prepared a proposition that Brown should retain the possession of the Armory, that he should release us, and that the firing should stop.

Capt. Brown. Were there two written propositions drawn up while you were prisoner?

Cross. Yes, there was another paper prepared by Kitzmiller and some others. I went out to stop the firing; a man went with me, and they took him prisoner and tied him; this was Thompson, who was afterwards taken out and shot; Brown's treatment of me was kind and respectful; heard him talk roughly to some men who were going in to where the blacks were confined.

Several witnesses for the defence were then called, but none of them answered to their subpœnas. They had not been returned. There was no doubt, now, that the trial would have been closed at once; for, up to this period, no earnest effort had been made, by the counsel for the defence, to compel the Court to grant a brief delay; when, unexpectedly, John Brown arose from his mattress and addressed the Judge.

JOHN BROWN'S SPEECH.

May it Please the Court — I discover that, notwithstanding all the assurances I have received of a fair trial, nothing like a fair trial

is to be given me, as it would seem. I gave the names, as soon
as I could get them, of the persons I wished to have called as witnesses, and was assured that they would be subpœnaed. I wrote
down a memorandum to that effect, saying where these parties were;
but it appears that they have not been subpœnaed, so far as I can
learn. And now I ask, if I am to have any thing at all deserving
the name and shadow of a fair trial, that this proceeding be deferred
until to-morrow morning; for I have no counsel, as I have before
stated, on whom I feel that I can rely; but I am in hopes counsel
may arrive who will attend to seeing that I get the witnesses who are
necessary for my defence. I am myself unable to attend to it. I have
given all the attention I possibly could to it, but am unable to see or
know about them, and can't even find out their names; and I have
nobody to do any errands, for my money was all taken from me
when I was sacked and stabbed, and I have not a dime. I had two
hundred and fifty or sixty dollars in gold and silver taken from my
pocket, and now I have no possible means of getting any body to do
my errands for me, and I have not had all the witnesses subpœnaed.
They are not within reach, and are not here. I ask at least until
to-morrow morning to have something done, if any thing is designed;
if not, I am ready for any thing that may come up.

The old man lay down again, drew his blanket over
him, closed his eyes, and appeared to sink in tranquil
slumber.

This bold speech, with its modest request, (which
was seconded by Mr. Hoyt, who, we are told, "arose
amid great sensation," and stated that other counsel
would arrive to-night,) shamed the unfaithful Virginia
advocates into an immediate resignation, and the Court
into an adjournment till the following morning. But
t is due to the reputation of Mr. Hunter to say, that
he resolutely resisted this action.

"The town," flashed the telegraph, "is greatly
excited; the guard has been increased; the conduct
of Brown is regarded as a trick." The very appearance of decency alarmed the citizens of Charlestown!

V.

The Defence.

JOHN BROWN cared little for posthumous fame; but for his reputation, as a help or hinderance to the cause of the slave, he had a just degree of solicitude. He did not wish to die with the character of a robber or a murderer. He desired to show that he had shed no blood, committed no violence, done no uncourteous act, uttered no unkind or vindictive saying, beyond what the furtherance of his plan demanded — above or outside of the absolute necessities of his holy scheme and dangerous situation. While freely admitting every act that he committed, therefore, and having no hope whatever of a verdict of acquital, or of a pardon, he sought to prove in Court, by the evidence of his enemies, that he had not in any way transcended the obligations of his divinely-appointed mission. This · design, of course, was not acceptable to Virginia; and her loyal sons, therefore, — Messrs. Botts and Green, — although they often stated their determination to see justice done, took no efficient steps to secure its fulfilment. This is a copy of the brief directions given to them at the commencement of the trial: it is transcribed from the original, in the old hero's handwriting :

JOHN BROWN'S DIRECTIONS TO HIS COUNSEL.

We gave to numerous prisoners perfect liberty.

Get all their names.

We allowed numerous other prisoners to visit their families, to quiet their fears.

Get all their names.

We allowed the conductor to pass his train over the bridge with all his passengers, I myself crossing the bridge with him, and assuring all the passengers of their perfect safety.

Get that conductor's name, and the names of the passengers, so far as may be.

We treated all our prisoners with the utmost kindness and humanity.

Get all their names, so far as may be.

Our orders, from the first and throughout, were, that no unarmed person should be injured, under any circumstances whatever.

Prove that by ALL *the prisoners.*

We committed no destruction or waste of property.

Prove that.

The Court assembled at ten o'clock on Saturday. John Brown was brought in and laid on his pallet. Mr. Samuel Chilton, of Washington City, and Mr. Henry Griswold, of Ohio, appeared as additional counsel for the prisoner.

Mr. Chilton rose and said, that, on his arrival in Charlestown, after finding that the counsel whom he had come to assist had retired from the case, he hesitated about undertaking it ; it was only at the urgent solicitation of the prisoner and his friends, that he had now consented to do so ; but, not having had time to read the indictment or the evidence already given, it was impossible for him to discharge the full duty of a counsel. So, also, with Mr. Griswold. A short delay —a few hours only—would enable them to make some preparation.

28

The Court, as usual, refused the request, and referred, with some asperity, to the recent speech of the plain-spoken prisoner. "This term," said the Judge, "will very soon end ; *and it is my duty to endeavor to get through with all the cases if possible, in justice to the prisoners*, and in justice to the State. The trial must proceed."

Mr. Hoyt, after objecting to certain papers, (which were withdrawn,) and asking certain questions relative to the witnesses he had summoned, called on John P. Dangerfield, of Harper's Ferry, to testify. From the evidence for the defence, it is unnecessary to quote more than those passages which refer to the object that John Brown had in view, and a few brief incidents of the conflict not elsewhere noted :

John P. Dangerfield. Was a prisoner in the hands of Capt. Brown at the engine house. About a dozen black men were there, armed with pikes, which they carried most awkwardly and unwillingly. During the firing they were lying about asleep, some of them having crawled under the engines. From the treatment of Capt. Brown he had no personal fear of him or his men during his confinement. Saw one of John Brown's sons shot in the engine house ; he fell back, exclaiming, "It's all up with me," and died in a few moments. Another son came in and commenced to vomit blood ; *he was wounded while out with Mr. Kitzmuller*, (carrying a flag of truce.) The prisoner frequently complained that his men were shot down while carrying a flag of truce.

Mr. Hunter again tried to arrest the production of evidence so disgraceful to the Virginians ; but even the barbarous code of his native State did not prevent the presentation of proof tending to show the absence of malice. The witness was allowed to proceed :

"Brown promised safety to all descriptions of property except slave property. After the first attack Capt. Brown cried out to surrender. Saw Brown wounded on the hip by a thrust from a sabre, and several sabre cuts on his head. *When the latter wounds were given, Capt. Brown appeared to be shielding himself with his head down, but making no resistance.* The parties outside appeared to be firing as they pleased."

Major Mills, master of the armory, was next sworn.

" Was one of the hostages of Capt. Brown in the engine house. . . . *Brown's son went out with a flag of truce, and was shot.* Heard Brown frequently complain that the citizens had acted in a barbarous manner. He did not appear to have any malicious feeling. His intentions were to shoot nobody unless they were carrying or using arms."

John Brown here asked whether the witness saw any firing on his part that was not purely defensive.

" *Witness.* It might be considered in that light, perhaps; the balls came into the engine house pretty thick."

A conversation here ensued between John Brown, lying on his cot, and Mr. Dangerfield, as to the part taken by the prisoner in not unnecessarily exposing his hostages to danger. The witness generally corroborated the Liberator's version of the circumstances attending the attack on the engine house, but could not testify to all the incidents that he enumerated. He did not hear him say that he surrendered. The wife and daughter of the witness were permitted to visit him unmolested, and free verbal communication was allowed with those outside. " We were treated kindly, but were compelled to stay where we didn't want to be "

Samuel Snider, the next witness, corroborated the evidence of Mr. Dangerfield; asserting that the prisoner honestly endeavored to protect his hostages, and wished to make peace more for their sake than his personal safety.

Mr. Hoyt's sudden indisposition caused the Court to adjourn for an hour.

At two o'clock in the afternoon, the testimony was

resumed, and the examination conducted by Mr. Griswold.

Captain Simms, commander of the Frederick Volunteers, was the first witness.

"Brown complained," he said, "that his men were shot down like dogs while bearing a flag of truce. I told him that they must expect to be shot down like dogs, if they took up arms in that way."

What an appalling declaration for an American citizen to make — that men who interfere in behalf of the heavily oppressed, the despised poor, for whom Jesus suffered on the Cross of Calvary, but whom Virginia converts into mere articles of merchandise, "must expect" — in a country which boasts of its freedom and devotion to human rights — "to be shot down like dogs"! How horrible, and how horribly true!

"Brown said he knew what he had to undergo when he came there. He had weighed the responsibility, and should not shrink from it; he said he had full possession of the town, and could have massacred all the inhabitants, had he thought proper to do so; but, as he had not, he considered himself entitled to some terms. He said he shot no one who had not carried arms. I told him that Mayor Beckham had been killed, and that I knew he was altogether unarmed. He seemed sorry to hear of his death, and said, 'I fight only those who fight me.' I saw Stevens at the hotel after he had been wounded [*while carrying a flag of truce*], and shamed some young men *who were endeavoring to shoot him, as he lay in his bed, apparently dying*. . . . He had no sympathy for the acts of the prisoner, but he regarded him as a brave man."

Two other witnesses corroborated these evidences of the old hero's courage and humanity, and of the cowardly barbarity of the Virginians. The defence here rested their case.

LAWYERS' TONGUE-FENCING.

Whereupon, the lawyers began their preliminary

duties — to submit various motions and make objections thereto. For such as admire this description of debate, I submit the official report of it.

A MOTION.

Mr. Chilton, for the prisoner, rose and submitted a motion that the prosecution in this case be compelled to elect one count of the indictment and abandon the others. The indictment consists of four counts, and is indorsed thus : 'An indictment for treason, and advising and conspiring with slaves and others to rebel.' The charge of treason is in the first, and the second count alleges a charge different from that which is indorsed on the back of the indictment, and which is upon record. The second count is under the following statute : "If a free person advise or conspire with a slave to rebel or make an insurrection, he shall be punished with death, whether such rebellion or insurrection be made or not." But the second count of the indictment is, that these parties, who are charged by the indictment, "conspired, together with other persons, to induce certain slaves, the property of of Messrs. Allstadt and Washington, to make rebellion and insurrection." There is a broad distinction between advising and conspiring with slaves to rebel, and conspiring with others to induce slaves to rebel. Whether he was to avail himself of their irregularity by instruction from the Court to the Jury to disregard this second count entirely, or whether it would be proper to wait until the conclusion of the trial, and then move an arrest of judgment, he left his Honor to decide. He proceeded to argue the motion that the prosecution be compelled to elect one count and abandon the others, quoting Archibald's Criminal Pleading in support of his view. He further alluded to the hardship which rests upon the prisoner to meet various and distinct charges in the same trial. From the authority he read, it would be seen that in a case of treason, different descriptions of treason could not be united in the same indictment : high treason could not be associated with other treason. If an inferior grade of the same character could not be included in separate counts, still less can offences of higher grade. Treason in this country is high treason. Treason against the State of Virginia is treason against her sovereignty. We have no other description of treason, because treason can only be committed against sovereignty, whether that of the United States or of a sovereign State.

OBJECTIONS.

Mr. Harding could not see the force of the objection made by the learned counsel on the other side. In regard to separate offences

28*

being charged, these were but different parts of the same transaction. Treason against the Government is properly made the subject of one of the counts. But we also have a count of murder, for it can hardly be supposed that treason can exist without being followed or accompanied by murder. Murder arose out of this treason, and was the natural result of this bloody conspiracy; yet, after all the evidence has been given on all these points, the objection is made that we must confine ourselves to a single one of them. He hoped that no such motion would be granted.

Mr. Hunter, in reply to the argument of Mr. Chilton, said that the discretion of the Court compelling the prosecution to elect on one count in the indictment, is only exercised where great embarrassment would otherwise result to the prisoner. As applied to this particular case, it involved this point, that notwithstanding the transaction, as has been disclosed by the evidence, be one transaction, a continued, closely-connected series of acts, which, according to our apprehension of the law of the land, involves the three great offences of treason, conspiring with and advising slaves to make insurrection, and the perpetration of murder; whether, in a case of this character, it is right and proper for the Court to put the prosecution upon their election, as to one of the three, and bar us from investigation of the two others, although they relate to facts involved in one grand fact. Notwithstanding the multiplicity of duties devolving upon the prosecutor and assistant prosecutors, yet we have found time to be guarded and careful in regard to the mode of framing the indictment. It is my work, and I propose to defend it as right and proper. He then proceeded to quote Chitty's Criminal Law and Robinson's Practice, to prove that the discretion of the Court there spoken of, in reference to the furthering of the great object in view, was the attainment of justice. Where the prisoner is not embarrassed in making his defence, this discretion is not to be exercised by the Court, and no case can be shown where the whole ground of the indictment referred to one and the same transaction. This very case in point would show the absurdity of the principle, if it were as broad as contended for by his learned friend. As to the other point of objection, it was too refined and subtle for his poor intellect.

REPLY TO THEM.

Mr. Chilton responded. In order to ascertain what a party is tried for, we must go to the finding of the Grand Jury. If the Grand Jury return an indictment charging the party with murder, finding a true bill for that, and he should be indicted for manslaughter, or any other offence, the Court would not have jurisdiction to try him on that count in the indictment. And the whole question turns on the construction of the section of the statute which has been read, viz., whether or not advising or conspiring with slaves to rebel is a separate and distinct offence from conspiring with other persons to induce it.

THE DECISION.

The *Court* said that the difference might perhaps be taken advantage of to move an arrest of judgment; but the Jury had been charged and had been sworn to try the prisoners on the indictment as drawn. The trial must go on, and counsel could afterwards move an arrest of judgment. As to the other objection, the Court made this answer : The very fact that the offence can be charged in different counts, varying the language and circumstances, is based upon the idea that distinct offences may be charged in the same indictment. The prisoners are to be tried on the various counts as if they were various circumstances. There is no legal objection against charging various crimes in the same indictment. The practice has been to put a party upon election where the prisoner would be embarrassed in his defence ; but that is not the law. In this case, these offences charged are all part of the same transaction, and no case is made out for the Court to interfere and put the parties upon an election.

APPEAL FOR TIME.

Mr. Chilton said he would reserve the motion as a basis for a motion in arrest of judgment.

•*Mr. Griswold* remarked that the position of all the present counsel of the prisoner was one of very great embarrassment. They had no disposition to interfere with the course of practice, but it was the desire of the defendant that the case should be argued. He supposed that counsel could obtain sufficient knowledge of the evidence previously taken by reading notes of it. But it was now nearly dark. If it was to be argued at all, he supposed the argument for the Commonwealth would probably occupy the attention of the Court until the usual time for adjournment, unless it was the intention to continue with a late evening session. From what had heretofore transpired, he felt a delicacy in making any request of the Court; but knowing that the case was now ended except for mere argument, he did not know that it would be asking too much for the Court to adjourn after the opening argument on behalf of the prosecution.

Mr. Hunter said that he would cheerfully bear testimony to the unexceptionable manner in which the counsel who had just taken his seat had conducted the examination of witnesses to-day. It would afford him very great pleasure, in all ordinary cases, to agree to the indulgence of such a request as the gentleman had just made, and which was entirely natural. But he was bound to remember, and respectfully remind the Court, that this state of things, which places counsel in a somewhat embarrassing position in conducting the defence, is purely and entirely the act of the prisoner. His counsel will not be responsible for it; the Court is not responsible for it; but the unfortunate prisoner is responsible for his own act in dismissing *his faithful, skilful, able, and zealous counsel on yesterday afternoon.* He would simply say that not only were the jurors kept away from their families by their delays, *but there could not be a female in this county, who, whether with good cause or not, was not trembling with anxiety and apprehension.* While their courtesy to the counsel and humanity to the prisoner should have due weight, yet the Commonwealth has its rights, the community has its rights, the Jury have their rights, and it was for his Honor to weigh these in opposite scales, and determine whether we should not go on and bring this case to a close to-night. We had until twelve o'clock to do it in.

ARGUMENT FOR AND AGAINST A DECENT DELAY.

Mr. Chilton said their client desired that they should argue his case. It was impossible for him to do so now, and he could not allow himself to make an attempt at argument on a case about which he knew so little. If he were to get up at all, it would be for the unworthy purpose of wasting time. He had no such design; but having undertaken this man's cause, he very much desired to comply with his wishes. He would be the last man in the world to subject the jurors to inconvenience unnecessarily; but although the prisoner may have been to blame, may have acted foolishly, and may have had an improper purpose in so doing, still he could not see that he should therefore be forced to have his case submitted without argument. *In a trial for life and death, we should not be too precipitate.*

The Court here consulted with the jurors, *who expressed themselves very anxious to get home.*

His Honor said he was desirous of trying this case precisely as he would try another, without any reference at all to outside feeling.

Mr. Hoyt remarked that he was physically incapable of speaking to-night, even if fully prepared. He had worked very hard last night to get the law points, until he fell unconscious from exhaustion and fatigue. For the last five days and nights he had only slept ten hours, and it seemed to him that justice to the person demanded the allowance of a little time in a case so extraordinary in all its aspects as this.

The Court suggested that we might have the opening argument for the prosecution to-night, at any rate.

Mr. Harding would not like to open the argument now, unless the case was to be finished to-night. He was willing, however, to submit tne case to the jury without a single word, *believing they would do the prisoner justice.* The prosecution had been met not only on the threshold, but at every step, with obstructions to the progress of the case. If the case was not to be closed to-night, he would like to ask the same indulgence given to the other side, that he might collate the notes of the evidence he had taken.

. The *Court* inquired what length of time the defence would require for argument on Monday morning. He could then decide whether to grant the request or not.

After consultation, *Mr. Chilton* stated that there would be only two speeches by himself and Mr. Griswold, not occupying more than two hours and a half in all.

Mr. Hunter again entered an earnest protest against delay.

The Court then ordered the prosecution to proceed. Mr. Hunter spoke forty minutes, and ridiculed as absurd the expectation of the prisoner — that he should have been dealt with by the rules of honorable warfare !

The Court then adjourned till Monday ; and the brave old man, satisfied that his motives were now correctly understood, and that no injury to the Cause would ensue from his heroic unsuccess, was carried back on the pallet to his cell in the prison. He returned there a conqueror.

VI.

LAWYERS' PLEAS.

THE Court reassembled early on Monday morning, October 31. John Brown was brought from prison between files of armed men, as the practice was, and laid down on his bed within the bar. "He looked better," we are told, "than on the previous day; his health is evidently improving, and he seemed to be at the most perfect ease of mind." The Court room and every approach to it were densely crowded.

From the opening of the Court until the afternoon session, the counsel for the defence — Messrs. Griswold and Chilton — and for the prosecution — Messrs. Hunter and Harding — occupied the attention of the jury in arguing for and against the prisoner. I do not intend to pollute my pages with any sketch of the lawyers' pleas. They were able, without doubt, and erudite, and ingenious; but they were founded, nevertheless, on an atrocious assumption. For they assumed (as all lawyers' speeches must) that the statutes of the State were just; and, therefore, if the prisoner should be prover. guilty of offending against them, that it was right that he should suffer the penalty they inflict. This doctrine every Christian heart must scorn; John

Brown, at least, despised it; and so also, to be faithful to his memory, and my own instincts, must I. Mr. Griswold proved conclusively that, even according to the laws of Virginia, John Brown had not been guilty either of treason, of inciting to insurrection, or of murder with malice prepense; although, undoubtedly, he had committed other offences against the peace and dignity of that ancient Commonwealth. In any civilized State — in Europe, England, or our North — these facts would have resulted in the acquittal of the prisoner; for, although a person may be proven guilty of murder, if he be arraigned for theft, that indictment — in every free country — must at once be abandoned. Mr. Chilton's speech is unworthy of further notice than that it began in falsehood and ended in cant. Two quotations will sustain my statement:

" He desired, and the whole State desired, and the whole South desired, that the trial should be fair: *and it had been fair!* . . . . He charged the jury to look on this case, as far as the law would allow, with an eye favorable to the prisoner, and when their verdict should be returned — no matter what it might be — *he trusted that every man in the country would acquiesce in it.* Unless the majesty of the law were supported, dissolution of the Union must soon ensue, with all the evils that must necessarily follow in its train."

Mr. Hunter was true to his barbaric instincts to the last; eulogizing Wise to begin with, filling up his speech with the infamous maxims of iniquitous laws, and closing it with anathemas on godly John Brown. The peroration of his speech is noteworthy from its audacity of assertion:

"We therefore ask his conviction to vindicate the *majesty* of the law. While we have patiently borne delays, as well here as outside in the community, in preservation of the character of Virginia, *that plumes itself on its moral character,* as well as physical, and on *its loyalty and its devotion to truth and right,* we ask you to discard any thing else, and render your verdict as you are sworn to do. . . . Justice is the centre upon which Deity sits. There is another column which represents its mercy. *You have nothing to do with that."*

Mr. Hunter closed his speech at half past one o'clock.

"During most of the arguments to-day, Brown lay on his back, with his eyes closed.

"Mr. Chilton asked the Court to instruct the Jury, if they believed the prisoner was not a citizen of Virginia, but of another State, they cannot convict on a count of treason.

"The Court declined, saying the Constitution did not give rights and immunities alone, but also imposed responsibilities.

"Mr. Chilton asked another instruction, that the Jury must be satisfied that the place where the offence was committed was within the boundaries of Jefferson County, which the Court granted."

The Jury then retired to consider their verdict, and the Court adjourned for half an hour.

THE VERDICT.

Thus far, for our record of the trial, we have been obliged to rely on pro-slavery authority. It was not till the following day that a truthful and impartial reporter succeeded in eluding the cowardly and inquisitorial vigilance of the Virginians, who, in their anxiety to prevent a fair trial or a true report, excluded all Northern men from their City — as had been done, a thousand times before, in each of the despotic Commonwealths south of the Potomac, by men who are ever, and in various ways, committing daily violence on the Federal Constitution, and accusing, in the same breath, the Northern men who submit to these infractions as guilty of assailing the rights of the South.

Thus far, then, they have been convicted out of their

TRIAL OF CAPT. JOHN BROWN.

own mouths; and, in order to complete their self-con-
demnation, I will conclude this report with an extract
from one of their own journals:

After an absence of three quarters of an hour, the Jury returned
into Court with a verdict. At this moment the crowd filled all the
space from the couch inside the bar, around the prisoner, beyond the
railing in the body of the Court, out through the wide hall, and beyond the doors. There stood the anxious but perfectly silent and
attentive populace, stretching head and neck to witness the closing
scene of Old Brown's trial. It was terrible to look upon such a
crowd of human faces, moved and agitated with but one dreadful ex-
pectancy — to let the eyes rest for a moment upon the only calm and
unruffled countenance there, and to think that he alone of all present
was the doomed one, above whose head hung the sword of fate. But
there he stood, a man of indomitable will and iron nerve, all collected
and unmoved, even while the verdict that consigned him to an ignominious doom was pronounced upon him. After recapitulating his
offences set forth in the indictment, the Clerk of the Court said:

Gentlemen of the Jury, what say you? Is the prisoner at the bar,
John Brown, guilty, or not guilty?

Foreman. Guilty.

Clerk. Guilty of treason, and conspiring and advising with slaves
and others to rebel, and murder in the first degree?

Foreman. Yes.

Not the slightest sound was heard in the vast crowd as this verdict
was thus returned and read. Not the slightest expression of elation
or triumph was uttered from the hundreds present, who, a moment
before, outside the Court, joined in heaping threats and imprecations on
his head; nor was this strange silence interrupted during the whole
of the time occupied by the forms of the Court. Old Brown himself
said not even a word, but, as on any previous day, turned to adjust
his pallet, and then composedly stretched himself upon it.

Mr. Chilton moved an arrest of judgment, both on account of errors
in the indictment and errors in the verdict. The objection in regard
to the indictment has already been stated. The prisoner has been
tried for an offence not appearing on the record of the Grand Jury.
The verdict was not on each count separately, but was a general verdict on the whole indictment.

Counsel on both sides being too much exhausted to go on, the motion was ordered to stand over till to-morrow, and Brown was again
removed unsentenced to prison.

"There he stood!" Alas! for the honor of the
29

Union, whom Virginia thus disgraced in the eyes of
the world, the brave old man was too feeble to stand.
" He sat up in his bed when the Jury entered," writes
another and more vindictive Virginia journalist, " and,
after listening to the rendition of the verdict, lay down
very composedly, without saying a word." The writer
adds, intending thereby to eulogize the Virginians,
" There was no demonstration of any kind whatever."
Thus thoroughly does Slavery corrupt the heart, that
the spectacle of an heroic old man, feeble from the loss
of blood poured out in behalf of God's despised poor,
unable to stand unsupported on his feet, and yet condemned to die on the scaffold, shocked no one Southern conscience — excited " no demonstration of any
kind whatever."

VII.

Condemned to Die.

THE first of November was devoted to the trial of
Coppoc, which was continued on the following day.
No witnesses were called for the defence. Mr. Harding for the State, and Messrs. Hoyt and Griswold for
the defence, followed by Mr. Hunter, who closed for the
prosecution, addressed the jury, who presently retired
to appear to consider their pre-determined verdict — of
GUILTY.

"During the absence of the Jury in Coppoc's case,"
says an eye witness, "in order that no time should be
wasted, John Brown was brought in from jail to be sentenced. He walked with considerable difficulty, and
every movement appeared to be attended with pain,
although his features gave no expression of it. It was
late, and the gaslights gave an almost deathly pallor to
his face. He seated himself near his counsel, and,
after once resting his head upon his right hand, remained entirely motionless, and for a time appeared
unconscious of all that passed around — especially unconscious of the execrations audibly whispered by spectators : ' D—d black-hearted villain ! heart as black

(339)

as a stove-pipe'!' and many such. While the Judge
read his decision on the points of exception which had
been submitted, Brown sat very firm, with lips tightly
compressed, but with no appearance of affectation of
sternness. He was like a block of stone. When the
clerk directed him to stand and say why sentence
should not be passed upon him, he rose and leaned
slightly forward, his hands resting on the table. He
spoke timidly — hesitatingly, indeed — and in a voice
singularly gentle and mild. But his sentences came
confused from his mouth, and he seemed to be wholly
unprepared to speak at this time.* Types can give no
intimation of the soft and tender tones, yet calm and
manly withal, that filled the Court room, and, I think,
touched the hearts of many who had come only to rejoice at the heaviest blow their victim was to suffer."

This is what he said :.

JOHN BROWN'S LAST SPEECH.

"I have, may it please the Court, a few words
to say.

"In the first place, I deny every thing but what I
have all along admitted — the design on my part to free
the slaves. I intended certainly to have made a clear
thing of that matter, as I did last winter, when I went
into Missouri, and there took slaves without the snap-
ping of a gun on either side, moved them through the
country, and finally left them in Canada. I designed
to have done the same thing again, on a larger scale.
That was all I intended. I never did intend murder,

---

* It was expected that all the prisoners would be condemned and executed on the
same day. Hence, John Brown was taken by surprise.

or treason, or the destruction of property, or to excite or incite slaves to rebellion, or to make insurrection.

"I have another objection: and that is, it is unjust that I should suffer such a penalty. Had I interfered in the manner which I admit, and which I admit has been fairly proved — (for I admire the truthfulness and candor of the greater portion of the witnesses who have testified in this case) — had I so interfered in behalf of the rich, the powerful, the intelligent, the so-called great, or in behalf of any of their friends, either father, mother, brother, sister, wife, or children, or any of that class, and suffered and sacrificed what I have in this interference, it would have been all right, and every man in this Court would have deemed it an act worthy of reward rather than punishment.

"This Court acknowledges, as I suppose, the validity of the Law of God. I see a book kissed here which I suppose to be the Bible, or, at least, the New Testament. That teaches me that all things 'whatsoever I would that men should do unto me I should do even so to them.' It teaches me further, to 'remember them that are in bonds as bound with them.' I endeavored to act up to that instruction. I say, I am yet too young to understand that God is any respecter of persons. I believe that to have interfered as I have done, as I have always freely admitted I have done, in behalf of His despised poor, was not wrong, but right. Now, if it is deemed necessary that I should forfeit my life for the futherance of the ends of justice, and mingle my blood further with the blood of my children, and with the blood of millions in this slave country whose

29 *

rights are disregarded by wicked, cruel, and unjust enactments — I submit: so let it be done.

"Let me say one word further.

"I feel entirely satisfied with the treatment I have received on my trial. Considering all the circumstances, it has been more generous than I expected. But I feel no consciousness of guilt. I have stated from the first what was my intention and what was not. I never had any design against the life of any person, nor any disposition to commit treason, or excite slaves to rebel, or make any general insurrection. I never encouraged any man to do so, but always discouraged any idea of that kind.

"Let me say, also, a word in regard to the statements made by some of those connected with me. I hear it has been stated by some of them that I have induced them to join me. But the contrary is true. I do not say this to injure them, but as regretting their weakness. There is not one of them but joined me of his own accord, and the greater part at their own expense. A number of them I never saw, and never had a word of conversation with, till the day they came to me, and that was for the purpose I have stated.

"Now I have done."

Perfect quiet prevailed while this speech was delivered; and, when he finished, the Judge proceeded to pass sentence on him. After a few preliminary remarks, he stated that no doubt could exist of the guilt of the prisoner, and sentenced him to be hanged by the neck till he was dead, on Friday, the 2d day of December. "At the announcement," said a spectator,

" that, for the sake of example, the execution would be
more than usually public, one indecent fellow, behind
the Judge's chair, shouted and clapped hands jubi-
lantly; but he was indignantly checked, and in a manner that induced him to believe that he would do best
to retire. It is a question, nevertheless, if the general
sentiment were not fairly expressed by this action.
John Brown was soon after led away again to his place
of confinement."

Was ever such a speech delivered in America — so
fearless, yet so gentle; so manly, modest, wise, God's-
heart-imbued ?

VIII.

THE CONQUERING PEN.

FROM the date of his incarceration in the jail of Charlestown, till the day of his execution, John Brown wrote a number of eminently characteristic letters to his friends in different parts of the country. Such of them as we have been able to obtain, are herewith subjoined:

LETTER FOR COUNSEL.

CHARLESTOWN, JEFFERSON Co., Oct. 22, 1859.

To THE HON. JUDGE TILDEN.

Dear Sir: I am here a prisoner, with several sabre cuts in my head, and bayonet stabs in my body. My object in writing is to obtain able and faithful counsel for myself and fellow-prisoners, five in all, as we have the faith of Virginia pledged through her governor, and numerous prominent citizens, to give us a fair trial. Without we can obtain such counsel from without the slave states, neither the facts in our case can come before the world, nor can we have the benefit of such facts as might be considered mitigating, in the view of others, upon our trial. I have money on hand here to the amount of two hundred and fifty dollars, and personal property sufficient to pay a most liberal fee to yourself, or any able man who will undertake our defence, if I can be allowed the benefit of said property. Can you, or some other good man, come on immediately, for the sake of the young men prisoners at least? My wounds are doing well.

Do not send an ultra abolitionist.

Very respectfully yours,

JOHN BROWN.

P. S. The trial is set for Wednesday next, the 26th instant.

J. W. CAMPBELL, *Sheriff Jefferson Co.*

(344)

A noble lady, a worthy friend of John Brown, when
the news of his "failure" and imprisonment reached
Boston, determined to go on to Virginia to nurse him;
but, prostrated by the shock thus given to her nervous
system, she was prevented, by physical incapacity, from
carrying out the generous and heroic impulse. On
suggesting the execution of this design to her distinguished relative, Mrs. Child, that lady at once sent a
letter to Captain Brown, forwarding it with a note to
Governor Wise, in which she asked permission to go
on to Charlestown and nurse the old hero.

LETTER TO CAPTAIN BROWN.

WAYLAND, MASS., Oct. 26, 1859.

Dear Captain Brown: Though personally unknown to you, you
will recognize in my name an earnest friend of Kansas, when circumstances made that territory the battle ground between the antagonis-
tic principles of slavery and freedom, which politicians so vainly
strive to reconcile in the government of the United States.

Believing in peace principles, I cannot sympathize with the method
you chose to advance the cause of freedom; but I honor your generous intentions; I admire your courage, moral and physical; I reverence you for the humanity which tempered your zeal; I sympathize
with you in your cruel bereavement, your sufferings, and your
wrongs. In brief, I love you and bless you.

Thousands of hearts are throbbing with sympathy as warm as mine.
I think of you night and day, bleeding in prison, surrounded by hostile faces, sustained only by trust in God and your own strong heart.
I long to nurse you — to speak to you sisterly words of sympathy and
consolation. I have asked the permission of Governor Wise to do so.
If the request is not granted, I cherish the hope that these few words
may at least reach your hands, and afford you some little solace.
May you be strengthened by the conviction that no honest man ever
sheds blood for freedom in vain, however much he may be mistaken in
his efforts. May God sustain you, and carry you through whatsoever
may be in store for you. Yours, with heartfelt respect, sympathy,
and affection.   L. MARIA CHILD.

Governor Wise's answer to Mrs. Child's request was
respectful, but crafty and characteristic. He would

forward the letter, he said, to the Commonwealth's Attorney, "with the request that he will ask the permission of the Court to hand it to the prisoner." After asserting that Virginia and Massachusetts were not involved in a civil war; that the Federal Constitution gave to citizens of Massachusetts going to Virginia the immunities of a citizen of the United States; that, coming to minister to the captive in prison — a mission merciful and humane — she had the right to visit Charlestown, and would "not only be allowed, but be respected, if not welcomed," the politician added, that "a few unenlightened and inconsiderate persons, fanatical in their modes of thought and action to *maintain justice and right*, might molest you, or be disposed to do so, and this might suggest the imprudence of risking any experiment upon the peace of a society very much excited by the crimes with whose chief author you seem to sympathize so much." Declaring the readiness of Virginia to protect Mrs. Child against the fury of the populace, the next sentence of the let ter was worthy of Mark Antony : "I could not permit an insult, even to woman in her walk of charity among us, *though it be to one who whetted knives of butchery for our mothers, sisters, daughters, and babes. . . .* His attempt was the natural consequence of your sympathy." He concluded by announcing that whether the lady should see him or not, when she should arrive in Charlestown, would be for the Court and its officers to say. The Executive, he intimates, and the Judiciary are separate branches of the Government; a statement that the first attempt to try Stevens will explain.

The gilded threat of this letter caused Mrs. Child to delay her departure until she should hear from the old hero himself. When his letter came, it prevented her journey.

JOHN BROWN'S LETTER TO MRS. CHILD.

[No date.]

Mrs. L. Maria Child.

My dear Friend: (such you prove to be, though a stranger:) Your most kind letter has reached me, with the kind offer to come here and take care of me. Allow me to express my gratitude for your great sympathy, and at the same time to propose to you a different course, together with my reasons for wishing it. I should certainly be greatly pleased to become personally acquainted with one so gifted and so kind; but I cannot avoid seeing some objections to it, under present circumstances. First, I am in charge of a most humane gentleman, who, with his family, have rendered me every possible attention I have desired, or that could be of the least advantage; and I am so far recovered from my wounds as no longer to require nursing. Then, again, it would subject you to great personal inconvenience and heavy expense, without doing me any good.

Allow me to name to you another channel through which you may reach me with your sympathies much more effectually. I have at home a wife and three young daughters — the youngest but little over five years old, the oldest nearly sixteen. I have also two daughters-in-law, whose husbands have both fallen near me here. There is also another widow, Mrs. Thompson, whose husband fell here. Whether she is a mother or not I cannot say. All these, my wife included, live at North Elba, Essex County, New York. I have a middle-aged son, who has been, in some degree, a cripple from his childhood, who would have as much as he could well do to earn a living. He was a most dreadful sufferer in Kansas, and lost all he had laid up. He has not enough to clothe himself for the winter comfortably. I have no living son, or son-in-law, who did not suffer terribly in Kansas.

Now, dear friend, would you not as soon contribute fifty cents now, and a like sum yearly, for the relief of those very poor and deeply afflicted persons, to enable them to supply themselves and their children with bread and very plain clothing, and to enable the children to receive a common English education? Will you also devote your own energies to induce others to join in giving a like amount, or any other amount, to constitute a little fund for the purpose named?

I cannot see how your coming here can do me the least good , and I am quite certain you can do me immense good where you are. I am quite cheerful under all my afflicting circumstances and prospects ; having, as I humbly trust, " the peace of God, which passeth all understanding," to rule in my heart. You may make such use of this as you see fit. God Almighty bless and reward you a thousand fold.
    Yours, in sincerity and truth,   JOHN BROWN.

LETTER FROM THE QUAKER LADY.

NEWPORT, R. I., Tenth Month, 27th, 1859.
CAPT. JOHN BROWN.
    Dear Friend : Since thy arrest, I have often thought of thee, and have wished that, like Elizabeth Fry towards her prison friends, so I might console thee in thy confinement. But that can *never* be, and so I can only write thee a few lines, which, if they contain any comfort, may come to thee like some little ray of light. You can never know how very many dear friends love thee with all their hearts, for thy brave efforts in behalf of the poor oppressed; and though we, who are non-resistants, and religiously believe it better to reform by moral, and not by carnal, weapons, could not approve of bloodshed, yet we know thee was animated by the most generous and philanthropic motives. Very many thousands openly approve thy intentions, though most friends would not think it right to take up arms. Thousands pray for thee every day; and, O, I do pray that God will be with thy soul. Posterity will do thee justice. If Moses led out the thousands of Jewish slaves from their bondage, and God destroyed the Egyptians in the sea because they went after the Israelites to bring them back to slavery, then, surely, by the same reasoning, we may judge thee a deliverer who wished to release millions from a more cruel oppression. If the American people honor Washington for resisting with bloodshed for seven years an unjust tax, how much more ought thou to be honored for seeking to free the poor slaves ! O, I wish I could plead for thee, as some of the other sex can plead; how I would seek to defend thee ! If I had now the eloquence of Portia ; how I would turn the scale in thy favor ! But I can only pray, " God bless thee ! " God pardon thee, and, through our Redeemer, give thee safety and happiness now and always.   From thy friend,   E. B.

JOHN BROWN'S REPLY.

CHARLESTOWN, JEFFERSON CO., VA., November 1, 1859.
    My dear Friend, E. B. of R. I.: Your most cheering letter of 27th of October is received, and may the Lord reward you a thousand fold for the kind feeling you express towards me ; but more especially

for your fidelity to the "poor that cry, and those that have no help." For this I am a prisoner in bonds. It is solely my own fault, in a military point of view, that we met with our disaster — I mean that I mingled with our prisoners, and so far sympathized with them and their families, that I neglected my duty *in other* respects. But God's will, not mine, be done.

You know that Christ once armed Peter. So also in my case; I think he put a sword into my hand, and there continued it, so long as he saw best, and then kindly took it from me. I mean when I first went to Kansas. I wish you could know with what cheerfulness I am now wielding the "sword of the Spirit" on the right hand and on the left. I bless God that it proves "mighty to the pulling down of strongholds." I always loved my Quaker friends, and I commend to their kind regard my poor, bereaved, widowed wife, and my daughters and daughters-in-law, whose husbands fell at my side. One is a mother, and the other likely to become so soon. They, as well as my own sorrow-stricken daughter, are left very poor, and have much greater need of sympathy than I, who, through Infinite Grace and the kindness of strangers, am "joyful in all my tribulations."

Dear sister, write them at North Elba, Essex Co., N. Y., to comfort their sad hearts. Direct to Mary A. Brown, wife of John Brown. There is also another, a widow, wife of Thompson, who fell with my poor boys in the affair at Harper's Ferry, at the same place.

I do not feel conscious of guilt in taking up arms; and had it been on behalf of the rich and powerful, the intelligent, the great, — as men count greatness, — of those who form enactments to suit themselves and corrupt others, or some of their friends, that I interfered, suffered, sacrificed, and fell, it would have been doing very well. But enough of this.

These light afflictions, which endure for a moment, shall work out for me *a far more exceeding and eternal weight of glory*. I would be very grateful for another letter from you. My wounds are healing. *Farewell.* God will surely attend to his own cause in the best possible way and time, and he will not forget the work of his own hands.

Your friend,

John Brown.

LETTER TO HIS FAMILY.

Charlestown, Jefferson Co., Va., 8th Nov., 1859.

Dear Wife and Children — Every One: I will begin by saying that I have in some degree recovered from my wounds, but that I am quite weak in my back, and sore about my left kidney. My appetite has been quite good for most of the time since I was hurt. I am supplied with almost every thing I could desire to make me comfortable, and

the little I do lack (some articles of clothing, which I lost) I may
perhaps soon get again. I am, besides, quite cheerful, having (as I
trust) the peace of God, which "passeth all understanding," to "rule
in my heart," and the testimony (in some degree) of a good conscience
that I have not lived altogether in vain. I can trust God with both
the time and the manner of my death, believing, as I now do, that for
me at this time to seal my testimony (for God and humanity) with my
blood, will do vastly more towards advancing the cause I have earnestly endeavored to promote, than all I have done in my life before.
I beg of you all meekly and quietly to submit to this; not feeling
yourselves in the least *degraded* on that account. Remember, dear
wife and children all, that Jesus of Nazareth suffered a most excru-
ciating death on the cross as a felon, under the most aggravating
circumstances. Think, also, of the prophets, and apostles, and Christians of former days, who went through greater tribulations than you
or I; and (try to) be reconciled. May God Almighty comfort all
your hearts, and soon wipe away all tears from your eyes. To him be
endless praise. Think, too, of the crushed millions who "have no
comforter." I charge you all never (in your trials) to forget the
griefs of " the poor that cry, and of those that have none to help them."
I wrote most earnestly to my dear and afflicted wife not to come on
for the present at any rate. I will now give her my reasons for doing
so. First, it would use up all the scanty means she has, or is at all
likely to have, to make herself and children comfortable hereafter.
For let me tell you that the sympathy that is now aroused in your
behalf may not always follow you. There is but little more of the
romantic about helping poor widows and their children than there is
about trying to relieve poor " niggers." Again, the little comfort it
might afford us to meet again would be dearly bought by the pains of
a final separation. We must part, and, I feel assured, for us to meet
under such dreadful circumstances would only add to our distress.
If she come on here, she must be only a gazing stock throughout the
whole journey, to be remarked upon in every look, word, and action,
and by all sorts of creatures, and by all sorts of papers throughout the
whole country. Again, it is my most decided judgment that in quietly
and submissively staying at home, vastly more of generous sympathy
will reach her, without such dreadful sacrifice of feeling as she must
put up with if she comes on. The visits of one or two female friends
that have come on here have produced great excitement, which is very
annoying, and they cannot possibly do me any good. O Mary, do
not come ; but patiently wait for the meeting (of those who love God
and their fellow-men) where no separation must follow. " They shall
go no more out forever." I greatly long to hear from some one of

you, and to learn any thing that in any way affects your welfare. I sent you ten dollars the other day. Did you get it? I have also endeavored to stir up Christian friends to visit and write to you in your deep affliction. I have no doubt that some of them at least will heed the call. Write to me, care of Capt. John Avis, Charlestown, Jefferson County, Va.

"Finally, my beloved, be of good comfort." May all your names be "written on the Lamb's book of life" — may you all have the purifying and sustaining influence of the Christian religion — is the earnest prayer of your affectionate husband and father.

JOHN BROWN.

P. S. I cannot remember a night so dark as to have hindered the coming day, nor a storm so furious or dreadful as to prevent the return of warm sunshine and a cloudless sky. But, beloved ones, to remember that this is not your rest, that in this world you have no abiding place or continuing city. To God and his infinite mercy I always commend you.   J. B.

Nov. 9.

LETTER TO HIS HALF BROTHER.

CHARLESTOWN, JEFFERSON CO., VA., Nov. 12, 1859.

Dear Brother Jeremiah: Your kind letter of the 9th instant is received, and also one from Mr. Tilden, for both of which I am greatly obliged. You inquire, "Can I do any thing for you or your family?" I would answer that my sons, as well as my wife and daughter, are all very poor, and that any thing that may hereafter be due me from my father's estate I wish paid to them, as I will endeavor *hereafter to describe*, without legal formalities to consume it all. One of my boys has been so entirely used up as very likely to be in want of comfortable clothing for the winter. I have, through the kindness of friends, fifteen dollars to send him, which I will remit shortly. If you know where to reach *him*, please send him that amount at once, as I shall remit the same to *you* by a safe conveyance. If I had a plain statement from Mr. Thompson of the state of my accounts, with the estate of my father, I should then better know what to say about that matter. As it is, I have not the least memorandum left me to refer to. If Mr. Thompson will make me a statement, and charge *my dividend fully for his trouble*, I would be greatly obliged to him. In that case you can send me any remarks of your own. I am gaining in health slowly, and am *quite cheerful* in view of my approaching end, being fully persuaded that I am worth inconceivably more to *hang* than for any other purpose. God Almighty bless and save you all.

Your affectionate brother,   JOHN BROWN.

P. S. Nov. 13. — Say to my poor boys never to grieve for one moment on my account; and should many of you live to see the time when you will not blush to own your relation to Old John Brown, it will not be more strange than many things that have happened. I feel a thousand times more on account of my sorrowing friends than on my own account. So far as *I am concerned*, I "count it all joy." "I have fought the good fight," and have, as I trust, "finished my course." Please show this to any of my family that you may see. My love to all; and may God, in his infinite mercy, for Christ's sake, bless and save you all. Your affectionate brother,   J. Brown.

LETTER FROM A CHRISTIAN CONSERVATIVE.

WEST NEWTON, MASS., Nov. 5, 1859.

CAPT. JOHN BROWN.

Dear Brother: Withholding any expression of opinion respecting the outbreak at Harper's Ferry, I cannot but admire your bravery and effort to save life during the conflict. But, above all, your unwavering faith in God and fidelity to principle, your fearless answers, your faithful testimony against slavery, and your noble, self-sacrificing spirit excite the admiration of all who venerate justice, truth, and humanity.

While I cannot approve of all your acts, I stand in awe of your position since your capture, and dare not oppose you lest I be found fighting against God; for you speak as one having authority, and seem to be strengthened from on high. Look only to God for aid in these your trying hours, which if they be brief, may the illumination of his Spirit and of a lifetime be centred in the time allotted you here. If called to ascend the gallows, may you do it joyfully, praising God that you have been counted worthy to die for those ready to perish; and, like his Son, may you feel to forgive and bless those who take your life. Many, yes, a multitude, appreciate you *now;* and were you ambitious of immortal fame, you might now enjoy a foretaste of that which is to come, if you die as you have lived since a prisoner.

Your family will not be forgotten; their wants will be attended to abundantly by those who love heroism and integrity to principle, and by the Father who suffers not a sparrow to fall to the ground without his notice. My prayers you have. May God give you strength and resignation, and inspire you to utter words of wisdom, warning, courage, and love to those you leave.

I would imprint on your sacred face the kiss of sympathy and love ere you join the multitude of martyrs who have gone before you. But this cannot be. God bless you. I would ask a line from you, but would not tax your brief time; for never having seen you, I should

sacredly cherish a line from your hand. Believing God reigns, I feel
to view these recent events as his providence, which in time may be
fully manifested, although at present inscrutable. A host of friends
love and remember you, and I speak for many in my immediate neighborhood. Farewell, dear brother. God bless you.

JOHN BROWN'S REPLY TO A CHRISTIAN CONSERVATIVE.

CHARLESTOWN, JEFFERSON Co., VA., Nov. 15, 1859.

My dear Sir: Your kind mention of *some* things in my conduct
here, which you approve, is very comforting indeed to my mind. Yet
I am conscious that you do me no more than justice. I do certainly
feel that through divine grace *I have endeavored* to be "faithful in a
very few things," mingling with even these much of imperfection. I
am certainly "unworthy even to suffer affliction with the *people of
God;*" yet in infinite grace he has THUS honored me. May the *same*
grace enable me to serve him in a "*new obedience*," through my little
remainder of this life, and to rejoice in him forever. I cannot feel
that God will suffer even the poorest service we may any of us render
him or his cause to be lost or in vain. I do feel, "dear brother,"
that I am wonderfully "strengthened from on high."

May I use that strength in "*showing his strength* unto this generation," and his power to every one that is to come. I am most grateful for your assurance that my poor, shattered, heart-broken "family
will not be forgotten." I have long tried to recommend them to "the
God of my fathers." I have *many* opportunities for *faithful plain deal-
ing* with the more powerful, influential, and intelligent classes in this
region, which, I trust, are not entirely misimproved. I *humbly trust
that I* firmly believe that "God reigns," and I think I can truly say,
'Let the earth rejoice." May God take care of his *own cause, and of
his own great name,* as well as of those who love their neighbors.

Farewell!   Yours, in truth,   JOHN BROWN.

The next letter was addressed to his old school-
master, in Litchfield, Connecticut, and is thus introduced by the Rev. L. W. Bacon:

"My aged friend, the Rev. H. L. Vaill, of this place, remembers
John Brown as having been under his instruction in the year 1817,
at Morris Academy. He was a godly youth, laboring to recover from
his disadvantages of early education, in the hope of entering the ministry of the gospel. Since then, the teacher and pupil have met but
once to take 'a retrospective look over the route by which God had
led them.' But a short time since, Mr. Vaill wrote to Brown, in his

30 *

prison, a letter of Christian friendship, to which he has received the following heroic and sublime reply. Has ever such an epistle been written from a condemned cell since the letter 'to Timotheus,' when Paul 'was brought before Nero the second time'?

"I have copied it faithfully from the autograph that lies before me, without the change or omission of a word, except to omit the full name of the friends to whom he sends his message. The words in Italics and capitals are so underscored in the original. The handwriting is clear and firm; but towards the end of the sheet seems to show that the sick old man's hand was growing weary. The very characters make an appeal to us for our sympathy and prayers. 'His salutation with his own hand. Remember his bonds.'"

LETTER TO HIS SCHOOLMASTER.

CHARLESTOWN, JEFFERSON CO., VA., Nov. 15, 1859.

REV. H. L. VAILL.

My dear, steadfast Friend: Your most kind and most welcome letter of the 8th instant reached me in due time.

I am very grateful for all the good feeling you express, and also for the kind counsels you give, together with your prayers in my behalf. Allow me here to say, that notwithstanding "my soul is amongst lions," still I believe that "God in very deed is with me." You will not, therefore, feel surprised when I tell you that I am "joyful in all my tribulations;" that I do not feel condemned of Him whose judgment is just, nor of my own conscience. Nor do I feel degraded by my imprisonment, my chain, or prospect of the gallows. I have not only been (though utterly unworthy) permitted to "suffer affliction with God's people," but have also had a great many rare opportunities for "preaching *righteousness* in the great congregation." I trust it will not all be lost. The jailer (in whose charge I am) and his family and assistants have all been most kind; and, notwithstanding he was one of the bravest of all who *fought me*, he is *now* being abused for his humanity. So far as my observation goes, none but *brave* men are likely to be *humane* to a fallen foe. Cowards prove their *courage* by their *ferocity*. It may be done in that way with but little risk.

I wish I could write you about a few only of the interesting times I here experience with different classes of men — clergymen among others. Christ, the great Captain of liberty as well as of salvation, and who began his mission, as foretold of him, by proclaiming it, saw fit to take from me a sword of steel after I had carried it for a time; but he has put another in my hand, ("the sword of the Spirit;") and I pray God to make me a faithful soldier wherever he may send me — not less on the scaffold than when surrounded by my warmest sympathizers.

My dear old friend, I do assure you I have not forgotten our last meeting, nor our retrospective look over the route by which God had then led us; and I bless his name that he has again enabled me to hear your words of cheering and comfort at a time when I, at least, am on the "brink of Jordan." See Bunyan's Pilgrim. God in infinite mercy grant us soon another meeting on the opposite shore. I have often passed under the rod of Him whom I call my Father; and certainly no son ever needed it oftener; and yet I have enjoyed much of life, as I was enabled to discover the secret of this somewhat early. It has been in making the prosperity and the happiness, of others my own; so that really I have had a great deal of prosperity. I am very prosperous still, and looking forward to a time when "peace on earth and good will to men" shall every where prevail; I have no murmuring thoughts or envious feelings to fret my mind. "I'll praise my Maker with my breath."

Your assurance of the earnest sympathy of the friends in my native land is very grateful to my feelings; and allow me to say a word of comfort to them:

As I believe most firmly that God reigns, I cannot believe that any thing I have *done*, *suffered*, *or may yet suffer*, *will be lost to the cause of God or of humanity.* And before I began my work at Harper's Ferry, I felt assured that in the *worst event* it would certainly PAY. I often expressed that belief, and can now see no possible cause to alter my mind. I am not as yet, in the *main*, at all disappointed. I have been a *good deal* disappointed as it regards *myself* in not keeping up to *my own plans;* but I now feel entirely reconciled to that, even; for God's plan was infinitely better, *no doubt*, or I should have kept to my own. Had Samson kept to his determination of not telling Delilah wherein his great strength lay, he would probably have never overturned the house. I did not tell Delilah; but I was induced to act very *contrary to my better judgment;* and I have lost my *two* noble boys, and other friends, if not my *two eyes*.

But "God's will, *not mine*, be done." I feel a comfortable hope that like that erring servant of whom I have just been writing, *even I* may (through infinite mercy in Christ Jesus) yet "*die in faith.*" As to both the time and manner of my death, I have but very little trouble on that score, and *am able* to be (as you exhort) "of good cheer."

I send through you my best wishes to Mrs. W——— and her son George, and to all dear friends. May the God of the *poor and oppressed* be the God and Saviour of you all.

Farewell, till we *meet again*.

Your friend, in truth,   JOHN BROWN.

CHARLESTOWN, JEFFERSON CO., VA., 16th Nov., 1859.

My dear Wife: I write you in answer to a most kind letter, of November 13, from dear Mrs. ——. I owe her ten thousand thanks for her kindness to *you particularly, and more especially* than for what she has done, and is doing, in a more direct way for me personally. Although I feel grateful for every expression of kindness or sympathy towards me, yet nothing can so effectually minister to my comfort as acts of kindness done to relieve the wants or mitigate the sufferings of my poor, distressed family. May *God Almighty and their own consciousness* be their eternal rewarders. I am exceedingly rejoiced to have you make the acquaintance, and be surrounded by, such choice friends as I have *long known* some of those to be, with whom you are staying, by reputation. I am most glad to have you meet with one *of a family* (or I would rather say of two families) *most beloved and never to be forgotten by me.* I mean *dear, gentle* ——. *Many and many* a time has she, her *father, mother, brother, sisters, uncle and aunt* (like angels of mercy) ministered to the wants of myself and of my poor sons, both in sickness and in health. Only last year I lay sick for quite a number of weeks with them, and was cared for *by all*, as though I had been a most affectionate brother or father. *Tell her* that I ask God to bless and reward them *all* forever. "*I was* a stranger, and they took me in." It may possibly be that —— would like to copy this letter, and send it to her home. If so, by all means let her do so. *I would write them* if I had the power.

Now let me say a word about the effort to educate our daughters. I am no longer able to provide means to help towards that object, and it therefore becomes me not to dictate in the matter. I shall gratefully submit the direction of the whole thing to those whose generosity may lead them to undertake it in their behalf, while I give *anew* a little expression of my own choice respecting it. You, my wife, *perfectly well know* that I have always expressed a decided preference for a very *plain, but perfectly practical*, education for both *sons and daughters.* I do not mean an education so very miserable as that *you and I* received in early life, nor as some of our children enjoyed. When I say plain, but practical, I mean enough of the learning of the schools to enable them to transact the common business of life comfortably and respectably, together with that thorough training to good business habits which best prepares both men and women to be *useful, though poor,* and to meet the *stern* REALITIES of life with a good grace. You well know that I always claimed that the *music* of the broom, wash-tub, needle, spindle, loom, axe, scythe, hoe, flail, &c., should first be learned at all events, and that of the piano, &c., AFTERWARDS. I put them in that order as most conductive to health of body and mind;

and for the obvious reason that, after a life of some *experience and of much observation*, I have found *ten women* as well as *ten men* who have made their mark in life *right*, whose early training was of that *plain, practical* kind, to *one* who had a more popular and fashionable *early* training. But enough of this.

Now, in regard to your coming here: If you feel sure that you can endure the trials and the shock, which will be *unavoidable*, (if you come,) I should be most glad to see you *once more;* but when I think of your being insulted on the road, and perhaps *while here*, and of only seeing your wretchedness made complete, *I shrink* from it. Your composure and fortitude of mind may be *quite equal to it all;* but I am in *dreadful doubt* of it. *If you do come*, defer your journey till about the 27th or 28th of this month. The scenes which you will have to pass through on coming here will be *any thing but those* you now pass, with tender-hearted friends, and kind faces to meet you every where. *Do consider the matter well* before you make the *plunge*. I think I had better say *no more* on this *most painful* subject. My health improves a little ; my mind is very tranquil, I may say joyous, and I continue to receive every kind attention that I have any possible need of. I wish you to send copies of all my letters to all our poor children. What I write to one must answer for all, till I have more strength. I get numerous kind letters from friends in almost all directions, to encourage me to " be of good cheer," and I still have, *as I trust*, " the peace of God to rule in my heart." May God, for Christ's sake, ever make his face to shine on you all.

Your affectionate husband, JOHN BROWN.

LETTER TO A YOUNG FRIEND.

CHARLESTOWN, JEFFERSON CO., VA., NOV. 17, 1859.

My Dear Young Friend : — I have just received your most kind and welcome letter of the 15th inst., but did not get any other from you. I am under many obligations to you, and to your father, for all the kindness you have shown me, especially since my disaster. May God and your own consciences ever be your rewarders. Tell your father that I am quite cheerful — that I do not feel myself in the least :e-graded by my imprisonment, my chains, or the near prospect of the gallows. Men cannot imprison, or chain, or hang the soul. I go joyfully in behalf of millions that " have no rights " that this *great and glorious*, this *Christian* Republic is " bound to respect." Strange change in morals, political as well as Christian, since 1776 ! I look forward to other changes to take place in God's good time, fully believing that the " fashion of this world passeth away."

Farewell. May God abundantly bless you all !

Your friend, JOHN BROWN.

LETTER TO HIS SON JASON.

CHARLESTOWN, JEFFERSON Co., VA., Nov. 22, 1859

Dear Children: Your most welcome letters of the 16th inst. I have just received, and I bless God that he has enabled you to bear the heavy tidings of our disaster with so much seeming resignation and composure of mind. That is exactly the thing I have wished you all to do for me — to be cheerful and perfectly resigned to the holy will of a wise and good God. I bless his most holy name, that I am, (I trust,) in some good measure, able to do the same. I am even "joyful in all my tribulations," even since my confinement, and I humbly trust that "I know in whom I have trusted." A calm peace (perhaps) like that which your own dear mother felt, in view of her last change, seems to fill my mind by day and by night. Of this, neither the powers of "earth or hell" can deprive me. Do not, dear children, any of you, grieve for a single moment on my account. As I trust my life has not been thrown away, so I also humbly trust that my death shall not be in vain. God can make it to be a thousand times more valuable to his own cause than all the miserable service (at best) that I have rendered it during my life. When I was first taken, I was too feeble to write much; so I wrote what I could to North Elba, requesting Ruth and Anne to send you copies of all my letters to them. I hope they have done so, and that you, Ellen, will do the same with what I may send to you, as it is still quite a labor for me to write all that I need to. I want your brothers to know what I write, if you know where to reach them. I wrote Jeremiah, a few days since, to supply a trifling assistance, fifteen dollars, to such of you as might be most destitute. I got his letter, but do not know as he got mine. I hope to get another letter from him soon. I also asked him to show you my letter. I know of nothing you can any of you now do for me, unless it is to comfort your own hearts, and cheer and encourage each other to trust in God, and Jesus Christ, whom he hath sent. If you will keep his sayings, you shall certainly "know of his doctrine, whether it be of God or no." Nothing can be more grateful to me than your earnest sympathy, except it be to know that you are fully persuaded to be Christians. And now, dear children, farewell for this time. I hope to be able to write you again. The God of my father take you for his children.

Your affectionate father,　　　　　JOHN BROWN.

NOTE. — The remittance referred to was unquestionably intended for Owen Brown, who escaped from Harper's Ferry, but is supposed to be destitute even of a change of clothing. The significant allusion in the letter shows that the father was confident of Owen's safety. — *Akron (O.) Beacon.*

LETTER TO AN OHIO CLERGYMAN.

JAIL, CHARLESTOWN, Wednesday, Nov. 23, 1859.

Rev. McFARLAND.

Dear Friend: Although you write to me as a stranger, the spirit you show towards me and the cause for which I am in bonds, makes me feel towards you as a dear friend. I would be glad to have you, or any of my liberty-loving ministerial friends here, to talk and pray with me. I am not a stranger to the way of salvation by Christ. From my youth I have studied much on that subject, and at one time hoped to be a minister myself; but God had another work for me to do. To me it is given in behalf of Christ, not only to believe on him, but also to *suffer* for his sake. But while I trust that I have some experimental and saving knowledge of religion, it would be a great pleasure to me to nave some one better qualified than myself to lead my mind in prayer and meditation, now that my time is so near a close. You may wonder, are there no ministers of the gospel here? I answer, No. There are no ministers of *Christ* here. These ministers who profess to be Christian, and hold slaves or advocate slavery, I cannot abide them. 'My knees will not bend in prayer with them while their hands are stained with the blood of souls. The subject you mention as having been preaching on, the day before you wrote to me, is one which I have often thought of since my imprisonment. I think I feel as happy as Paul did when he lay in prison. He knew if they killed him it would greatly advance the cause of Christ; that was the reason he rejoiced so. On that same ground "I do rejoice, yea, and will rejoice." Let them hang me; I forgive them, and may God forgive them, for they know not what they do. I have no regret for the transaction for which I am condemned. I went against the laws of men, it is true; but "whether it be right to obey *God* or *men*, judge ye." Christ told me to remember them that are in bonds, as *bound with them*, to do towards them as I would wish them to do towards me in similar circumstances. My conscience bade me do that. I tried to do it, but failed. Therefore I have no regret on that score. I have no sorrow either as to the result, only for my poor wife and children. They have suffered much, and it is hard to leave them uncared for. But God will be a husband to the widow, and a father to the fatherless.

I have frequently been in Wooster; and if any of my old friends from about Akron are there, you can show them this letter. I have but a few more days, and I feel anxious to be away, "where the wicked cease from troubling, and the weary are at rest." Farewell.

Your friend, and the friend of all friends of liberty,

JOHN BROWN.

From a subsequent letter, dated Nov. 24, we make the following extract:

I have had many interesting visits from pro-slavery persons, almost daily, and I endeavor to *improve them faithfully, plainly, and kindly*. I do not think I ever enjoyed life better than since my confinement here. For this I am indebted to *Infinite Grace*, and kind letters from friends from different quarters. I wish I could only know that all my poor family were as composed and as happy as *I*. I think nothing but the Christian religion could ever make any one so composed.

"My willing soul would stay
In such a frame as this."

JOHN BROWN.

LETTER TO MR. HOYT.

CHARLESTOWN, JEFFERSON CO., VA., Nov. 24, 1859.
GEORGE H. HOYT, ESQ.

Dear Sir: Your kind letter of the 22d inst. is received. I exceedingly regret my inability to make you some other acknowledgment for all your efforts in my behalf than that which consists merely in words; but so it is. May God and a good conscience be your continual reward. I really do not see what you can do with me any further. I commend my poor family to the kind *remembrance* of all friends, but I well understand that *they are not the only poor* in our world. I ought to begin to leave off saying our world. I have but very little idea of the charges made against Mr. Griswold, as I get to see but little of what is afloat. *I am very sorry for any wrong that may be done him;* but I have no means of contradicting any thing that may be said, not knowing what is said. I cannot see how it should be *any more dishonorable* for him to receive some compensation for his expenses and service, than for Mr. Chilton, and I am not aware that any blame is attached to him on that score. I am getting more letters constantly than I well know how to answer. *My kind friends* appear to have very wrong ideas of my condition as regards *replying* to all the kind communications I receive.

Your friend, in truth, JOHN BROWN.

This letter needs a word of comment. Mr. Chilton, "John Brown's chivalrous Southern lawyer," demanded a fee of one thousand dollars, which was paid out of the fund contributed for his family and cause in the New England States. Mr. Griswold accepted a fee of two hundred and fifty dollars for travelling expenses and services from John Brown personally; supposing — as every one at Charlestown thought at the time — that he was a man of independent fortune. For receiving this fee, Mr. Griswold has been denounced in hundreds of democratic papers, while not one of them has printed a reproachful word against the " distinguished lawyer " from Maryland. Neither is to blame, or both are ; and if to blame, let a fourfold punishment be meted out to Mr. Chilton.

LETTER TO HIS WIFE — EXTRACTS.

Before Mrs. Brown started from Philadelphia for Charlestown, she received a letter from her husband, dated November 25, in which, after referring to the fact that she was then staying with Lucretia Mott, he says:

. . . I remember the faithful old lady well, but presume she has no recollection of me. I once set myself to oppose a mob at Boston, where she was. After I interfered, the police immediately took up the matter, and soon put a stop to mob proceedings. The meeting was, I think, in Marlboro' Street Church, or Hotel, perhaps. I am glad to have you make the acquaintance of such old "Pioneers" in the cause. I have just received from Mr. John Jay, of New York, a draft for $50 (fifty dollars) for the benefit of my family, and will enclose it made payable to your order. I have also $15 (fifteen dollars) to send to our crippled and destitute unmarried son; when I can, I intend to send you, by express, two or three little articles to carry home. Should you happen to meet with Mr. Jay, say to him that you fully appreciate his great kindness both to me and my family. God bless all such friends. It is out of my power to reply to all the kind and encouraging letters I get; I wish I could do so. I have been so much relieved from my lameness for the last three or four days as to be able to sit up to read and write pretty much all day, as well as part of the night; and I do assure you and all other friends that I am quite busy, and none the less happy on that account. The time passes quite pleasantly, and the near approach of my great change is not the occasion of any particular dread.

I trust that God, who has sustained me so long, will not forsake me when I most feel my need of Fatherly aid and support. Should He hide His face, my spirit will droop and die; but not otherwise, be assured. My only anxiety is to be properly assured of my fitness for the company of those who are "washed from all filthiness," and for the presence of Him who is infinitely pure. I certainly think I do have some "hunger and thirst after righteousness." If it be only genuine, I make no doubt I "shall be filled." Please let all our friends read my letters when you can; and ask them to accept of it as in part for them. I am inclined to think you will not be likely to succeed well about getting away the bodies of your family; but should that be so, do not let that grieve you. It can make but little difference what is done with them.

You can well remember the changes you have passed through. Life is made up of a series of changes, and let us try to meet them in the best manner possible. You will not wish to make yourself and children any more burdensome to friends than you are really compelled to do. I would not.

I will close this by saying that, if you now feel that you are equal to the undertaking, do exactly as you feel disposed to do about coming to see me before I suffer. I am entirely willing.

Your affectionate husband,   JOHN BROWN.

LETTER TO THADDEUS HYATT.

CHARLESTOWN, JEFFERSON CO., VA., Nov. 27, 1859.

THADDEUS HYATT, ESQ.

My dear Sir: Your very acceptable letter of the 24th instant has just been handed to me. I am certainly most obliged to you for it, and for all your efforts in behalf of my family and myself. . . . It, your effort, at any rate, takes from my mind the greatest burden I have felt since my imprisonment, to feel assured that, in some way, my shattered and broken-hearted wife and children would be so far relieved as to save them from great physical suffering. Others may have devised a better way of doing it. I had no advice in regard to it, and felt very grateful to know, while I was yet living, of almost any active measure being taken. I hope no offence is taken at yourself or me in the matter. I am beginning to familiarize my mind with new and very different scenes. Am very cheerful.

Farewell, my friend.   JOHN BROWN.

LETTER TO A YOUNG LADY.

CHARLESTOWN, JEFFERSON CO., VA., Nov. 27, 1859.

My dear Miss —— : Your most kind and cheering letter of the 18th instant is received. Although I have not been at all low-spirited nor cast down in feeling since being imprisoned and under sentence, which I am fully aware is soon to be carried out, it is exceedingly gratifying to learn from friends that there are not wanting in this generation some to sympathize with me and appreciate my motive, even now that I am whipped. Success is in general the standard of all merit. I have passed my time here quite cheerfully; still trusting that neither my life nor my death will prove a total loss. As regards both, however, I am liable to mistake. It affords me some satisfaction to feel conscious of having at least *tried* to better the condition of those who are always on the under-hill side, and am in hope of being able to meet the consequences without a murmur. I am endeavoring to get ready for another field of action, where no defeat befalls the truly brave. That "God reigns," and most wisely, and controls all events, might, it would seem, reconcile those who believe it to much that appears to be very disastrous. I am one who have tried to believe that, and still keep trying. Those who die for the truth may prove to be courageous at last; so I continue "hoping on," till I shall find that the truth must finally prevail. I do not feel in the least degree despondent nor degraded by my circumstances, and I entreat my friends not to grieve on my account. You will please excuse a very poor and short letter, as I get more than I can possibly answer. I send my best wishes to your kind mother, and to all the family, and to all the true friends of humanity. And now, dear friends, God be with you all, and ever guide and bless you.

Your friend,   John Brown.

LETTER TO JUDGE TILDEN.

CHARLESTOWN, JEFFERSON Co., VA., Monday, Nov. 28, 1859.
Hon. D. R. TILDEN.

My dear Sir: Your *most kind and comforting* letter of the 23d inst. is received.

I have no language to express the feelings of gratitude and obligation I am under for your kind interest in my behalf ever since my disaster.

The great bulk of mankind estimate each other's actions *and motives* by the measure of success or *otherwise* that attends them through life. By that rule I have been one of the *worst* and one of the *best* of men. *I do* not claim to have been one of the *latter ;* and I leave it to an impartial tribunal to decide whether the world has been the *worse* or the better of my *living* and *dying* in it. My present great anxiety is to get as near in readiness for a different field of action as I well *can*, since being in a good measure *relieved from the fear* that my poor, *broken-hearted wife and children* would come to immediate want. May God reward, *a thousand fold*, all the kind efforts made in their behalf.

I have enjoyed *remarkable cheerfulness and composure of mind* ever since my confinement; and it is a great comfort to *feel assured* that *I am permitted* to die (*for a cause*) not *merely* to pay the debt of nature, (as all must.) I feel myself to be *most* unworthy of *so great* distinction. The particular manner of dying *assigned* to me, gives me but very little *uneasiness*. I wish I had the time and the ability to give you (my dear friend) some little idea of what is *daily, and, I might almost say, hourly*, passing within my *prison walls;* and could my friends but witness only a few of those scenes just as they occur, I think they would feel very well reconciled to my being here *just what I am, and just as I am.* My *whole* life *before* had not afforded me one half the opportunity to plead *for the right. In this*, also, *I find* much to reconcile me to both my present condition and my immediate prospect. I may be *very insane*, (and *I am so*, if insane at all.) But if that be so, *insanity* is like a very pleasant dream to me. I am not in the least degree conscious of my *ravings*, of my fears, or of any terrible visions whatever; but *fancy* myself entirely composed, and that my *sleep, in particular*, is as sweet as that of a healthy, joyous little infant. I pray God that he will grant me a continuance of the same calm, but delightful, *dream*, until I come to know of those realities which " eyes have not seen, and which ears have not heard." I have scarce realized that I am in prison, or in irons, at all. I certainly think I was never more cheerful in my life. I intend to take the liberty of sending, by express, to your care, some trifling articles for those of my family who may be in Ohio, which you can hand to my brother JEREMIAH, when you may see him, together with fifteen dollars I have asked him to advance to them. Please excuse me so often troubling you with my letters, or any of my matters. Please also remember me *most* kindly to MR. GRISWOLD, and to all others who love their neighbors. I write JER-EMIAH to your care.   Your friend, in truth,   JOHN BROWN.

LETTER TO MR. SEWALL.

CHARLESTOWN, JEFFERSON CO., VA., Nov. 29, 1859.

S. E. SEWALL, ESQ.

My dear Sir: Your most kind letter of the 24th inst. is received. It does, indeed, give me "pleasure," and the greatest encouragement to know of any efforts that have been made in behalf of my poor and deeply afflicted family. It takes from my mind the greatest cause of sadness I have experienced during my imprisonment here. I feel quite cheerful, and ready to die. I can only say, for want of time, may the *God of the oppressed* and the poor, *in great mercy, remember* all those to whom we are so deeply indebted.

Farewell.   Your friend,   JOHN BROWN.

JOHN BROWN'S LAST LETTER TO HIS FAMILY.

CHARLESTOWN PRISON, JEFFERSON CO., VA., Nov. 30, 1859.

My dearly beloved Wife, Sons and Daughters, Every One: As I now begin what is probably the last letter I shall ever write to any of you, I conclude to write to all at the same time. I will mention some little matters particularly applicable to little property concerns in another place.

I recently received a letter from my wife, from near Philadelphia, dated Nov. 22, by which it would seem that she was about giving up the idea of seeing me again. I had written her to come on if she felt equal to the undertaking, but I do not know that she will get my letter in time. It was on her own account chiefly that I asked her to stay back. At first I had a most strong desire to see her again, but there appeared to be very serious objections; and should we never meet in this life, I trust that she will in the end be satisfied it was for the best at least, if not most for her comfort. I enclosed in my last letter to her a draft of $50 from John Jay, made payable to her order. I have now another to send her, from my excellent old friend Edward Harris of Woonsocket, R. I., for $100, which I shall also make payable to her order.

I am waiting the hour of my public murder with great composure of mind and cheerfulness, feeling the strong assurance that in no other possible way could I be used to so much advantage to the cause of God and of humanity, and that nothing that either I or all my family have sacrificed or suffered will be lost. The reflection that a wise and merciful, as well as just and holy God rules not only the affairs of this world, but of all worlds, is a rock to set our feet upon under all circumstances — even those more severely trying ones into which our own feelings and wrongs have placed us. I have now no doubt but that our seeming disaster will ultimately result in the most glorious success. So, my dear shattered and broken family, be of good cheer, and believe and trust in God with all your heart, and with all your soul, for he doeth all things well. Do not feel ashamed on my account, nor for one moment despair of the cause or grow weary of well doing. I bless God I never felt stronger confidence in the certain and near approach of a bright morning and glorious day than I have felt, and do now feel, since my confinement here. I am endeavoring to return, like a poor prodigal as I am, to my Father, against whom I have always sinned, in the hope that he may kindly and forgivingly meet me, though a very great way off.

O, my dear wife and children, would to God you could know how I have been travailing in birth for you all, that no one of you may fail of the grace of God through Jesus Christ; that no one of you

31 *

may be blind to the truth and glorious light of his Word, in which life and immortality are brought to light. I beseech you, every one, to make the Bible your daily and nightly study, with a child-like, honest, candid, teachable spirit of love and respect for your husband and father.

And I beseech the God of my fathers to open all your eyes to the discovery of the truth. You cannot imagine how much you may soon need the consolations of the Christian religion. Circumstances like my own, for more than a month past, have convinced me beyond all doubt of our great need of some theories treasured up when our prejudices are excited, our vanity worked up to the highest pitch. O, do not trust your eternal all upon the boisterous ocean without even a helm or compass to aid you in steering. I do not ask of you to throw away your reason; I only ask you to make a candid, sober use of your reason.

My dear young children, will you listen to this last poor admonition of one who can only love you? O, be determined at once to give your whole heart to God, and let nothing shake or alter that resolution. You need have no fears of regretting it. Do not be vain and thoughtless, but sober-minded; and let me entreat you all to love the whole remnant of our once great family. Try and build up again your broken walls, and to make the utmost of every stone that is left. Nothing can so tend to make life a blessing as the consciousness that your life and example bless and leave you the stronger. Still, it is ground of the utmost comfort to my mind to know that so many of you as have had the opportunity have given some proof of your fidelity to the great family of men. Be faithful unto death; from the exercise of habitual love to man it cannot be very hard to love his Maker.

I must yet insert the reason for my firm belief in the divine inspiration of the Bible, notwithstanding I am, perhaps, naturally sceptical; certainly not credulous. I wish all to consider it most thoroughly when you read that blessed book, and see whether you cannot discover such evidence yourselves. It is the purity of heart, filling our minds as well as work and actions, which is every where insisted on, that distinguishes it from all the other teachings, that commends it to my conscience. Whether my heart be willing and obedient or not, the inducement that it holds out is another reason of my convictions of its truth and genuineness; but I do not here omit this my last argument on the Bible, that eternal life is what my soul is panting after this moment. I mention this as a reason for endeavoring to leave a valuable copy of the Bible, to be carefully preserved in remembrance of me, to so many of my posterity, instead of some other book at equal cost.

I beseech you all to live in habitual contentment with moderate

ircumstances and gains of worldly store, and earnestly to teach this
to your children and children's children after you, by example as well
as precept. Be determined to know by experience, as soon as may be,
whether Bible instruction is of divine origin or not. Be sure to owe
no man any thing, but to love one another. John Rogers wrote to his
children, "Abhor that arrant whore of Rome." John Brown writes
to his children to abhor, with undying hatred also, that sum of all
villanies — slavery. Remember, he that is slow to anger is better than
the mighty, and he that ruleth his spirit than he that taketh a city.
Remember, also, that they, being wise, shall shine, and they that turn
many to righteousness, as the stars forever and ever.

And now, dearly beloved family, to God and the work of his grace
I commend you all.

Your affectionate husband and father, JOHN BROWN.

JOHN BROWN'S WILL.

CHARLESTOWN, JEFFERSON Co., VA., Dec. 1, 1859.

I give to my son John Brown, Jr., my surveyor's compass and other
surveyor's articles if found; also, my old granite monument, now at
North Elba, N. Y., to receive upon its two sides a further inscription,
as I will hereafter direct; said stone monument, however, to remain
at North Elba so long as *any of my children and my wife* may remain
there as residents.

I give to my son Jason Brown my silver watch with my name en-
graved on inner case.

I give to my son Owen Brown my double-spring opera-glass, and
my rifle gun, (if found,) presented to me at Worcester, Mass. It is
globe-sighted and new. I give also to the same son fifty dollars in
cash, to be paid him from the proceeds of my father's estate, in consideration of his terrible suffering in Kansas, and his crippled condition
from his childhood.

I give to my son Solomon Brown fifty dollars in cash, to be paid
him from my father's estate, as an offset to the first two cases above
named.

I give to my daughter Ruth Thompson my large old Bible, containing the family record.

I give to each of my sons, and to each of my *other* daughters, my
son-in-law Henry Thompson, and to each of my daughters-in-law,
a good a copy of the Bible as can be purchased at some bookstore in
New York or Boston, at a cost of five dollars each in cash, to be paid
out of the proceeds of my father's estate.

I give to each of my grandchildren that may be living when my
father's estate is settled, as good a copy of the Bible as can be purchased (as above) at a cost of three dollars each.

All the Bibles to be purchased at one and the same time, for cash, on the best terms.

I desire to have ($50) fifty dollars *each* paid out of the final proceeds of my father's estate to the following named persons, to wit: To Allen Hammond, Esq., of Rockville, Tolland County, Conn., *or* to George Kellogg, Esq., former agent of the New England Company at that place, *for the use and benefit of that company.* Also, fifty dollars to Silas Havens, formerly of Lewisburg, Summit County, O., if he can be found; also, fifty dollars to a man of Storck County, O., at Canton, who sued my father in his lifetime, through Judge Humphrey and Mr. Upson of Akron, to be paid by J. R. Brown to the man in person, if he can be found. His name I cannot remember. My father made a compromise with the man by taking our house and lot at Manneville. I desire that any remaining balance that may become my due from my father's estate may be paid in equal amounts to my wife, and to each of my children, and to the widows of Watson and Owen Brown, by my brother.

John Avis, *Witness.*   John Brown.

A FINAL CODICIL.

Charlestown, Jefferson Co., Va., Dec. 2, 1859.

It is my desire that my wife have all my personal property not previously disposed of by me, and the entire use of all my landed property during her natural life; and that, after her death, the proceeds of such land be equally divided between all my then living children; and that what would be a child's share be given to the children of each of my two sons who fell at Harper's Ferry, and that a child's share be divided among the children of my now living children who may die before their mother, (my present beloved wife.) No formal will can be of use when my expressed wishes are made known to my *dutiful* and beloved family.   John Brown.

My dear Wife: I have time to enclose the within and the above, which I forgot yesterday, and to bid you another farewell. "Be of good cheer," and God Almighty bless, save, comfort, guide, and keep you to "the end." Your affectionate husband,   John Brown.

LETTER TO JAMES FORMAN.

Charlestown Prison, Jefferson Co., Va., Dec. 1, 1859.
James Forman, Esq.

My dear Friend: I have only time to say I got your kind letter of the 26th Nov. this evening. Am very grateful for all the good feeling expressed by yourself and wife. May God abundantly bless and save you all. I am very cheerful, in hopes of entering on a better state of existence, in a few hours, through infinite grace in "Christ Jesus, my Lord." Remember the "poor that cry," and "them that are in bonds as bound with them."

Your friend as ever,   JOHN BROWN.

LETTER TO MR. HUNTER.

CHARLESTOWN, VA., Nov. 22, 1859.

ANDREW HUNTER, ESQ., *Present.*

Dear Sir: I have just had my attention called to a seeming confliction between the statement I at first made to Governor Wise and that which I made at the time I received my sentence, regarding my intentions respecting the slaves we took about the Ferry. There need be no such confliction, and a few words of explanation will, I think, be quite sufficient. I had given Governor Wise a full and particular account of that; and when called in court to say whether I had any thing further to urge, I was taken wholly by surprise, as I did not expect my sentence before the others. In the hurry of the moment, I forgot much that I had before intended to say, and did not consider the full bearing of what I then said. I intended to convey this idea: that it was my intention to place the slaves in a condition to defend their liberties if they would, without any bloodshed, but not that I intended to run them out of the Slave States. I was not aware of any such apparent confliction until my attention was called to it, and I do not suppose that a man in my then circumstances should be superhuman in respect to the exact purport of every word he might utter. What I said to Governor Wise was spoken with all the deliberation I was master of, and was intended for truth; and what I said in court was equally intended for truth, but required a more full explanation than I there gave. Please make such use of this as you think calculated to correct any wrong impression I may have given.

JOHN BROWN.

The three following letters have never hitherto been published :

CHARLESTOWN, JEFFERSON Co., VA., Oct. 31, 1859.

My dear Wife and Children, Every One: I suppose you have learned before this by the newspapers that two weeks ago to-day we were fighting for our lives at Harper's Ferry; that during the fight Watson was mortally wounded, Oliver killed, Wm. Thompson killed, and Dauphin slightly wounded; that on the following day I was taken prisoner, immediately after which I received several sabre cuts in my head, and bayonet stabs in my body. As nearly as I can learn, Watson died of his wound on Wednesday the second, or on Thursday the third day after I was taken. Dauphin was killed when I was taken, and Anderson, I suppose, also. I have since been tried, and found guilty of treason, &c., and of murder in the first degree. I have not yet received my sentence. No others of the company with whom you were acquainted were, so far as *I can learn*, either killed or taken. Under all these terrible calamities, I feel quite cheerful in the assurance that God reigns, and will overrule all for his glory and the best possible good. I feel *no* consciousness of *guilt* in the matter, nor even mortification on account of my imprisonment and iron; and I feel perfectly assured that very soon no member of my family will feel any possible disposition to "blush on my account." Already dear friends at a distance, with kindest sympathy, are cheering me with the assurance that *posterity* at least will do me justice. I shall commend you all together, with my beloved, but bereaved, daughters-in-law, to their sympathies, which I have no doubt will soon reach you. I also commend you all to Him "whose mercy endureth forever" — to the God of my fathers, "whose I am, and whom I serve." "He will never leave you or forsake you" unless you forsake Him. Finally, my dearly beloved, be of good comfort. Be sure to remember and *to follow my advice*, and my example *too*, so far as it has been consistent with the holy religion of Jesus Christ, in which I remain a most firm and humble believer. Never forget the poor, nor think any thing you bestow on them to be lost to you, even though they may be as *black* as Ebedmelech, the Ethiopian eunuch, who cared for Jeremiah in the pit of the dungeon, or as *black* as the one to whom Philip preached Christ. Be sure to entertain strangers, for thereby some have —— "Remember them that are in bonds as bound with them." I am in charge of a jailer *like* the one who took charge of "Paul and Silas;" and you may rest assured that both *kind hearts and kind faces* are more or less about me, whilst thousands are thirsting for my blood. "These *light* afflictions, which are but *for a moment*, shall work out for us a *far more exceeding and eternal* weight of glory." I hope to be able to write you again. My wounds are doing well. Copy this, and send it to your sorrow-stricken brothers, Ruth, to comfort them. Write me a few words in regard to the welfare of all. God Almighty bless you. all, and make you "joyful in the midst of all your tribulations." Write to John Brown, Charlestown, Jefferson Co., Va., care of Captain John Avis. Your affectionate husband and father.   JOHN BROWN.

Nov. 3, 1859.

P. S. — Yesterday, Nov. 2, I was sentenced to be hanged on Dec. 2d next. Do not grieve on my account. I am still quite cheerful. God bless you.   Yours ever,   JOHN BROWN.

LETTER TO HIS WIFE.

CHARLESTOWN, JEFFERSON CO., VA., Nov. 12, 1859.

My dear Wife: Your most welcome letter of the 13th instant I got yesterday. I am very glad to learn from *yourself* that you feel so much resigned to your circumstances, so much confidence in a wise and good Providence, and such composure of mind in the midst of all your deep afflictions. This is "*just as it should be;*" and let me still say, "Be of good cheer;" for we shall soon "come out of all our great tribulations," and very soon (if we trust in him) "God shall wipe away all tears from our eyes." Soon "we shall be satisfied when we are awake in his likeness." There *is now here* a source of much *lisquietude* to me, viz., *the fires* which are almost of *daily and nightly* occurrence in this *immediate* neighborhood. Whilst I well know that no one of them is the work of our friends, I know at the same time that by more or less of the inhabitants we shall be charged with them, the same as with the ominous and threatening letters to Governor Wise. In the existing *state* of public feeling, I can easily see a further objection to your coming here at present; *but I did not intend* saying another word to you on that subject. Why will you not say to me whether you had any crops *mature* this season? If so, what ones? Although I may never more intermeddle with your worldly affairs, I have not *yet lost all* interest in them. A little history of your *success* or *of your failures*, I should very much prize; and I would gratify you and other friends some way were it in my power. I am still quite cheerful, and by no means "cast down." I "remember that the time is short." The little trunk and all its contents (so far as I can judge) reached me safe. May God reward all the contributors. I wrote you under cover to our excellent friend Mrs. Spring on the 16th instant. I presume you have it before now. When you return it is most *likely* the Lake will *not* be open; so you must get your ticket at Troy for Moreau Station, or *Glens Falls*, (*for Glens Falls if you can get one,*) or get one for Vergennes in Vermont, and take your chance of crossing over *on the ice* to Westport. If you go soon, the route by Glens Falls to Elizabethtown will *probably be the best.* I have just learned that our poor Watson lingered with his wound until Wednesday about noon of the 19th Oct. Oliver died near my side in a few moments after he was shot. Dauphin died the next morning after Oliver and William were killed, viz., Monday. He died almost instantly — was by my side. William was shot by several persons. Anderson was killed with Dauphin.

Keep this letter to refer to. God Almighty bless and keep you all. Your affectionate husband, JOHN BROWN.

Dear Mrs. Spring: I send this to your care, because I am at a loss where it will reach my wife. Your friend, in truth, J. BROWN.

LETTER TO HIS CHILDREN.

CHARLESTOWN, JEFFERSON Co., VA., Nov. 22, 1859.

Dear Children All : I address this letter to you, supposing that your mother is not yet with you. She has not yet come here, as I have requested her not to do at present, *if at all*. She may think it best for her not to come at all. *She has*, (or will,) I presume, written you before this. Annie's letter to us both of the 9th has but just reached me. I am very glad to get it, and to learn that you are *in any* measure cheerful. This is the greatest comfort I can have, *except* that *it would be to know* that you are all *Christians*. God in mercy grant you all may be so. That is what you all will *certainly* need. *When* and in what *form* death may come is of but small moment. I feel just as content to die for *God's Eternal Truth, and for suffering humanity's, on the scaffold as in any other way;* and I do not say this from any disposition to *" brave it out."* No ; I would readily *own* my wrong, were I *in the least convinced of it.* I have now been confined over a month, with a good opportunity to look the whole thing as "fair in the face" as I am capable of doing ; and I now feel it most grateful that I am counted (*in the least possible degree*) worthy to suffer for the truth. I want you all to "be of good cheer." This life *is intended* as a season of training, chastisement, temptation, affliction, and trial, and "the righteous shall come out of" it all. O my dear children, let me again entreat you all to "forsake the foolish and *live*." What can you possibly lose by such a course? "Godliness with contentment is great gain, having the promise of *the life that now is, and of that which* is to come." "Trust in the Lord and *do good*, so shalt thou dwell in the land ; and verily thou shalt be fed." I have enjoyed life much ; why should I complain on leaving it? I want some of you to write me a little more particularly about all that concerns your welfare. I intend to write you as often as I can. "To God and the word of his grace I commend you all."

Your affectionate father,   JOHN BROWN.

P. S. — I am very grateful to all our friends.

Yours,   J. B.

IX.

Forty Days in Chains.

THE old man was imprisoned in the jail of Charles-town for forty-two days. The preceding chapter contains the principal letters that he wrote during this long period of confinement. His conduct while in jail was in keeping with his previous character. He never wavered in his faith; never faltered in the presence of any man. From his first commitment, on the 19th of October, till the 7th of November, no clean clothing was given to him; he lay as he had fallen at Harper's Ferry, in his dirty and blood-stained garments.

Such brief notes as have been published of his life in prison, from reliable authorities, I will now record in their chronological order:

DURING THE TRIAL.

The first is a telegraphic despatch to the Associated Press, of October 26:

"Brown has made no confession; but, on the contrary, says he has full confidence in the goodness of God, and is confident that he will rescue him from the perils that surround him. He says he has had rifles levelled at him, knives at his throat, and his life in as great peril as it is now, but that God has always been at his side. He knows God is with him, and fears nothing."

32 (373)

On the 2d of November, Judge Russell, of Boston, and his wife,* arrived in Charlestown, and had an interview with John Brown. The Judge spoke of the charge preferred by an administration journalist in Kansas against the Captain, which charged him with having killed the ruffians of Pottawattomie. The old man declared that he did not, in any way, participate in their execution ; but thought here, in jail, as he had believed in Kansas, that the act was just and necessary. A reliable writer, who was admitted to the cell on the same day, thus speaks of the old man :

"He is permitted to receive such visitors as he desires to see. He states that he welcomes every one, and that he is preaching, even in jail, with great effect, upon the enormities of slavery, and with arguments that every body fails to answer."

Another newspaper correspondent who visited him at this time — the days of his sentence — says :

"He said that Captain Avis, his jailer, showed as much kindness in treating him, as he had shown courage in attacking him. 'It is what I should expect from a brave man.' Seeing that one of the deputy jailers was present, he added: 'I don't say this to flatter; it isn't my way. I say it because it is true.' Capt. Brown appears perfectly fearless in all respects, — says that he has no feeling about death on a scaffold, and believes that every act, 'even all the follies that led to this disaster, were decreed to happen ages before the world was made.' The only anxiety he expressed was in regard to the circumstances of his family. He asked and obtained leave to add a postscript to a letter to his wife, telling her that he was to be hanged on the second of December, and requested that it should be directed to Mrs. John Brown, 'for there are some other widow Browns in North Elba.' He speaks highly of his medical attendants, but rejects the offered counsel of all ministers who believe that slavery is right. He will die as fearlessly as he has lived."

* "When that Boston wife went down to John Brown's prison, and stood mending the sabre cut of his coat, a young Virginian, doubtless of the first families, who had on a uniform, although requested by a friend to retire for the purpose of letting her and Brown talk of old times alone, looked in through the window. But the wit of the woman got rid of him; for, having finished her needlework, she turned round and said, 'Young man, get me a brush to clean this coat with;' but the chivalry of the old State was so livid hot with rage at being asked to do any thing useful, that he went off, and was not seen again for half an hour. Now, that is a specimen of this white race in working." — *Speech of Wendell Phillips*, New York, December 15.

The visit of Judge Russell and his wife was not liked by the self-styled hospitable Virginians, but they were permitted to visit the jail unmolested by the populace, and were not uncourteously received.

AFTER THE TRIAL.

The next Northern visitor — a Boston sculptor — who had come to take a likeness and a measure of John Brown's head, was less tenderly treated by the authorities. Captain Brown refused, at first, to permit the measurements to be made; but, when told that a lady, who had been a friend to him in other days, requested it as a personal favor, he at once expressed his willingness to permit it to be done. But the judicial, official, and jail authorities interposed, and the sculptor was refused all access to him. A reporter who had access to the cell on the same day — November 3 — writes:

"Brown's cheerfulness never fails him. He converses with all who visit him in a manner so free from restraint and with so much unconcern, that none can doubt his real convictions of self-approval. His daring courage has strongly impressed the people, and I have more than once heard public avowals of admiration of his fearlessness in spite of ominous murmurs of disapprobation from bystanders. A telegraphic despatch, dated Boston, was this morning received from T. W. Higginson. It said, 'John Brown's wife wishes to go on and see him. Can you obtain permission for her?' This was answered affirmatively; but when the matter was mentioned to Brown, he directed that this message should be immediately sent : 'Do not, for God's sake, come here now. John Brown.'"

In his next letter he adds :

"November 4. Certain Northern papers convey the impressions of a very general belief in John Brown's safety from execution. They assume, that, for political or other reasons, Governor Wise will be induced to show clemency to this condemned man. Such ideas are received here with indignation. It is evident that any attempt to remove him alive from this town would fail. The people say that a regiment of soldiers, with the Governor at their head, could not accomplish it. You, at a distance, can hardly form an impression of the rage for vengeance which is felt by the citizens of this place.

When Brown was in court on trial, there were always faces. burning with hatred hanging over him, fiercely watching every movement that he made. In the event of an attempt to rescue, which has been the great fear all along, the jailers have been instructed to shoot him. The populace are resolute in their determination that their victims shall never be taken from them, and it does not seem that this determination is to be shaken by any expedient.

"Brown's own ideas on the subject are characteristic. He tranquilly says, 'I do not know that I ought to encourage any attempt to save my life. I am not sure that it would not be better for me to die at this time. I am not incapable of error, and I may be wrong; but I think that perhaps my object would be nearer fulfilment if I should die. I must give it some thought.' There is no insincerity about this, you may be sure. Brown does not value his life; or, at least, is wholly unmoved at the prospect of losing it. He was never more firm than at this moment. The only compunctions he expresses are in relation to his management at Harper's Ferry, by which he lost not only himself, but sacrificed his associates. He sometimes says that if he had pursued his original plan of immediate escape to the mountains, he could never have been taken, for he and his men had studied the vicinity thoroughly, and knew it a hundred times better than any of the inhabitants. It was, he says, his weakness in yielding to the entreaties of his prisoners, and delaying his departure, that ruined him. 'It was the first time,' are his own words, 'that I ever lost command of myself, and now I am punished for it.'

"The reason Brown has given for asking his wife to remain away, is also characteristic. He knows it would cause great suffering, and will, possibly, shatter his composure in a manner which he is resolved against, lest his captors should esteem it an evidence of regret for what he has done. The despatch which I told you was sent to Mrs. Brown did not reach her, and to-day another was received, announcing that she was about to leave Philadelphia for this town. Brown will still make another effort to check her. Nothing seems to give Brown greater annoyance than hearing of those threatening anonymous letters that are continually sent to Governor Wise, and to the authorities of Charlestown, respecting his fate. He protests against them, and feels unwilling to believe that they proceed from his own friends.".

A pro-slavery reporter of the New York Herald visited John Brown on the same days, and thus records the results of the interview :

"I have just seen 'Old Captain Brown.' I inquired after his health and condition; he replied that his recent wounds had caused some inflammation in an old one, received, doubtless, in some of his 'Kansas work;' with that exception he was easy in mind and body, and thought he had done his duty to God and man. If it was decreed that he should suffer for it, very well; it was of but small consequence to him. He cared but little, any way. I asked him if he had no regret for the valuable lives he had destroyed. The old sinner replied he had not intended that. In answer to the query, 'If he thought his designs could be carried out without bloodshed?' he replied, 'It had been done in Missouri.' Just at that point the interview terminated.

"The prisoners are still guarded with the greatest vigilance. Hundreds of men all the time under arms are stationed at the jail, which, by the way, in its external appearance looks much more like a private residence than a jail, with its curtained windows and porch or stoop, to speak in Yankee parlance, leading out on the street — but it is very strong and secure within."

On the 5th of November, a Northern lady — Mrs. Spring—arrived in Charlestown to nurse John Brown; and, on the following day, was admitted to his cell. From her account of this interview, all that has not hitherto been published is subjoined:

"On our way we spent a night at Harper's Ferry. In the parlor we heard a young lady describing to a gentleman the horrors of the night of terror. 'I wished,' she said, 'I could shoot them all.' She told the story of poor Thompson, brought wounded into the hotel, followed by the infuriated people, protected for a time by Mr. Foulke's sister, at last dragged out and killed on the bridge. She said, 'It was dreadful to drag him out so; but they did right to kill him. *I would*. . . .'

"Between Mr. Brown and his jailer there has grown up a most friendly feeling. Captain Avis, who is too brave to be afraid to be kind, has done all he could for the prisoners, and been cursed accordingly. Still their condition was very cheerless, and Mr. Brown was in the same clothes in which he was taken. A cloth under his head was much stained with blood from a still open wound. It was hard for me to forget the presence of the jailer, (I had that morning seen his advertisement of 'fifty negroes for sale;') but I soon lost all thought of him in listening to Mr. Brown, who spoke at once of his plans and his failure. Twenty years he has labored, and waited, and suffered, and at last he believed the time of fulfilment had come. But he failed; and instead of being free on the mountains, strong to break every yoke, and let the oppressed go free, he was shorn of his strength, with prison walls about him. 'But,' he said, 'I do not now reproach myself; I did what I could.' I said, 'The Lord often leads us in strange ways.' 'Yes,' he answered; 'and *I think I cannot now better serve the cause I love so much than to die for it; and in my death I may do more than in my life.*' A pleasant smile came over his face when I exclaimed, 'Then you will be our martyr!' I continued, 'I want to ask one question for others, not for myself— Have you been actuated by any feeling of revenge?' He raised his head, and gave me a surprised look; then, lying back, he answered slowly, but firmly, 'I am not conscious of having had a feeling of the kind. No, not in all the wrong done to me and my family in Kansas, have I had a feeling of revenge.'. 'That would not sustain you now,' I remarked. 'No, indeed,' he replied quickly; 'but I sleep peacefully as an infant, or if I am wakeful, glorious thoughts come to me, entertaining

32 *

my mind.' Presently he added, 'The sentence they have pronounced against me did not disturb me in the least; it is not the first time that I have looked death in the face.' 'It is not the hardest thing for a brave man to die,' I answered; 'but how will it be in the long days before you, shut up here? If you can be true to yourself in all this, how glad we shall be!' '*I cannot say,*' he responded, '*but I do not believe I shall deny my Lord and Master, Jesus Christ; and I should be if I denied my principles against slavery.* Why, I preach against it all the time — Captain Avis knows I do.' The jailer smiled, and said, 'Yes.' We spoke of those who, in times of trial, forgot themselves, and he said, 'There seems to be just that difference in people; some can bear more than others, and not suffer so much. He had been through all kinds of hardships, and did not mind them.' My son remarked it was a great thing to have confidence in one's own strength. 'I did not mean to say that,' was the answer. 'It was only a constitutional difference, and I have been trained to hardships.' When twelve years old he went with his father to furnish the American army with cattle. This had led him far away from home, and subjected him to much exposure. Sometimes he slept in graveyards, but without any superstitious fears, and in forests a hundred miles from human habitations, surrounded by hostile English and Indians. 'But,' he added, smiling, 'I have one unconquerable weakness; I have always been more afraid of being taken into an evening party of ladies and gentlemen than of meeting a company of men with guns.' I think he is still more afraid of giving trouble to others. He seems to me to be purely unselfish, and in all that he has done to have never thought of himself, but always of others. In a noble letter to his wife, which I brought away with me, he entreats his 'dear wife and children, every one, *Never in all your trials forget the poor that cry, and him that hath none to help him.*'

"While he was talking to me with deepest solicitude of his family, the rabble, ever hanging about the Court House and prison, fearful that we were plotting treason inside, became restless. The sheriff was frightened, and called the jailer, so that I had only a moment to speak to Stevens, and to say farewell to Mr. Brown, who stood up to take leave of us, saying, 'The Lord will bless you for coming here.'

"There was, I learned afterwards, an angry mob outside the jail, but I did not see it. In a moment we reached the hotel, and at once recorded all we could remember of this interesting visit. That night there were rumors of an attack on the jail, and it was thought best that I should not repeat my visit.

"But the evening before we left Charlestown, a telegram announced to me that Mrs. Brown was in Philadelphia; and I was anxious therefore to have another interview with her husband. In the morning I sent for the Judge, who went with us to the prison door. Mr. Brown was sitting at the table, where he had just finished a letter to his wife, and a note to me. He looked better, and brighter, and happier than at my first visit, and Stevens also looked better. The old man said little except about his family, whom he commended to the kindness of good people."

The next account that we have, is from the correspondence of a pro-slavery paper, — the New York

Herald, — and from so very prejudiced a source, it is an important testimony to John Brown's character and courage :

" A person visiting Brown in jail, and seeing him for the first time, with an estimate formed of the man from his conduct during the trial and the speeches there delivered by him, would find his preconceived opinions rapidly disappear before the subject of them. It is true that, acting under excitement and from the consciousness that he was surrounded by his enemies, Brown frequently indulged in irascible remarks, feeling somewhat secure in the protection of the law whose victim he must be, while, at the same time, he dared, and, indeed, seemed to court, the worst his foes could do, thinking, perhaps, that he might escape the slower and more vengeful process of the law. In this state of feeling, sensitive as an enthusiast in giving to the world the motives of an act which, to his own diseased mind, was great and good, but which the world must condemn, he claimed with petulance and impatience those delays in the administration of the law which neither his crimes nor the circumstances of the court could fairly admit of. His object in this was, as he himself said, to give the world a fair opportunity of judging of his motives. If this opportunity was to be denied him, a summary quietus from one of the Sharpe's rifles in the hands of his enemies was all he next most desired. Now that he has received at the hands of justice and fair play all the delay that he could possibly hope for — a trial protracted over five days — with the fullest publicity given to the statements of those witnesses who testified most directly and generously to his humanity to his prisoners in the Armory at Harper's Ferry, he is satisfied, and awaits the result with that calm firmness which is the sure characteristic of a brave man.

" What Brown was most anxious to establish in the eyes of the world, during the trial, was his claim to being considered humane and merciful from his conduct to his prisoners. Whatever good quality a man possesses in any marked degree he is most anxious to have acknowledged at a time when circumstances point the other way; and so it was with Brown. Though his deeds in the Kansas border wars did not entitle him to be considered either as humane, or as averse to the shedding of blood, certainly his prisoners at Harper's Ferry had no fault to find with him on that score. They frankly acknowledged his humanity and courtesy towards them. At all events, the opinions formed of the man from the darker features of his life would fade before the influence of a personal interview with him in prison. Now that his fate has been decided by the just and proper process of law, he feels resigned to it. He no longer indulges in complaints and invectives. He rarely adverts to his trial ; but whenever he does, he pays a tribute to all concerned — Judge, counsel, and witnesses. He speaks freely upon all subjects but one, and that is the death of his sons. From his taciturnity he has been adjudged as entirely callous as to the fate of his sons and the other unfortunate victims of his mad enterprise ; but this is a very great mistake, and arises from ignorance of the human heart. He avoids the subject, it is true, but in waiving it, should it be started, the observer can mark and understand the feeling which confines it to his own heart. He speaks freely

enough of his wife and daughters, and he has been some time considering the propriety of allowing them to visit him. They are now on
their way to visit him, although he had resolved on avoiding an interview with them until some few days previous to that fixed for his
death, and which he has not the slightest hope of seeing put off a
single hour.

"Mrs. Russell, wife of Judge Russell, visited him the other day,
and had a long chat with him. He appeared very much pleased with
the lady's manner, and was very communicative with her. In illustrating his own character, he said that he had never known what fear
was when brought into opposition or collision with his fellow-man,
but that he had a strange feeling of that nature on his first introduction to the higher class of men with whom his peculiar and wayward
life brought him into contact. This feeling, he said, was very awk-
ward, and very painful, also, when entering the society of women.
The interview with Mrs. Russell seemed to touch the old man's heart,
and no woman could turn from him, so full of trials and sorrow —
for woman at such a moment rarely looks back to first causes — without emotion.

"Brown frequently indulges in amusing narratives of his encoun-
ters with his border enemies of Kansas and Missouri. He related to
me that upon one occasion he had succeeded in running away with a
party of slaves from Missouri, but that he was so hotly pursued that
some stratagem was necessary to prevent them from being overtaken,
in the event of which a severe fight and consequent sacrifice of life
must be the result. To avoid this, Brown himself turned off the
track of the retreating party, and having completely disguised himself, joined as an amateur the pursuers. With them he remained a
day and a night, entering into their counsels and effectually controlling their motions, so that he turned them off the right track, and gave
his friends an opportunity to escape. The old man laughed as he
recalled the scene, and said, 'I never was good at a disguise, but that
time I deceived several in the party who had seen and known me
before.' With all who come in a kindly spirit to visit him Brown is
exceedingly free and open. He esteems such as friends, and seems to
view their leave-taking with regret. But these visits are but as angels'-
visits, few and far between, for the jealousy and suspicion with which
the people of Charlestown regard all who are likely to feel for and
sympathize with the prisoner — in fact, all strangers — keep barred
the prison doors. It is not so, however, in regard to those about
whose earnest hostility to all abolition movements there is no doubt
entertained. They enter in flocks, and gape, and stare, and follow
the jailer in and out. He is in the same cell with Stevens, at whose
bedside he is constantly found sitting, with the Bible (just closed as
the visitor enters) placed upon his knees. This is the Bible he always
carried with him. It was found, after the final attack and recapture
of Harper's Ferry, in the Armory, and was by some kind person restored to its owner in captivity. It is almost needless to say that
Brown awaits death with that resignation and tranquillity which disarm the dreaded phantom of all terror."

A republican correspondent, writing under date of
November 8, informs us that,

"Brown's conversation is singularly attractive. His manner is magnetic. It attracts every one who approaches him, and while he talks he reigns. The other prisoners venerate him. Stevens sits in his bed, usually with his face away from the window, and listens all day to 'the Captain's' words, seldom offering a syllable except when called upon. Sometimes he gets a little excited, and springs forward to make clear some point about which 'the Captain' is in doubt; but his five bullets, in head and breast, weigh him down, and he is soon exhausted. As for the other men, — Copeland, Green, and Coppic, — they are always sending messages to 'the Captain,' assuring him that 'it was not they who confessed, and he mustn't growl at them, but at Cook.' I cannot forget hearing Brown express himself on the subject of the threatening anonymous letters that have been received by Gov. Wise relating to his case. 'Well, gentlemen,' he said, 'I tell you what I think of them. They come from no friends of mine. I have nothing to do with such friends. Why, gentlemen, of all the things in the world that I despise, anonymous letters are the worst. If I had a little job to do, I would sooner take one half the men I brought down here to help me than as many of these fellows as could fill all Jefferson County, standing close upon every inch. If I don't get out of this jail before such people as they are take me out, I shan't go very soon.'"

During all this time, John Brown received large numbers of letters daily. All anonymous notes he burned without reading. He replied to as many of the others as•he had time to answer. Previous to this date, also, two militia companies paid him a visit, — the Continentals and the Frederickburg Guards. He received them cordially ; but objected, he said, "to be made a monkey show of." He told the Continentals that he had seen their uniform on the border during the war of 1812.

WRIT OF ERROR REFUSED.

On November 16, says the New York Tribune,

"John Brown, by counsel, made his last appeal to a Virginia tribunal. Within a few hours' time, the five judges of the Supreme Court of Appeals uttered their unanimous opinion that the judgment of the Jefferson County Court, under which the old man awaits death by hanging on the 2d day of December, was right; and therefore they denied his petition for a writ of error. The indictment upon which Brown was tried contained four counts — for treason, for advising and conspiring with slaves and others to rebel, and for murder. Charged jointly with others, he was tried alone. One general judgment of death was entered upon the whole of it. The grounds of his application for a writ of error were few. He claimed, first, that the judgment against him was erroneous, because it was not averred in the treason count, that at the time of the offence charged he was a citizen of the State of Virginia or of the United States. The law is well settled, that treason is a breach of allegiance, and can be committed only by one who owes allegiance, either temporary or perpetual. Brown appealed to the Court, that if the judgment against him on all the counts, including this defective one of treason, was to stand, he would be put out of all possible reach of the Executive clemency. That clemency could have reached him, on the contrary, if the judgment had only been on the other counts of the indictment. Secondly, he claimed that the judgment under which he now awaits death was erroneous, in that the Court below denied his application that the prosecution be made to elect some one count upon which to try him, and abandon the rest. He was entitled to that election : *First*, Because the offence of treason is not pardonable by the Governor of Virginia, and therefore a count charging it should not have been united in an indictment with counts for offences that are pardonable. *Second*, Because the punishment upon conviction upon each of the counts was not necessarily the same ; that while it was inevitably capital upon one of them, upon the others he might have been found guilty only of a misdemeanor, or of a simple manslaughter. *Thirdly*, he insisted that the Court below should have instructed the Jury that if they believed,·from the evidence, that at the time of the committing of the acts charged in the count for treason, he was not a citizen of Virginia, but of another State, he could not be convicted under it. *Fourthly*, he claimed that the finding by the Jury upon the counts for conspiring with slaves to rebel, and for killing ' four white men and one free negro,' ' in manner and form as aforesaid,' was too uncertain and inconsistent to warrant a judgment of death. Briefly, and without any delay painful to the tense expectation of the Virginia mind, did the five Judges of the Appeals Court say to John Brown, through his counsel, ' The judgment under which you are to be hung by the neck until you are dead, is plainly right.' *His counsel were not allowed to be heard.''* ·

JOHN BROWN AND THE SOUTHERN CLERGY.

John Brown had frequent calls from the Virginia clergy, but with none of them would he bow the knee to their Baal. Mr. Lowry, an old neighbor, who visited him in prison, states that :

" Mr. Brown is a member of the Old-School Presbyterian Church, and a decidedly religious man, though he strictly and sternly refuses to be aided in his prayers by the pro-slavery divines of Virginia. One of these gentlemen, in conversation with me, said that he had called on Brown to pray with him. He said that Brown asked if he was ready to fight, if necessity required it, for the freedom of the slave. On his answering in the negative, Brown said that he would thank him to retire from his cell; that his prayers would be an abomination to his God. To another clergyman he said that he would not insult his God by bowing down with any one who had the blood of the slave upon his skirts.''

A correspondent of the Baltimore American gives this additional testimony to John Brown's fidelity:

"Captain Brown has also recovered, and is getting quite active. He refuses to receive any ministers who countenance slavery, telling them to go home and read their Bibles. Rev. Alfred Griffith had an interview with him a few days since, which lasted for nearly an hour, principally on the subject of slavery. They quoted Scripture to sustain their views, and had quite a clashing time of it; but neither was able to convince the other of the correctness of their peculiar doctrines."

Another writer says:

"Brown was visited yesterday by Rev. James H. March, of the M. E. Church. The reverend gentleman having advanced an argument in favor of the institution of slavery as it now exists, Brown replied to him, saying, 'My dear sir, you know nothing about Christianity; you will have to learn the A B C's in the lesson of Christianity, as I find you entirely ignorant of the meaning of the word. I, of course, respect you as a gentleman; but it is as a *heathen* gentleman.' The reverend gentleman here thought it best to draw such a discussion to a close, and therefore withdrew."

Let the churches of America blush in shame in presence of the faithful Christian of Charlestown jail. Was ever testimony against slavery so firmly or so worthily borne? The effect of it was noteworthy. The clergymen of Charlestown refused to pray for John Brown before his execution, although that custom is immemorial, and Christianity enjoins the duty of praying even for our enemies.

To Mr. Lowry, in speaking of the Pottawattomie executions, and the person who accused him of having killed the ruffians, he said that he was mistaken in supposing that the charge needed any refutation from him. "Time and the honest verdict of posterity," he said, "will approve of every act of mine to prevent slavery from being established in Kansas. *I never shed the blood of a fellow-man, except in self-defence or in promotion of a righteous cause.*" Mr. Lowry adds:

"During our conversation, the martial music (where Governor Wise was reviewing his army near the prison) made a great noise, and, thinking it must annoy him, I asked him if it did not. 'No,' said the man; 'it is inspiring!'

"And here, as I parted with him, telling him I would see him again, if possible, he repeated to me: 'Tell those without that I am cheerful.' My time was up, and I was invited to leave."

During this week five fires, caused by incendiaries, occurred within a circuit of fifteen miles. The frightened Virginians attributed them to anti-slavery invaders; but the planters, knowing the feelings of their slaves, slept every night in the town. A cow approached the guards, one evening, and, refusing to give the countersign, was shot. In a few days afterwards, companies of infantry and artillery arrived from Petersburg and Richmond, to protect the citizens.

On their arrival in Charlestown, on November 22, these protectors of Virginia from her graminivorous enemies paid a visit to the old man in prison; but no one cared or was permitted to describe the interview. Governor Wise, who accompanied them to Charlestown, had a conversation with John Brown, who "justified and defended his course."

On the 24th, the militia Colonel hitherto in command was superseded by General Taliaferro, and martial law was at once proclaimed. The telegraph was seized by the Government of Virginia, and every train that entered the State was searched and put under guard. The Austrian passport system was inaugurated — for the first time in American history.

The next and only published record of John Brown's life in his cell, until the day preceding his sublime victory over death, is from the pen of a very prejudiced authority, but bears, nevertheless, internal evidenees of its truthfulness :

"Colonel Smith, of the Virginia Military Institute, paid a visit to John Brown to-day, in company with Mr. O. Jennings Wise, son of Governor Wise, who is attached to Company F, of Richmond. I had an interview with one of the jail officials who was present at the conversation that took place between Captain Brown and these gentlemen, and I give you, word for word, what transpired during our interview:

Reporter. Did Colonel Smith question Brown as to whether he had any desire to have a clergyman to administer to him the consolations of religion ?

Jail Official. Yes, he did; but Brown said he did not recognize any slaveholder, lay or clerical, or any man sympathizing with slavery, as a Christian. He gave the same reason yesterday for his refusal to accept the services of some clergymen who called upon him. He also said he would as soon be attended to the scaffold by blacklegs or robbers of the worst kind as by slaveholding ministers, or ministers sympathizing with slavery, and that if he had his choice he would prefer being followed to the scaffold by barefooted, barelegged, ragged negro children, and their old gray-headed slave-mother, than by clergymen of this character. He would feel, he said, much prouder of such an escort, and wished he could have it.

Reporter. Has he said any thing on the subject of religion to the clergymen who have called upon him ?

Official. Yes, he argues with them; but winds up frequently by telling them that they, and all slaveholders and sympathizers with slavery, have far more need of prayers themselves than he has, and he accordingly advises them to pray for themselves, and exhibit no concern about him. While making these remarks, he requests that he would not be understood as designing to offer any insult.

Reporter. Does his health seem impaired by the anxiety which he must necessarily feel in view of his impending fate ?

Official. No, sir; he looks much better to-day than he did at any period since his imprisonment. He eats his meals regularly, and seems to be in better spirits this morning than he has been for ten days.

Reporter. Does he make any reference to his sons who were shot at Harper's Ferry ?

Official. He expressed some anxiety to get the bodies of his sons together, and requested the jailer to give his wife any assistance in his power to get them together.

Reporter. What does he mean by getting them together ?

Official. He is aware that the body of one of his sons was taken to the Winchester Medical College for dissection, and in using the words getting them together he meant to have their bones collected and given to his wife. He also expressed a desire to have the bones of two men, named Thompson, from his neighborhood, who were shot at Harper's Ferry, given to his wife. He expressed an idea that it would be well to have the flesh burned off the bodies of all, and their bones boxed up, so that they might be carried home with more convenience. In expressing this wish he remarked that he meant to do no violence to

33

the feelings or Christian sentiments of the people of Virginia. His sole object was to prevent inconvenience in their transportation, and avoid any disagreeable odor.

Reporter. There was a rumor on the streets during yesterday that he was engaged in writing out, or had written, his autobiography. Is there any truth in the rumor?

Official. No, sir; there is no truth in it. He is, however, writing a long communication to his family.*

Reporter. Does he exhibit much concern about his wife and children?

Official. Some time since he felt deeply concerned lest they may be reduced to want. Now, however, he has less concern on that head, doubtless because of the assurance he received of a purpose to make provision for them. He often speaks of his three youngest daughters, the eldest of whom, he says, is rising sixteen, and the youngest six.

Reporter. Does he say any thing relative to Governor Wise?

Official. He speaks of him in the highest terms, and expressed himself much pleased at seeing his son to-day, on account of his father's treatment of him. He observed that the Governor treated him much better than he expected he would have done under the circumstances.

Reporter. Does he seek to justify himself for the murder of the men at Pottawattomie Creek, when questioned upon the subject?

Official. He says he did not kill any of them, but that he approved of their being killed.

Reporter. Has he any intercourse with the rest of his confederates now in jail?

Official. He has not, except with Stevens, who occupies the same cell with him.

Reporter. Did he seem pleased when he was informed that the Governor agreed to hand over his body to his wife?

Official. He was very much pleased when he read the Governor's letter to the Sheriff, requesting his body to be given to his wife after execution.

At this stage of the dialogue a Presbyterian clergyman of this town, named Dutton, entered the jailer's dwelling, and requested to have his name reported to Mr. Brown, with a request for an interview if convenient. The message was delivered, but Mr. Brown declined an interview, on the ground that he was then too busy. Mr. Dutton then left.

Reporter. What is it keeps him busy?

Official. He is engaged in reading about two dozen letters, sent to him this morning. In declining an interview with Mr. Dutton, he desired that he (Mr. D.) be informed of his (Brown's) willingness to see him in the course of the day, and argue with him on the subject of religion.

Reporter. What is generally the character of the letters sent to him?

Official. They are generally letters of sympathy and condolence.

Reporter. Does he receive any assuring him of a purpose to rescue him?

Official. Yes; several. These, however, are mostly anonymous, and he invariably commits them to the flames. I have observed him

* Which they never received.

throwing them into the fire upon finding them to be anonymous. Recently he reads no anonymous letter. Any communication, however, applauding him as a martyr to the anti-slavery cause, he carefully files away. Referring to his execution this morning, during his conversation with Mr. O. J. Wise and Colonel Smith, he said he was not to be executed, but publicly murdered.

Reporter. · Does he profess any religion?

Official. Yes; he says he is a member of the Congregationalist Church, and represents himself as a good Christian.

Reporter. Have you any idea whether he has written, or intends to write, any thing which he would wish to have published?

Official. ·He has written nothing that I am aware of, except a short note to a gentleman across the street, stating that his commentaries on Beecher's sermon were not published as he gave them. Some of his commentaries, he said, were omitted, while others were materially altered.

Reporter. Does he exhibit any lack of firmness when spoken to on the subject of his approaching doom?

Official. I remarked to him this morning that the question was frequently asked, "Whether there was any caving in. on his part," and his reply was, that there was no caving in about him; that he would hold up to the last moment as he did at the start.

Reporter. What does he say regarding the prospects of his rescue?

· *Official.* He said he was sure his sons could hardly contemplate his fate without using some efforts to rescue him; but this, he presumed, they would only do if he was allowed to remain in jail without any thing more than. ordinary precaution· to prevent his escape or rescue being exercised. He said, however, that such an attempt would not be made in view of the precautions now taken. He had no idea that any attempt at rescue would be made with so large a military force as he understood was now present.

· *Reporter.* Is he aware that he will not be permitted to make any speech from the scaffold?

Official. Yes, he is; and when informed of that fact, he said he did not care about saying any thing."

"In all his conversation," wrote another reporter, "Brown showed the utmost gentleness and tranquillity, and a quiet courtesy withal, that contrasted rather strongly with the bearing of some of his visitors."

X.

HUSBAND AND WIFE.

MRS. BROWN, on her return to Philadelphia from Baltimore, wrote a letter to Governor Wise, asking for the bodies of her slain sons, and of her husband, after his execution. He sent her the orders for them, addressed to the Sheriff and the General in command. On Wednesday evening, Mrs. Brown, carrying these sad certificates, arrived at Harper's Ferry, under the escort of two gentlemen from Philadelphia. She intended to have gone to Charlestown with them, on the following morning, to have her last earthly interview with her husband. When the morning came, a despatch from head-quarters ordered the officers to detain the sorrow-stricken wife and her friends until further orders. A trustworthy correspondent says :

"I learned at Charlestown that for several hours a triangular correspondence by telegraph was going on between Charlestown, Richmond, and Harper's Ferry, which ultimated in a despatch from General Taliaferro, saying that he had sent a file of dragoons to escort Mrs. Brown, but not the others. The mortification of the citizens of Harper's Ferry was not less than that of Mrs. Brown, and her friends, at so cruel and unlooked-for an act on the part of the chivalrous sons of Virginia. But as a cow will frighten a private doing sentry duty, one live Northern woman and two Northern men might reasonably be expected to intimidate a Virginia army.

"The escort consisted of a file of eight mounted riflemen, under a sergeant. Captain Moore, of the Montgomery Guards, stationed at this place, very kindly offered his own services as a personal escort to Mrs. Brown, and she gladly accepted it.

"The Captain referred frequently, as they came along, to the unfortunate situation of her husband. She exhibited no sorrow or regret, so far as he could observe."

The gallant Captain had the brutality to attempt to argue with a wife, thus circumstanced, in favor of that great crime against God and man, for assailing whose power her husband was doomed to die.

The writer, above quoted, continues:

"I was in sight when the formidable cavalcade arrived. The military went through manœuvres in Scott's Manual, named and nameless, and which were well calculated to impress the beholder with the wonderful effectiveness of a Virginia regiment at a general muster, but in a no more sanguinary conflict. At last, however, Mrs. Brown was admitted. She was kindly received by Captain and Mrs. Avis. Mrs. Avis, by order of the powers that be, conducted Mrs. Brown into a private apartment, where her clothing was searched for concealed weapons, or other means which the morbid suspicion of the Virginia army of occupation suggested Mrs. Brown might surreptitiously convey to her husband.

"In the mean time Captain Brown had been informed that his wife had arrived. The announcement was made by General Taliaferro, when the following dialogue took place:

"'Captain Brown, how long do you desire this interview to last?' asked the Virginian.

"'Not long; three or four hours will do,' said Captain Brown.

"'I am very sorry, Captain Brown,' said the Virginia General, 'that I shall not be able to oblige you. Mrs. Brown must return to-night to Harper's Ferry.'

"'General, execute your orders; I have no favors to ask of the State of Virginia,' was the brave old man's reply.

"This fact was related to an acquaintance of mine by a Virginia gentleman, as an illustration of Captain Brown's courage and bravery. He did not see in it the scathing rebuke to the pusillanimity of a great State, which, with a cordon of twenty-five hundred men, would not protract the last interview between a brave man and his sorrow-stricken wife."

33 *

Mrs. Brown, we are told, was led into the cell by the
jailer. Her husband rose, and, as she entered, received
her in his arms. For some minutes they stood speech-
less, — Mrs. Brown resting her head upon her husband's breast, and clasping his neck with her arms.
At length they sat down and spoke ; and from Captain
Avis, who was the only witness of that sorrowful scene,
(his fellow-prisoner, Stevens, having been placed in an
adjoining cell before the entrance of the wife,) the following record comes :

John Brown spoke first. "Wife, I am glad to see you," he said.

"My dear husband, it is a hard fate."

"Well, well; cheer up, cheer up, Mary. We must all bear it in
the best manner we can. I believe it is all for the best."

"Our poor children — God help them."

"Those that are dead to this world are angels in another. How are
all those still living ? Tell them their father died without a single regret for the course he has pursued — that he is satisfied he is right in
the eyes of God and of all just men."

Mrs. Brown then spoke of their remaining children and their home.
Brown's voice, as he alluded to the bereavements of his family, was
broken with emotion. After a brief pause, Brown said:

"Mary, I would like you to get the bodies of our two boys who
were killed at Harper's Ferry, also the bodies of the two Thompsons,
and, after I am dead, place us all together on a wood pile, and set fire
to the wood ; burn the flesh, then collect our bones and put them in
a large box, then have the box carried to our farm in Essex County,
and there bury us."

Mrs. Brown said, "I really cannot consent to do this. I hope you
will change your mind on this subject. I do not think permission
would be granted to do any such thing. For my sake, think no more
of such an idea."

"Well, well," Brown answered, "do not worry or fret about it; I
thought the plan would save considerable expense, and was the best."

Mrs. Brown observed a chain about the ankles of her husband. To
avoid its galling his limbs, he had put on two pairs of woollen socks.
Mrs. Brown said she was desirous of procuring the chain as a family
relic. She had already at her home the one with which the limbs of
John Brown, Jr., were inhumanly shackled in Kansas, and in which

he was goaded on by the Border devils until he was mad, and the chain had worn through his flesh to the bone; and this, too, she desired. Captain Brown said he had himself asked that it be given to his family, and had been refused.

The conversation then turned upon matters of business, which Brown desired to have arranged after his death. He gave his wife all the letters and papers which were needed for this purpose, and read to her the will which had been drawn up for him by Mr. Hunter, carefully explaining every portion of it.

Speaking of the parties to whom sums are directed to be paid, he said: "Dear Mary, if you can find these, pay them personally; but do not pay any one who may present himself as their attorneys, for if it gets into the hands of attorneys, we do not know what will become of it."

Subsequently he requested his wife to make a denial of the statement that had gained publicity, that he had said in his interview with Governor Wise that he had been actuated by feelings of revenge. He denied that he had ever made such statement, and wished his denial made known; and he denied further that any such base motives had ever been his incentive action.

After this conversation they took supper together. This occupied only a few minutes. Their last sorrowful meal being concluded, and the time approaching at which they must part, Mrs. Brown asked to be permitted to speak to the other prisoners. But Gen. Taliaferro's orders forbade this, though Capt. Avis expressed a willingness to permit her to see them even at the risk of violating orders. She declined to see them under the circumstances.

Brown then touched upon business affairs, until an order was received from the Commander-in-Chief, saying that the interview must terminate. Brown then said, "Mary, I hope you will always live in Essex County. I hope you will be able to get all our children together, and impress the inculcation of the right principles to each succeeding generation. I give you all the letters and papers which have been sent me since my arrest. I wish you also to take all my clothes that are here, and carry them home. Good by, good by. God bless you!"

Mrs. Brown was escorted back to Harper's Ferry, and reached there, greatly exhausted, at nine o'clock.

THREE STRAY FACTS.

The rope with which the old man was to be hanged was publicly exhibited several days before the date of his official murder. South Carolina sent one, Missouri

another, and Kentucky a third rope, with which to
strangle the fearless man who had dared to beard the
lion which the nation dreaded in its oldest and strongest
den. The gifts of South Carolina and Missouri were
found to be wanting in strength ; and Kentucky had
the infamous preference in this choice of the necessities of assassination.

A forged letter, purporting to be written by Mrs.
Doyle, the widow of one of the ruffians of Pottawattomie, was published before John Brown's execution, in
order to avert from Virginia the indignation which the
slaughter of a hero would inevitably excite in every
manly heart in Christendom. It was a fit expedient
for its authors ; but it failed to effect its purpose. It
proved the brutality of Slavery ; not the crime of its
pure-hearted assailant.

On this day, also, the old man presented to a mer-
chant of Charlestown, who had shown him great kindness, a copy of the Bible, bearing on the fly-leaf this
dedication :

"With the best wishes of the *undersigned, and his sincere thanks* for
many acts of kindness received. There is no Commentary in the
world so good in order to a right understanding of this Blessed Book
as an honest, child-like, and teachable spirit.   JOHN BROWN.

"*Charlestown, 29th November,* 1859."

The opposite page was thus inscribed :

"John Brown. The leaves were turned down and marked by him
while in prison at Charlestown, Va. But a small portion of those
passages, which in the most positive terms condemn oppression and
violence, are marked."

"Many hundred passages," writes a correspondent of a Southern
paper, "which can by any possibility of interpretation be tortured into
a support of his peculiar theory, are carefully marked, both by having
the corner of the pages turned over, and by being surrounded by
heavy pencil marks."

XI.

The Victory over Death.

THE sun rose clear and bright on the 2d of December. A haze, that presently veiled it, soon disappeared; and ere the hour appointed for the hero's death, not a cloud was to be seen in the ethereal expanse. The temperature was so exceedingly genial, that, until late in the afternoon, the windows of all the houses were open.

THE SCAFFOLD.

On the previous evening, the timber for the scaffold had been removed from "the enclosure of the new Baptist church," to a field about half a mile distant from the jail, which had been fixed on by the General in command, and marked out with white flags on short stakes, to indicate the position the several sentries should occupy. At seven o'clock the carpenters began the work of erecting the scaffold. When finished, it was about six feet high, twelve wide, and fifteen or eighteen in length. A hand rail extended around three sides and down the flight of steps. On the other side, stout uprights, with a cross beam, which was supported by strong braces. In the centre of the cross beam was an iron hook, from which the rope was suspended. The trap beneath was arranged to swing on hinges, attached to the platform so slightly as to break from

it when the cord was cut that upheld the trap. The
cord, knotted at the end, passed through a hole in the
trap, through another hole in the cross beam, over the
corner, and down the upright, to a hook near the
ground, to which it was tied. Thus, the weight of a
man being placed on it, when the cord near the hook
was cut, the trap would fall at once.

THE MILITARY PARADE.

. At eight o'clock the troops began to arrive ; and at
nine the first company took position. Horsemen clothed
in scarlet jackets were posted around the field at fifty
feet apart, and a double line of sentries was stationed
farther in. As each company arrived, it took its allotted
position. The following diagram will explain the position of the military forces :

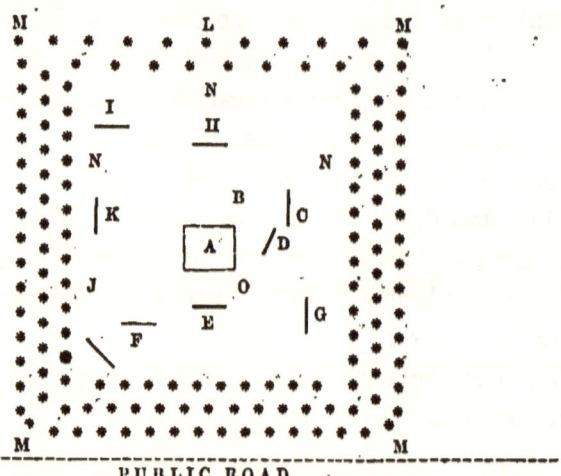

DESCRIPTION OF THE FIELD. — A, Scaffold; B, Generals and Staff; C, Virginia Cadets;
D, Cadet Howitzers, with cannon pointed at scaffold; E, Richmond Company; F, Win-
chester Continentals; G, Fauquier Cavalry; H, Company A of Richmond; I, Alexandria
Riflemen; K, Riflemen, and part of Capt. Ashby's Cavalry, to keep order in the small
crowd. J, Hunter's Guard, at entrance gate, supported by a piece of Artillery under
command of Lieut. Green of the United States Marines; L, Woods scoured by the
Woods Rifles, to have the first brush at the enemy, if approaching from Harper's
Ferry; M M M M, Pickets of the Fauquier Cavalry; N N N, Two lines of Sentries; O,
Petersburg Grays as Body Guard to prisoner in wagon.

The first companies of infantry and cavalry having taken their position, the artillery then arrived, with a huge brass cannon, which was so placed and pointed that, in the event of an attempted rescue, the prisoner might be blown into shreds by the heavy charge of grape shot that lay hidden in it. Other cannon were stationed, with equal care, to sweep the jail and every approach to it. From eight o'clock till ten, the military were in constant motion. The extent of these precautions may be inferred from the fact that lines of pickets and patrols encircled the field of death for fifteen miles, and that over five hundred troops were posted about the scaffold. Nearly three thousand militia soldiers were on the ground. There were not more than four hundred citizens present; for the fears of a servile insurrection, or an anti-slavery invasion, had kept them at home to watch the movements of their slaves.

IN JAIL.

John Brown rose at daybreak, resumed his correspondence with undiminished energy, and continued to write till half past ten o'clock, when the Sheriff, Jailer, and assistants entered, and told him that he must prepare to die.

The Sheriff bade him farewell in his cell. The old man quietly thanked him for his kindness, and spoke of Captain Avis, his jailer, as a brave man. He was then led to the cell of Copeland and Green. This interview is thus reported:

"He told them to stand up like men, and not betray their friends. He then handed them a quarter of a dollar each, saying he had no more use for money, and bade them adieu. He then visited Cook and

Coppoc, who were chained together, and remarked to Cook: ' You have made false statements.'

"Cook asked: ' What do you mean ? '

"Brown answered: ' Why, by stating that I sent you to Harper's Ferry.'

"Cook replied: ' Did you not tell me in Pittsburg to come to Harper's Ferry and see if Forbes had made any disclosures ? '

"Brown: ' No, sir ; you knew I protested against your coming.'

"Cook replied : ' Captain Brown, we remember differently,' at the same time dropping his head.

"Brown then turned to Coppic and said: ' Coppoc, you also made false statements, but I am glad to hear you have contradicted them. Stand up like a man.' He also handed him a quarter. He shook both by the hand, and they parted.

"The prisoner was then taken to Stevens's cell, and they kindly interchanged greetings.

"Stevens: ' Good by, Captain; I know you are going to a better land.'

"Brown replied:' ' I know I am.' Brown told him to bear up, and not betray his friends, giving him a quarter.

"He did not visit Hazlett, as he has always persisted in denying any knowledge of him."

How touchingly manly, and yet what childlike simplicity! "I know I am" — "he gave them a quarter," are both equally characteristic of the man.

A TRIUMPHAL MARCH.

At eleven o'clock, John Brown came out of jail. An eye witness said of his appearance at this solemn moment: "He seemed to walk out of the Gates of Fame ; his countenance was radiant ; he walked with the step of a conqueror." Another spectator — every one, in truth, who saw the old man — corroborated this report: On leaving the jail, he wrote, John Brown had on his face an expression of calmness and serenity characteristic of the patriot who is about to die, with a living consciousness that he is laying down his life for the good of his fellow-creatures. His face was even joyous, and a forgiving smile rested upon his lips.

His was the lightest heart, among friend or foe, in the whole of Charlestown that day ; and not a word was spoken that was not an intuitive appreciation of his manly courage. Firmly, with elastic step, he moved forward. No flinching of a coward's heart there. He stood in the midst of that organized mob, from whose despotic hearts petty tyranny seemed for the nonce eliminated by the admiration they had on once beholding A MAN ; for John Brown was there every inch a man.

As he stepped out of the door, a black woman, with a little child in her arms, stood near his way. The twain were of the despised race for whose emancipation and elevation to the dignity of children of God he was about to lay down his life. His thoughts at that moment none can know except as his acts interpret them. He stopped for a moment in his course, stooped over, and with the tenderness of one whose love is as broad as the brotherhood of man, kissed it affectionately. That mother will be proud of that mark of distinction for her offspring ; and some day, when over the ashes of John Brown the temple of Virginia liberty is reared, she may join in the joyful song of praise which on that soil will do justice to his memory. As he passed along, a black woman with a child in her arms, ejaculated, " God bless you, old man ; I wish I could help you, but I cannot." He heard her, and, as he looked at her, a tear stood in his eye.

The vehicle which was to convey John Brown to the scaffold was a furniture wagon. On the front seat was the driver, a man named Hawks,* said to be a native

* Reader, is not this symbolical ? Think and say and act accordingly.

34

of Massachusetts, but for many years a resident of Virginia, and by his side was seated Mr. Saddler, the undertaker. In the box was placed the coffin, made of black walnut, enclosed in a poplar box with a flat lid, in which coffin and remains were to be transported to the North. John Brown mounted the wagon, and took his place in the seat with Captain Avis, the jailer, whose admiration of his prisoner is of the profoundest nature. Mr. Saddler, too, was one of John Brown's stanchest friends in his confinement, and pays a noble tribute to his manly qualities.

He mounted the wagon with perfect calmness. It was immediately surrounded with cavalry. This military escort of the warrior of the Lord to the scene of his last earthly victory, consisted of Captain Scott's company of cavalry, one company of Major Loring's battalion of defensibles, Captain Williams's Montpelier Guard, Captain Scott's Petersburg Greys, Company D, Captain Miller, of the Virginia Volunteers, and the Young Guard, Captain Rady; the whole under the command of Colonel T. P. August, assisted by Major Loring — the cavalry at the head and rear of the column.

The wagon was drawn by two white horses. From the time of leaving jail until he mounted the gallows stairs, he wore a smile upon his countenance, and his keen eye took in every detail of the scene. There was no blenching, nor the remotest approach to cowardice nor nervousness. As he was leaving jail, when asked if he thought he could endure his fate, he said, "I can endure almost any thing but parting from friends; that is very hard." On the road to the scaffold, he said, in reply to an inquiry, "It has been a characteristic of me, from infancy, not to suffer from physical fear. I have suffered a thousand times more from bashfulness than from fear."

"I was very near the old man," writes an eye witness, "and scrutinized him closely. He seemed to take in the whole scene at a glance; and he straightened himself up proudly, as if to set to the soldiers an example of a soldier's courage. The only motion he made, beyond a swaying to and fro of his body, was that same patting of his knees with his hands that we noticed throughout his trial and while in jail. As he came upon an eminence near the gallows, he cast his eye over the. beautiful landscape, and followed the windings of the Blue Ridge Mountains in the distance. He looked up earnestly at the sun, and sky, and all about, and then remarked, 'This is a beautiful country. I have not cast my eyes over it before — that is, while passing through the field.'"

"Yes," was the sad reply of the brave Captain Avis.

"You are a game man, Captain Brown," said Mr. Saddler.

"Yes," he said, "I was so trained up; it was one of the lessons of my mother; but it is hard to part from friends, though newly made."

"You are more cheerful than I am, Captain Brown," responded Mr. Saddler.

"Yes," said the hero, "*I ought to be.*"

THE FIELD OF DEATH.

By this time, the wagon had reached the field of death — the warrior's last battle ground. It is thus described:

"The field contained about forty acres, I should say, part of it in corn stubble, but the greater part in grass. The surface is undulating, and a broad hillock near the public road was selected as the site for the gallows, because it would afford the distant spectators a fair view, and place the prisoner so high that if compelled to fire upon him, the soldiers need not shoot each other or the civilians. The field was bounded on the south by the road, on the north by a pretty bit of woodland, and on the remaining two sides by enclosed fields."

The sun shone with great splendor as the condemned hero's escort came up, and afar off could be seen the bright gleaming muskets and bayonets of his body guard, hedging him in, in close ranks, all about. On the field the several companies glittered with the same sparkle of guns and trappings; and the gay colors of their uniforms, made more intense in the glare, came out into strong relief, with the dead tints of sod and woods. Away off to the east and south, the splendid mass of the Blue Ridge loomed against the sky and shut in the horizon. Over the woods towards the northeast, long, thin stripes of cloud had gradually accumulated, and foreboded the storm that came in due time; while, looking towards the south, the eye took in an undulating fertile country, stretching out to the distant mountains. All nature seemed at peace, and the shadow of the approaching solemnity seemed to have been cast over the soldiers, for there was not a sound to be heard as the column came slowly up the road. There was no band of musicians to heighten the effect of the scene by playing the march of the dead, but with solemn tread the heavy footfalls came as of those of one man. Thus they passed to their station to the easterly side of the scaffold.

As the procession entered the field, the old hero, as

if surprised at the absence of the people, remarked:
"I see no citizens here — where are they?"

"The citizens are not allowed to be present — none
but the troops," was the reply.

"That ought not to be," said the old man; "citizens
should be allowed to be present as well as others."

THE MARTYR CROWNED.

The wagon halted. The troops composing the escort
took up their assigned position; but the Petersburg
Greys, as the immediate body guard, remained as
before, closely hemming the old hero in — as if still as
afraid of his sword of Gideon, as the State had proved
itself to be of his sword of the Lord, by preventing the
people from listening to his last words. They finally
opened ranks to let him pass out; when, with the
assistance of two men, he descended from the wagon.
Mr. Hunter and Mayor Green were standing near by.
"Gentlemen, good by," the old man said in an unfal-
tering tone; and then, with firm step and erect form,
he calmly walked past jailers, sheriff, and officers, and
mounted the scaffold steps. He was the first man that
stood on it. As he quietly awaited the necessary
arrangements, he surveyed the scenery unmoved, looking principally in the direction of the people in the far
distance. "There is no faltering in his step," wrote
one who saw him, "but firmly and erect he stands
amid the almost breathless lines of soldiery that surround him. With a graceful motion of his pinioned
right arm he takes the slouched hat from his head and
carelessly casts it upon the platform by his side." "I
know," said another witness, "that every one within

34 *

view was greatly impressed with the dignity of his bearing. I have since heard men of the South say that his courageous fortitude and insensibility to fear filled them with amazement."

The hour had now come. The officer approached him. To Captain Avis he said: "I have no words to thank you for all your kindness to me."

His elbows and ankles are pinioned, the white cap is drawn over his eyes, the hangman's rope is adjusted around his neck. John Brown is ready to be ushered into the land of the hereafter.

"Captain Brown," said the Sheriff, "you are not standing on the drop. Will you come forward?"

"I can't see, gentlemen," was the old man's answer, unfalteringly spoken, "you must lead me."

The Sheriff led his prisoner forward to the centre of the drop.

"Shall I give you a handkerchief," asked the Sheriff, "and let you drop it as a signal?"

"No; I am ready at any time; but do not keep me needlessly waiting."

This was the last of John Brown's requests of Virginia; and this, like all the others, was refused. When he pleaded for delay during the progress of his trial, the State refused it, and hurried him to his doom; and now, when he asked, standing on the gallows, blindfolded, and with the rope that was to strangle him around his neck, for no unnecessary delay, the demoniacal spirit of slavery again turned a deaf ear to his request. Instead of permitting the execution to be at once consummated, the proceedings were checked by the martial order — "Not ready yet;" and the hideous mockery of a vast military display began. For ten minutes at least, under the orders of the commanding officer, the troops trod heavily over the ground, hither and thither, now advancing towards the gallows, now turning about in sham defiance of an imaginary enemy.

Each moment to every humane man seemed an hour, and some of the people, unable to restrain an expression of their sense of the outrage, murmured — *Shame! Shame!*

At last the order was given, and the rope was severed with a hatchet. As the trap fell, its hinges gave a wailing sort of screak, that could be heard at every point on the fields.[*]

John Brown is slowly strangling — for the shortness of the rope prevents a speedy death.

"There was but one spasmodic effort of the hands to clutch at the neck, but for nearly five minutes the limbs jerked and quivered. He seemed to retain an extraordinary hold upon life. One who has seen numbers of men hung before, told me he had never seen so hard a struggle. After the body had dangled in mid air for twenty minutes, it was examined by the surgeons for signs of life. First the Charlestown physicians went up and made their examination, and after them the military surgeons, the prisoner being executed by the civil power, and with military assistance as well. To see them lifting up the arms, now powerless, that

---

[*] "Was this symbolic," asks an able writer, "of the wail of grief that went up at the moment from thousands of friends to the cause of emancipation throughout the land? In the dead stillness of the hour it went to my heart like the wail for the departed that may be heard in some highland glen."

once were so strong, and placing their ears to the breast of the corpse, holding it steady by passing an arm around it, was revolting in the extreme. And so the body dangled and swung by its neck, turning to this side or that when moved by the surgeons, and swinging pendulum like, from the force of the south wind that was blowing, until, after thirty-eight minutes from the time of swinging off, it was ordered to be cut down, the authorities being quite satisfied that their dreaded enemy was dead. The body was lifted upon the scaffold, and fell into a heap. It was then put into the black walnut coffin, the body guard closed in about the wagon, the cavalry led the van, and the mournful procession moved off."

There was another procession at that moment — unseen by the Virginians : a procession of earth's holiest martyrs before the Throne of God : and from among them came a voice, which said :

 . "Come, ye blessed of my Father, inherit the kingdom prepared for you from the foundations of the world. . . . Inasmuch as ye have done it unto one of the least of these my brethren, ye have done it unto me."

 The soul of John Brown stood at the right hand of the Eternal. He had fought the good fight, and now wore the crown of victory.

In the prison of Charlestown a plaintive wail was heard. Sustained by no religious convictions, one prisoner was in great agony of mind. The scaffold from which the stainless soul of John Brown leaped from earth into the bosom of the God of the oppressed, was only half a mile behind the jail in which his body had been confined. "From the windows of his cell Cook had an unobstructed view of the whole proceedings. He watched his old Captain until the trap fell and his body swung into mid air, when he turned away and gave vent to his feelings."

With his sword and his voice John Brown had demonstrated the unutterable villany of slavery. His corpse was destined to continue the lesson. The surgeons pronounced the old man dead; they declared that his spinal column had been ruptured; they said that the countenance was now purple and distorted; they knew that the cord had cut a finger's depth into the neck of the strangled corpse.

Yet, as the animal heat still remained in the body, it was not permitted to be taken away until it should cool. Even this precaution against an earthly resurrection did not satisfy the hearts corrupted by slavery.

"I heard it suggested by a Captain," writes a witness of unquestioned veracity, "that a good dose of · arsenic should be administered to the corpse to make sure work; and many others wished that at least the head might be cut off and retained by them, since the body was to be embalmed, and, on gorgeous catafalques, carried in procession through Northern cities. This bloodthirstiness is on a par," the writer adds, "with that of the students at the Winchester Medical College, who have skinned the body of one of Brown's sons, separated the nervous and muscular and venous

systems, dried and varnished, and have the whole hung
up as a nice anatomical illustration. Some of the students wished to stuff the skin ; others to make it into
game pouches."

Such is the spirit of Southern Slavery !

" The body once in its coffin and on its way back to
the jail," wrote a correspondent, " the field was quickly
deserted, the cannon, limbered up again, rumbled away,
and the companies of infantry and troops of cavalry in
solid column marched away. The body had not left
the field before the carpenters began to take the scaffold
to pieces, that it might be stored up against the 16th
instant, when it will be used to hang Cook and Coppic together. A separate gallows will be built for the
two negroes."

" The night after the execution has set in dark and
stormy. The south wind has brought up a violent
storm."

The body of John Brown was delivered to his widow
at Harper's Ferry, and by her it was carried to North
Elba, where it now lies at rest on the bosom of the
majestic mountain region that he loved when living.
It was interred as only dead heroes should be buried.
There was no vast assemblage of " the so-called great;"
no pompous parade ; no gorgeous processions; but loyal
worth and noble genius stood at the grave of departed
heroism ; for his friends and his family wept as the
Heaven-inspired soul of Wendell Phillips pronounced
the eulogium of John Brown, — the latest and our
greatest martyr to the teachings of the Bible and the
American Idea.

As the coffin was lowered into the grave, a clergy man, with prophetic voice, repeated these words of the Apostle Paul:

"I have fought the good fight; I have finished my course; I have kept the faith: henceforth there is laid up for me a crown of righteousness, which the Lord, the righteous Judge, shall give me; and not to me only, but unto all that love his appearing."

SAMSON AGONISTES.

December 2, 1859.

YOU bound and made your ſport of him, Philiſtia!
  You ſet your ſons at him to flout and jeer;
You loaded down his limbs with heavy fetters;
  Your mildeſt mercy was a ſmiling ſneer.

One man, among a thouſand who defied him,
  One man from whom his awful ſtrength had fled—
You brought him out to laſh him with your vengeance;
  Ten thouſand curſes on one hoary head!

You think his eyes are cloſed and blind forever,
  Becauſe you feared them to this mortal day;
You draw a longer breath of exultation,
  Becauſe your conqueror's power is torn away.

Oh fools! his arms are round your temple pillars:
  Oh blind! his ſtrength divine begins to wake,
Hark! the great roof-tree trembles from its centre—
  Hark! how the rafters bend, and ſwerve, and ſhake!